Dramatists Sourcebook

1999–2000 EDITION

Dramatists Sourcebook

1999–2000 Edition

Complete opportunities for playwrights, translators, composers, lyricists and librettists

EDITED BY
Kathy Sova
Tim Cusick
Samantha Rachel Rabetz

Theatre Communications Group • New York

Published by Theatre Communications Group, Inc.
355 Lexington Ave., New York, NY 10017-0217.

This publication is made possible in part with public funds from the New York State Council on the Arts, a State Agency.

TCG books are exclusively distributed to the book trade by Consortium Book Sales and Distribution, 1045 Westgate Dr., St. Paul, MN 55114.

Manufactured in the United States of America

ISSN 0733-1606
ISBN 1-55936-175-1

Contents

Preface

Welcome friends to the *1999–2000 Dramatists Sourcebook*'s 19th edition.

It is exciting as we begin to think about the new millennium to see that there are many, many organizations still searching for and awarding new work. We have added many new listings. And though some organizations have disbanded or stopped offering prizes or providing programs due to lack of funding, other organizations on hiatus during previous years have once again begun to look for new work, and other organizations have found new ways to assist young writers and develop new theatre in their communities. This year the *Sourcebook* includes more than 1,100 listings—more than any previous edition. This is good news.

Every year the *Sourcebook* is fully updated. This means that every organization listed is contacted, and all information checked for accuracy—from addresses and Web site information to special interests and submission requirements. If an organization doesn't respond (and numerous attempts are made), we do not include them. We can't be sure their information is still accurate or that they will be responsive to you if they aren't to us. We can safely say that at press time all the listings included here are in existence and their information correct.

Since each listing is updated annually, it is important that you work with the most current *Sourcebook* (in addition to the inclusion and deletion of listings, most addresses and contact information, not to mention deadlines and guidelines, are modified in some way every year).

Using the *Sourcebook*. Select those listings your work is best suited for and follow the guidelines meticulously. The Special Interests Index is helpful in finding those listings that may be specifically searching for your type of work. When instructed to write for guidelines, do so. This is a good idea in general as sometimes dates and guidelines change after the *Sourcebook* publishes. Most important is to ALWAYS enclose an SASE with every mailed script if you'd like it returned (unless the entry specifies that scripts will not be returned). If a listing says it accepts scripts, it is always assumed that an SASE must be sent along for return; we do not restate this for every listing. Also, always assume the deadline dates in this book refer to the day materials should arrive, not the postmark date.

Study—and restudy—Tony Kushner's "A Simple Working Guide for Playwrights" (page ix, the Prologue). It's filled with great advice on everything from preparing the physical manuscript to what to do while waiting, while waiting, while waiting...

You should know that throughout this book, "full-length play" means just that—a full-length, original work for adult audiences, without a score or libretto. One-acts, musicals, adaptations, translations, plays for young audiences, solo pieces, performance art and screenplays are listed separately. "Young audiences" refers to audiences age 18 or younger, "young playwrights" refers to playwrights age 18 or younger, "students" refers to college students or students in an affiliated writing program.

Entries are alphabetized by first word (excluding "the") even if they start with a proper name. So, for example, Mark Taper Forum is listed under M. In the index, you will also find this theatre cross-listed under T. Regardless of the way "theatre" is spelled in an organization's name, we alphabetize it as if it were spelled "re," not "er."

We try to improve the *Sourcebook* with each edition. And we rely on your feedback. Because of previous comments we have weeded out some listings that weren't serving you properly, and corrected others to reflect their policies more accurately. So, please contact us: write/E-mail: sova@tcg.org; Kathy Sova, *Dramatists Sourcebook* Editor, TCG, 355 Lexington Ave, New York, NY 10017.

I want to offer my gratitude to Tim Cusick, who served as a wonderful editor for this volume. In addition to editing most of the listings, he spent countless hours phoning many of the organizations listed here and improved greatly on the quality of this *Sourcebook*. And much thanks to Samantha Rachel Rabetz for her careful eye and cheerful willingness in helping with even the smallest details throughout this daunting project. Thanks to Wendy Weiner for guiding us through some troubled moments.

Most of all, we want to thank all of you out there doing the work. We hope we have somehow made your ambitious task a little easier. We wish you joy, health and success in 2000!

Kathy Sova
July 1999

A Simple Working Guide for Playwrights
by Tony Kushner

A) *Format:* Most playwrights use a format in which character headings are placed centered above the line and capitalized:

<u>LIONEL</u>

I don't possess a mansion, a car, or a string of polo ponies...

Lines should be single-spaced. Stage directions should be indented and single-spaced. If a character's line is interrupted at the end of the page, its continuance on the following page should be marked as such:

<u>LIONEL</u> (cont'd)

or a string of polo ponies...

There are denser, and thus more economical, formats; since Xeroxing is expensive, and heavy scripts cost more to ship, you may be tempted to use these, but a generously spaced format is much easier to read, and in these matters it doesn't pay to be parsimonious.

B) *Typing and reproducing:* Scripts should be typed neatly and reproduced clearly. Remember that everyone who reads your script will be reading many others additionally, and it will work to your serious disadvantage if the copy's sloppy, faded, or otherwise unappealing. If you use a computer printer, eschew old-fashioned dot-matrix and other robotic kinds of print. Also, I think it's best to avoid using incredibly fancy word-processing printing programs with eight different typefaces and decorative borders. Simple typescript, carefully done, is best. Check for typos. A playwright's punctuation may be idiosyncratic for purposes of expressiveness, but not too idiosyncratic, and spelling should be correct.

C) *Sending the script:*

1) The script should have a title page with the title, your name, address and phone number, or that of your agent or representative. Scripts are now automatically copyrighted at the moment of creation, but simply writing © and the date on the title page can serve as a kind of scarecrow for thievish magpies.

2) Never, never send an unbound script. Loose pages held together by a rubber band don't qualify as bound, nor do pages clamped together with a mega-paperclip. A heavy paper cover will protect the script as it passes from hand to hand.

3) Always, always enclose a self-addressed stamped envelope (SASE) or you will never see your script again. You may enclose a note telling the theatre to dispose of the copy instead of returning it; but you must have the ultimate fate of the script planned for in the eventuality of its not being selected for production. Don't leave this up to the theatre! If you want receipt of the script acknowledged, include a self-addressed, stamped postcard (SASP).

D) *Letter of inquiry and synopsis:* If a theatre states, in its entry in the *Sourcebook,* that it does not accept unsolicited scripts, believe it. Don't call and ask if there are exceptions; there aren't. A well-written and concise letter of inquiry, however, accompanied by a synopsis possessed of similar virtues *can* get you an invitation to submit your play. It's prudent, then, to spend time on both letter and synopsis. It is, admittedly, very hard for a writer to sum up his or her work in less than a page, but this kind of boiling-down can be of value beyond its necessity as a tool for marketing;

use it to help clarify for yourself what's central and essential about your play. A good synopsis should *briefly* summarize the basic features of the plot without going into excessive detail; it should evoke both the style and the thematic substance of the play without recourse to clichéd description ("This play is about what happens when people lose their dreams..."); and it should convey essential information, such as cast size, gender breakdown, period, location, or anything else a literary manager deciding whether to send for the play might want to know. Make reference to other productions in your letter, but don't send thick packets of reviews and photos. And don't offer your opinion of the play's worth, which will be inferred as being positive from the fact that you are its parent.

E)   *Waiting:*   Theatres almost always take a long time to respond to playwrights about a specific play, frequently far in excess of the time given in their listings in the *Sourcebook.* This is due neither to spite nor indolence. Literary departments are usually understaffed and their workload is fearsome. Then, too, the process of selection invariably involves a host of people and considerations of all kinds. In my opinion you do yourself no good by repeatedly calling after the status of your script; you will become identified as a pest. It's terribly expensive to copy and mail scripts, but you must be prepared to shoulder the expense and keep making copies if they don't get returned. If, after a certain length of time past the deadline, you haven't heard from a theatre, send a letter inquiring politely about the play, reminding the appropriate people that you'd sent an SASE with the script; and then forget about it. In most cases, you will get a response and the script returned eventually.

One way to cut down on the expenses involved is to be selective about venues for submission. Reading *Sourcebook* entries and scrutinizing a copy of *Theatre Profiles* (see Useful Publications) will help you select the theatres most compatible with your work. If you've written a musical celebration of the life of Phyllis Schlafly, for example, you won't want to send it to theatres with an interest in radical feminist dramas. Or you won't necessarily want to send your play about the history of Western imperialism to a theatre that produces an annual season of musical comedy.

F)   *Produce yourself!*   In *Endgame,* Clov asks Hamm, "Do you believe in the life to come?" and Hamm responds, "Mine was always that." The condition of endless deferment is one that modern American playwrights share with Beckett's characters and other denizens of the postmodern world. Don't spend your life waiting. You may not be an actor, but that doesn't mean that action is forbidden you. Playwrights can, with very little expense, mount readings of their work; they can band together with other playwrights for readings and discussions; and they can, if they want to, produce their work themselves. Growth as a writer for the stage depends on seeing your work on stage, and if no one else will put it there, the job is up to you. At the very least, and above all else, while waiting, waiting, waiting for responses and offers, keep reading, thinking and writing.

Tony Kushner's plays include *Angels in America, A Gay Fantasia on National Themes, Part One: Millennium Approaches* and *Part Two: Perestroika; A Bright Room Called Day; Hydriotaphia or the Death of Doctor Browne; The Illusion,* freely adapted from Corneille's *L'Illusion Comique; Slavs! (Thinking About the Longstanding Problems of Virtue and Happiness)*; and adaptations of Goethe's *Stella,* Brecht's *The Good Person of Setzuan* and Ansky's *The Dybbuk.* His work has been produced by theatres throughout the United States, including Mark Taper Forum, The Joseph Papp Public Theater/New York Shakespeare Festival, New York Theatre Workshop, Hartford Stage Company, Berkeley Repertory Theatre and Los Angeles Theatre Center, as well as other theatres around the country and abroad. *Angels in America* has been produced in over 30 countries. Mr. Kushner is the recipient of numerous awards, including the 1993 Pulitzer Prize for Drama.

Script Opportunities

- Production
- Prizes
- Publication
- Development

Production

What theatres are included in this section?

The overwhelming majority of the not-for-profit professional theatres through-out the United States is represented here. In order to be included, a theatre must have been operating for at least two years and must meet professional standards of staffing, programming and budget. *Commercial and amateur producers are not included.*

How should I go about deciding where to submit my play?

Don't send it out indiscriminately. Take time to study the listings and select those theatres most likely to be receptive to your material. Find out all you can about each of the theatres you select. Look to TCG's *Theatre Profiles 12* for information on most of these theatres, including seasonal lists of plays each performed from 1993–95. Read *American Theatre* to see what plays the theatres are currently presenting and what their other activities are (see Useful Publications for more information). Whenever possible, go to see the theatre's work.

When I submit my play, what can I do to maximize its chances?

First, read carefully the Simple Working Guide for Playwrights in the Prologue of this *Sourcebook* for good advice on script submission. Then follow each theatre's guidelines meticulously. Pay particular attention to the Special Interests section: If a theatre specifies "gay and lesbian themes only," do not send them your heterosexual romantic comedy, however witty and well written it is. Also, bear in mind the following points about the various submission procedures:

1) "Accepts unsolicited scripts": Don't waste the theatre's time and yours by writing to ask permission to submit your play—just send it. If you want an acknowledgment of receipt, say so and enclose a self-addressed stamped postcard (SASP) for this purpose. *Always* **enclose a self-addressed stamped envelope (SASE) for the return of the script.** Note that you may not receive any response to your work if you don't include this SASE. Many theatres enclose their response letter with the script when returning it.

2) "Synopsis and letter of inquiry": An increasing number of theatres require a synopsis rather than the script itself. Never send an unsolicited script to these theatres. Prepare a clear, cogent and *brief* synopsis of your play and send it along with any other materials requested in the listing. The letter of inquiry is a cover note asking for permission to submit the script; if there is something about your play or about yourself as a writer that you think may spark the theatre's interest, by all means mention it, but keep the letter brief. Unless the theatre specifies that it only responds if it wants to see the script, always enclose an SASP for the theatre's response.

3) "Professional recommendation": Send a script (not a letter of inquiry) accompanied by a letter of recommendation from a theatre professional. Wait until you can obtain such a letter before approaching these theatres.

4) "Agent submission": If you do not have an agent yet, do not submit to these theatres. Wait until you have had a production or two and have acquired a representative who can submit your script for you.

5) "Direct solicitation to playwright or agent": Do not submit to these theatres. If they are interested in your work you will hear from them!

6) Do not E-mail your submissions. E-mail and Web addresses are included for the purpose of general inquiries and, in some cases where stated, to obtain quidelines or applications. Perhaps in the future, producing organizations may open up their E-mail channels to accept brief synopsis submissions, but for now there are very few willing to do so. Respect their submission procedures.

Note: we've persuaded theatres requiring letters and synopses to give us two response times—one for letters and one for scripts should they ask to see one. All response times are approximate, and theatres may take longer to respond.

A CONTEMPORARY THEATRE
(Founded 1965)
The Eagles Building, 700 Union St; Seattle, WA 98101-2330; (206) 292-7660,
FAX 292-7670; Web http://www.acttheatre.org
Gordon Edelstein, *Artistic Director*

Submission procedure: no unsolicited scripts; direct solicitation to playwright or agent; will accept synopsis, 10-page dialogue sample and letter of inquiry from Northwest playwrights only. **Types of material:** full-length plays, translations, adaptations, musicals, solo pieces. **Special interests:** current social, political and psychological issues; plays theatrical in imagination and execution; multicultural themes; not keen on "kitchen-sink" realism or "message" plays. **Facilities:** 390 seats, thrust stage; 390 seats, arena stage; 150 seats, cabaret. **Best submission time:** Sep–Apr. **Response time:** 1 month letter for Northwest playwrights; 4–6 months script for Northwest playwrights. **Special programs:** new play development workshops. FirstACT: play commissions and workshops. ACT/Hedgebrook Women Playwrights Festival (see Development).

A. D. PLAYERS
(Founded 1967)
2710 West Alabama St; Houston, TX 77098; (713) 526-2721, FAX 439-0905
Literary Manager

Submission procedure: no unsolicited scripts; synopsis, resume and letter of inquiry. **Types of material:** full-length plays, one-acts, adaptations, plays for young audiences, musicals. **Special interests:** works that "state or affirm the centrality of God's love and power in the issue of life." **Facilities:** Grace Theater, 212 seats, proscenium stage. **Production considerations:** cast limit of 12, prefers less than 10; no more than 2 sets, maximum height 11' 6"; no fly space, minimal lighting. **Best submission time:** year-round. **Response time:** 2 months letter; 12 months script. **Special programs:** staged reading series. Theater Arts Academy: includes playwriting classes; contact theatre for information.

A NOISE WITHIN
(Founded 1991)
234 South Brand Blvd; Glendale, CA 91204; (818) 546-1449, FAX 240-3004
Art Manke, *Artistic Co-Director*

Submission procedure: accepts unsolicited scripts. **Types of material:** translations, adaptations. **Special interests:** translations and adaptations of classical material only. **Facilities:** A Noise Within, 144 seats, thrust stage. **Best submission time:** fall. **Response time:** 6–8 months.

ABOUT FACE THEATRE
(Founded 1995)
3212 North Broadway; Chicago, IL 60657; (773) 549-7943, FAX 935-4483;
  E-mail faceline1@aol.com; Web http://www.aboutface.base.org
Carl Hippensteel, *Literary Manager*

Submission procedure: no unsolicited scripts; synopsis, first 10 pages of script, cast list, resume and letter of inquiry with SASE for response. **Types of material:** full-length plays, one-acts, adaptations, musicals, performance art. **Special interests:** "queer" plays only, especially by and about lesbians; material that challenges ideas about gender and sexuality in historical or contemporary contexts; imaginative scripts of literary caliber that break traditional ideas about dramatic form, structure and presentation. **Facilities:** About Face Theatre, 99 seats, flexible thrust stage. **Production considerations:** no fly space. **Best submission time:** year-round. **Response time:** 3 months letter; 6 months script. **Special programs:** Face to Face Workshop Series: developmental program of readings and workshop stagings with audience response.

THE ACTING COMPANY
(Founded 1972)
Box 898, Times Square Station; New York, NY 10108; (212) 564-3510,
  FAX 714-2643; E-mail mail@theactingcompany.org;
  Web http://www.theactingcompany.org
Margot Harley, *Producing Director*
Richard Corley, *Associate Producing Director*

Submission procedure: no unsolicited scripts; professional recommendation. **Types of material:** full-length plays, one-acts, translations, adaptations, musicals. **Special interests:** mainly classical repertory but occasionally produces new works suited to acting ensemble of approximately 8 men, 3 women, age range 24–45; prefers works with poetic dimension and heightened language. **Facilities:** no permanent facility; touring company which plays in New York City for 1 or 2 weeks a year. **Production considerations:** productions tour in repertory; simple, transportable proscenium-stage set. **Best submission time:** Nov–Jan. **Response time:** 3 months.

ACTORS ALLEY
(Founded 1971)
El Portal Center for the Arts; 5269 Lankershim Blvd;
  North Hollywood, CA 91601; (818) 508-4234, FAX 508-5113
Jeremiah Morris, *Artistic Director*

Submission procedure: accepts unsolicited scripts. **Types of material:** full-length plays, one-acts, translations, adaptations, plays for young audiences. **Special interests:** works by southern CA-based writers. **Facilities:** Pavilion, 350 seats, proscenium/thrust stage; Circle Forum, 99 seats, flexible stage; Store Front Theatre, 42 seats, proscenium stage. **Production considerations:** small cast for Store Front. **Best submission time:** Nov. **Response time:** 12 months. **Special programs:** year-round reading series.

ACTORS & PLAYWRIGHTS' INITIATIVE
(Founded 1989)
Box 50051; Kalamazoo, MI 49005-0051; (616) 343-8310, FAX 343-8450;
Robert C. Walker, *Artistic Director*

Submission procedure: no unsolicited scripts; professional recommendation. **Types of material:** full-length plays, one-acts, translations, adaptations, plays for young audiences, musicals, solo pieces. **Special interests:** aggressive and provocative social-political plays; plays that explore heterosexual, gay and bisexual relationships. **Facilities:** API Theatre, 60 seats, thrust stage. **Production considerations:** cast limit of 10; minimal set, costumes, props; no fly space. **Best submission time:** Oct–Feb. **Response time:** 6 months. **Special programs:** Firstage Script Development Reader's Theatre: developmental year-round reading series.

ACTOR'S EXPRESS
(Founded 1988)
King Plow Arts Center, J-107; 887 West Marietta St NW; Atlanta, GA 30318;
    (404) 875-1606, FAX 875-2791; E-mail actorsexpress@mindspring.com
Literary Manager

Submission procedure: no unsolicited scripts; 10-page dialogue sample, character breakdown, professional recommendation and letter of inquiry. **Types of material:** full-length plays, translations, adaptations, musicals. **Special interests:** new musicals; socially relevant material; minority and gay themes; works with poetic dimension. **Facilities:** Actor's Express, 150 seats, black box. **Production considerations:** modest production demands; no fly space. **Best submission time:** Nov–Jan. **Response time:** 6 weeks letter; 4–6 months script.

ACTORS' GANG THEATER
(Founded 1981)
6201 Santa Monica Blvd; Hollywood, CA 90038; (323) 465-0566,
    FAX 467-1246; E-mail actorsgng1@aol.com
Chris Wells, *Literary Manager*

Submission procedure: accepts unsolicited scripts. **Types of material:** full-length plays, plays for young audiences. **Special interests:** highly theatrical political or avant-garde works. **Facilities:** Actors' Gang Theater, 99 seats, flexible stage; Actors' Gang El Centro, 40 seats, flexible stage. **Best submission time:** year-round. **Response time:** 2 months.

ACTORS' THEATRE
(Founded 1983)
Box 780; Talent, OR 97540; (541) 535-5250
Peter Alzado, *Artistic Director*

Submission procedure: no unsolicited scripts; synopsis, dialogue sample and letter of inquiry. **Types of material:** full-length plays, one-acts, translations, adaptations. **Facilities:** Actors' Theatre, 108 seats, thrust stage. **Best submission time:** year-round. **Response time:** 3 months letter; 4 months script.

ACTORS THEATRE OF LOUISVILLE
(Founded 1964)
316 West Main St; Louisville, KY 40202-4218; (502) 584-1265, FAX 561-3300;
     E-mail actors@aye.net
Michael Bigelow Dixon, *Literary Manager*
Amy Wegener, *Assistant Literary Manager*

Submission procedure: Humana Festival (see below): no unsolicited scripts; synopsis and 10-page dialogue sample; prefers agent submission or professional recommendation. National Ten-Minute Play Contest (see Prizes): accepts unsolicited 10-page one-acts. **Types of material** full-length plays, one-acts, translations, adaptations, solo pieces. **Special interests:** plays of ideas; language-oriented plays; plays with passion, humor and experimentation. **Facilities:** Pamela Brown Auditorium, 637 seats, thrust stage; Bingham Theatre, 320 seats, arena stage; Victor Jory Theatre, 159 seats, thrust stage. **Best submission time:** year-round. **Response time:** 6–9 months (most scripts returned in fall). **Special programs:** National Ten-Minute Play Contest (see Prizes); Humana Festival of New American Plays: annual presentation of new work in rotating rep; *deadline:* ongoing; *notification:* fall 1999; *dates:* Feb–Mar 2000.

ADOBE THEATRE COMPANY
(Founded 1991)
453 West 16th St; New York, NY 10011; (212) 352-0441,
     FAX 352-0441 (call first); Web http://www.adobe.org
Jordan Schildcrout, *Literary Manager*

Submission procedure: no unsolicited scripts; synopsis, dialogue sample and letter of inquiry. **Types of material:** full-length plays, one-acts, adaptations. **Special interests:** comedies that subvert conventional theatrical form and genre. **Facilities:** Ohio Theatre, 75 seats, flexible stage. **Production considerations:** prefers large cast and characters in their thirties. **Best submission time:** year-round. **Response time:** 2 months letter; 4 months script.

ALABAMA SHAKESPEARE FESTIVAL
(Founded 1972)
1 Festival Dr; Montgomery, AL 36117-4605; (334) 271-5300
Kent Thompson, *Artistic Director*
Jennifer Hebblethwaite, *Literary Associate*

Submission procedure: accepts unsolicited scripts with letter of inquiry for Southern Writers' Project only (see below); agent submission for all other plays. **Types of material:** full-length plays, adaptations, plays for young audiences. **Special interests:** new plays with southern or African-American themes; plays for young audiences. **Facilities:** Festival Stage, 750 seats, modified thrust stage; Octagon, 225 seats, flexible stage. **Best submission time:** year-round. **Response time:** 2 months letter; 12 months script. **Special programs:** Southern Writers' Project: project to commission and develop plays based on southern and/or African-American issues; address submissions to Southern Writers' Project.

ALLEY THEATRE
(Founded 1947)
615 Texas Ave; Houston, TX 77002; (713) 228-9341
Gregory Boyd, *Artistic Director*

Submission procedure: no unsolicited scripts; professional recommendation. **Types of material:** full-length plays, translations, adaptations, musicals. **Facilities:** Main Stage, 800 seats, thrust stage; Arena Stage, 300 seats, arena stage. **Best submission time:** year-round. **Response time:** 2–6 months.

ALLIANCE THEATRE COMPANY
(Founded 1968)
1280 Peachtree St NE; Atlanta, GA 30309; (404) 733-4650,
    FAX 733-4625; Web http://www.alliancetheatre.org
Literary Department

Submission procedure: no unsolicited scripts; synopsis, maximum 10-page dialogue sample and letter of inquiry. **Types of material:** full-length plays, one-acts, plays for young audiences, musicals. **Special interests:** work that especially speaks to a culturally diverse community; plays with compelling stories and engaging characters, told in adventurous ways. **Facilities:** Alliance Theatre, 800 seats, proscenium stage; Studio Theatre, 200 seats, flexible stage. **Best submission time:** Mar–Sep. **Response time:** 1–2 months letter; 6 months script.

AMAS MUSICAL THEATRE, INC.
(Founded 1968)
450 West 42nd St, Suite 2J; New York, NY 10036; (212) 563-2565,
    FAX 268-5501; E-mail amas@westegg.com;
    Web http://www.westegg.com/amas
Donna Trinkoff, *Producing Director*

Submission procedure: accepts unsolicited scripts. **Types of material:** musicals, cabaret/revues. **Special interests:** multicultural casts and themes. **Facilities:** no permanent facility; company performs in various proscenium or black box venues with 74–99 seats. **Production considerations:** cast limit of 15. **Best submission time:** summer, winter. **Response time:** 3–6 months. **Special programs:** AMAS Six O'Clock Musical Theatre Lab: a reading series for new musicals open to composers, lyricists and librettists; writer must supply cast and musical director; AMAS provides theatre and publicity.

AMERICAN CABARET THEATRE
(Founded 1989)
401 East Michigan St; Indianapolis, IN 46204; (317) 631-0334, FAX 686-5443;
    E-mail cabaret@indy.net; Web http://americancabarettheatre.com
Claude McNeal, *Artistic Director/Founder*

Submission procedure: no unsolicited scripts; synopsis and letter of inquiry; prefers professional recommendation. **Types of material:** cabaret/revues. **Special**

interests: cabaret/revues dealing with original American themes. **Facilities:** Mainstage, 400 seats, proscenium stage; Second Stage, 150 seats, proscenium stage. **Production considerations:** cast size of 6–12; limited fly, wing and storage space. **Best submission time:** Jul–Sep. **Response time:** 1–2 months letter; 2–3 months script.

AMERICAN CONSERVATORY THEATER
(Founded 1965)
30 Grant Ave, 6th Floor; San Francisco, CA 94108-5800; (415) 439-2445,
     FAX 834-3360
Paul Walsh, *Dramaturg*

Submission procedure: no unsolicited scripts; agents and theatre professionals only may send synopsis, maximum 10-page dialogue sample and letter of inquiry. **Types of material:** full-length plays, translations, adaptations. **Facilities:** Geary Theater, 1,000 seats, proscenium stage. **Best submission time:** year-round. **Response time:** 6–12 months.

AMERICAN MUSIC THEATER FESTIVAL/PRINCE MUSIC THEATER
(Founded 1984)
100 South Broad St, Suite 650; Philadelphia, PA 19110; (215) 972-1000,
     FAX 972-1020; Web http://www.amtf.org
Ben Levit, *Artistic Director*

Submission procedure: no unsolicited scripts; synopsis, sample cassette and letter of inquiry. **Types of material:** music-theatre works including musical comedy, music drama, opera, experimental works, solo pieces. **Facilities:** Prince Music Theater, 450 seats, proscenium stage. **Best submission time:** year-round. **Response time:** 3 weeks letter; 6 months script.

THE AMERICAN PLACE THEATRE
(Founded 1964)
111 West 46th St; New York, NY 10036; (212) 840-2960
Literary Department

Submission procedure: no unsolicited scripts; agent submission. **Types of material:** full-length plays, adaptations, performance art. **Special interests:** works by American playwrights only. **Facilities:** Main Stage, 180–299 seats, flexible stage; Cabaret Space, 75 seats, flexible stage; First Floor Theatre, 75 seats, flexible stage. **Best submission time:** Sep–Jun. **Response time:** 3–4 months. **Special programs:** The Humor Hatchery: developmental program of humorous plays by American playwrights.

AMERICAN RENEGADE THEATRE COMPANY
(Founded 1991)
11136 Magnolia Blvd; North Hollywood, CA 91601; (818) 763-4430
Barry Thompson, *Literary Manager*

Submission procedure: accepts unsolicited scripts. **Types of material:** full-length plays. **Special interests:** contemporary American plays. **Facilities:** Front Theatre, 99 seats, proscenium stage; Back Theatre, 45 seats, black box. **Best submission time:** year-round. **Response time:** 3–6 months.

AMERICAN REPERTORY THEATRE
(Founded 1979)
64 Brattle St; Cambridge, MA 02138; (617) 495-2668;
     Web http://www.amrep.org
Scott Zigler, *Artistic Associate*

Submission procedure: no unsolicited scripts; agent submission. **Types of material:** full-length plays, translations, adaptations, musicals, cabaret/revues. **Special interests:** prefers plays "which lend themselves to poetic use of the stage." **Facilities:** Loeb Drama Center, 556 seats, flexible stage; Holyoke Street Theatre, 350 seats, proscenium stage; Church Street Theatre, 200 seats, black box. **Production considerations:** cast limit of 15.

AMERICAN STAGE
(Founded 1977)
Box 1560; St. Petersburg, FL 33731; (813) 823-1600, FAX 823-7529
Kenneth Noel Mitchell, *Artistic Director*

Submission procedure: no unsolicited scripts; professional recommendation. **Types of material:** full-length plays, adaptations, plays for young audiences. **Facilities:** American Stage, 130 seats, thrust stage. **Production considerations:** cast limit of 8; 1 set. **Best submission time:** year-round. **Response time:** 12 months. **Special programs:** New Visions: new play festival.

AMERICAN STAGE COMPANY
(Founded 1986)
Box 336; Teaneck, NJ 07666
James Vagias, *Executive Producer*

Submission procedure: no unsolicited scripts. **Types of material:** full-length plays, musicals. **Facilities:** American Stage in Residence at Fairleigh Dickinson University, 290 seats, proscenium stage. **Production considerations:** cast limit of 6–15.

AMERICAN STAGE FESTIVAL
(Founded 1974)
14 Court St; Nashua, NH 03060; (603) 889-2336
Attn: New Scripts, EARLY STAGES

Submission procedure: no unsolicited scripts; synopsis, 10-page dialogue sample and letter of inquiry with SASE for response; include cassette of 2–3 songs for musicals. **Types of material:** full-length plays, musicals. **Special interests:** material with strong emotional content that tells a compelling story, especially one that explores what used to be called "The American Dream." **Facilities:** Summer Stage, 492 seats, proscenium stage; Year-Round Stage, 277 seats, thrust. **Production considerations:** cast limit of 10 for plays, 15 plus 5 musicians for musicals. **Best submission time:** Sep–Dec. **Response time:** 2–3 months letter; 4–6 months script.

AMERICAN THEATER COMPANY
(Founded 1985)
1909 West Byron St; Chicago, IL 60613; (773) 929-5009, FAX 929-5171;
        E-mail atcdir@aol.com
Brian Russell, *Artistic Director*

Submission procedure: no unsolicited scripts; synopsis and letter of inquiry with SASP for response. **Types of material:** full-length plays, translations, adaptations, musicals. **Special interests:** language-oriented plays that utilize heightened theatrical reality; musicals; substantive comedies; social and political themes. **Facilities:** American Theater Company, 137 seats, modified thrust stage. **Production considerations:** prefers cast limit of 15; modest technical demands. **Best submission time:** year-round. **Response time:** 2–4 months letter; 6–12 months script.

AMERICAN THEATRE OF ACTORS, INC.
(Founded 1976)
314 West 54th St; New York, NY 10019; (212) 581-3044
James Jennings, *Artistic Director*

Submission procedure: accepts unsolicited scripts. **Types of material:** full-length plays, one-acts. **Special interests:** realistic plays dealing with contemporary social issues. **Facilities:** Chernuchin Theatre, 140 seats, proscenium stage; Sargent Theatre, 65 seats, proscenium stage; Beckmann Theatre, 35 seats, arena stage. **Production considerations:** cast limit of 8; minimal sets. **Best submission time:** year-round. **Response time:** 2 weeks.

APPLE TREE THEATRE

(Founded 1983)
595 Elm Place, Suite 210; Highland Park, IL 60035; (847) 432-8223,
   FAX 432-5214; Web http://www.appletreetheatre.com

Submission procedure: no unsolicited scripts; direct solicitation to playwright or agent. **Types of material:** full-length plays, adaptations, plays for young audiences, musicals. **Facilities:** Apple Tree Theatre, 177 seats, modified thrust stage. **Production considerations:** cast limit of 9; unit set. **Response time:** 4 months. **Special programs:** staged readings.

ARDEN THEATRE COMPANY

(Founded 1988)
40 North 2nd St; Philadelphia, PA 19106; (215) 922-8900; FAX 922-7011;
   Web http://www.libertynet.org/~arden
Terrence J. Nolen, *Producing Artistic Director*

Submission procedure: no unsolicited scripts; synopsis and letter of inquiry. **Types of material:** full-length plays, translations, adaptations, musicals. **Special interests:** new adaptations of literary works. **Facilities:** Haas Stage/Mainstage, 400 seats, flexible stage; Arcadia Stage/Studio Theatre, 175 seats, flexible stage. **Best submission time:** year-round. **Response time:** 3 months letter; 6 months script.

ARENA STAGE

(Founded 1950)
1101 6th St SW; Washington, DC 20024; (202) 554-9066, FAX 488-4056
Cathy Madison, *Literary Manager*

Submission procedure: no unsolicited scripts; synopsis, bio and letter of inquiry; submissions will be considered for developmental program. **Types of material:** full-length plays, translations, adaptations, solo pieces. **Special interests:** unproduced works; plays for a multicultural company; plays by women, writers of color, physically disabled writers and other "nonmainstream" artists; Latin American plays; Canadian plays. **Facilities:** Fichandler Stage, 827 seats, arena stage; The Kreeger Theater, 514 seats, modified thrust stage; The Old Vat Room, 110 seats, cabaret stage. **Best submission time:** year-round. **Response time:** 1 day letter; 6–12 months script.

ARIZONA THEATRE COMPANY

(Founded 1966)
Box 1631; Tucson, AZ 85702-1631; (520) 884-8210
Samantha K. Wyer, *Assistant to the Artistic Director*

Submission procedure: no unsolicited scripts; synopsis, 10-page dialogue sample, production history, resume and letter of inquiry. **Types of material:** full-length plays, translations, adaptations, musicals. **Facilities:** Herberger Theater Center (in Phoenix), 800 seats, proscenium stage; Temple of Music and Art (in Tucson), 600 seats, proscenium stage. **Best submission time:** spring–summer. **Response time:**

1 month letter; 4–6 months script. **Special programs:** New Play Reading Series: rehearsed readings followed by discussion with audience. National Hispanic Playwriting Award (see Prizes).

ARKANSAS REPERTORY THEATRE
(Founded 1976)
Box 110; Little Rock, AR 72203-0110; (501) 378-0445, FAX 378-0012
Brad Mooy, *Literary Manager*

Submission procedure: no unsolicited scripts; synopsis and letter of inquiry. **Types of material:** full-length plays, musicals, cabaret/revues, solo pieces. **Facilities:** Arkansas Repertory Theatre, 354 seats, proscenium stage; Second Stage, 99 seats, black box. **Production considerations:** prefers small cast. **Best submission time:** year-round. **Response time:** 3 months letter; 3–6 months script. **Special programs:** New Playreading Series.

ARROW ROCK LYCEUM THEATRE
(Founded 1961)
High St; Arrow Rock, MO 65320; (660) 837-3311, FAX 837-3112
Michael Bollinger, *Artistic Producing Director*

Submission procedure: no unsolicited scripts; direct solicitation to playwright or agent. **Types of material:** full-length plays, translations, adaptations, musicals. **Facilities:** Arrow Rock Lyceum Theatre, 408 seats, semithrust stage.

ART STATION
(Founded 1986)
Box 1998; Stone Mountain, GA 30086; (770) 469-1105, FAX 469-0355;
    E-mail info@artstation.org; Web http://www.artstation.org
Jon Goldstein, *Literary Manager*

Submission procedure: accepts unsolicited scripts. **Types of material:** full-length plays, adaptations, musicals, solo pieces. **Special interests:** professionally unproduced works; new works by southern playwrights. **Facilities:** ART Station Theatre, 100 seats, proscenium/thrust stage. **Production considerations:** cast limit of 6; single set; no fly space. **Best submission time:** Jun–Dec. **Response time:** 4 months. **Special programs:** I.T.C. Playwrights Project: year-round playwrights group meets bimonthly to critique and develop new works; presents monthly staged readings.

ARTISTS REPERTORY THEATRE
(Founded 1981)
1516 Southwest Alder St; Portland, OR 97205; (503) 241-9807, FAX 241-8268;
    E-mail allen@artistsrep.org; Web http://www.artistsrep.org
Allen Nause, *Artistic Director*

Submission procedure: no unsolicited scripts; synopsis and letter of inquiry. **Types of material:** full-length plays, adaptations. **Facilities:** Reiersgaard Theatre, 150–170 seats, flexible black box. **Production considerations:** cast limit of 10; 1 set or unit set. **Best submission time:** year-round. **Response time:** 1 month letter; 6 months script. **Special programs:** Play Lab: staged reading series.

ARTS AT ST. ANN'S
(Founded 1979)
157 Montague St; Brooklyn, NY 11201; (718) 834-8794, FAX 522-2470
Susan Feldman, *Artistic Director*

Submission procedure: no unsolicited scripts; synopsis and letter of inquiry. **Types of material:** full-length plays, musicals. **Special interests:** musical theatre works. **Facilities:** Church of St. Ann and Holy Trinity, 652 seats, flexible stage; Parish Hall, 100 seats, flexible stage. **Best submission time:** year-round. **Response time:** 2 months letter; 3 months script.

ARVADA CENTER FOR THE ARTS & HUMANITIES
(Founded 1976)
6901 Wadsworth Blvd; Arvada, CO 80003; (303) 431-3080, FAX 431-3083
Kathy Kuehn, *Performing Arts Director*

Submission procedure: no unsolicited scripts; synopsis and letter of inquiry. **Types of material:** plays for young audiences only. **Facilities:** Arvada Center Amphitheater, 1200 seats, proscenium stage; Arvada Center Main Stage, 498 seats, thrust stage. **Production considerations:** cast limit of 6–9; minimal set. **Best submission time:** year-round. **Response time:** 3–5 months letter; 5–8 months script.

ASIAN AMERICAN THEATER COMPANY
(Founded 1973)
1840 Sutter St, Suite 207; San Francisco, CA 94115; (415) 440-5545,
    FAX 440-5597; E-mail aatc@wenet.net
Pamela A. Wu, *Producing Director*

Submission procedure: accepts unsolicited scripts with synopsis, character breakdown, resume and letter of inquiry. **Types of material:** full-length plays, adaptations, plays for young audiences. **Special interests:** plays that explore diversity of the Asian-Pacific–American experience. **Facilities:** no permanent facility. **Best submission time:** year-round. **Response time:** 3–6 months.

ASOLO THEATRE COMPANY
(Founded 1960)
5555 North Tamiami Trail; Sarasota, FL 34243; (941) 351-9010, FAX 351-5796;
    E-mail bruce_rodgers@asolo.org; Web http://www.asolo.org
Bruce E. Rodgers, *Associate Artistic Director*

Submission procedure: no unsolicited scripts; 1-page synopsis and letter of inquiry with SASE for response. **Types of material:** full-length plays, translations, adaptations, solo pieces. **Special interests:** adaptations of great literature. **Facilities:** The Mertz Theatre, 499 seats, proscenium stage; The Cook Theatre, 161 seats, proscenium stage. **Best submission time:** Jun–Aug. **Response time:** 2 months letter; 6 months script.

ATLANTIC THEATER COMPANY

(Founded 1984)
453 West 16th St; New York, NY 10011; (212) 691-5919, FAX 691-6280
Toni Amicarella, *Literary Manager*

Submission procedure: no unsolicited scripts; agent submission. **Types of material:** full-length plays, one-acts, adaptations. **Facilities:** Atlantic Theater Mainstage, 160 seats, proscenium stage; Black Box, 70 seats, proscenium stage. **Best submission time:** fall–winter. **Response time:** 3–6 months. **Special programs:** Atlantic 453: year-round play readings, workshops and productions in Black Box Space.

ATTIC THEATRE CENTRE

(Founded 1987)
6562½ Santa Monica Blvd; Hollywood, CA 90038; (323) 469-3786,
      FAX 463-9571
James Carey, *Producing Artistic Director*

Submission procedure: no unsolicited scripts; synopsis, dialogue sample and letter of inquiry with SASE for response. **Types of material:** full-length plays, one-acts, solo pieces. **Facilities:** Mainstage, 53 seats, black box; Attic 2, 43 seats, black box. **Production considerations:** simple sets; no fly or wing space. **Best submission time:** year-round. **Response time:** 1 month letter; 3–6 months script. **Special programs:** play reading series; developmental workshops; Attic Theatre Ensemble's One-Act Marathon (see Prizes).

AULIS COLLECTIVE FOR THEATER AND MEDIA, INC.

(Founded 1996)
Box 673, Prince St Station; New York, NY 10012
Literary Manager

Submission procedure: no unsolicited scripts; synopsis, resume and letter of inquiry with SASE for response. **Types of material:** full-length plays, one-acts, solo pieces, performance art. **Special interests:** works that explore the connections between domestic violence against children and global violence; plays with music. **Facilities:** no permanent space; various black box theatres under 99 seats. **Best submission time:** year-round. **Response time:** 3 months letter; 6 months script.

AURORA THEATRE COMPANY
(Founded 1992)
2315 Durant Ave; Berkeley, CA 94704; (510) 843-4822, FAX 843-4826;
    Web http://auroratheatre.org
Literary Manager

Submission procedure: no unsolicited scripts; synopsis and letter of inquiry. **Types of material:** full-length plays, adaptations. **Special interests:** plays emphasizing language and ideas. **Facilities:** Aurora Theatre, 67 seats, arena stage. **Production considerations:** cast limit of 8; minimal production demands. **Best submission time:** year-round. **Response time:** 6 months letter; 6 months script.

THE B STREET THEATRE
(Founded 1992)
2711 B St; Sacramento, CA 95816; (916) 443-5391;
    Web http://www.sna.com/bstreet/
Buck Busfield, *Producing Director*

Submission procedure: no unsolicited scripts; agent submission. **Types of material:** full-length plays. **Special interests:** contemporary comedies and dramas with an edge; no "TV writing." **Facilities:** The B Street Theatre, 150 seats, black box. **Production considerations:** cast limit of 6; no fly space; modest production demands. **Best submission time:** year-round. **Response time:** 3–6 months.

BAILIWICK REPERTORY
(Founded 1982)
Bailiwick Arts Center; 1229 West Belmont; Chicago, IL 60657-3205;
    (773) 883-1090; E-mail bailiwickr@aol.com
David Zak, *Artistic Director*

Submission procedure: send SASE for manuscript submission guidelines. **Types of material:** full-length plays, translations, adaptations, musicals, solo pieces. **Special interests:** translations and adaptations; theatrically inventive and/or politically intriguing works; plays by women for Women's Work series; work appropriate for Deaf Bailiwick Artists, especially work by deaf or hard-of-hearing writers. **Facilities:** mainstage, 150 seats, flexible/thrust stage; cabaret/studio, 100 seats, flexible stage. **Best submission time:** year-round. **Response time:** 8–12 months. **Special programs:** note: all playwrights submitting to these programs must first send SASE for submission guidelines. Pride Performance Series: year-round exploration of works of interest to the lesbian and gay communities, culminating in summer festival. Director's Festival: annual directors' showcase of 48 plays, 10–50 minutes long, staged in black-box setting. Studio Series: workshops and readings of plays, performance pieces and musicals.

BARKSDALE THEATRE
(Founded 1953)
1601 Willow Lawn Dr, Suite 301E; Richmond, VA 23230; (804) 282-9440,
    FAX 288-6470; E-mail barksdalev@aol.com
Randy Strawderman, *Artistic Director*

Submission procedure: no unsolicited scripts; synopsis and letter of inquiry. **Types of material:** full-length plays, one-acts, translations, adaptations, plays for young audiences, musicals, cabaret/revues, solo pieces. **Facilities:** Mainstage, 214 seats, arena stage. **Production considerations:** small cast, minimal production demands; no fly or wing space. **Best submission time:** summer. **Response time:** 6 months letter; 12 months script.

THE BARROW GROUP
(Founded 1986)
Box 5112; New York, NY 10185; (212) 522-1421, FAX 522-1402
Assistant Literary Manager

Submission procedure: no unsolicited scripts; professional recommendation. **Types of material:** full-length plays, translations, adaptations. **Facilities:** no permanent facility. **Production considerations:** cast limit of 12; minimal sets. **Best submission time:** year-round. **Response time:** 1–6 months.

BARTER THEATRE
(Founded 1933)
Box 867; Abingdon, VA 24212-0867; (540) 628-2281, FAX 628-4551;
    E-mail barter@naxs.com; Web http://www.bartertheatre.com
Richard Rose, *Producing Artistic Director*

Submission procedure: no unsolicited scripts; synopsis, dialogue sample and letter of inquiry; send sample cassette for musicals. **Types of material:** full-length plays, translations, adaptations, plays for young audiences, musicals. **Special interests:** social issues and current events; works that expand theatrical form; nonurban-oriented material. **Facilities:** Barter Theatre, 508 seats, proscenium stage; Barter's Stage II, 140 seats, flexible stage. **Production considerations:** cast of 4–10. **Best submission time:** Mar, Sep. **Response time:** 9 months letter; 12 months script. **Special programs:** Barter's Early Stages: script development program.

BAY STREET THEATRE
(Founded 1991)
Box 810; Sag Harbor, NY 11963; (516) 725-0818, FAX 725-0906;
    Web http://www.baystreet.org
Mia Emlen Grosjean, *Literary Manager*

Submission procedure: no unsolicited scripts; agent submission. **Types of material:** full-length plays, musicals, solo pieces. **Special interests:** plays that challenge as well as entertain; plays that "address the heart of our community and champion the human spirit." **Facilities:** Mainstage, 299 seats, thrust stage.

Production considerations: cast limit of 8–9; prefers unit set; no fly or wing space; small-scale musicals only. **Best submission time:** year-round. **Response time:** 3–6 months. **Special programs:** Reading series: readings of 2 new plays each fall and spring; playwright receives $50 honorarium and travel from New York City; scripts for special programs selected through theatre's normal submission procedure.

BERKELEY REPERTORY THEATRE
(Founded 1968)
2025 Addison St; Berkeley, CA 94704; (510) 204-8901, FAX 841-7711;
    E-mail litman@berkeleyrep.org
Literary Manager

Submission procedure: no unsolicited scripts; direct solicitation to playwright or agent. **Types of material:** full-length plays, translations, adaptations. **Facilities:** Mark Taper Mainstage, 400 seats, thrust stage. **Special programs:** Parallel Season: productions of 2–3 new plays each season. Commissioning program. In-house readings.

THE BELMONT PLAYHOUSE
(Founded 1991)
2385 Arthur Ave; Bronx, NY 10458; (718) 304-4348, FAX 563-5053;
    E-mail thebelmont@hotmail.com
Dante Albertie, *Artistic Director*

Submission procedure: accepts unsolicited scripts. **Types of material:** full-length plays, translations, adaptations. **Special interests:** plays with Italian-American or urban themes. **Facilities:** Belmont Playhouse, 75 seats, black box; Performance Space, 25–100 seats, platform. **Production considerations:** cast limit of 6; one set; no fly space. **Best submission time:** year-round. **Response time:** 3–5 months.

BERKSHIRE THEATRE FESTIVAL
(Founded 1928)
Box 797; Stockbridge, MA 01262; (413) 298-5536, FAX 298-3368;
    E-mail info@berkshiretheatre.org; Web http://www.berkshiretheatre.org
Kate Maguire, *Producing Director*

Submission procedure: no unsolicited scripts; agent submission. **Types of material:** full-length plays, musicals, solo pieces. **Special interests:** thought-provoking vacation entertainment; theatre on the "cutting edge." **Facilities:** Playhouse, 413 seats, proscenium stage; Unicorn Theatre, 124 seats, thrust stage. **Production considerations:** cast limit of 8 for plays; small orchestra for musicals. **Best submission time:** Oct–Dec. **Response time:** 3 months. **Special programs:** staged reading series.

BILINGUAL FOUNDATION OF THE ARTS

(Founded 1973)
421 North Ave 19; Los Angeles, CA 90031; (323) 225-4044, FAX 225-1250
Agustin Coppola, *Dramaturg*

Submission procedure: accepts unsolicited scripts. **Types of material:** full-length plays, translations, adaptations, plays for young audiences. **Special interests:** plays with Hispanic themes or by Hispanic playwrights only. **Facilities:** BFA's Little Theatre, 99 seats, thrust stage; uses theatres at Los Angeles Center for the Arts for some mainstage productions. **Production considerations:** cast limit of 10; simple set. **Best submission time:** year-round. **Response time:** 3–6 months.

BIRMINGHAM CHILDREN'S THEATRE

(Founded 1947)
Box 1362; Birmingham, AL 35201; (205) 458-8181, FAX 458-8895;
    Web http://www.bct123.org
Burt Brosowsky, *Executive Director*

Submission procedure: accepts scripts; prefers synopsis and letter of inquiry. **Types of material:** plays for young audiences. **Special interests:** interactive plays for preschool–grade 2; presentational plays for K–6. **Facilities:** Birmingham-Jefferson Civic Center Theatre, 1073 seats, thrust stage; Studio Theatre, up to 250 seats, lab space. **Production considerations:** prefers cast of 4–6. **Best submission time:** Sep–Dec. **Response time:** 2 weeks letter; minimum 2 months script.

BLOOMSBURG THEATRE ENSEMBLE

(Founded 1978)
226 Center St; Bloomsburg, PA 17815; (570) 784-5530, FAX 784-4912;
    Web http://www.bte.org
Tom Byrn, *Play Selection Chair*

Submission procedure: no unsolicited scripts; synopsis, dialogue sample, professional recommendation and letter of inquiry. **Types of material:** full-length plays, translations, adaptations. **Special interests:** new translations of classics; rural themes; plays suitable for small acting ensemble. **Facilities:** Alvina Krause Theatre, 369 seats, proscenium stage. **Production considerations:** small to mid-sized cast; 1 set or unit set. **Best submission time:** summer. **Response time:** 3 months letter; 6 months script.

BOARSHEAD THEATER

(Founded 1966)
425 South Grand Ave; Lansing, MI 48933; (517) 484-7800, FAX 484-2564
John Peakes, *Artistic Director*

Submission procedure: no unsolicited scripts; synopsis, character breakdown, 6–10-page dialogue sample and letter of inquiry with SASP for response. **Types of material:** full-length plays, plays for young audiences. **Special interests:** one-act plays for young audiences only; plays that make use of theatrical conventions or create new ones; social issues; comedies; no musicals. **Facilities:** Center for the Arts, 249 seats, thrust stage. **Production considerations:** cast limit of 4–6 for children's shows. **Best submission time:** year-round. **Response time:** 1 month letter; 3–6 months script. **Special programs:** staged readings of 5 new plays a year.

BORDERLANDS THEATER
(Founded 1986)
Box 2791; Tucson, AZ 85702; (520) 882-8607, FAX 882-7406 (call first);
 E-mail bltheater@aol.com

Submission procedure: no unsolicited scripts; synopsis and letter of inquiry. **Types of material:** full-length plays, translations, adaptations. **Special interests:** cultural diversity; race relations; "border" issues, including concerns of the geographical border region as well as the metaphorical borders of gender, class and race. **Facilities:** Pima Community College Center for the Arts: 1st theatre, 400 seats, proscenium stage; 2nd theatre, 160 seats, black box. **Production considerations:** cast limit of 12; minimal set. **Best submission time:** year-round. **Response time:** 1 month letter; 3–6 months script.

BRISTOL RIVERSIDE THEATRE
(Founded 1986)
Box 1250; Bristol, PA 19007; (215) 785-6664, FAX 785-2762;
 E-mail brtboss@aol.com; Web http://www.brtstage.org
David J. Abers, *Assistant to Artistic Director*

Submission procedure: accepts unsolicited scripts. **Types of material:** full-length plays, one-acts, translations, adaptations, musicals, solo pieces. **Special interests:** cutting-edge works; plays that experiment with form; translations; musicals. **Facilities:** Bristol Riverside Theatre, 302 seats, flexible stage. **Production considerations:** cast limit of 10 for plays, 18 for musicals, 9 for orchestra; minimal production demands. **Best submission time:** spring. **Response time:** 6–8 months. **Special programs:** year-round reading series.

CALIFORNIA REPERTORY COMPANY
(Founded 1989)
1250 Bellflower Blvd; Long Beach, CA 90840-2701; (562) 985-5357,
 FAX 985-2263
Howard Burman, *Artistic Producing Director*

Submission procedure: direct solicitation to playwright or agent. **Types of material:** full-length plays, translations, adaptations. **Special interests:** international works. **Facilities:** UT Theatre, 400 seats, proscenium stage; Studio Theatre, 225 seats, flexible stage; Players Theatre, 90 seats, proscenium stage. **Production considerations:** cast of 8–18. **Best submission time:** Sep, Mar. **Response time:** 3 weeks letter; 2 months script.

CALIFORNIA SHAKESPEARE FESTIVAL
(Founded 1973)
701 Heinz Ave; Berkeley, CA 94710; (510) 548-3422, FAX 843-9921;
E-mail letters@calshakes.org; Web http://www.calshakes.org
Artistic Associate

Submission procedure: no unsolicited scripts; synopis and letter of inquiry. **Types of material:** translations, adaptations. **Special interests:** new translations and adaptations of classical plays suitable for large-scale, outdoor production only. **Facilities:** Bruns Amphitheatre, 521 seats, outdoor proscenium. **Best submission time:** fall. **Response time:** 6 months letter; 6 months script.

CALIFORNIA THEATRE CENTER
(Founded 1976)
Box 2007; Sunnyvale, CA 94087; (408) 245-2979, FAX 245-0235;
E-mail ctc@ctcinc.org
Will Huddleston, *Resident Director*

Submission procedure: accepts unsolicited scripts; prefers synopsis and letter of inquiry. **Types of material:** plays for young audiences. **Special interests:** classics adapted for young audiences; comedies; historical material. **Facilities:** company primarily tours to large proscenium-stage theatres; Sunnyvale Performing Arts Center (home theatre), 200 seats, proscenium stage. **Production considerations:** cast limit of 8 for professional touring productions; minimum cast of 15 for conservatory productions; modest production demands. **Best submission time:** year-round. **Response time:** 1 month letter; 4–6 months script.

CAPITAL REPERTORY COMPANY
(Founded 1981)
111 North Pearl St; Albany, NY 12207; (562) 462-4531, ext 293, FAX 462-4531
Margaret Mancinelli-Cahill, *Producing Artistic Director*

Submission procedure: no unsolicited scripts; agent submission. **Types of material:** full-length plays, translations, adaptations, music-theatre works. **Facilities:** Capital Rep Theatre, 299 seats, thrust stage. **Production considerations:** simple set. **Best submission time:** late spring. **Response time:** 4–6 months.

CARMEL PERFORMING ARTS FESTIVAL
(Founded 1996)
Box 221473; Carmel, CA 93922; (408) 644-8383, FAX 647-0758;
E-mail rmckee@mbay.net; Web http://www.carmelfest.org
Robin McKee, *Producing Artistic Director*

Submission procedure: no unsolicited scripts; professional recommendation. **Types of material:** full-length plays, one-acts, translations, adaptations, plays for young audiences, solo pieces, performance art. **Facilities:** Golden Bough, 305 seats, proscenium stage; Circle Theatre, 99 seats, thrust stage; Cherry Center for the Arts, 48 seats, proscenium stage. **Production considerations:** prefers cast limit of 10. **Best submission time:** Mar. **Response time:** 4–5 months. **Special programs:** CPAF Reading Series: annual staged readings and workshops; playwright receives modest honorarium, travel, housing; submit synopsis and letter of inquiry to Readings Coordinator; *deadline:* 15 April 2000; *notification:* 15 May 2000; *dates:* Oct 2000.

THE CAST THEATRE
(Founded 1976)
804 North El Centro Ave; Hollywood, CA 90038; (323) 462-0265
Literary Manager

Submission procedure: accepts unsolicited scripts. **Types of material:** full-length plays. **Special interests:** previously unproduced works. **Facilities:** Cast at the Circle, 99 seats, proscenium stage; Cast, 65 seats, proscenium stage. **Best submission time:** year-round. **Response time:** 6 months.

CASTILLO THEATRE
(Founded 1983)
500 Greenwich St, Suite 201; New York, NY 10013; (212) 941-5800,
    FAX 941-8340; E-mail castilloth@aol.com;
    Web http://www.castillo.org
Fred Newman, *Artistic Director*

Submission procedure: no unsolicited scripts; synopsis, 5–10 page dialogue sample and letter of inquiry; prefers playwright see theatre production before submitting. **Types of material:** full-length plays, one-acts. **Special interests:** plays that address social, cultural and political concerns and challenge theatrical and social convention; multiracial/multicultural issues. **Facilities:** Castillo Theatre, 71 seats, thrust stage. **Best submission time:** year-round. **Response time:** 2 months letter; 6 months script. **Special programs:** weekly playwriting workshop; contact Dan Friedman, dramaturg, for information.

CELEBRATION THEATRE
(Founded 1982)
7985 Santa Monica Blvd; Los Angeles, CA 90046; (323) 957-1884,
    FAX 957-1826; Web http://www.celebrationtheatre.com
Tom Jacobson, *Literary Manager*

Submission procedure: accepts unsolicited scripts. **Types of material:** full-length plays, one-acts, adaptations, musicals, cabaret/revues. **Special interests:** plays not previously produced on the West Coast with gay and lesbian themes. **Facilities:** Celebration Theatre, 65 seats, thrust stage. **Production considerations:** cast limit of 12; single set. **Best submission time:** year-round. **Response time:** 6 months.

CENTER STAGE
(Founded 1963)
700 North Calvert St; Baltimore, MD 21202-3686; (410) 685-3200,
   FAX 539-3912
James Magruder, *Resident Dramaturg*

Submission procedure: no unsolicited scripts; synopsis, sample pages and letter of inquiry. **Types of material:** full-length plays, translations, adaptations, music-theatre works, solo pieces. **Special interests:** plays with no previous mainstage production. **Facilities:** Pearlstone Theater, 541 seats, modified thrust stage; Head Theater, 100–400 seats, flexible space. **Best submission time:** year-round. **Response time:** 5–7 weeks letter; 4–6 months script.

CENTRE STAGE–SOUTH CAROLINA!
(Founded 1983)
Box 8451; Greenville, SC 29604-8451; (864) 233-6733, FAX 233-3901;
   E-mail cbla@infoave.net
Claude W. Blakely, *Administrative Director*

Submission procedure: accepts unsolicited scripts. **Types of material:** full-length plays, one-acts, plays for young audiences, musicals, cabaret/revues. **Special interests:** plays for young audiences; issues of interest to senior citizens and minorities; musical revues. **Facilities:** Mainstage, 300 seats, thrust stage; Youth Theatre, 175 seats, thrust stage. **Production considerations:** 2 sets; no fly space; limited wing space. **Best submission time:** year-round. **Response time:** 2 months. **Special programs:** Sunday Evenings Readers Theatre: regularly scheduled rehearsed readings presented for public followed by audience discussion.

CENTER THEATER ENSEMBLE
(Founded 1985)
1346 West Devon Ave; Chicago, IL 60660; (773) 508-0200
Dale Calandra, *Literary Manager*

Submission procedure: no unsolicited scripts; synopsis, resume and letter of inquiry with SASE for response. **Types of material:** full-length plays, translations, adaptations, musicals, solo pieces. **Special interests:** comedies; plays creating a heightened reality; language-oriented plays; dramas of substance; original musicals only. **Facilities:** Mainstage, 75 seats, modified thrust stage; Studio, 35 seats, black box. **Production considerations:** cast limit of approximately 12; limited wing space, no fly space. **Best submission time:** year-round. **Response time:** 3 months letter; 3 months script. **Special programs:** Playwrights Workshop Series: participation by invitation only. Actor/Director/Playwright Unit: participants meet monthly to work on scripts; some scripts given staged reading, possibly leads to 2-week developmental workshop and performances and/or full production; participants selected through personal interview; Chicago-area playwrights contact Dale Calandra, Workshop Coordinator, for appointment. Center Theater International Playwrighting Contest (see Prizes).

THE CHANGING SCENE
(Founded 1968)
1527½ Champa St; Denver, CO 80202; (303) 893-5775
Maxine Munt, *Literary Manager*

Submission procedure: accepts unsolicited scripts. **Types of material:** full-length plays, performance art. **Special interests:** previously unproduced work only; nonrealistic plays. **Facilities:** The Changing Scene, 76 seats, black box. **Production considerations:** cast limit of 10; prefers single adjustable set. **Best submission time:** year-round. **Response time:** 4–6 months.

CHARLOTTE REPERTORY THEATRE
(Founded 1976)
129 West Trade St; Charlotte, NC 28202; (704) 333-8587,
      FAX 333-0224
Claudia Carter Covington, *Literary Manager*

Submission procedure: accepts unsolicited scripts. **Types of material:** full-length plays. **Special interests:** professionally unproduced work; no children's works. **Facilities:** Booth Theatre at North Carolina Blumenthal Performing Arts Center, 450 seats, flexible stage. **Best submission time:** year-round. **Response time:** 3–6 months. **Special programs:** Festival of New American Plays: annual festival of staged readings; stipend, transportation and housing provided.

CHICAGO DRAMATISTS

See Membership and Service Organizations.

THE CHILDREN'S THEATRE COMPANY
(Founded 1965)
2400 Third Ave S; Minneapolis, MN 55404-3597; (612) 874-0500,
      FAX 874-8119
Elissa Adams, *Director of New Play Development*

Submission procedure: no unsolicited scripts; synopsis, first 20 pages of script, resume and letter of inquiry. **Types of material:** full-length plays, one-acts, translations, adaptations, plays for young audiences, musicals. **Special interests:** adaptations or original plays for young audiences; work samples from writer's with no previous experience writing for children's theatre. **Facilities:** Children's Theatre Company, 745 seats, proscenium stage. **Best submission time:** Jul–Feb. **Response time:** 1 month letter; 6 months script. **Special programs:** Threshold: 1–4 works for young audiences commissioned each year for developmental laboratory.

CHILDSPLAY
(Founded 1977)
Box 517; Tempe, AZ 85280; (602) 350-8101, FAX 350-8584
David Saar, *Artistic Director*

Submission procedure: no unsolicited scripts; synopsis, 10-page dialogue sample and letter of inquiry. **Types of material:** plays for young audiences, including full-length plays, adaptations, musicals, performance pieces. **Special interests:** nontraditional plays; material that entertains and challenges both performers and audiences; 2nd and 3rd productions of unpublished work. **Facilities:** Herberger Theater Center Stage, 800 seats, proscenium stage; Scottsdale Center for the Arts, 800 seats, proscenium stage; Stage West, 350 seats, proscenium stage; Tempe Performing Arts Center, 175 seats, black box; also performs in Tucson (no permanent space). **Production considerations:** some van-sized touring productions. **Best submission time:** Jun–Oct. **Response time:** 1 month letter; 3 months script. **Special programs:** commissioning program.

CINCINNATI PLAYHOUSE IN THE PARK
(Founded 1960)
Box 6537; Cincinnati, OH 45206-0537; (513) 345-2242
Edward Stern, *Producing Artistic Director*

Submission procedure: no unsolicited scripts; agent submission. Rosenthal New Play Prize (see Prizes) accepts synopsis and dialogue sample. **Types of material:** full-length plays, translations, adaptations, musicals. **Facilities:** Robert S. Marx Theatre, 629 seats, thrust stage; Thompson Shelterhouse, 220 seats, thrust stage. **Best submission time:** year-round. **Response time:** 4-6 months. **Special programs:** Lois and Richard Rosenthal New Play Prize (see Prizes).

CITY THEATRE COMPANY
(Founded 1974)
57 South 13th St; Pittsburgh, PA 15203; (412) 431-4400, FAX 431-5535;
        E-mail theatre@citytheatre-pgh.org; Web http://www.citytheatre-pgh.org
Marc Masterson, *Producing Director*

Submission procedure: no unsolicited scripts; agent submission. **Types of material:** full-length plays, chamber musicals, solo pieces. **Special interests:** plays of substance with strong storyline. **Facilities:** mainstage, 250 seats, proscenium/thrust stage; laboratory theatre, 99 seats, black box. **Production considerations:** cast limit of 8. **Best submission time:** year-round. **Response time:** 4 months.

CIVIC THEATRES OF CENTRAL FLORIDA
(Founded 1926)
1001 East Princeton St; Orlando, FL 32803; (407) 896-7365, FAX 897-3284
Ellen Jones, *Producing Artistic Director*

Submission procedure: no unsolicited scripts; synopsis, production history, resume, professional recommendation and letter of inquiry. **Types of material:** full-length plays, plays for young audiences, musicals. **Facilities:** Family Classics, 350 seats, thrust stage; Mainstage, 350 seats, proscenium stage; Secondstage, 100 seats, thrust stage. **Best submission time:** year-round. **Response time:** 3 months letter; 6 months script.

CLARENCE BROWN THEATRE COMPANY
(Founded 1974)
206 McClung Tower; Knoxville, TN 37996; (423) 974-6011, FAX 974-4867;
    E-mail cbt@utk.edu; Web http://web.utk.edu/~cbt/
Thomas P. Cooke, *Producing Artistic Director*

Submission procedure: no unsolicited scripts; synopsis, character breakdown, 1–2 pages of dialogue and letter of inquiry. **Types of material:** full-length plays. **Special interests:** contemporary American plays. **Facilities:** Clarence Brown Theatre, 600 seats, proscenium stage; Carousel Theatre, 250 seats, arena stage. **Best submission time:** year-round. **Response time:** 1 month letter; 1 month script.

CLASSIC STAGE COMPANY
(Founded 1969)
136 East 13th St; New York, NY 10003; (212) 677-4210, FAX 477-7504
Artistic Associate

Submission procedure: no unsolicited scripts; synopsis, dialogue sample and letter of inquiry. **Types of material:** translations and adaptations of "classic literature and themes only." **Special interests:** translations and adaptations of classic plays; adaptations of major nondramatic classics; prefers highly theatrical work. **Facilities:** Classic Stage Company, 180 seats, flexible stage. **Best submission time:** year-round. **Response time:** 2 months letter; 3 months script. **Special programs:** developmental program of rehearsed readings.

THE CLEVELAND PLAY HOUSE
(Founded 1916)
8500 Euclid Ave; Cleveland, OH 44106-0189; (216) 795-7010, FAX 795-7005
Scott Kanoff, *Literary Manager/Resident Director*

Submission procedure: no unsolicited scripts; resume and letter of inquiry with SASE for response. **Types of material:** full-length plays, adaptations, musicals. **Facilities:** Kenyon C. Bolton Theatre, 612 seats, proscenium stage; Francis E. Drury Theatre, 501 seats, proscenium stage. **Best submission time:** Sep–Dec. **Response time:** 1–2 months letter; 1–3 months script. **Special programs:** The Next Stage (see Development).

CLEVELAND PUBLIC THEATRE
(Founded 1981)
6415 Detroit Ave; Cleveland, OH 44102-3011; (216) 631-2727, FAX 631-2575;
    E-mail cpt@en.com; Web http://www.clevelandartists.net/cpt
James A. Levin, *Artistic Director*

Submission procedure: no unsolicited scripts; synopsis, 5–page dialogue sample and letter of inquiry. **Types of material:** full-length plays, one-acts, solo pieces. **Special interests:** experimental, poetic, politically, intellectually and spiritually challenging works; voices not heard in the mainstream (people of color, women, gays and lesbians, seniors, youth under 18); no standard commercial fare or "anything you might see on TV." **Facilities:** Gordon Square Theatre, 550 seats, flexible thrust; Cleveland Public Theatre, 150–175 seats, flexible stage (arena/proscenium); Down Stage, 60 seats, black box. **Production considerations:** cast limit of 10; simple set. **Best submission time:** year-round. **Response time:** 6 weeks letter; 9 months script. **Special programs:** New Plays Festival: 2-week developmental workshops of 6 plays culminating in stage readings; scripts selected through theatre's normal submission procedure; *deadline:* 1 Aug 2000; *notification:* Dec 2000; *dates:* Jan–Mar 2001.

COCONUT GROVE PLAYHOUSE
(Founded 1954)
3500 Main Highway; Miami, FL 33133; (305) 442-2662, FAX 444-6437
Arnold Mittelman, *Producing Artistic Director*

Submission procedure: no unsolicited scripts; synopsis and letter of inquiry. **Types of material:** full-length plays, translations, musicals, cabaret/revues. **Special interests:** dramas, musicals. **Facilities:** Mainstage, 1100 seats, proscenium stage; Encore Room, 150 seats, cabaret. **Best submission time:** year-round. **Response time:** 1 week letter; 2 months script.

THE COLONY STUDIO THEATRE
(Founded 1975)
1944 Riverside Dr; Los Angeles, CA 90039; (323) 665-0280, FAX 667-3235;
    E-mail theatrecol@aol.com

Submission procedure: no unsolicited scripts; professional recommendation. **Types of material:** full-length plays, adaptations. **Facilities:** Studio Theatre, 99 seats, thrust stage. **Production considerations:** cast of 6–20; plays cast from resident company. **Best submission time:** year-round. **Response time:** 6 months.

COMMONWEAL THEATRE COMPANY

(Founded 1989)
Box 15; Lanesboro, MN 55949; (507) 467-2525, FAX 467-2468;
    E-mail cmmnweal@polaristel.net
Hal Cropp, *Core Artist*

Submission procedure: no unsolicited scripts; professional recommendation. **Types of material:** full-length plays, translations, adaptations. **Facilities:** St. Mane Theatre, 126 seats, proscenium stage. **Production considerations:** prefers cast limit of 9; 1 set; no wing space. **Best submission time:** Oct–Dec. **Response time:** 1 month. **Special programs:** Commonweal New Play Workshop: annual 2-week developmental workshop for 1 script chosen from regular submissions; play receives rehearsals culminating in staged reading for invited audience; playwright receives housing during workshop.

CONEY ISLAND, USA

(Founded 1980)
1208 Surf Ave; Coney Island, NY 11224; (718) 372-5159, FAX 372-5101;
    E-mail dzigun@echonyc.com; Web http://www.coneyislandusa.com
Dick D. Zigun, *Artistic Director*

Submission procedure: no unsolicited scripts; synopsis, resume, reviews of prior work and letter of inquiry. **Types of material:** company books in already existing productions of plays and performance art. **Special interests:** new and old vaudeville; pop music; pop culture; Americana bizarro. **Facilities:** Sideshows by the Seashore, 150 seats, arena stage; also open-air performances on streets. **Best submission time:** year-round. **Response time:** 1 month letter; 6 months script.

CONTEMPORARY AMERICAN THEATER FESTIVAL

(Founded 1991)
Box 429; Shepherdstown, WV 25443; (304) 876-3473, FAX 876-0955;
    Web http://www.catf.org
Ed Herendeen, *Producing Director*

Submission procedure: no unsolicited scripts; synopsis and letter of inquiry. **Types of material:** full-length plays. **Special interests:** new American plays; contemporary issues. **Facilities:** Main Stage, 350 seats, proscenium stage; Studio Theater, 99 seats, black box. **Best submission time:** fall. **Response time:** 1 month letter; 3–6 months script. **Special programs:** staged readings each Tuesday night during summer season.

CORNERSTONE THEATER COMPANY
(Founded 1986)
708 Traction Ave; Los Angeles, CA 90013; (213) 613-1700, FAX 613-1714;
E-mail cornerstn@aol.com
Daniel Forcey, *Administrative Associate*

Submission procedure: no unsolicited scripts; letter of inquiry only. **Types of material:** full-length plays, adaptations, musicals. **Special interests:** company primarily interested in collaborating with playwrights to develop new works or contemporary adaptations of classics, focusing on specific communities. **Facilities:** no permanent facility. **Best submission time:** year-round. **Response time:** 2 months.

THE COTERIE THEATRE
(Founded 1979)
2450 Grand Ave; Kansas City, MO 64108-2520; (816) 474-6785,
FAX 474-7112; E-mail jefchurch@aol.com; Web http://www.thecoterie.com
Jeff Church, *Producing Artistic Director*

Submission procedure: accepts unsolicited scripts from established playwrights in youth-theatre field; others send brief synopsis, dialogue sample, resume and letter of inquiry. **Types of material:** works for young and family audiences, including adaptations, musicals and solo pieces. **Special interests:** ground-breaking works only; plays with culturally diverse casts or themes; social issues; adaptations of classic or contemporary literature; musicals. **Facilities:** The Coterie Theatre, 240 seats, flexible stage. **Production considerations:** cast limit of 12, prefers 5–7; no fly or wing space. **Best submission time:** year-round. **Response time:** 4 months letter; 10 months script.

COURT THEATRE
(Founded 1955)
5535 South Ellis Ave; Chicago, IL 60637; (773) 702-7005, FAX 834-1897
Resident Dramaturg

Submission procedure: no unsolicited scripts; synopsis, dialogue sample and letter of inquiry; theatre usually only produces commissioned work. **Types of material:** translations and adaptations of classic texs only. **Special interests:** infrequently produced or "undiscovered" material. **Facilities:** Abelson Auditorium, 253 seats, thrust stage. **Production considerations:** cast of 6–8; 1–2 sets; limited fly space. **Best submission time:** summer. **Response time:** 6 weeks letter; 1–6 months script.

CROSSROADS THEATRE COMPANY
(Founded 1978)
7 Livingston Ave; New Brunswick, NJ 08901; (732) 249-5581, FAX 249-1861
Literary Department

Submission procedure: no unsolicited scripts; synopsis, 10-page dialogue sample, bio and/or resume and letter of inquiry. **Types of material:** full-length plays, one-acts, translations, adaptations, musicals, cabaret/revues, performance art. **Special interests:** African-American, African and West Indian issue-oriented, experimental plays that examine the complexity of the human experience. **Facilities:** Crossroads Theatre, 264 seats, thrust stage. **Best submission time:** year-round. **Response time:** 3 months letter; 12 months script. **Special programs:** The Genesis Festival: A Celebration of New Voices in African-American Theatre: spring series of public readings and special events for the purpose of developing new plays; scripts selected through theatre's normal submission procedure.

CUMBERLAND COUNTY PLAYHOUSE
(Founded 1965)
Box 830; Crossville, TN 38557; (931) 484-4324, FAX 484-6299
Jim Crabtree, *Producing Director*

Submission procedure: no unsolicited scripts; synopsis and letter of inquiry. **Types of material:** full-length plays, adaptations, plays for young audiences, musicals. **Special interests:** works for family audiences; works with southern or rural background; works about Tennessee history or culture. **Facilities:** Cumberland County Playhouse, 490 seats, proscenium stage; Theater-in-the-Woods, 200 seats, outdoor arena; Adventure Theater, 180–220 seats, flexible black box. **Best submission time:** Aug–Dec. **Response time:** 2 weeks letter (if interested); 6–12 months script.

DALLAS CHILDREN'S THEATER
(Founded 1984)
2215 Cedar Springs; Dallas, TX 75201; (214) 978-0110, FAX 978-0118;
    Web http://www.dct.org
Artie Olaisen, *Administrative Artist*

Submission procedure: no unsolicited scripts; synopsis, character/set breakdown and letter of inquiry. **Types of material:** full-length plays, adaptations, plays for young audiences. **Special interests:** works for family audiences; adaptations of classics; historical plays; socially relevant works. **Facilities:** El Centro Theater, 500 seats, proscenium stage; Crescent Theater, 180 seats, flexible stage. **Best submission time:** year-round. **Response time:** 3 months letter; 6 months script.

DALLAS THEATER CENTER
(Founded 1959)
3636 Turtle Creek Blvd; Dallas, TX 75219-5598; (214) 526-8210,
    FAX 521-7666
Preston Lane, *Literary Office*

Submission procedure: no unsolicited scripts; professional recommendation. **Types of material:** full-length plays, adaptations, translations, solo pieces. **Special interests:** plays that explore language or form; material relating to the African-American or Hispanic experience. **Facilities:** Arts District Theater, 530 seats, flexible stage; Kalita Humphreys Theater, 466 seats, thrust stage. **Best submission time:** year-round. **Response time:** 9–12 months.

DELAWARE THEATRE COMPANY
(Founded 1978)
200 Water St; Wilmington, DE 19801-5030; (302) 594-1104, FAX 594-1107
Fontaine Syer, *Artistic Director*

Submission procedure: no unsolicited scripts; agent submission; synopsis and letter of inquiry from DE, MD and PA playwrights only. **Types of material:** full-length plays, translations, adaptations. **Facilities:** Delaware Theatre Company, 390 seats, thrust stage. **Production considerations:** cast limit of 10. **Best submission time:** Feb–May. **Response time:** 1 month letter; 3 months script.

DELL'ARTE PLAYERS COMPANY
(Founded 1971)
Box 816; Blue Lake, CA 95525; (707) 668-5663, FAX 668-5665;
   E-mail dellarte@aol.com; Web http://www.dellarte.com
Michael Fields, *Managing Artistic Director*

Submission procedure: no unsolicited scripts; synopsis and letter of inquiry; company customarily creates its own original works but may from time to time produce plays by or collaborate with other writers. **Types of material:** full-length plays, translations, adaptations, plays for young audiences, solo pieces. **Special interests:** comedies; issue-oriented works in commedia dell'arte style; Christmas plays for young audiences. **Facilities:** Dell'Arte Players, 100 seats, flexible stage. **Production considerations:** company of 3–4 actors; production demands adaptable to touring. **Best submission time:** Jan–Mar. **Response time:** 3 weeks letter; 6 weeks script.

DENVER CENTER THEATRE COMPANY
(Founded 1979)
1050 13th St; Denver, CO 80204; (303) 446-4856
Bruce K. Sevy, *Associate Artistic Director/New Play Development*

Submission procedure: accepts unsolicited scripts from Rocky Mountain region playwrights only; others send synopsis, 10-page dialogue sample, resume of writing experience and letter of inquiry. **Types of material:** full-length plays. **Special interests:** work not previously professionally produced. **Facilities:** The Stage, 642 seats, thrust stage; The Space, 450 seats, arena stage; The Ricketson, 250 seats, proscenium stage; The Source, 200 seats, thrust stage. **Best submission time:** year-round. **Response time:** 4–6 weeks letter; 4–6 months script. **Special programs:** Denver Center Theatre Company U S WEST Theatre Fest (see Development); The Francesca Primus Prize (see Prizes).

DETROIT REPERTORY THEATRE

(Founded 1957)

13103 Woodrow Wilson Ave; Detroit, MI 48238; (313) 868-1347, FAX 868-1705

Barbara Busby, *Literary Manager*

Submission procedure: accepts unsolicited scripts. **Types of material:** full-length plays. **Special interests:** issue-oriented plays. **Facilities:** Detroit Repertory Theatre, 194 seats, proscenium stage. **Production considerations:** prefers cast limit of 8. **Best submission time:** Sep–Feb. **Response time:** 3–6 months.

DIAMOND HEAD THEATRE

See Diamond Head Theatre Originals in Development.

DIXON PLACE

(Founded 1986)

258 Bowery; New York, NY 10012; (212) 219-3088, FAX 274-9114

Andrew J. Mellen and Micah Schraft, *Curators of New Play Reading Series*

Submission procedure: no unsolicited scripts; direct solicitation to playwright or agent. **Types of material:** full-length plays, one-acts, musicals. **Special interests:** works by New York City–based writers only; works by women; writers of color; "adventurous settings"; no "kitchen-sink soap operas." **Facilities:** Dixon Place, 70 seats, thrust stage. **Production considerations:** readings only; small stage; no sets; minimal lighting. **Best submission time:** year-round. **Response time:** 6 months.

DO GOODER PRODUCTIONS, INC.

(Founded 1994)

359 West 54th St, Suite 4FS; New York, NY 10019; (212) 581-8852,
    FAX 541-7928; E-mail dogooder@panix.com;
    Web http://www.panix.com/~dogooder

Mark Robert Gordon, *Founding Artistic Director*

Submission procedure: no unsolicited scripts; agent submission. **Types of material:** full-length plays, one-acts, solo pieces. **Facilities:** no permanent facility; performs in various 99–150-seat venues. **Best submission time:** 1 Sep–15 Oct. **Response time:** 8 months. **Special programs:** DGP New Playwright Award; write for guidelines; *deadline:* 15 Oct 1999; *notification:* May 2000.

DOBAMA THEATRE

(Founded 1960)

1846 Coventry Rd; Cleveland Heights, OH 44118; (216) 932-6838,
    FAX 932-3259

Submission procedure: accepts unsolicited scripts from OH playwrights only; others send synopsis, sample pages and letter of inquiry. **Types of material:** full-length plays, solo pieces. **Special interests:** plays with opportunities for ethnically diverse casting; plays that make a statement about contemporary life. **Facilities:** Dobama Theatre, 200 seats, thrust stage. **Production considerations:** prefers cast limit of 9; limited production demands; no fly space. **Best submission time:** year-round. **Response time:** 9 months letter; 9–12 months script. **Special programs:** One world premiere: production of 1 new play included in mainstage season each year; preference given to OH writers. Owen Kelly Adopt-a-Playwright Program: 2 full-length plays by OH residents each given 2 weeks of developmental work with director, dramaturg and cast, culminating in workshop production; playwright must be available to participate; to apply, submit script to the attention of the program; *deadline:* 1 Feb 2000; *notification:* 15 May 2000; *dates:* Jun 2000. Marilyn Bianchi Kids' Playwriting Festival: annual short-play competition open to students attending Cuyahoga County schools, grades 1–12; winners receive savings bonds, publication and/or full production; write for application starting Sep 1999; *deadline:* Feb 2000; exact date TBA.

DORSET THEATRE FESTIVAL
(Founded 1976)
Box 510; Dorset, VT 05251; (802) 867-2223, FAX 867-0144;
E-mail theatre@sover.net; Web http://www.theatredirectories.com
Jill Charles, *Artistic Director*

Submission procedure: no unsolicited scripts; synopsis, 10-page dialogue sample, character/set breakdown and letter of inquiry with SASP for response; include production history of readings in New York City–New England area if available. **Types of material:** full-length plays. **Special interests:** plays with broad commercial appeal. **Facilities:** Dorset Playhouse, 218 seats, proscenium stage. **Production considerations:** cast limit of 8; prefers 1 set or unit set. **Best submission time:** Sep–Dec. **Response time:** 3 months letter; 6–12 months script. **Special programs:** Dorset Colony for Writers (see Colonies).

DRAMA DEPT., INCORPORATED
(Founded 1995)
630 Ninth Ave, Suite 214; New York, NY 10036-3708; (212) 541-8299, -8441,
FAX 541-8489; E-mail dramadept@aol.com;
Web http://www.dramadept.com
Michael S. Rosenberg, *Managing Director*

Submission procedure: no unsolicited scripts; all projects initiated by company members. **Types of material:** full-length plays, one-acts, translations, adaptations, musicals, cabaret/revues. **Special interests:** neglected classics. **Facilities:** no permanent facility.

DUDLEY RIGGS INSTANT THEATRE COMPANY

(Founded 1954)
1586 Burton St; St. Paul, MN 55108; (612) 647-6748, FAX 647-5637
Dudley Riggs, *Producing Director*

Submission procedure: accepts unsolicited scripts with synopsis and letter of inquiry; include cassette for musicals. **Types of material:** capsule musicals/songs, cabaret/revues, solo pieces. **Special interests:** prefers work with no previous main stage productions; satiric comedies about contemporary issues such as intergenerational relationships, aging, retirement, loss and recovery. **Facilities:** Dudley Riggs Theatre, 260 seats, modified thrust stage. **Production considerations:** cast limit of 3–7. **Best submission time:** year-round. **Response time:** 8 months.

EAST WEST PLAYERS

(Founded 1965)
244 South San Pedro St, Suite 301; Los Angeles, CA 90012; (213) 625-7000,
      FAX 625-7111; E-mail info@eastwestplayers.com;
      Web http://eastwestplayers.com
Ken Narasaki, *Literary Manager*

Submission procedure: accepts unsolicited scripts with SASE for response. **Types of material:** full-length plays, translations, adaptations, plays for young audiences, musicals. **Special interests:** plays by or about Asian-Pacific–Americans. **Facilities:** The David Henry Hwang Theatre at Union Center for the Arts, 265 seats, proscenium stage. **Production considerations:** minimal production demands. **Best submission time:** year-round. **Response time:** 3–8 months.

EDYVEAN REPERTORY THEATRE

(Founded 1967)
Box 47509; Indianapolis, IN 46227-7509; (317) 788-2072, FAX 788-2079;
      E-mail ert@indy.net; Web http://www.edyvean.org
Karla Ries, *Marketing Sales Director*

Submission procedure: no unsolicited scripts; synopsis and letter of inquiry. **Types of material:** full-length plays, one-acts, translations, adaptations, plays for young audiences, musicals, solo pieces, cabaret/revues. **Facilities:** Mainstage, 750 seats, proscenium stage. **Best submission time:** year-round. **Response time:** 6 months letter; 6 months script.

EL TEATRO CAMPESINO

(Founded 1965)
Box 1240; San Juan Bautista, CA 95045; (831) 623-2444, FAX 623-4127;
      E-mail teatro@hollinet.com
Luis Valdez, *Artistic Director*

Submission procedure: no unsolicited scripts; direct solicitation to playwright or agent. **Types of material:** full-length plays, one-acts, translations, adaptations, plays for young audiences, musicals, cabaret/revues, solo pieces. **Special interests:**

socially relevant works; works that reflect a multiethnic world; contemporary adaptations of classics. **Facilities:** El Teatro Campesino Playhouse, 150 seats, flexible stage. **Best submission time:** Jan–Apr. **Response time:** 12 months.

THE EMELIN THEATRE FOR THE PERFORMING ARTS
(Founded 1973)
Library Lane; Mamaroneck, NY 10543; (914) 698-3045, FAX 698-1404;
        E-mail emelin98@aol.com; Web http://www.emelin.org
John Raymond, *Managing Director*

Submission procedure: accepts unsolicited scripts with professional recommendation only; include video for solo pieces. **Types of material:** full-length plays, chamber musicals, cabaret/revues, solo pieces. **Facilities:** The Emelin Theatre, 280 seats, proscenium stage. **Production considerations:** small cast; no fly space. **Best submission time:** year-round. **Response time:** 2 months.

THE EMPTY SPACE THEATRE
(Founded 1970)
3509 Fremont Ave N; Seattle, WA 98103-8813; (206) 547-7633,
        FAX 547-7635; Web http://emptyspace.com
Eddie Levi Lee, *Artistic Director*

Submission procedure: no unsolicited scripts; direct solicitation to playwright or agent. **Types of material:** full-length plays, translations, adaptations, musicals, solo pieces. **Special interests:** bold, provocative, celebratory work. **Facilities:** The Empty Space Theatre at the Fremont Palace, 150 seats, endstage. **Production considerations:** prefers small casts. **Best submission time:** year-round. **Response time:** 1–2 months.

ENSEMBLE STUDIO THEATRE
(Founded 1972)
549 West 52nd St; New York, NY 10019; (212) 247-4982, FAX 664-0041
Jamie Richards, *Executive Producer*

Submission procedure: accepts unsolicited scripts. **Types of material:** full-length plays, one-acts. **Facilities:** Mainstage, 99 seats, black box; Studio, 60 seats, proscenium stage. **Best submission time:** year-round. **Response time:** 6 months. **Special programs:** summer reading series and playwriting workshops. First Look: reading series of full-length plays. Annual Marathon of One-Act Plays: one-act play festival; *deadline:* 1 Dec 1999; *dates:* May–Jun 2000.

THE ENSEMBLE THEATRE
(Founded 1977)
3535 Main St; Houston, TX 77002-9529; (713) 520-0055, FAX 520-1269
Eileen J. Morris, *Artistic Director*

Submission procedure: accepts unsolicited scripts. **Types of material:** full-length plays, adaptations, plays for young audiences, musicals, solo pieces. **Special**

interests: works reflecting the African-American experience. **Facilities:** Hawkins Stage, 199 seats, proscenium stage; Arena Stage, 80 seats, black box. **Production considerations:** cast limit of 10; maximum 2 sets. **Best submission time:** Aug. **Response time:** 5 months.

ENSEMBLE THEATRE OF CINCINNATI
(Founded 1986)
1127 Vine St; Cincinnati, OH 45210; (513) 421-3555, FAX 421-8002
D. Lynn Meyers, *Producing Artistic Director*

Submission procedure: no unsolicited scripts; synopsis, dialogue sample, resume and letter of inquiry. **Types of material:** full-length plays, adaptations, plays for young audiences. **Special interests:** contemporary and social issues. **Facilities:** Ensemble Theatre of Cincinnati, 202 seats, thrust stage. **Production considerations:** cast limit of 6; simple set. **Best submission time:** Sep. **Response time:** 1 month letter; 4 months script.

ESSENTIAL THEATRE
(Founded 1987)
995 Greenwood Ave, #6; Atlanta, GA 30306; (404) 876-8471
Peter Hardy, *Producing Artistic Director*

Submission procedure: accepts unsolicited scripts. **Types of material:** full-length plays. **Special interests:** work not professionally produced; will also consider second or third production. **Facilities:** no permanent facility. **Best submission time:** spring. **Response time:** 6 months.

EUREKA THEATRE COMPANY
(Founded 1972)
330 Townsend St, Suite 210; San Francisco, CA 94107; (415) 243-9899,
    FAX 243-0789
Bill Schwartz, *Executive Producing Director*

Submission procedure: accepts unsolicited scripts. **Types of material:** full-length plays, one-acts, translations, adaptations, solo pieces. **Special interests:** dynamic contemporary plays "strongly theatrical with an eye toward the millennium." **Facilities:** Mainstage, 200–300 seats, flexible stage. **Best submission time:** year-round. **Response time:** 6 months. **Special programs:** Discovery Series: regularly scheduled rehearsed readings of new plays presented for public and followed by audience discussion.

FIRST STAGE MILWAUKEE
(Founded 1987)
929 North Water St; Milwaukee, WI 53202; (414) 273-2314, FAX 273-5595
Rob Goodman, *Producer/Artistic Director*

Submission procedure: no unsolicited scripts; synopsis, resume and letter of inquiry. **Types of material:** works for young audiences, including translations, adaptations and musicals. **Facilities:** Marcus Center for the Performing Arts's Todd Wehr Theater, 500 seats, thrust stage. **Best submission time:** spring–summer. **Response time:** 1 month letter; 3 months script.

FLEETWOOD STAGE
(Founded 1993)
44 Wildcliff Dr; New Rochelle, NY 10805; (914) 654-8533, FAX 235-4459
Lewis Arlt, *Producing Director*

Submission procedure: accepts unsolicited scripts; prefers professional recommendation. **Types of material:** full-length plays. **Facilities:** Playhouse at Wildcliff, 100 seats, proscenium stage. **Production considerations:** cast limit of 8; prefers unit set. **Best submission time:** year-round. **Response time:** 6–9 months. **Special programs:** Playwright's Forum: developmental program for playwrights in Westchester and Fairfield Counties; send SASE for application and guidelines.

FLORIDA STAGE
(Founded 1987)
262 South Ocean Blvd; Manalapan, FL 33462; (561) 585-3404, FAX 588-4708;
    E-mail flastage@aol.com; Web http://www.floridastage.org
Louis Tyrrell, *Producing Director*

Submission procedure: no unsolicited scripts; agent submission. **Types of material:** full-length plays, plays for young audiences. **Special interests:** contemporary issues and ideas. **Facilities:** Florida Stage, 250 seats, thrust stage. **Production considerations:** cast limit of 2–6; 1 set. **Best submission time:** year-round. **Response time:** 3–4 months. **Special programs:** reading series.

FLORIDA STUDIO THEATRE
(Founded 1973)
1241 North Palm Ave; Sarasota, FL 34236; (941) 366-9017
Chris Angermann, *Associate Director*

Submission procedure: no unsolicited scripts; synopsis and letter of inquiry. **Types of material:** full-length plays, translations, adaptations, musicals, cabaret/revues, solo pieces. **Facilities:** Florida Studio Theatre, 173 seats, semi-thrust stage; FST Cabaret Club, 100 seats, cabaret space. **Best submission time:** Aug–Apr. **Response time:** 1–2 weeks letter; 6 months script. **Special programs:** Sarasota Festival of New Plays: 4-tier festival includes Young Playwrights Festival: workshop productions of plays by playwrights grades 2–12; *deadline:* 1 Apr 2000; *dates:* May 2000. Burdick New Play Festival: workshop productions of 3 new plays; playwright receives stipend, travel, housing; scripts selected through theatre's normal submission procedure; *dates:* May 2000. New Play Summer Fest: workshop productions of 3 new plays; playwright receives stipend, travel, housing; scripts selected through theatre's normal submission procedure; *dates:* Jul–Aug 2000. Fall staged reading series. American Sketches Contest (see Prizes).

THE FOOTHILL THEATRE COMPANY
(Founded 1977)
Box 1812; Nevada City, CA 95959; (530) 265-9320
Philip Charles Sneed, *Artistic Director*

Submission procedure: accepts unsolicited scripts. **Types of material:** full-length plays, one-acts, translations, adaptations, plays for young audiences, solo pieces. **Special interests:** plays dealing with history of northern CA and/or the rural western U.S. **Facilities:** The Nevada Theatre, 246 seats, proscenium stage; also rents small spaces with 50–100 seats. **Production considerations:** very limited fly and wing space. **Best submission time:** year-round. **Response time:** 6–12 months.

FORD'S THEATRE
(Founded 1968)
511 Tenth St NW; Washington, DC 20004; (202) 638-2941, FAX 347-6269
John Rogers, *Literary Associate*

Submission procedure: no unsolicited scripts; synopsis, sample pages and letter of inquiry. **Types of material:** full-length plays, musicals. **Special interests:** small-scale musicals and works celebrating the African-American experience. **Facilities:** Ford's Theatre, 699 seats, proscenium/thrust stage. **Production considerations:** cast limit of 15. **Best submission time:** spring–summer. **Response time:** 3 months letter; 6–12 months script.

THE FOUNTAIN THEATRE
(Founded 1990)
5060 Fountain Ave; Los Angeles, CA 90029; (323) 663-2235, FAX 663-1629
Simon Levy, *Producing Director/Dramaturg*

Submission procedure: no unsolicited scripts; synopsis, and letter of inquiry. **Types of material:** full-length plays, translations, adaptations. **Special interests:** lyrical dramas; contemporary comedies; works with dance; adaptations of American literature. **Facilities:** Fountain Theatre Mainstage, 78 seats, thrust stage. **Production considerations:** cast limit of 12; 1 set; no fly space; low ceiling. **Best submission time:** year-round. **Response time:** 3 months letter; 6 months script.

FREE STREET PROGRAMS
(Founded 1969)
1419 West Blackhawk St; Chicago, IL 60622; (773) 772-7248, FAX 772-7248;
E-mail free@mcs.net
Ron Bieganski, *Artistic Director*
David Schein, *Executive Director*

Submission procedure: no unsolicited scripts; letter from writer with "a concept for a show or a brilliant idea for a new theatre program for inner-city kids/teens." **Types of material:** plays and performance pieces, including shows to be performed in public places or outdoors. **Special interests:** inner-city kids/teenagers; "cultural empowerment of new populations"; developing works with communities; enhancing literacy through the arts; new work by Chicago-area artists. **Facilities:** national/international touring company (teens). **Production considerations:** no expensive production demands. **Response time:** 2 months letter; 2 months script.

FREEDOM REPERTORY THEATRE
(Founded 1966)
1346 North Broad St; Philadelphia, PA 19121; (215) 765-2793, FAX 765-4191
Barbara Silzle, *Director of Artistic Initiatives*

Submission procedure: no unsolicited scripts; synopsis, 5–10-page work sample, resume and letter of inquiry. **Types of material:** full-length plays, musicals, caba-ret/revues. **Special interests:** contemporary plays with African-American themes. **Facilities:** John E. Allen Theatre, 298 seats, proscenium stage; Freedom Cabaret Theatre, 120 seats, flexible stage. **Best submission time:** year-round. **Response time:** 6–12 weeks. **Special programs:** Freedom Fest: play reading series; resident playwright program; commissioning program; all programs are by invitation only.

FRONTERA @ HYDE PARK THEATRE
(Founded 1992)
511 West 43rd St; Austin, TX 78751; (512) 302-4933, FAX 302-5041
Vicky Boone, *Artistic Director*

Submission procedure: no unsolicited scripts; synopsis and letter of inquiry. **Types of material:** full-length plays, translations, adaptations, musicals, solo pieces. **Facilities:** Hyde Park Theatre, 90 seats, flexible. **Best submission time:** year-round. **Response time:** 3 months letter; 6 months script.

FULTON OPERA HOUSE/ACTOR'S COMPANY OF PENNSYLVANIA
(Formerly Actor's Company of Pennsylvania)
(Founded 1963)
Box 1865; Lancaster, PA 17608-1865; (717) 394-7133, FAX 397-3780;
      E-mail artdir@fultontheatre.org; Web http://www.fultontheatre.org
Michael Mitchell, *Artistic Director*

Submission procedure: no unsolicited scripts; synopsis and letter of inquiry. **Types of material:** full-length plays, adaptations. **Special interests:** mainstream works on contemporary issues; plays that embrace diversity. **Facilities:** Fulton Opera House, 630 seats, proscenium stage; Studio Theatre, 100 seats, black box. **Production considerations:** cast limit of 10. **Best submission time:** fall. **Response time:** 3–6 months letter; 6 months script. **Special programs:** Mondays in May: annual concert reading series of new plays.

GALA HISPANIC THEATRE
(Founded 1976)
Box 43209; Washington, DC 20010; (202) 234-7174, FAX 332-1247;
E-mail galadc@aol.com; Web http://www.galadc.org
Hugo J. Medrano, *Producing/Artistic Director*

Submission procedure: accepts unsolicited scripts; prefers synopsis/description of play and letter of inquiry. **Types of material:** full-length plays, solo pieces. **Special interests:** plays by Spanish, Latino or Hispanic-American writers in Spanish or English only; prefers Spanish-language works with accompanying English translation; works that reflect sociocultural realities of Hispanics in Latin America, the Caribbean or Spain, as well as the Hispanic-American experience. **Facilities:** GALA Hispanic Theatre, 200 seats, proscenium stage. **Production considerations:** cast limit of 6–8. **Best submission time:** Apr–May. **Response time:** 1 month letter; 12 months script. **Special programs:** poetry onstage.

GEFFEN PLAYHOUSE
(Founded 1995)
10886 LeConte Ave; Los Angeles, CA 90024; (310) 208-6500, FAX 208-0341
Amy Levinson, *Literary Associate*

Submission procedure: no unsolicited scripts; synopsis, dialogue sample and letter of inquiry. **Types of material:** full-length plays, adaptations, musicals. **Facilities:** Geffen Playhouse, 498 seats, proscenium stage. **Best submission time:** year-round. **Response time:** 1 month letter; 6 months script.

GEORGE STREET PLAYHOUSE
(Founded 1974)
9 Livingston Ave; New Brunswick, NJ 08901; (732) 846-2895, FAX 247-9151
Maxine Kern, *Literary Manager*

Submission procedure: no unsolicited scripts; professional recommendation. **Types of material:** full-length plays, one-acts for young audiences, musicals. **Special interests:** social issue one-acts suitable for touring to schools (not seeking any other type of one-act for young audiences); comedies and dramas that present a fresh perspective on our society; "work that tells a compelling, personal human story while entertaining, challenging and stretching the imagination." **Facilities:** Mainstage, 367 seats, proscenium/thrust stage. **Production considerations:** prefers cast limit of 7 for plays, 10 for musicals. **Best submission time:** year-round. **Response time:** 8-10 months. **Special programs:** Next Stage Festival: workshops of 3 new plays. The Diva Project: presentation of new material by 4 solo female performers.

GEORGIA REPERTORY THEATRE

(Founded 1990)

Department of Drama, University of Georgia; Athens, GA 30602-3154;
(706) 542-2836, FAX 542-2080; E-mail longman@uga.cc.uga.edu
Stanley V. Longman, *Dramaturg*

Submission procedure: accepts unsolicited scripts. **Types of material:** full-length plays. **Special interests:** plays not previously professionally produced. **Facilities:** Fine Arts Theatre, 750 seats, proscenium stage; Cellar Theatre, 100 seats, proscenium stage. **Production considerations:** cast limit of 8; minimal set. **Best submission time:** after Oct 1999 only. **Response time:** 3–6 months.

GERMINAL STAGE DENVER

(Founded 1974)

2450 West 44th Ave; Denver, CO 80211; (303) 455-7108;
E-mail gsden@privatei.com; Web http://www2.privatei.com/~gsden
Ed Baierlein, *Director/Manager*

Submission procedure: no unsolicited scripts; synopsis, 5-page dialogue sample and letter of inquiry with SASP for response. **Types of material:** full-length plays, translations, adaptations. **Special interests:** adaptations that use both dialogue and narration. **Facilities:** Germinal Stage Denver, 100 seats, thrust stage. **Production considerations:** cast limit of 10; minimal production requirements. **Best submission time:** year-round. **Response time:** 2 weeks letter; 6 months script.

GEVA THEATRE

(Founded 1972)

75 Woodbury Blvd; Rochester, NY 14607-1717; (716) 232-1366
Jean Ryon, *New Plays Coordinator*

Submission procedure: no unsolicited scripts; synopsis, dialogue sample, production history, resume and letter of inquiry. **Types of material:** full-length plays, translations, adaptations. **Facilities:** Elaine P. Wilson Theatre, 552 seats, modified thrust stage; Ronald and Donna Fielding Nextstage, 175 seats, flexible stage. **Best submission time:** year-round. **Response time:** 1 week letter; 6 months script. **Special programs:** American Voices New Play Reading Series; Hibernatus Interruptus, A Winter Festival of New Plays: 2-week workshops of 3 plays; Regional Playwrights and Young Writers Festival; scripts selected through theatre's normal submission procedure.

THE GLINES

(Founded 1976)

240 West 44th St; New York, NY 10036; (212) 354-8899

Submission procedure: accepts unsolicited scripts. **Types of material:** full-length plays. **Special interests:** plays dealing with gay experience only; plays not previously produced in New York City. **Facilities:** no permanent facility. **Best submission time:** year-round. **Response time:** 2 months.

GOODMAN THEATRE
(Founded 1925)
200 South Columbus Dr; Chicago, IL 60603-6491; (312) 443-3811,
FAX 263-6004; E-mail staff@goodman-theatre.org
Susan V. Booth, *Director of New Play Development*

Submission procedure: no unsolicited scripts; synopsis, professional recommendation and letter of inquiry. **Types of material:** full-length plays, translations, musicals, solo pieces. **Special interests:** social or political themes. **Facilities:** Goodman Mainstage, 683 seats, proscenium stage; Goodman Studio, 135 seats, proscenium stage. **Best submission time:** year-round. **Response time:** 2–3 months letter; 6–8 months script.

GOODSPEED OPERA HOUSE
(Founded 1963)
Box A; East Haddam, CT 06423; (860) 873-8664, FAX 873-2329;
E-mail info@goodspeed.org
Sue Frost, *Associate Producer*

Submission procedure: no unsolicited scripts; synopsis, sample cassette and letter of inquiry. **Types of material:** original musicals only. **Facilities:**
Goodspeed Opera House, 400 seats, proscenium stage; Goodspeed-at-Chester, 200 seats, adaptable proscenium stage. **Best submission time:** Jan–Mar. **Response time:** 3 months letter; 12 months script.

GREAT AMERICAN HISTORY THEATRE
(Founded 1978)
30 East Tenth St; St. Paul, MN 55101; (612) 292-4323, FAX 292-4322
Ron Peluso, *Artistic Director*

Submission procedure: no unsolicited scripts; synopsis and letter of inquiry. **Types of material:** full-length plays, adaptations, musicals, solo pieces. **Special interests:** full-length plays involving Midwest or Minnesota history only; no pageants. **Facilities:** Crawford Livingston Theatre, 597 seats, thrust stage. **Production considerations:** cast limit of 8; moderate production demands; small musicals only. **Best submission time:** spring. **Response time:** 4–6 months letter; 4–6 months script.

GRETNA THEATRE
(Founded 1926)
Box 578; Mt. Gretna, PA 17064; (717) 964-3322, FAX 964-2189

Submission procedure: no unsolicited scripts; synopsis, 5-page dialogue sample, character list with descriptions, production history and letter of inquiry; include cassette for musicals. **Types of material:** full-length plays, musicals. **Special interests:** plays suitable for summer audiences; prefers comedies; musicals. **Facilities:** Mt. Gretna Playhouse, 700 seats, proscenium stage. **Production**

considerations: open-air facility; 14' ceiling over stage. **Best submission time:** Aug–Apr. **Response time:** 1 month letter; 3 months script.

THE GUTHRIE THEATER
(Founded 1963)
725 Vineland Place; Minneapolis, MN 55403; (612) 347-1185, FAX 347-1188;
   E-mail joh@guthrietheater.org
Literary Department

Submission procedure: no unsolicited scripts; professional recommendation with SASE for response. **Types of material:** full-length plays, translations, adaptations. **Special interests:** well-crafted, highly theatrical plays of depth and significance dealing with universal themes; contemporary international plays; new translations/adaptations from classic literature; adaptations of folktales from diverse cultures exploring themes of universal scope; no sitcoms. **Facilities:** Guthrie Theater, 1309 seats, thrust stage; Guthrie Lab, 350 seats, flexible stage. **Best submission time:** year-round. **Response time:** 3–4 months.

HANGAR THEATRE
(Founded 1964)
Box 205; Ithaca, NY 14850; (607) 273-8588, FAX 273-4516;
   Web http://hangartheatre.org
Jamie Grady, *Managing Director*

Submission procedure: no unsolicited scripts; agent submission. **Types of material:** full-length plays, one-acts. **Facilities:** Mainstage, 377 seats, thrust stage. **Best submission time:** Sep–Dec. **Response time:** 3 months.

THE HARBOR THEATRE
(Founded 1998)
160 West 71st St, PHA; New York, NY 10023; (212) 787-1945
Stuart Warmflash, *Artistic Director*

Submission procedure: no unsolicited scripts; synopsis and letter of inquiry. **Types of material:** full-length plays, musicals. **Facilities:** no permanent facility. **Best submission time:** year-round. **Response time:** 2 weeks letter; 3 months script. **Special programs:** The Harbor Theatre Workshop (see Membership and Service Organizations).

HARTFORD STAGE COMPANY
(Founded 1964)
50 Church St; Hartford, CT 06103; (860) 525-5601, FAX 525-4420
Shawn René Graham, *Literary Associate*

Submission procedure: no unsolicited scripts; professional recommendation. **Types of material:** full-length plays, translations, adaptations. **Facilities:** John W. Huntington Theatre, 489 seats, thrust stage. **Best submission time:** year-round. **Response time:** 6–9 months.

THE HASTY PUDDING THEATRE
(Founded 1795)
12 Holyoke St; Cambridge, MA 02138; (617) 496-6757, FAX 495-5205
Michael McClung, *Executive Director*

Submission procedure: accepts unsolicited scripts. **Types of material:** full-length plays, translations, adaptations, plays for young audiences, musicals, solo pieces, performance art, cabaret/revues. **Special interests:** plays exploring gender issues. **Facilities:** The Hasty Pudding Theatre, 360 seats, proscenium stage. **Best submission time:** year-round. **Response time:** 2–3 months. **Special programs:** monthly reading series.

HEDGEROW THEATRE
(Founded 1923)
146 West Rose Valley Rd; Wallingford, PA 19086; (610) 565-4211;
    Web http://www.libertynet.org/~hedgerow
Walt Vail, *Literary Manager*

Submission procedure: no unsolicited scripts; synopsis and letter of inquiry. **Types of material:** full-length plays, plays for young audiences. **Special interests:** new plays by DE, NJ and PA playwrights; mysteries; comedies. **Facilities:** Mainstage, 144 seats, proscenium stage. **Production considerations:** small stage; minimal production demands. **Best submission time:** year-round. **Response time:** 2 months letter; 4 months script.

HIDDEN THEATRE
(Founded 1994)
2301 Franklin Ave E; Minneapolis, MN 55406; (612) 339-4949, FAX 332-6037;
    Web http://www.hiddentheatre.org
David Schulner, *Artistic Associate*

Submission procedure: no unsolicited scripts; synopsis, 10-page dialogue sample, bio and letter of inquiry. **Types of material:** full-length plays, translations, adaptations. **Special interests:** theatrically inventive new material that asks challenging questions suitable for core ensemble 20–30 years old. **Facilities:** no permanent facility. **Best submission time:** year-round. **Response time:** 6–10 weeks letter; 6–10 months script.

HIP POCKET THEATRE
(Founded 1977)
Box 136758; Fort Worth, TX 76135; (817) 246-9775, FAX 272-2697;
    E-mail mdmolemo@aol.com;
    Web http://www.startext.net/homes/hippocket
Johnny Simons, *Artistic Director*

Submission procedure: accepts unsolicited scripts; include cassette for musicals. **Types of material:** full-length plays, translations, adaptations, plays for young audiences, musicals, solo pieces, multimedia works. **Special interests:** well-crafted stories with poetic, mythic slant that incorporate ritual and ensemble; works utilizing masks, puppetry, music, dance, mime and strong visual elements. **Facilities:** Oak Acres Amphitheatre, 175 seats, outdoor amphitheatre. **Production considerations:** simple sets. **Best submission time:** Oct–Feb. **Response time:** 6 weeks.

THE HIPPODROME STATE THEATRE
(Founded 1973)
25 Southeast Second Place; Gainesville, FL 32601-6596; (352) 373-5968,
      FAX 371-9130; Web http://hipp.gator.net
Tamerin Dygert, *Dramaturg*

Submission procedure: no unsolicited scripts; synopsis, dialogue sample and letter of inquiry with SASE for response. **Types of material:** full-length plays, one-acts, translations, adaptations. **Special interests:** multicultural plays. **Facilities:** Mainstage Theatre, 266 seats, thrust stage; Second Stage, 87 seats, flexible stage. **Production considerations:** cast limit of 8; unit set. **Best submission time:** May–Aug. **Response time:** 1–2 months letter; 3–5 months script. **Special programs:** informal play reading series: developmental series held Jan–Aug; possibility of later full production on second stage or in site-specific gallery and bar spaces; scripts selected through theatre's normal submission procedure.

HONOLULU THEATRE FOR YOUTH
(Founded 1955)
2846 Ualena St; Honolulu, HI 96819-1910; (808) 839-9885, FAX 839-7018;
      E-mail hnlty@aol.com; Web http://alaike./cchawaii.edu/openstudio/hty
Jane Campbell, *Producing Director*

Submission procedure: no unsolicited scripts; synopsis, resume and letter of inquiry. **Types of material:** one-acts, plays for young audiences. **Special interests:** plays for audiences up to high school age, with contemporary themes; adaptations of literary classics; new works based on Pacific Rim cultures; plays with compelling language that are imaginative and socially relevant. **Facilities:** Leeward Community College Theatre, 650 seats, proscenium stage; McCoy Pavilion, 300 seats, flexible stage. **Production considerations:** cast limit of 6. **Best submission time:** year-round. **Response time:** 1 month letter; 4–5 months script.

HORIZON THEATRE COMPANY
(Founded 1983)
Box 5376; Atlanta, GA 31107; (404) 523-1477, FAX 584-8815;
      E-mail horizonco@mindspring.com;
      Web http://www.mindspring.com/~horizonco
Jennifer Hebblethwaite, *Literary Manager*

Submission procedure: no unsolicited scripts, except for Festival (see below); synopsis, resume and letter of inquiry. **Types of material:** full-length plays, translations, adaptations, musicals. **Special interests:** contemporary issues; plays by women; southern urban themes; comedies. **Facilities:** Horizon Theatre,

170–200 seats, flexible stage. **Production considerations:** plays cast from ensemble of up to 12 actors. **Best submission time:** Sep–Dec. **Response time:** 6 months letter; 12 months script. **Special programs:** Teen Ensemble: one-acts about teen issues to be performed by teens. Senior Citizens Ensemble: one-acts about senior citizen issues to be performed by senior citizens. New South for the New Century Festival: annual festival of readings, workshops and full productions of plays by playwrights speaking from, for and about the South; *deadline:* 15 Jan 2000; *notification:* 1 Apr 2000; *dates:* May–Jun 2000.

HORSE CAVE THEATRE
(Founded 1977)
Box 215; Horse Cave, KY 42749; (502) 786-1200, FAX 786-5298;
    Web http://www.horsecavetheatre.org
Warren Hammack, *Artistic Director*

Submission procedure: no unsolicited scripts; professional recommendation. **Types of material:** full-length plays. **Special interests:** KY-based plays by KY playwrights. **Facilities:** Horse Cave Theatre, 346 seats, thrust stage. **Production considerations:** cast limit of 10; 1 set. **Best submission time:** Oct–Apr. **Response time:** varies.

HUDSON THEATRE
(Founded 1991)
6539 Santa Monica Blvd; Hollywood, CA 90038; (323) 856-4252,
    FAX 856-4316; E-mail hudsonthr@aol.com
Elizabeth Reilly, *Artistic Director*

Submission procedure: no unsolicited scripts; synopsis and letter of inquiry. **Types of material:** full-length plays, one-acts, musicals, solo pieces. **Facilities:** Mainstage, 99 seats, modified thrust stage; Avenue Theatre, 99 seats, runway; Guild Theatre, 43 seats, proscenium stage. **Best submission time:** year-round. **Response time:** 1 month letter; 6 months script.

THE HUMAN RACE THEATRE COMPANY
(Founded 1986)
126 North Main St, Suite 300; Dayton, OH 45402-1710; (937) 461-3823,
    FAX 461-7223; E-mail hrtheatre@aol.com;
    Web http://www.humanracetheatre.org
Tony Dallas, *Playwright in Residence*

Submission procedure: no unsolicited scripts; professional recommendation. **Types of material:** full-length plays, one-acts, adaptations; plays for young audiences. **Special interests:** OH playwrights; adaptations and original works for junior and senior high school audiences; contemporary issues. **Facilities:** The Loft, 219 seats, thrust stage. **Production considerations:** small cast; no fly space; plays for young audiences tour to schools. **Best submission time:** Dec–Feb. **Response time:** 6 months.

HUNTINGTON THEATRE COMPANY
(Founded 1981)
264 Huntington Ave; Boston MA 02115-4606; (617) 266-7900, FAX 353-8300
Scott Edmiston, *Literary Associate*

Submission procedure: no unsolicited scripts; synopsis and letter of inquiry. **Types of material:** full-length plays, translations, adaptations. **Facilities:** Huntington Theatre, 850 seats, proscenium stage. **Best submission time:** May–Sep. **Response time:** 2 months letter; 4 months script.

ILLINOIS THEATRE CENTER
(Founded 1976)
400A Lakewood Blvd; Park Forest, IL 60466; (708) 481-3510, FAX 481-3693;
  E-mail itcbillig@juno.com
Etel Billig, *Producing Director*

Submission procedure: no unsolicited scripts; synopsis and letter of inquiry with SASE for response. **Types of material:** full-length plays, musicals. **Facilities:** Illinois Theatre Center, 180 seats, proscenium/thrust stage. **Production considerations:** cast limit of 9 for plays, 14 for musicals. **Best submission time:** year-round. **Response time:** 1 month letter; 2 months script.

ILLUSION THEATER
(Founded 1974)
528 Hennepin Ave, Suite 704; Minneapolis, MN 55403; (612) 339-4944,
  FAX 337-8042; E-mail illusiontheater@juno.com
Michael Robins, *Executive Producing Director*

Submission procedure: no unsolicited scripts; professional recommendation. **Types of material:** full-length plays, one-acts, translations, adaptations, musicals, solo pieces. **Special interests:** writers to collaborate on new works with company. **Facilities:** Illusion Theater, 250 seats, semi-thrust stage. **Best submission time:** Jul–Nov. **Response time:** 6–12 months. **Special programs:** Fresh Ink Series: 5–6 plays each presented with minimal set and costumes for 1 weekend; post-performance discussion with audience, who are seated onstage; scripts selected through theatre's normal submission procedure.

INDIANA REPERTORY THEATRE
(Founded 1972)
140 West Washington St; Indianapolis, IN 46204-3465; (317) 635-5277,
  FAX 236-0767
Emily Nicoson, *Literary Manager*

Submission procedure: no unsolicited scripts; synopsis and letter of inquiry with SASE for response. **Types of material:** full-length plays, translations, adaptations, solo pieces. **Special interests:** adaptations of classic literature; plays that explore cultural/ethnic issues "with a Midwestern voice." **Facilities:** Mainstage, 600 seats, modified proscenium stage; Upperstage, 300 seats, modified thrust stage.

Production considerations: cast limit of 6–8. **Best submission time:** year-round (season chosen by Jan each year). **Response time:** 3–4 months letter; 6 months script. **Special programs:** Discovery Series: presentation of plays for family audiences with a focus on youth and culturally/ethnically diverse plays with an emphasis on history and literature; scripts selected through theatre's normal submission procedure.

INTAR HISPANIC AMERICAN ARTS CENTER
(Founded 1966)
Box 788; New York, NY 10108; (212) 695-6134, -6135, ext 17, FAX 268-0102
Lorenzo Mans, *Literary Manager*

Submission procedure: accepts unsolicited scripts. **Types of material:** full-length plays, one-acts, translations, adaptations, musicals, solo pieces. **Special interests:** new plays by Hispanic-American writers and translations and adaptations of Hispanic works only. **Facilities:** INTAR on Theatre Row, 99 seats, proscenium stage; INTAR Stage Two, 75 seats, proscenium stage. **Production considerations:** prefers cast limit of 8; no wing space. **Best submission time:** year-round (season chosen late summer–early fall). **Response time:** 3–6 months. **Special programs:** New Works Lab: workshop productions. Reading series.

INTERACT THEATRE COMPANY
(Founded 1988)
2030 Sansom St; Philadelphia, PA 19103; (215) 568-8077, FAX 568-8095
Seth Rozin, *Producing Artistic Director*
Larry Loebell, *Literary Manager*

Submission procedure: no unsolicited scripts; synopsis, 10-page dialogue sample and letter of inquiry. **Types of material:** full-length plays. **Special interests:** plays that theatrically explore issues of cultural, political and/or social significance. **Facilities:** The Adrienne, 106 seats, proscenium stage. **Production considerations:** cast limit of 10. **Best submission time:** year-round. **Response time:** 1 month letter; 3 months script. **Special programs:** annual Showcase of New Plays in Jan, including both developmental and fully staged readings; primarily local playwrights.

INTIMAN THEATRE
(Founded 1972)
Box 19760; Seattle, WA 98109; (206) 269-1901, FAX 269-1928;
        E-mail scripts@intiman.org; Web http://www.seattlesquare.com/intiman
Steven Alter, *Artistic Associate*

Submission procedure: no unsolicited scripts; professional recommendation. **Types of material:** full-length plays, translations, adaptations. **Special interests:** well-crafted plays that fully utilize the power of language and character relationships to explore enduring themes. **Facilities:** Intiman Playhouse, 480 seats, thrust stage. **Production considerations:** prefers cast limit of 12. **Best submission time: Dec–Mar. **Response time:** 6 months. **Special programs:** New Voices at Intiman: developmental readings of unproduced new plays.

INVISIBLE THEATRE
(Founded 1976)
1400 North 1st Ave; Tucson, AZ 85719; (520) 882-9721, FAX 884-5410
Deborah Dickey, *Literary Manager*

Submission procedure: no unsolicited scripts; professional recommendation. **Types of material:** full-length plays, one-acts, musicals, solo pieces. **Special interests:** mainly but not exclusively works with contemporary settings; works with strong female roles; social and political issues. **Facilities:** Invisible Theatre, 78 seats, black box. **Production considerations:** cast limit of 10; simple set; minimal props; small-cast musicals only. **Best submission time:** Oct–Dec. **Response time:** 6–12 months.

IRONDALE ENSEMBLE PROJECT
(Founded 1983)
Box 1314, Old Chelsea Station; New York, NY 10011-1314; (212) 633-1292,
     FAX 633-2078; E-mail irondalert@aol.com; Web http://www.irondale.org
Jim Niesen, *Artistic Director*

Submission procedure: no unsolicited scripts; letter of inquiry from playwright interested in developing work with ensemble through ongoing workshop process. **Types of material:** full-length plays, adaptations, plays with music. **Special interests:** works with political or social relevance. **Facilities:** no permanent facility. **Production considerations:** cast limit of 8–9. **Best submission time:** Apr–Sep. **Response time:** 10 weeks.

JEWISH ENSEMBLE THEATRE
(Founded 1989)
6600 West Maple Rd; West Bloomfield, MI 48322-3002; (248) 788-2900,
     FAX 788-2900; E-mail jetplay@aol.com; Web http://www.comnet.org/jet
Evelyn Orbach, *Artistic Director*

Submission procedure: accepts unsolicited scripts. **Types of material:** full-length plays, one-acts, plays for young audiences. **Special interests:** works on Jewish themes and/or by Jewish writers; work not previously professionally produced. **Facilities:** Aaron DeRoy Theatre, 193 seats, thrust stage. **Production considerations:** no fly space. **Best submission time:** late spring–early fall. **Response time:** 6 months. **Special programs:** Festival of New Plays in Staged Readings: 4 plays given readings, possibly leading to mainstage production; scripts selected through theatre's normal submission procedure.

JEWISH REPERTORY THEATRE
(Founded 1974)
92nd Street Y; 1395 Lexington Ave; New York, NY 10128; (212) 415-5550;
  E-mail jrep@echonyc.com; Web http://jrt.org
Ran Avni, *Artistic Director*

Submission procedure: accepts unsolicited scripts. **Types of material:** full-length plays, musicals. **Special interests:** works that address some aspect of Jewish life; plays not reviewed in New York during the past 5 years. **Facilities:** Playhouse 91, 299 seats, thrust stage. **Production considerations:** small cast. **Best submission time:** Sep–May. **Response time:** 1 month. **Special programs:** Lee Guber Playwrights' Lab: readings of new plays.

JOHN DREW THEATER
(Founded 1931)
158 Main St; East Hampton, NY 11937; (516) 324-0806, FAX 324-2722
Leonard Ziemkiewicz, *General Manager*

Submission procedure: no unsolicited scripts; 1-page synopsis, character/set breakdown and letter of inquiry. **Types of material:** full-length plays, solo pieces. **Special interests:** comedies; plays with contemporary setting. **Facilities:** John Drew Theater, 387 seats, proscenium stage. **Production considerations:** cast limit of 4; unit set; no fly space. **Best submission time:** year-round. **Response time:** 3 months letter; 3 months script.

JOMANDI PRODUCTIONS
(Founded 1978)
1444 Mayson St NE; Atlanta, GA 30324; (404) 876-6346, FAX 872-5764;
  E-mail jomandi@bellsouth.net
Literary Manager

Submission procedure: no unsolicited scripts; synopsis, dialogue sample, resume and letter of inquiry. **Types of material:** full-length plays, adaptations, plays for young audiences, musicals, solo pieces. **Special interests:** historical or contemporary portrayals of the African-American experience; adaptations of African-American literature. **Facilities:** 14th Street Playhouse, 370 seats, proscenium/thrust stage. **Production considerations:** produces some large-cast plays but prefers cast of 7; prefers unit set. **Best submission time:** spring–summer. **Response time:** 3 months letter; 4–6 months script.

THE JOSEPH PAPP PUBLIC THEATER/NEW YORK SHAKESPEARE FESTIVAL
(Founded 1954)
The Joseph Papp Public Theater; 425 Lafayette St; New York, NY 10003;
(212) 539-8530, FAX 539-8505
John Dias, *Literary Director*
Wiley Hausam, *Associate Producer, Musicals*

Submission procedure: no unsolicited scripts; synopsis, 10-page sample scene and letter of inquiry; include cassette of 3–5 songs for musicals and operas. **Types of material:** full-length plays, translations, adaptations, musicals, operas, solo pieces. **Facilities:** Newman Theater, 299 seats, proscenium stage; Anspacher Theater, 275 seats, thrust stage; Martinson Hall, 200 seats, proscenium stage; LuEsther Hall, 150 seats, flexible stage; Shiva Theater, 100 seats, flexible stage. **Best submission time:** year-round. **Response time:** 1 month letter; 6 months script.

JUNGLE THEATER
(Founded 1990)
2951 South Lyndale Ave; Minneapolis, MN 55408; (612) 822-4002,
FAX 822-9408; E-mail bain@jungletheater.com
Bain Boehlke, *Artistic Director*

Submission procedure: no unsolicited scripts; synopsis, sample pages, resume and letter of inquiry. **Types of material:** full-length plays. **Facilities:** The New Jungle Theater, 140 seats, proscenium stage. **Best submission time:** year-round. **Response time:** 1 month letter; 3 months script. **Special programs:** Emerging Playwrights Reading Series: sit down and staged readings of new plays by early-career playwrights; scripts selected through theater's normal submission procedure and by professional recommendation; *dates:* Sep 1999.

THE KAVINOKY THEATRE
(Founded 1981)
320 Porter Ave; Buffalo, NY 14221; (716) 881-7652, (FAX) 881-7790
David Lamb, *Artistic Director*

Submission procedure: no unsolicited scripts; professional recommendation. **Types of material:** full-length plays, adaptations. **Special interests:** comedies. **Facilities:** Kavinoky Theatre, 260 seats, proscenium/thrust stage. **Production considerations:** prefers cast limit of 7; no fly and limited wing space. **Best submission time:** Jun–Aug. **Response time:** 1 month.

KITCHEN DOG THEATER COMPANY
(Founded 1990)
3120 McKinney Ave; Dallas, TX 75204; (214) 953-1055, FAX (214) 953-1873;
E-mail kdog@the-mac.org
Dan Day, *Artistic Director*

Submission procedure: accepts unsolicited scripts. **Types of material:** full-length plays, translations, adaptations, solo pieces. **Special interests:** plays by TX and

Southwest playwrights. **Facilities:** The McKinney Avenue Contemporary, 100–150 seats, thrust stage; Second Space, 75–100 seats, black box. **Production considerations:** cast limit of 5; moderate production demands; moderate set. **Best submission time:** year-round. **Response time:** 6–8 months. **Special programs:** New Works Festival: annual presentation of new plays including one full production, staged readings, mini workshops and artist residencies; submit script with SASP for response; *deadline:* 15 Feb 2000; *notification:* 15 Mar 2000; *dates:* May–Jun 2000.

L. A. THEATRE WORKS
(Founded 1974)
681 Venice Blvd; Venice, CA 90291; (310) 827-0808, FAX 827-4949;
    E-mail latworks@aol.com
Kirsten Dahl, *Literary Manager*

Submission procedure: no unsolicited scripts; agent submission. **Types of material:** full-length plays, one-acts, adaptations. **Special interests:** highly theatrical, nonrealistic new plays; contemporary adaptations of classic themes. **Facilities:** no permanent facility. **Best submission time:** year-round. **Response time:** 4–6 months.

LA JOLLA PLAYHOUSE
(Founded 1947)
Box 12039; La Jolla, CA 92039; (858) 550-1070, FAX 550-1075
Elizabeth Bennett, *Literary Manager*

Submission procedure: no unsolicited scripts; professional recommendation. **Types of material:** full-length plays, translations, musicals. **Special interests:** material pertinent to the lives we are leading at the end of this century; innovative form and language. **Facilities:** Mandell Weiss Center for the Performing Arts, 500 seats, proscenium stage; Weiss Forum, 400 seats, thrust stage. **Best submission time:** Jun–Nov. **Response time:** 6 months.

LA MAMA EXPERIMENTAL THEATER CLUB
(Founded 1961)
74A East 4th St; New York, NY 10003; (212) 254-6468, FAX 254-7597;
    E-mail lamama@lamama.org; Web http://www.lamama.org
Ellen Stewart, *Artistic Director*
Beverly Petty, *Associate Director*

Submission procedure: no unsolicited scripts; accepts unsolicited videotapes of projects with synopsis; prefers professional recommendation. **Types of material:** full-length plays, one-acts, musicals, solo pieces, performance art. **Special interests:** culturally diverse works with music, movement and media. **Facilities:** Annex Theater, 199 seats, flexible stage; The Club Theater, 99 seats, black box; First Floor Theater, 99 seats, black box. **Best submission time:** year-round. **Response time:** 2–6 months. **Special programs:** Experiment '99: a weekly concert play reading series curated by George Ferencz. Cross Cultural Institute of Theater Art Studies (C.C.I.T.A.S.): theatrical workshops and premiere productions involving collaboration among artists of varying geographic and ethnic origins that promote intercultural understanding and artistic exchange. La MaMa Umbria: summer artist's residency program outside of Spoleto in Umbria, Italy; contact theatre for more information.

LAGUNA PLAYHOUSE
(Founded 1920)
606 Laguna Canyon Rd; Laguna Beach, CA 92651; (714) 494-8022,
    FAX 497-6948
Andrew Barnicle, *Artistic Director*

Submission procedure: no unsolicited scripts; direct solicitation to playwright or agent. **Types of material:** full-length plays, plays for young audiences, musicals. **Facilities:** Moulton Theater, 418 seats, proscenium stage.

LAMB'S PLAYERS THEATRE
(Founded 1971)
Box 182229; Coronado, CA 92178; (619) 437-6050, FAX 437-6053
Jeffrey S. Miller, *Director of Outreach*

Submission procedure: no unsolicited scripts; synopsis, maximum 10-page dialogue sample and letter of inquiry; include cassette for musicals. **Types of material:** full-length plays, one-acts, plays for young audiences, musicals, cabaret/revues. **Facilities:** Harder Stage, 350 seats, thrust stage; Hahn, 250 seats, proscenium stage; Lyceum, 200 seats, flexible stage. **Best submission time:** year-round. **Response time:** 4–6 weeks letter; 4–6 months script.

LIFELINE THEATRE
(Founded 1982)
6912 North Glenwood Ave; Chicago, IL 60626; (773) 761-0667, FAX 761-4582;
    E-mail lifeline@suba.com
Dorothy Milne, *Artistic Director*

Submission procedure: no unsolicited scripts; synopsis and letter of inquiry. **Types of material:** adaptations only. **Facilities:** Lifeline Theatre, 100 seats, proscenium stage. **Best submission time:** year-round. **Response time:** 1 month letter; 6 months script.

LINCOLN CENTER THEATER
(Founded 1966)
150 West 65th St; New York, NY 10023; (212) 362-7600
Anne Cattaneo, *Dramaturg*

Submission procedure: no unsolicited scripts; agent submission. **Types of material:** full-length plays, one-acts, translations, adaptations, musicals. **Facilities:** Vivian Beaumont, 1000 seats, thrust stage; Mitzi E. Newhouse, 300 seats, thrust stage. **Best submission time:** year-round. **Response time:** 2–4 months.

LIVE BAIT THEATRICAL COMPANY
(Founded 1987)
3914 North Clark; Chicago, IL 60613; (773) 871-1212, FAX 871-3191;
    Web http://www.livebaittheater.org
Ryan C. LaFleur, *Managing Director*

Submission procedure: no unsolicited scripts; synopsis and letter of inquiry from Chicago-area playwrights only; no other submissions accepted. **Types of material:** full-length plays, translations, adaptations, solo pieces, performance art. **Special interests:** nonrealistic plays; performance poetry; performance art; multimedia works; works that emphasize visual aspects of staging. **Facilities:** Live Bait Theater, 70 seats, black box. **Production considerations:** prefers cast limit of 9; 1 set; no fly or wing space. **Best submission time:** year-round. **Response time:** 6 weeks letter; 6 months script.

THE LIVING THEATRE
(Founded 1947)
800 West End Ave, #5A; New York, NY 10025; (212) 865-3957, FAX 865-3234
Craig Peritz, *Administrative Assistant*

Submission procedure: no unsolicited scripts; synopsis and letter of inquiry. **Types of material:** full-length plays, translations, adaptations. **Special interests:** plays that creatively incorporate audience participation; experimental works; new theatre forms; nonfictional plays dealing with current issues performed by actors who play themselves. **Facilities:** no permanent facility; touring company; street and various outdoor venues. **Production considerations:** plays must accommodate ensemble of 12. **Best submission time:** year-round. **Response time:** 6 months letter; 6 months script.

LONG BEACH PLAYHOUSE
(Founded 1929)
5021 East Anaheim St; Long Beach, CA 90804; (562) 494-1014, FAX 494-1014;
    Web http://www.longbeachplayhouse.com
Robert Leigh, *Managing Director*

Submission procedure: accepts unsolicited scripts. **Types of material:** full-length plays, one-acts, translations, adaptations, plays for young audiences, musicals, cabaret/revues, solo pieces. **Special interests:** plays not previously professionally produced; ethnically inclusive and diverse projects with strong social themes and/or unusual theatricality. **Facilities:** Mainstage, 200 seats, thrust stage; Studio, 98 seats, proscenium stage. **Production considerations:** simple sets; no wing space. **Best submission time:** year-round. **Response time:** 3–6 months. **Special programs:** New Works Festival: 4 plays chosen for annual staged reading attended by professional critics who provide written and oral feedback; playwright receives $100 honorarium and videotape of reading; *deadline:* 15 Dec 1999. *notification:* Feb 2000. *dates:* spring 2000.

LONG WHARF THEATRE
(Founded 1965)
222 Sargent Dr; New Haven, CT 06511; (203) 787-4284, FAX 776-2287
Stefan Lanfer, *Literary Associate*

Submission procedure: no unsolicited scripts; synopsis, dialogue sample, resume and letter of inquiry. **Types of material:** full-length plays, translations, adaptations. **Special interests:** dramatic plays and comedies about human relationships, social concerns, ethical and moral dilemmas. **Facilities:** Newton Schenck Stage, 484 seats, thrust stage; Stage II, 199 seats, proscenium stage. **Best submission time:** year-round. **Response time:** 1 month letter; 3–6 months script.

MABOU MINES
(Founded 1970)
150 First Ave; New York, NY 10009; (212) 473-0559, FAX 473-2410
Sharon Fogarty, *Managing Director*

Submission procedure: no unsolicited scripts; professional recommendation. **Types of material:** full-length plays, one-acts, translations, adaptations. **Special interests:** contemporary works on contemporary issues. **Facilities:** The TOny, ROn, NAncy & DAvid–TORO NADA: NO BULL Theater at the 122 Community Center, 60 seats, flexible stage. **Best submission time:** year-round. **Response time:** 6 months.

MAD RIVER THEATER WORKS
(Founded 1978)
Box 248; West Liberty, OH 43357; (937) 465-6751; E-mail madriver@bright.net
Jeff Hooper, *Producing Director*

Submission procedure: no unsolicited scripts; direct solicitation to playwright or agent. **Types of material:** full-length plays, one-acts, adaptations. **Special interests:** company-developed works; Midwestern or rural subject matter. **Facilities:** Center Stage, 150 seats, flexible stage. **Production considerations:** cast limit of 6; simple set and costumes. **Best submission time:** year-round. **Response time:** 3–4 months.

MADISON REPERTORY THEATRE
(Founded 1969)
122 State St, Suite 201; Madison, WI 53703-2500; (608) 256-0029,
       FAX 256-7433; E-mail madisonrep@aol.com
D. Scott Glasser, *Artistic Director*

Submission procedure: no unsolicited scripts; synopsis and letter of inquiry. **Types of material:** full-length plays, translations, adaptations, musicals. **Facilities:** Isthmus Playhouse, 330 seats, thrust stage. **Production considerations:** cast limit of 15; no fly space. **Best submission time:** year-round. **Response time:** 4–6 months letter; 4–6 months script. **Special programs:** reading series for plays in development.

MAGIC THEATRE
(Founded 1967)
Fort Mason Center, Bldg D; San Francisco, CA 94123; (415) 441-8001,
    FAX 771-5505
Kent Nicholson, *Literary Manager*

Submission procedure: no unsolicited scripts; synopsis, first 10 pages of play, resume and letter of inquiry. **Types of material:** full-length plays, solo pieces. **Special interests:** new plays that are innovative and/or nonlinear in form and content; political themes. **Facilities:** Magic Theatre Southside, 170 seats, proscenium stage; Magic Theatre Northside, 155 seats, thrust stage. **Production considerations:** prefers cast limit of 6. **Best submission time:** Sep–May. **Response time:** 6 weeks letter; 6–8 months script.

MAIN STREET ARTS
(Founded 1993)
94 Main St; Nyack, NY 10960; (914) 358-7701, FAX 358-7701;
    E-mail msapaul@juno.com
Literary Manager

Submission procedure: no unsolicited scripts; synopsis, dialogue sample and letter of inquiry. **Types of material:** full-length plays, one-acts. **Facilities:** Mainstage, 65 seats, black box. **Production considerations:** cast limit of 6 for full-length plays; cast limit of 4 for one-acts. **Best submission time:** year-round. **Response time:** 3 weeks letter; 6 weeks script. **Special programs:** Developmental Reading Series: monthly rehearsed reading of one new play with director and actors followed by audience question and answer period; local authors preferred. Midsummernights Shorts One Act Festival: festival of 6–9 one-acts; *deadline:* 1 Mar 2000; no submissions prior to 1 Nov 1999; *notification:* 31 Mar 2000; *dates:* Jul–Aug 2000. Flying Blind Festival: presentation of short one-acts with no set requirements; $5 reading fee; *deadline:* 30 Jun 2000; *notification:* 15 July 2000; *dates:* Sep–Oct 2000.

MANHATTAN THEATRE CLUB
(Founded 1972)
311 West 43rd St, 8th Floor; New York, NY 10036; (212) 399-3000,
    FAX 399-4329; Web http://www.mtc-nyc.org
Christian Parker, *Literary Associate*
Clifford Lee Johnson III, *Director of Musical Theatre Program*

Submission procedure: no unsolicited scripts; agent submission. **Types of material:** full-length plays, musicals. **Facilities:** Stage I at City Center, 299 seats, proscenium stage; Stage II, 150 seats, thrust stage. **Production considerations:** prefers cast of 6–8; 1 set or unit set. **Best submission time:** year-round. **Response time:** 4 months. **Special programs:** readings and workshop productions of new musicals. "First-hearing" readings: in-house readings of new plays or first drafts. Manhattan Theatre Club Playwriting Fellowships (see Fellowships and Grants).

MARIN SHAKESPEARE COMPANY

(Founded 1989)
Box 4053; San Rafael, CA 94913; (415) 499-1108, FAX 499-1492;
    Web http://www.marinshakespeare.org
Robert Currier, *Artistic Director*

Submission procedure: no unsolicited scripts; synopsis, production history and letter of inquiry. **Types of material:** full-length plays, translations, adaptations. **Special interests:** classical, family-oriented or Shakespeare-related plays suitable for outdoor production. **Facilities:** Forest Meadows Amphitheatre, 600 seats, proscenium/thrust stage. **Best submission time:** year-round. **Response time:** 2 months letter; 2 months script.

MARIN THEATRE COMPANY

(Founded 1967)
397 Miller Ave; Mill Valley, CA 94941; (415) 388-5200, FAX 388-0768
Lee Sankowich, *Artistic Director*

Submission procedure: no unsolicited scripts; agent submission. **Types of material:** full-length plays, translations, adaptations, plays for young audiences. **Facilities:** Marin Theatre, 250 seats, proscenium stage; 2nd theatre, 109 seats, black box. **Best submission time:** Jun–Aug. **Response time:** 6 months.

MARK TAPER FORUM

(Founded 1967)
135 North Grand Ave; Los Angeles, CA 90012; (213) 972-8033
Pier Carlo Talenti, *Literary Manager*

Submission procedure: no unsolicited scripts; description of work, 5–10 sample pages and letter of inquiry. **Types of material:** full-length plays, one-acts, translations, adaptations, plays for young audiences, musicals, literary cabaret, solo pieces, performance art. **Facilities:** Mark Taper Forum, 742 seats, thrust stage. **Best submission time:** year-round. **Response time:** 4–6 weeks letter; 8–10 weeks script. **Special programs:** Performing for Los Angeles Youth: 55-minute plays that tour Southern CA schools; maximum 6 actors; suitable for grades K–8; scripts selected through theatre's normal submission procedure. Mark Taper Forum Developmental Programs (see Development).

MCC THEATER

(Founded 1986)
120 West 28th St; New York, NY 10001; (212) 727-7722, FAX 727-7780
Stephen Willems, *Literary Manager*

Submission procedure: no unsolicited scripts; synopsis and letter of inquiry with SASE or SASP for response. **Types of material:** full-length plays, one-acts, translations, adaptations, musicals. **Facilities:** MCC Theater, 99 seats, black box. **Production considerations:** cast limit of 10. **Best submission time:** year-round. **Response time:** 2 weeks letter; 2 months script.

McCarter Theatre Center for the Performing Arts
(Founded 1972)
91 University Place; Princeton, NJ 08540; (609) 683-9100, FAX 497-0369;
    E-mail cmcnulty@mccarter.org; Web http://www.mccarter.org
Charles McNulty, *Literary Manager*

Submission procedure: no unsolicited scripts; synopsis, 10-page dialogue sample and letter of inquiry. **Types of material:** full-length plays, musicals. **Facilities:** McCarter Theatre, 1077 seats, proscenium stage. **Best submission time:** Sep–May. **Response time:** 1 month letter; 3 months script.

Meadow Brook Theatre
(Founded 1967)
Wilson Hall; Rochester, MI 48309-4401; (248) 370-3310, FAX 370-3108;
    E-mail mbrkthea@oakland.edu
Karim Alrawi, *Literary Manager*

Submission procedure: no unsolicited scripts; synopsis, sample pages and letter of inquiry. **Types of material:** full-length plays, plays for young audiences, musicals. **Special interests:** plays with a Michigan location or subject matter; educational one-act plays suitable for touring; comedies. **Facilities:** Meadow Brook Theatre, 608 seats, proscenium stage. **Best submission time:** year-round. **Response time:** 1–2 months letter; 3–5 months script.

Merrimack Repertory Theatre
(Founded 1979)
50 East Merrimack St; Lowell, MA 01852; (978) 454-6324, FAX 934-0166;
    Web http://www.mrtlowell.com
David G. Kent, *Producing Artistic Director*

Submission procedure: no unsolicited scripts; synopsis and letter of inquiry. **Types of material:** full-length plays, translations, adaptations, plays for young audiences, musicals. **Special interests:** well-crafted stories with a poetic and human focus; varied ethnic tapestries of American life and love. **Facilities:** Liberty Hall, 372 seats, thrust stage. **Production considerations:** moderate cast size; simple set. **Best submission time:** spring–summer. **Response time:** 1 month letter (if interested); 6 months script.

Merry-Go-Round Playhouse
(Founded 1958)
Box 506; Auburn, NY 13021; (315) 255-1305, FAX 252-3815
Beth Ann Scanlon, *Literary Manager*

Submission procedure: accepts unsolicited scripts. **Types of material:** full-length plays, translations, adaptations, plays for young audiences, musicals. **Special interests:** participatory plays for young audiences with cast limit of 3–4; plays for grades K–12. **Facilities:** Merry-Go-Round Playhouse (adaptable), 325 seats, proscenium stage or 100 seats, thrust stage. **Production considerations:** cast limit of 5. **Best submission time:** Jan–Feb. **Response time:** 2 months.

METRO THEATER COMPANY
(Founded 1973)
8308 Olive Blvd; St. Louis, MO 63132-2814; (314) 997-6777, FAX 997-1811; E-mail bravomtc@aol.com
Carol North, *Producing Director*

Submission procedure: no unsolicited scripts; professional recommendation. **Types of material:** plays and musicals for young audiences. **Special interests:** no works longer than 60 minutes; plays with music that are not dramatically limited by traditional concepts of "children's theatre." **Facilities:** no permanent facility; touring company. **Production considerations:** works cast from ensemble of 5; sets suitable for touring. **Best submission time:** year-round. **Response time:** 2–3 months. **Special programs:** new plays readings; commissioning program; interested writers send letter of inquiry with recommendations from theatres who have produced writer's work.

METROSTAGE
(Founded 1984)
1201 North Royal St; Alexandria, VA 22314; (703) 548-9044, FAX 548-9089
Carolyn Griffin, *Producing Artistic Director*

Submission procedure: no unsolicited scripts; synopsis, first 10 pages of dialogue, list of productions/readings and letter of inquiry. **Types of material:** full-length plays. **Facilities:** MetroStage, 150 seats, thrust stage. **Production considerations:** cast limit of 8, prefers 4; prefers 1 set. **Best submission time:** year-round. **Response time:** 1 month letter; 1 month script. **Special programs:** First Stage: staged reading series Oct–May.

MILL MOUNTAIN THEATRE
(Founded 1964)
1 Market Square SE; Roanoke, VA 24011-1437; (540) 342-5749, FAX 342-5745; E-mail mmtmail@millmountain.org; Web http://www.millmountain.org
Literary Manager

Submission procedure: accepts unsolicited one-acts only; synopsis, 10-page dialogue sample and letter of inquiry for all other submissions; include cassette for musicals. **Types of material:** full-length plays, one-acts, musicals, solo pieces. **Special interests:** plays with racially mixed casts. **Facilities:** Mill Mountain Theatre, 400 seats, flexible proscenium stage; Theatre B, 125 seats, flexible stage. **Production considerations:** cast limit of 15 for plays, 24 for musicals; prefers unit set. **Best submission time:** year-round. **Response time:** 6 weeks letter; 6–8 months script. **Special programs:** Centerpieces: monthly lunchtime staged readings of one-acts by emerging playwrights; unpublished one-acts 25–35 minutes long (no 10-minute plays). ScriptTease: roundtable readings 2–3 times each year of full-length new plays at Hollins University. The Mill Mountain Theatre New Play Competition: The Norfolk Southern Festival of New Works (see Prizes).

MILWAUKEE CHAMBER THEATRE
(Founded 1975)
158 North Broadway; Milwaukee, WI 53202; (414) 276-8842, FAX 277-4477;
E-mail mct@execpc.com
Montgomery Davis, *Artistic Director*

Submission procedure: no unsolicited scripts; professional recommendation. **Types of material:** full-length plays, one-acts, translations, adaptations. **Special interests:** strong, well-crafted plays; plays about Shaw for annual Shaw Festival. **Facilities:** Broadway Theatre Center: Cabot Theatre, 358 seats, proscenium stage; studio, 96 seats, black box. **Production considerations:** 1 set or unit set. **Best submission time:** summer. **Response time:** 2 months.

MILWAUKEE PUBLIC THEATRE
(Founded 1974)
626 East Kilbourn Ave, #802; Milwaukee, WI 53202-3237; (414) 347-1685,
FAX 347-1690; E-mail bleigh@execpc.com;
Web http://www.execpc.com/mpt
Barbara Leigh, *Co-Artistic/Producing Director*

Submission procedure: no unsolicited scripts; direct solicitation to playwright or agent. **Types of material:** full-length plays, one-acts, translations, adaptations, plays for young audiences, solo pieces, cabaret/revues, clown/vaudeville shows. **Special interests:** works with cast of 1–3 playing multiple roles; political satire; social-political and regional or local themes; plays dealing with disabilities; interart works; new clown/vaudeville shows; works for young and family audiences. **Facilities:** no permanent facility. **Production considerations:** simple production demands, productions tour. **Response time:** 12 months. **Special programs:** outdoor park performances.

MILWAUKEE REPERTORY THEATER
(Founded 1954)
108 East Wells St; Milwaukee, WI 53202; (414) 224-1761, FAX 224-9097;
E-mail milwaukrep@aol.com
Paul Kosidowski, *Literary Manager*

Submission procedure: no unsolicited scripts; agent submission. **Types of material:** full-length plays, translations, adaptations, cabaret/revues. **Facilities:** Quadracci Powerhouse Theatre, 720 seats, thrust stage; Stiemke Theatre, 200 seats, flexible stage; Stackner Cabaret, 100 seats, cabaret stage. **Production considerations:** works for cabaret must not exceed 80 minutes in length. **Best submission time:** year-round. **Response time:** 2–3 months.

MINT THEATER COMPANY
(Founded 1992)
311 West 43rd St, 5th Floor; New York, NY 10036; (212) 315-9434
Jonathan Bank, *Artistic Director*

Submission procedure: no unsolicited scripts; direct solicitation to playwright or agent. **Types of material:** full-length plays, translations, adaptations. **Facilities:** Mint Space, 74 seats, black box.

MISSOURI REPERTORY THEATRE
(Founded 1964)
4949 Cherry St; Kansas City, MO 64110-2263; (816) 235-2727, FAX 235-5367;
    E-mail theatre@umkc.edu; Web http://www.missourireptheatre.org
George Keathley, *Artistic Director*

Submission procedure: no unsolicited scripts. **Types of material:** full-length plays, translations, adaptations. **Facilities:** Helen F. Spencer Theatre, 740 seats, modified thrust stage. **Best submission time:** theatre not accepting submissions until after 1 Jun 2000.

MIXED BLOOD THEATRE COMPANY
(Founded 1975)
1501 South Fourth St; Minneapolis, MN 55454; (612) 338-0937
David Kunz, *Script Czar*

Submission procedure: no unsolicited scripts; synopsis and letter of inquiry. **Types of material:** full-length plays, musicals, cabaret/revues. **Special interests:** comedies dealing with racial issues, politics or sports. **Facilities:** Main Stage, 200 seats, flexible stage. **Best submission time:** Aug–Jan. **Response time:** 1 month letter; 2–6 months script. **Special programs:** We Don't Need No Stinkin' Dramas (see Prizes).

MOVING ARTS
(Founded 1992)
1822 Hyperion Ave; Los Angeles, CA 90027; (213) 665-8961, FAX 665-1816;
    E-mail movnarts@primenet.com;
    Web http://www.primenet.com/~movnarts
Trey Nichols, *Literary Director*

Submission procedure: no unsolicited scripts; synopsis, dialogue sample, resume and letter of inquiry. **Types of material:** full-length plays, translations, adaptations. **Special interests:** work previously unproduced on West Coast. **Facilities:** Moving Arts Theatre, 36 seats, black box. **Production considerations:** cast limit of 7; modest production demands; no wing or fly space. **Best submission time:** year-round. **Response time:** 1–3 months letter; 6–8 months script.

MUSIC-THEATRE GROUP
(Founded 1971)
30 West 26th St, Suite 1001; New York, NY 10010; (212) 366-5260, ext 22,
FAX 366-5265
Lyn Austin, *Producing Director*

Submission procedure: no unsolicited scripts; direct solicitation to playwright or agent. **Types of material:** music-theatre works, operas, cabaret. **Special interests:** experimental musical works; collaborations between music-theatre, dance and the visual arts. **Facilities:** no permanent facility; various sites in New York City, The Berkshires and other national and international venues.

NATIONAL THEATRE OF THE DEAF
(Founded 1967)
Box 659; Chester, CT 06412; (860) 526-4971 (voice), -4974 (TTY),
FAX 526-0066; E-mail bookntd@aol.com
Will Rhys, *Artistic Director*

Submission procedure: no unsolicited scripts; synopsis, character breakdown, sample pages and letter of inquiry with SASE for response. **Types of material:** full-length plays, adaptations, plays for young audiences. **Special interests:** work not previously professionally produced only; deaf issues; culturally diverse plays. **Facilities:** no permanent facility; touring company. **Production considerations:** cast limit of 10; production must tour. **Best submission time:** year-round. **Response time:** 1 month letter; 3–6 months script.

NEBRASKA REPERTORY THEATRE
(Founded 1968)
215 Temple Bldg; 12th and R Sts; Lincoln, NE 68588-0201; (402) 472-2072,
FAX 472-9055
Jeffrey Elwell, *Executive Director*

Submission procedure: no unsolicited scripts; direct solicitation to playwright or agent. **Types of material:** full-length plays, plays for young audiences. **Special interests:** plays that contribute to multicultural awareness. **Facilities:** Studio Theatre, 180 seats, black box. **Production considerations:** cast limit of 10; simple set. **Response time:** 2–6 months. **Special programs:** Theatre for Family Audiences.

NEBRASKA THEATRE CARAVAN
(Founded 1976)
6915 Cass St; Omaha, NE 68132; (402) 553-4890, FAX 553-6288;
E-mail necaravan@aol.com
Marya Lucca-Thyberg, *Director of the Caravan*

Submission procedure: no unsolicited scripts; synopsis and letter of inquiry. **Types of material:** adaptations, plays for young audiences, musicals. **Special interests:** work suitable for elementary, intermediate and high school audiences only. **Facilities:** no permanent facility; touring company. **Production considerations:** cast limit of 8; 1 set. **Best submission time:** Sep–Dec. **Response time:** 1 month letter; 3 months script.

NEW AMERICAN THEATER

(Founded 1972)
118 North Main St; Rockford, IL 61101; (815) 963-9454,
    FAX 963-7215
William Gregg, *Producing Artistic Director*

Submission procedure: no unsolicited scripts; agent submission. **Types of material:** full-length plays, adaptations, cabaret/revues. **Facilities:** Mainstage, 282 seats, thrust stage; Second stage, 90 seats, flexible stage. **Production considerations:** small-to-medium cast size; modest production demands. **Best submission time:** fall. **Response time:** 3 months.

THE NEW CONSERVATORY THEATRE CENTER

(Founded 1981)
25 Van Ness, Lower Lobby; San Francisco, CA 94102; (415) 861-4914,
    FAX 861-6988; E-mail nctcsf@yahoo.com
Ed Decker, *Artistic Director*

Submission procedure: no unsolicited scripts; synopsis and letter of inquiry. **Types of material:** full-length plays, plays for young audiences. **Special interests:** work with gay, Latino or African-American themes. **Facilities:** Decker Theatre, 125 seats, proscenium stage; Walker Theatre, 60 seats, black box; Theatre III, 55 seats, black box. **Production considerations:** small cast; 1 set. **Best submission time:** year-round. **Response time:** 6 months letter; 1 year script.

NEW DRAMATISTS

See Membership and Service Organizations.

NEW FEDERAL THEATRE

(Founded 1970)
292 Henry St; New York, NY 10002; (212) 353-1176, FAX 353-1088;
    E-mail newfederal@aol.com
Woodie King, Jr., *Producing Director*

Submission procedure: no unsolicited scripts; professional recommendation. **Types of material:** full-length plays. **Special interests:** social and political issues; family and community themes related to minorities and women. **Facilities:** Henry Street Settlement: Harry Dejour Playhouse, 300 seats, proscenium stage; Experimental Theatre, 100 seats, black box; Recital Hall, 100 seats, thrust stage. **Production considerations:** small cast, no more than 2 sets. **Best submission time:** year-round. **Response time:** 5 months.

NEW GEORGES

(Founded 1992)

90 Hudson St, #2E; New York, NY 10013; (212) 620-0113, FAX 334-9239;
E-mail newgeorges@aol.com; Web http://www.newgeorges.org

Susan Bernfield, *Artistic Director*

Submission procedure: accepts unsolicited scripts; prefers synopsis and letter of inquiry. **Types of material:** full-length plays. **Special interests:** plays by women only; works with "vigorous use of language and heightened perspectives on reality." **Facilities:** no permanent facility. **Best submission time:** year-round. **Response time:** 3 months letter; 6–9 months script.

THE NEW GROUP

(Founded 1991)

85 Fifth Ave, New York, NY 10003

Kevin Scott, *Literary Manager*

Submission procedure: accepts unsolicited scripts with resume (only 1 submission per playwright per year). **Types of material:** full-length plays. **Special interests:** works not previously produced in New York City; "plays which reflect the spirit of our times and tell their stories with immediacy, fearlessness and discipline." **Facilities:** no permanent facility. **Best submission time:** year-round. **Response time:** 6–9 months. **Special programs:** Playwrights Unit: weekly developmental workshop with playwrights and actors; writers admitted for 3 months based on quality of submitted script.

NEW JERSEY REPERTORY COMPANY

(Founded 1997)

Box 138; Oakhurst, NJ 07755; (732) 229-3166, FAX 229-3167;
E-mail info@njrep.org; Web http://www.njrep.org

(Ms) Dana Benningfield, *Literary Manager*

Submission procedure: accepts unsolicited scripts with synopsis and character breakdown. **Types of material:** full-length plays, one-acts, musicals. **Special interests:** work not previously professionally produced; social, humanistic themes. **Facilities:** Main Stage, 72 seats, black box; Second Stage, 50 seats, flexible stage. **Production considerations:** cast limit of 7; unit or simple set. **Best submission time:** year-round. **Response time:** 6–12 months. **Special programs:** Script-in-Hand: year-round reading series for more than 20 plays; of these, up to 6 selected for Main Stage production.

NEW JERSEY SHAKESPEARE FESTIVAL

(Founded 1962)

36 Madison Ave; Madison, NJ 07940; (973) 408-3278, FAX 408-3361

Bonnie J. Monte, *Artistic Director*

Submission procedure: no unsolicited scripts; synopsis and letter of inquiry. **Types of material:** full-length plays, translations, adaptations, solo pieces. **Special**

interests: translations and/or adaptations of classic works only. **Facilities:** Festival Theatre, 308 seats, thrust stage; The Other Stage, 108 seats, black box. **Production considerations:** modest technical demands. **Best submission time:** theatre not accepting scripts until after Sep 2000. **Response time:** 2 months letter; 1 month script.

NEW REPERTORY THEATRE
(Founded 1985)
Box 610418; Newton Highlands, MA 02461; (617) 928-9831, FAX 527-5217;
    E-mail newrepthtr@aol.com;
    Web http://www.theatermirror.com/newrep/index.html
Rick Lombardo, *Producing Artistic Director*

Submission procedure: no unsolicited scripts; synopsis, dialogue sample and letter of inquiry. **Types of material:** full-length plays, translations, adaptations. **Special interests:** plays of ideas that center around pressing issues of our time; multicultural themes; intimate, interpersonal themes. **Facilities:** New Repertory Theatre, 160 seats, thrust stage. **Production considerations:** cast limit of 7. **Best submission time:** May–Aug. **Response time:** 2 months letter; 6 months script. **Special programs:** reading series.

NEW STAGE THEATRE
(Founded 1966)
Box 4792; Jackson, MS 39296-4792; (601) 948-0143, FAX 948-3538
John Maxwell, *Artistic Director*

Submission procedure: no unsolicited scripts; synopsis and letter of inquiry. **Types of material:** full-length plays, one-acts, solo pieces. **Facilities:** Meyer Crystal Auditorium, 364 seats, proscenium stage. **Production considerations:** cast limit of 3–8. **Best submission time:** summer–fall. **Response time:** 1 month letter; 3 months script. **Special programs:** Eudora Welty New Play Series; theatre produces one new play every season.

NEW TUNERS THEATRE
(Founded 1969)
1225 West Belmont; Chicago, IL 60657; (773) 929-7367, ext 10, FAX 327-1404;
    E-mail judytune@aol.com
Warner Crocker, *Artistic Director*

Submission procedure: no unsolicited scripts; synopsis, dialogue sample, 3-song cassette, professional recommendation and letter of inquiry. **Types of material:** musicals. **Facilities:** North Theatre, 150 seats, thrust stage; South Theatre, 150 seats, proscenium stage; West Theatre, 150 seats, thrust stage. **Best submission time:** Jan. **Response time:** 2 months letter; 6 months script. **Special programs:** Annual Festival of Staged Readings in summer; New Tuners Workshop: new musical developmental workshop; *deadline:* 1 Jan 2000; *dates:* Aug 2000.

NEW YORK STAGE AND FILM
(Founded 1984)
151 West 30th St, Suite 905; New York, NY 10001; (212) 239-2334,
FAX 239-2996
Johanna Pfaelzer, *Managing Producer*

Submission procedure: no unsolicited scripts; synopsis, resume and letter of inquiry. **Types of material:** full-length plays. **Facilities:** Powerhouse Theatre, 135 seats, proscenium stage; Coal Bin, 110 seats, black box. **Best submission time:** 1 Sep–31 Oct only. **Response time:** 1 month letter; 2 months script.

NEW YORK STATE THEATRE INSTITUTE
(Founded 1974)
155 River St; Troy, NY 12180; (518) 274-3200, FAX 274-3815
Patricia Di Benedetto Snyder, *Producing Artistic Director*

Submission procedure: no unsolicited scripts; synopsis, cast/scene breakdown and letter of inquiry. **Types of material:** full-length plays, adaptations, musicals. **Special interests:** works for family audiences only. **Facilities:** Schacht Fine Arts Center, 800 seats, proscenium stage. **Best submission time:** Mar–Sep. **Response time:** 2 months letter; 6 months script. **Special programs:** new work developmental workshops; playwrights receive staged reading or workshop production, negotiable remuneration, travel and housing.

NEW YORK THEATRE WORKSHOP
(Founded 1979)
79 East 4th St; New York, NY 10003; (212) 780-9037
Mandy Mishell Hackett, *Artistic Associate, Literary*

Submission procedure: no unsolicited scripts; synopsis, 10-page sample scene, resume and letter of inquiry. **Types of material:** full-length plays, one-acts, translations, music-theatre works, solo pieces, proposals only for performance art. **Special interests:** socially relevant and/or minority issues; innovative form and language. **Facilities:** 79 East 4th Street Theatre, 150 seats, proscenium stage. **Best submission time:** fall–spring. **Response time:** 1 month letter; 5 months script. **Special programs:** Mondays at Three: reading series, developmental workshops and symposiums. Summer writing residency. New York Theatre Workshop Playwriting Fellowship for emerging writers of color based in New York (see Fellowships and Grants).

NEXT ACT THEATRE
(Founded 1990)
Box 394; Milwaukee, WI 53201; (414) 278-7780, FAX 278-5930
David Cecsarini, *Producing Director*

Submission procedure: no unsolicited scripts; synopsis and letter of inquiry. **Types of material:** full-length plays, adaptations, solo pieces. **Facilities:** Stiemke Theatre, 198 seats, flexible stage; Studio Space, 99 seats, thrust stage. **Production**

considerations: small cast size; minimal production requirements. **Best submission time:** spring. **Response time:** 1 month letter; 6 months script.

NEXT THEATRE COMPANY
(Founded 1981)
927 Noyes St; Evanston, IL 60201; (847) 475-6763, FAX 475-6767;
    E-mail tucker@lightoperaworks.org; Web http://www.nexttheatre.org
Sarah Tucker, *Associate Artistic Director*

Submission procedure: no unsolicited scripts; synopsis, 10–15 pages of dialogue and letter of inquiry. **Types of material:** full-length plays, translations, adaptations. **Facilities:** Mainstage, 175 seats, proscenium stage. **Production considerations:** no fly space; limited wing space. **Best submission time:** year-round. **Response time:** 1 month letter; 3–6 months script.

NORTH SHORE MUSIC THEATRE
(Founded 1955)
62 Dunham Rd; Beverly, MA 01915; (978) 922-8500, FAX 921-0793;
    Web http://www.nsmt.org
John LaRock, *Associate Producer*

Submission procedure: no unsolicited scripts; synopsis and letter of inquiry with SASE for response; include cassette for musicals. **Types of material:** musicals. **Special interests:** musicals only. **Facilities:** Main Stage, 1800 seats, arena stage; Workshop, 100 seats, flexible stage. **Production considerations:** prefers cast limit of 12 for Workshop productions. **Best submission time:** year-round. **Response time:** 1 month letter; 3–6 months script. **Special programs:** New Works Development Program: spring and fall workshop productions of new works with authors in residence; theatre pays (rate varies) and houses writers; contact theatre for information.

NORTH STAR THEATRE
(Founded 1991)
347 Gerard St; Mandeville, LA 70448; (504) 624-5266, FAX 626-1692
Lori Bennett, *Producing Director*

Submission procedure: accepts unsolicited scripts with SASE for response. **Types of material:** full-length plays, one-acts, plays for young audiences. **Special interests:** one-act plays suitable for children. **Facilities:** North Star Theatre, 150 seats, thrust stage. **Production considerations:** minimal production demands; simple sets. **Best submission time:** year-round. **Response time:** 3 months.

NORTHLIGHT THEATRE
(Founded 1975)
9501 North Skokie Blvd; Skokie, IL 60076; (847) 679-9501, ext 3303,
     FAX 679-1879
Cecilie Keenan, *Assistant Artistic Director*

Submission procedure: no unsolicited scripts; synopsis and letter of inquiry. **Types of material:** full-length plays, translations, adaptations, musicals, solo pieces. **Special interests:** translations and adaptations of "lost" plays; the public world and public issues; plays of ideas; works that are passionate and/or hilarious; stylistic exploration and complexity; no domestic realism. **Facilities:** Center East Theatre, 850 seats, proscenium stage; Northlight Theatre, 345 seats, thrust stage. **Best submission time:** year-round. **Response time:** 1 month letter; 2–4 months script.

ODYSSEY THEATRE ENSEMBLE
(Founded 1969)
2055 South Sepulveda Blvd; Los Angeles, CA 90025; (310) 477-2055
Sally Essex-Lopresti, *Director of Literary Programs*

Submission procedure: no unsolicited scripts; synopsis, 8–10-page dialogue sample, play's production history (if any), resume and letter of inquiry with SASE for response; include cassette for musicals. **Types of material:** full-length plays, translations, adaptations, musicals. **Special interests:** culturally diverse works; works with innovative form or provocative subject matter; works exploring the enduring questions of human existence and the possibilities of the live theatre experience; works with political or sociological impact. **Facilities:** Odyssey 1, 99 seats, flexible stage; Odyssey 2, 99 seats, thrust stage; Odyssey 3, 99 seats, endstage. **Production considerations:** plays must be 90 minutes or longer. **Best submission time:** year-round. **Response time:** 2–4 weeks letter; 6 months script.

OLD GLOBE THEATRE
(Founded 1935)
Box 2171; San Diego, CA 92112-2171; (619) 231-1941
Raúl Moncada, *Literary Manager*

Submission procedure: no unsolicited scripts; synopsis and letter of inquiry with SASE for response. **Types of material:** full-length plays, translations, adaptations. **Special interests:** well-crafted, strongly theatrical material. **Facilities:** Lowell Davies Festival Stage, 620 seats, outdoor stage; Old Globe Theatre, 581 seats, modified thrust stage; Cassius Carter Centre Stage, 225 seats, arena stage. **Production considerations:** prefers cast limit of 8. **Best submission time:** year-round. **Response time:** 2–3 months letter; 6–10 months script.

OLDCASTLE THEATRE COMPANY
(Founded 1972)
Box 1555; Bennington, VT 05201-1555; (802) 447-1267, FAX 442-3704
Eric Peterson, *Producing Artistic Director*

Submission procedure: accepts unsolicited scripts. **Types of material:** full-length plays, musicals. **Facilities:** Bennington Center for the Arts, 300 seats, modified proscenium stage. **Best submission time:** winter. **Response time:** 4–6 months.

OLNEY THEATRE CENTER FOR THE ARTS
(Founded 1937)
2001 Olney-Sandy Spring Rd; Olney, MD 20832; (301) 924-4485, FAX 924-2654
David Jackson, *Literary Manager*

Submission procedure: no unsolicited scripts; professional recommendation. **Types of material:** full-length plays, translations, adaptations, solo pieces. **Facilities:** Mainstage, 500 seats, proscenium stage. **Production considerations:** cast limit of 8. **Best submission time:** year-round. **Response time:** 6 months.

OMAHA THEATER COMPANY FOR YOUNG PEOPLE
(Founded 1949)
2001 Farnam St; Omaha, NE 68102; (402) 345-4852, FAX 345-7255
James Larson, *Artistic Director*

Submission procedure: no unsolicited scripts; professional recommendation. **Types of material:** one-acts. **Special interests:** plays for family audiences only; plays based on children's literature and contemporary issues; multicultural themes. **Facilities:** Omaha Theater Company, 932 seats, proscenium stage; second stage, 175 seats, black box. **Production considerations:** cast limit of 10; prefers unit set. **Best submission time:** year-round. **Response time:** 6 months.

ONTOLOGICAL-HYSTERIC THEATER
(Founded 1968)
260 West Broadway; New York, NY 10013; (212) 941-8911, FAX 334-5149

Submission procedure: no unsolicited scripts; direct solicitation to playwright or agent. **Types of material:** full-length plays. **Facilities:** Ontological at St. Mark's Theater, 80 seats, black box.

OPEN CIRCLE THEATER
(Founded 1992)
429 Boren Ave N; Seattle, WA 98109; (206) 382-4250;
    Web http://www.opencircletheater.org
Scott Bradley, *Artistic Director*

Submission procedure: no unsolicited scripts; synopsis, 10-page dialogue sample, resume and letter of inquiry. **Types of material:** full-length plays, musicals, adaptations. **Special interests:** adaptations of fantastical or mythic themes only;

plays suitable for site-specific staging; plays incorporating new music and dance or movement; no realism. **Facilities:** Open Circle Theater, 50 seats, flexible stage. **Best submission time:** year-round. **Response time:** 2–3 months letter; 6 months script.

THE OPEN EYE THEATER
(Founded 1972)
Box 959; Margaretville, NY 12455; (914) 586-1660, FAX 586-1660;
        E-mail openeye@catskill.net; Web http://www.theopeneye.com
Amie Brockway, *Producing Artistic Director*

Submission procedure: no unsolicited scripts; synopsis and letter of inquiry with SASE for response. **Types of material:** full-length plays, one-acts, translations, adaptations. **Special interests:** plays for multigenerational audiences; culturally diverse themes; plays with music; ensemble plays; plays of any length (10 minutes or more); Catskill Mountain-area writers. **Facilities:** no permanent facility. **Production considerations:** minimal set. **Best submission time:** Oct–Apr. **Response time:** 1 week letter (if interested); 3–6 months script. **Special programs:** New Play Works: new-play developmental program of readings and workshop productions.

OREGON SHAKESPEARE FESTIVAL
(Founded 1935)
Box 158; Ashland, OR 97520; (541) 482-2111, FAX 482-0446
Lue Douthit, *Literary Manager*

Submission procedure: no unsolicited scripts; professional recommendation. **Types of material:** full-length plays. **Special interests:** plays of ideas; language-oriented plays; submissions by women and minority writers encouraged. **Facilities:** Elizabethan Theatre, 1194 seats, outdoor Elizabethan stage; Angus Bowmer Theatre, 600 seats, thrust stage; Black Swan, 140 seats, black box. **Best submission time:** fall. **Response time:** 3 months. **Special programs:** reading series; commissioning programs.

ORGANIC THEATER COMPANY
(Founded 1969)
1420 Maple Ave; Evanston, IL 60201; (847) 475-0600, FAX 475-9200
Ina Marlowe, *Producing Artistic Director*

Submission procedure: no unsolicited scripts; direct solicitation to playwright or agent. **Types of material:** full-length plays, long one-acts. **Facilities:** Mainstage, 200 seats, modified thrust stage.

PAN ASIAN REPERTORY THEATRE
(Founded 1977)
47 Great Jones St; New York, NY 10012; (212) 505-5655, FAX 505-6014;
     E-mail panasian@aol.com; Web http://www.panasian.org
Tisa Chang, *Artistic/Producing Director*

Submission procedure: no unsolicited scripts; synopsis and letter of inquiry. **Types of material:** full-length plays, translations, adaptations, musicals. **Special interests:** Asian or Asian-American themes only. **Facilities:** no permanent facility. **Production considerations:** prefers cast limit of 8. **Best submission time:** summer. **Response time:** 9 months letter; 9 months script. **Special programs:** staged readings and workshops.

THE PASADENA PLAYHOUSE
(Founded 1917)
80 South Lake Ave, Suite 500; Pasadena, CA 91101; (626) 792-8672,
     FAX 792-7343; E-mail patroninfo@pasadenaplayhouse.com;
     Web http://www.pasadenaplayhouse.org
David A. Tucker II, *Literary Manager*

Submission procedure: no unsolicited scripts; agent submission. **Types of material:** full-length plays, musicals. **Facilities:** The Pasadena Playhouse, 686 seats, proscenium stage. **Production considerations:** cast limit of 2–7; 1 set or unit set; modest musical requirements. **Best submission time:** year-round. **Response time:** 6–12 months.

PEGASUS PLAYERS
(Founded 1978)
1145 West Wilson; Chicago, IL 60640; (773) 878-9761, FAX 271-8057;
     E-mail pegasusp@megsinet.net
Alex Levy, *Literary Manager*

Submission procedure: no unsolicited scripts; synopsis and letter of inquiry. **Types of material:** full-length plays, translations, adaptations, musicals, solo pieces. **Facilities:** The O'Rourke Center for the Performing Arts, 250 seats, proscenium stage. **Best submission time:** year-round. **Response time:** 1 month letter; 4–6 months script. **Special programs:** Chicago Young Playwrights Festival: annual Jan festival of plays by Chicago-area high school students; write for information.

PEGASUS THEATRE
(Founded 1985)
3916 Main St; Dallas, TX 75226-1228; (214) 821-6005, FAX 826-1671
Steve Erwin, *Literary Manager*

Submission procedure: no unsolicited scripts; synopsis, 10-page dialogue sample, character breakdown and letter of inquiry. **Types of material:** full-length plays. **Special interests:** comedies only, especially contemporary satire; no mysteries. **Facilities:** Mainstage, 141 seats, proscenium stage. **Production considerations:** cast limit of 10; single set; limited fly space. **Best submission time:** Mar–Jun. **Response time:** 1 month letter; 6 months script.

PENDRAGON THEATRE

(Founded 1980)
148 River St; Saranac Lake, NY 12983-2031; (518) 891-1854, FAX 891-7012;
    E-mail pdragon@northnet.org; Web http://www.northnet.org/pendragon
Bob Pettee, *Managing Director*

Submission procedure: no unsolicited scripts; synopsis, dialogue sample and letter of inquiry with SASP for response. **Types of material:** full-length plays, plays for young audiences. **Special interests:** plays suitable for performance by adolescents ages 11–16. **Facilities:** Pendragon Theatre, 132 seats, black box. **Production considerations:** cast limit of 8; simple set. **Best submission time:** year-round. **Response time:** 3–4 weeks letter; 3 months script.

PENGUIN REPERTORY COMPANY

(Founded 1977)
Box 91; Stony Point, NY 10980; (914) 786-2873, FAX 786-3638
Joe Brancato, *Artistic Director*

Submission procedure: accepts unsolicited scripts. **Types of material:** full-length plays, adaptations. **Facilities:** Barn Playhouse, 108 seats, proscenium stage. **Production considerations:** cast limit of 5; simple set. **Best submission time:** Sep–Dec. **Response time:** 3 months.

PENOBSCOT THEATRE COMPANY

(Founded 1974)
183 Main St; Bangor, ME 04401; (207) 942-3333, FAX 947-6678;
    E-mail penthtr@agate.net
Mark Torres, *Producing Artistic Director*

Submission procedure: no unsolicited scripts; synopsis and letter of inquiry. **Types of material:** full-length plays. **Facilities:** Bangor Opera House, 299 seats, proscenium/thrust stage; Penobscot Theatre, 132 seats, proscenium/thrust stage. **Production considerations:** small cast; limited production requirements; small performance space. **Best submission time:** late fall. **Response time:** 1 month letter; 2 months script.

THE PENUMBRA THEATRE COMPANY

(Founded 1976)
The Martin Luther King Bldg; 270 North Kent St; St. Paul, MN 55102-1794;
    (651) 224-4601, FAX 224-7074
Lou Bellamy, *Artistic Director*

Submission procedure: accepts unsolicited scripts with resume. **Types of material:** full-length plays, one-acts, translations, adaptations, plays for young audiences, musicals. **Special interests:** works that address the African-American experience and the African diaspora. **Facilities:** Hallie Q. Brown Theatre, 260 seats, proscenium/thrust stage. **Best submission time:** year-round. **Response time:** 6–9 months. **Special programs:** Cornerstone Dramaturgy and Development Project (see Development).

THE PEOPLE'S LIGHT AND THEATRE COMPANY
(Founded 1974)
39 Conestoga Rd; Malvern, PA 19355-1798; (215) 647-1900
Alda Cortese, *Literary Manager*

Submission procedure: no unsolicited scripts; synopsis, cast list, 10-page dialogue sample and letter of inquiry. **Types of material:** full-length plays, translations, adaptations. **Special interests:** intelligent, original scripts for a family audience. **Facilities:** People's Light and Theatre, 350 seats, flexible stage; Steinbright Stage, 99–150 seats, flexible stage. **Production considerations:** cast limit of 6; 1 set or unit set. **Best submission time:** year-round. **Response time:** 2 weeks letter; 8–10 months script.

PERFORMANCE RIVERSIDE
(Founded 1983)
4800 Magnolia Ave; Riverside, CA 92506; (909) 222-8399, FAX 222-8940
William Freimuth, *Executive Director*

Submission procedure: no unsolicited scripts; synopsis and letter of inquiry. **Types of material:** musicals only. **Facilities:** Landis Auditorium, 850 seats, proscenium stage. **Production considerations:** cast limit of 25 inclusive of chorus; limited backstage and wing space. **Best submission time:** year-round. **Response time:** 1 month letter; 3 months script.

PERSEVERANCE THEATRE
(Founded 1979)
914 3rd St; Douglas, AK 99824; (907) 364-2421, FAX 364-2603;
     E-mail persthr@ptialaska.net; Web http://www.juneau.com/pt/
Peter DuBois, *Artistic Director*

Submission procedure: no unsolicited scripts; synopsis, list of previous productions, resume and letter of inquiry. **Types of material:** full-length plays, one-acts, solo pieces. **Special interests:** new plays by AK playwrights; plays about ethnic experiences, gender, sexual orientation and disabilities. **Facilities:** Mainstage, 150 seats, thrust stage; Phoenix Stage, 50–75 seats, flexible space. **Best submission time:** year-round. **Response time:** 2 months letter; 6 months script. **Special programs:** Cross-Cultural Playreading Festival: annual presentation of plays that represent a wide variety of views of America; *deadline:* ongoing; *dates:* spring 2000.

PHILADELPHIA THEATRE COMPANY
(Founded 1974)
The Belgravia, Suite 300; 1811 Chestnut St; Philadelphia, PA 19103;
(215) 568-1920, FAX 568-1944; E-mail ptcnet@aol.com;
Web http://www.phillytheatreco.com
John Rea, *Literary Manager*

Submission procedure: no unsolicited scripts; agent submission. **Types of material:** full-length plays, small-scale musicals, solo pieces. **Special interests:** new American plays; social/humanistic themes; sense of theatricality; no mysteries. **Facilities:** Plays and Players Theater, 324 seats, proscenium stage. **Best submission time:** year-round. **Response time:** 6–8 months. **Special programs:** STAGES: program of staged readings.

PHOENIX THEATRE
(Founded 1920)
100 East McDowell Rd; Phoenix, AZ 85004; (602) 258-1974, FAX 253-3626;
Web http://www.arde.com/phxth
Artistic Director

Submission procedure: no unsolicited scripts; synopsis, production history (if any) and letter of inquiry with SASE for response. **Types of material:** plays for young audiences, musicals, cabaret/revues. **Special interests:** plays with strong narratives suitable for a general audience. **Facilities:** Mainstage, 346 seats, proscenium stage; Cookie Company, 150 seats, arena stage. **Best submission time:** theatre not accepting submissions until after Sep 2000. **Response time:** 6 months letter; 6 months script.

THE PHOENIX THEATRE
(Founded 1983)
749 North Park Ave; Indianapolis, IN 46202; (317) 635-7529, FAX 635-0010;
E-mail phoenixt@oaktree.net; Web http://www.phoenixtheatre.org
Bryan Fonseca, *Producing Director*

Submission procedure: accepts unsolicited scripts. **Types of material:** full-length plays, one-acts. **Facilities:** Mainstage, 150 seats, proscenium stage; Underground, 75 seats, black box. **Best submission time:** Jan–Feb. **Response time:** 6 months. **Special programs:** The Festival of Emerging American Theatre (FEAT) Competition (see Prizes).

PILLSBURY HOUSE THEATRE
(Founded 1992)
3501 Chicago Ave S; Minneapolis, MN 55407; (612) 825-0459
Brian Goranson, *Dramaturg*

Submission procedure: no unsolicited scripts; synopsis and letter of inquiry. **Types of material:** full-length plays, one-acts, translations, adaptations. **Facilities:**

Pillsbury House Theatre, 100 seats, proscenium stage. **Best submission time:** year-round. **Response time:** 5 months letter; 6 months script.

PING CHONG & COMPANY
(Founded 1975)
47 Great Jones St, 2nd Floor; New York, NY 10012; (212) 529-1557,
    FAX 529-1703; E-mail 103034.434@compuserve.com

Submission procedure: no unsolicited scripts; direct solicitation to playwright. **Types of material:** full-length works by company only. **Facilities:** no permanent facility.

PIONEER THEATRE COMPANY
(Founded 1962)
University of Utah; Salt Lake City, UT 84112; (801) 581-6356, FAX 581-5472
Charles Morey, *Artistic Director*

Submission procedure: no unsolicited scripts; synopsis and letter of inquiry. **Types of material:** full-length plays, translations, adaptations, musicals. **Facilities:** Pioneer Memorial Theatre, 1000 seats, proscenium stage. **Best submission time:** fall. **Response time:** 1 month letter; 6 months script.

PIRATE PLAYHOUSE—ISLAND THEATRE
(Founded 1991)
2200 Periwinkle Way; Sanibel Island, FL 33957; (941) 472-4109, FAX 472-0055;
    E-mail pirateplay@aol.com
Ralph Elias, *Producing Artistic Director*

Submission procedure: no unsolicited scripts; synopsis, 10-page dialogue sample, character breakdown and letter of inquiry with SASP for response. **Types of material:** full-length plays, one-acts, musicals, solo pieces. **Special interests:** comedies, dramas and music-theatre pieces of universal significance that offer insight on the human condition. **Facilities:** Pirate Playhouse, 180 seats, flexible stage. **Best submission time:** year-round. **Response time:** 1–5 months letter; 6–8 months script.

PITTSBURGH PUBLIC THEATER
(Founded 1975)
6 Allegheny Square; Pittsburgh, PA 15212-5349; (412) 323-8200, FAX 323-8550
Todd Kreidler, *Assistant to the Artistic Director*

Submission procedure: no unsolicited scripts; synopsis, dialogue sample and letter of inquiry with SASE for response. **Types of material:** full-length plays, translations, adaptations, musicals. **Facilities:** Theodore L. Hazlett, Jr. Theater, 457 seats, flexible stage. **Best submission time:** year-round. **Response time:** 2 months letter; 6 months script.

PLAYHOUSE ON THE SQUARE
(Founded 1968)
51 South Cooper St; Memphis, TN 38104; (901) 725-0776, FAX 272-7530
Jackie Nichols, *Executive Producer*

Submission procedure: accepts unsolicited scripts. **Types of material:** full-length plays, musicals. **Facilities:** Playhouse on the Square, 250 seats, proscenium stage; Circuit Playhouse, 136 seats, proscenium stage. **Best submission time:** year-round. **Response time:** 3–5 months. **Special programs:** Playhouse on the Square New Play Competition (see Prizes).

PLAYMAKERS REPERTORY COMPANY
(Founded 1976)
CB# 3235 Center for Dramatic Art; Country Club Rd;
    Chapel Hill, NC 27599-3235; (919) 962-1132, FAX 962-4069
Milly S. Barranger, *Producing Director*

Submission procedure: no unsolicited scripts; agent submission. **Types of material:** full-length plays, translations, adaptations. **Facilities:** Paul Green Theatre, 498 seats, thrust stage. **Best submission time:** Aug–May. **Response time:** 6 months.

THE PLAYWRIGHTS' CENTER

See Membership and Service Organizations.

PLAYWRIGHTS HORIZONS *2/18*
(Founded 1971)
416 West 42nd St; New York, NY 10036-6896; (212) 564-1235, FAX 594-0296
Sonya Sobieski, *Literary Manager*

Submission procedure: accepts unsolicited scripts with resume and cover letter; if necessary, will accept synopsis, dialogue sample and letter of inquiry; for musicals, send script and cassette (no synopses). **Types of material:** full-length plays, musicals. **Special interests:** works by American writers only; works with strong sense of language that take theatrical risks. **Facilities:** Mainstage, 145 seats, proscenium stage; Studio Theater, 72 seats, black box. **Best submission time:** year-round. **Response time:** 1 month letter; 6–10 months script.

PORTLAND CENTER STAGE
(Founded 1988)
1111 Southwest Broadway; Portland, OR 97205; (503) 248-6309,
    FAX 796-6509; Web http://www.pcs.org
Elizabeth Huddle, *Producing Artistic Director*

Submission procedure: no unsolicited scripts; synopsis and letter of inquiry. **Types of material:** full-length plays, translations, adaptations. **Facilities:** Newmark Theatre, Portland Center for the Performing Arts, 860 seats, proscenium stage.

Production considerations: prefers cast limit of 8–12. **Best submission time:** year-round. **Response time:** 1–2 months letter; 2–3 months script.

PORTLAND STAGE COMPANY

(Founded 1970)
Box 1458; Portland, ME 04104; (207) 774-1043, FAX 774-0576;
E-mail portstage@aol.com; Web http://www.portlandstage.com
Peter Still, *Dramaturg/Literary Manager*

Submission procedure: no unsolicited scripts; synopsis, first 10 pages of play and letter of inquiry. **Types of material:** full-length plays, translations, adaptations. **Facilities:** Performing Arts Center Theatre, 290 seats, proscenium stage; PSC Rehearsal Hall, 90 seats, flexible space (readings only). **Best submission time:** May–Jan. **Response time:** 3 months letter; 6 months script.

PRIMARY STAGES

(Founded 1983)
584 9th Ave; New York, NY 10036; (212) 333-7471, FAX 333-2025
Tricia McDermott, *Literary Manager*

Submission procedure: no unsolicited scripts; agent submission. **Types of material:** full-length plays, musicals, solo pieces. **Special interests:** new American plays and small-cast musicals previously unproduced in New York City. **Facilities:** Primary Stages Theatre, 99 seats, proscenium stage; Phil Bosakowski Theatre, 65 seats, proscenium stage. **Production considerations:** small cast; single set or unit set; no fly or wing space. **Best submission time:** Sep–Jun. **Response time:** 6 months.

THE PUBLIC THEATRE

(Founded 1991)
2 Great Falls Plaza, Box 7; Auburn, ME 04210; (207) 782-2211, FAX 784-3856;
Web http://www.thepublictheatre.org
Janet Mitchko, *Associate Artistic Director*

Submission procedure: no unsolicited scripts; synopsis, dialogue sample and letter of inquiry. **Types of material:** full-length plays. **Facilities:** The Public Theatre, 307 seats, proscenium stage. **Production considerations:** cast limit of 7; minimal production demands. **Best submission time:** late spring–fall. **Response time:** 5 months letter; 10 months script.

THE PURPLE ROSE THEATRE COMPANY
(Founded 1991)
137 Park St; Chelsea, MI 48118; (734) 475-5817, FAX 475-0802;
 E-mail purplerose@earthlink.net;
 Web http://home.earthlink.net/~purplerose/
Anthony Caselli, *Literary Manager*

Submission procedure: no unsolicited scripts; synopsis, dialogue sample and letter of inquiry. **Types of material:** full-length plays. **Special interests:** plays that speak to a middle-American audience. **Facilities:** Garage Theatre, 119 seats, thrust stage. **Production considerations:** cast limit of 10; no fly or wing space. **Best submission time:** year-round. **Response time:** 2 months letter; 6–9 months script.

RED BARN THEATRE
(Founded 1981)
Box 707; Key West, FL 33040; (305) 293-3035, FAX 293-3035;
 E-mail mmcdon3444@aol.com
Mimi McDonald, *Managing Director*

Submission procedure: no unsolicited scripts; synopsis and letter of inquiry with professional recommendation. **Types of material:** full-length plays, musicals, cabaret/revues. **Facilities:** Red Barn Theatre, 88 seats, proscenium stage. **Production considerations:** cast limit of 8; small band for musicals; no fly space; limited wing space. **Best submission time:** Mar–Jul. **Response time:** 6 months letter (if interested); 6 months script.

RED EYE
(Founded 1983)
15 West 14th St; Minneapolis, MN 55403-2301; (612) 870-7531;
 E-mail redeye@mtn.org
Steve Busa, *Artistic Director*

Submission procedure: no unsolicited scripts; synopsis, 10-page dialogue sample and letter of inquiry with SASE for response. **Types of material:** full-length plays, solo pieces, performance art. **Special interests:** experimental drama and multimedia works only. **Facilities:** Mainstage, 76–120 seats, proscenium stage. **Best submission time:** year-round. **Response time:** 6 months letter (if interested); 6–9 months script. **Special programs:** Isolated Acts: annual multidisciplinary festival held Feb–Apr; by invitation only.

REPERTORIO ESPAÑOL
(Founded 1968)
138 East 27th St; New York, NY 10016
Robert Weber Federico, *Artistic Associate Producer*

Submission procedure: no unsolicited scripts; synopsis and letter of inquiry. **Types of material:** full-length plays, adaptations, plays for young audiences, musicals, operas. **Special interests:** plays dealing with Hispanic themes. **Facilities:** Gramercy

Arts Theatre, 135 seats, proscenium stage. **Production considerations:** small cast. **Best submission time:** summer. **Response time:** 1 month letter; 6 months script.

THE REPERTORY THEATRE OF ST. LOUIS
(Founded 1966)
Box 191730; St. Louis, MO 63119; (314) 968-7340
Susan Gregg, *Associate Artistic Director*

Submission procedure: no unsolicited scripts; synopsis, character breakdown, technical requirements and letter of inquiry. **Types of material:** full-length plays. **Special interests:** nonnaturalistic plays; contemporary social and political issues. **Facilities:** Main Stage, 750 seats, thrust stage; Studio Theatre, 130 seats, black box. **Production considerations:** small cast; modest production demands. **Best submission time:** year-round. **Response time:** 1 month letter; 2 years script. **Special programs:** developmental workshop for new plays; scripts selected through theatre's normal submission procedure.

RIVERSIDE THEATRE
(Founded 1981)
Box 1651; Iowa City, IA 52244; (319) 338-7672, FAX 887-1362;
     E-mail rtheatre@inav.net; Web http://soli.inav.net/~rtheatre
Ron Clark and Jody Hovland, *Artistic Directors*

Submission procedure: no unsolicited scripts; synopsis and letter of inquiry. **Types of material:** full-length plays, translations, adaptations, cabaret/revues, solo pieces. **Facilities:** Riverside Theatre, 118 seats, flexible stage. **Production considerations:** small cast; simple set. **Best submission time:** year-round. **Response time:** 1 month letter (if interested); 3–5 months script.

ROADSIDE THEATER
(Founded 1975)
91 Madison Ave; Whitesburg, KY 41858; (606) 633-0108, FAX 633-1009;
     E-mail roadside@appalshop.org; Web http://www.appalshop.org/rst
Dudley Cocke, *Director*

Submission procedure: no unsolicited scripts; synopsis, dialogue sample and letter of inquiry. **Types of material:** full-length plays. **Special interests:** plays about the Appalachian region only. **Facilities:** Appalshop Theater, 150 seats, thrust stage. **Production considerations:** small cast; simple sets suitable for touring. **Best submission time:** year-round. **Response time:** 3 weeks letter; 2 months script. **Special programs:** reading and workshop series. Playwright residencies initiated by theatre; playwright may not apply.

ROADWORKS PRODUCTIONS

(Founded 1992)

1144 West Fulton Market, Suite 105; Chicago, IL 60607; (312) 492-7150,
FAX 492-7155; E-mail shade@roadworks.org;
Web http://www.roadworks.org

Shade Murray, *Associate Artistic Director*

Submission procedure: no unsolicited scripts; professional recommendation.
Types of material: full-length plays. **Special interests:** scripts suitable for ensemble
aged 20–30; "explosive, high-energy" plays. **Facilities:** no permanent facility. **Best
submission time:** Sep–Nov. **Response time:** 2 months.

THE ROCKY MOUNTAIN PLAYWRIGHTING FESTIVAL

(Founded 1991)

Box 1626; Telluride, CO 81435; (970) 728-4052; E-mail PlayFest@aol.com;
Web http://members.aol.com/PlayFest/RMSTP.html

Owen Perkins, *Executive Director*

Submission procedure: accepts unsolicited scripts. **Types of material:** full-length
plays, one-acts, adaptations, solo pieces. **Facilities:** The Nugget Theatre, 220 seats,
proscenium stage. **Production considerations:** prefers small casts; simple sets. **Best
submission time:** year-round. **Response time:** 3 months. **Special programs:** The
Playwrighting Academy: 1–6 week workshops held on school campuses and in
communities nationwide on all aspects of theatre including playwrighting. The
Roy Barker Playwrighting Prize (see Prizes).

ROUND HOUSE THEATRE

(Founded 1978)

12210 Bushey Dr; Silver Spring, MD 20902; (301) 933-9530, FAX 933-2321

Jerry Whiddon, *Producing Artistic Director*

Submission procedure: no unsolicited scripts; synopsis, dialogue sample, cast
breakdown, technical requirements and letter of inquiry. **Types of material:** full-
length plays, translations, adaptations, plays for young audiences, musicals. **Special
interests:** contemporary issues; new translations of lesser-known classics;
experimental works; humorous plays. **Facilities:** Round House Theatre, 216 seats,
modified thrust stage. **Production considerations:** cast limit of 6; prefers 1 set.
Best submission time: year-round. **Response time:** 2 months letter (if interested);
minimum 12 months script.

SACRAMENTO THEATRE COMPANY

(Founded 1942)

1419 H St; Sacramento, CA 95814; (916) 446-7501, FAX 446-4066

Gary Armagnac, *Associate Artistic Director*

Submission procedure: no unsolicited scripts; agent submission. **Types of
material:** full-length plays, adaptations, cabaret/revues. **Special interests:**
contemporary social and political issues; craftsmanship; theatricality; vital

language. **Facilities:** McClatchy Mainstage, 300 seats, proscenium stage; Stage II, 90 seats, black box. **Production considerations:** cast limit of 3–5. **Best submission time:** Jun–Dec. **Response time:** 6 months.

THE SALT LAKE ACTING COMPANY
(Founded 1970)
168 West 500 N; Salt Lake City, UT 84103; (801) 363-0526, FAX 532-8513
David Mong, *Literary Manager*

Submission procedure: no unsolicited scripts; synopsis, 5–10-page dialogue sample, resume and letter of inquiry with SASE for response. **Types of material:** full-length plays, translations, adaptations, musicals. **Special interests:** western American writers "who understand the unique synergistic effect that playwright, actor and audience enjoy when a work is produced for the stage." **Facilities:** Upstairs, 99–130 seats, thrust stage; Chapel Theatre, 99 seats, thrust stage. **Best submission time:** year-round. **Response time:** 4 months letter; 8 months script. **Special programs:** reading series in winter, spring and fall.

SAN DIEGO REPERTORY THEATRE
(Founded 1976)
79 Horton Plaza; San Diego, CA 92101; (619) 231-3586, FAX 235-0939
Nakissa Etemad, *Resident Dramaturg*

Submission procedure: no unsolicited scripts; synopsis and letter of inquiry. **Types of material:** full-length plays, translations, adaptations, musicals, literary cabaret, mixed-media events. **Special interests:** multiethnic and intercultural work; hard-hitting social and political work; offbeat hip musicals; dramatic work with unusual incorporation of music; women's issues; sharp-edged comedy; poetic visions. **Facilities:** Lyceum Stage, 570 seats, modified thrust stage; Lyceum Space, 270 seats, flexible stage. **Production considerations:** no fly space in Lyceum Space. **Best submission time:** year-round. **Response time:** 3 months letter; 12 months script. **Special programs:** readings and workshop productions.

SAN JOSE REPERTORY THEATRE
(Founded 1980)
Box 2399; San Jose, CA 95109-2399; (408) 367-7266, FAX 367-7255
J. R. Orlando, *Assistant to the Artistic Director*

Submission procedure: no unsolicited scripts; agent submission. **Types of material:** full-length plays, translations, adaptations, musicals, solo pieces. **Special interests:** small-cast musicals. **Facilities:** San Jose Repertory Theatre, 525 seats, proscenium stage. **Best submission time:** Sep–Nov. **Response time:** 3–6 months.

SANTA FE STAGES

(Founded 1995)

105 East Marcy St, Suite 107; Santa Fe, NM 87501; (505) 982-6680,
   FAX 982-6682; E-mail sfstages@ix.netcom.com

Craig Strong, *Managing Director*

Submission procedure: no unsolicited scripts; agent submission. **Types of material:** full-length plays, translations, adaptations. **Special interests:** translations and adaptations of classics not in the standard repertoire; cutting-edge works. **Facilities:** Greer Garson Theatre, 525 seats, proscenium stage; Weckesser Studio Theatre, 100 seats, flexible stage. **Best submission time:** Sep–Apr. **Response time:** 1 week letter; 3 months script.

SANTA MONICA PLAYHOUSE

(Founded 1962)

1211 4th St; Santa Monica, CA 90401-1391; (310) 394-9779, FAX 393-5573

Chris DeCarlo and Evelyn Rudie, *Co-Artistic Directors*

Submission procedure: no unsolicited scripts; synopsis and letter of inquiry. **Types of material:** full-length plays, one-acts, translations, adaptations, plays for young audiences, musicals. **Facilities:** The Main Stage, 88 seats, arena/thrust stage; The Other Space, 70 seats, black box. **Production considerations:** cast limit of 8; simple production demands. **Best submission time:** year-round. **Response time:** 3 months letter; 6 months script.

SEACOAST REPERTORY THEATRE

(Founded 1986)

125 Bow St; Portsmouth, NH 03801; (603) 433-4793, FAX 431-7818;
   E-mail info@seacoastrep.org; Web http://www.seacoastrep.org

Roy M. Rogosin, *Producing Artistic Director*

Submission procedure: no unsolicited scripts; agent submission (1-page synopsis only; include cassette for musicals). **Types of material:** full-length plays, plays for young audiences, musicals. **Special interests:** new American plays; small-scale musicals; plays for young audiences. **Facilities:** Seacoast Repertory Theatre, 230 seats, thrust stage. **Best submission time:** year-round. **Response time:** 3–6 months.

SEASIDE MUSIC THEATER

(Founded 1977)

Box 2835; Daytona Beach, FL 32120; (904) 252-3394, FAX 252-8991;
   Web http://www.seasidemusictheater.org

Lester Malizia, *General Manager*

Submission procedure: no unsolicited scripts; synopsis, cassette of music and letter of inquiry. **Types of material:** musicals for young and adult audiences, cabaret/revues. **Facilities:** Winter Theater, 500 seats, proscenium stage; Summer Theater, 500 seats, proscenium stage; Theater for Children, 150 seats, modified thrust stage. **Production considerations:** cast limit of 8 for Winter Theater, 30 for

Summer Theater, 10 for Theater for Children; small musical combo for Theater for Children and Winter Theater, 25-member orchestra for Summer Theater; no wing or orchestra space in Winter Theater; no fly space except in Summer Theater. **Best submission time:** Sep–Nov. **Response time:** 1–3 months letter; 3–6 months script.

SEATTLE CHILDREN'S THEATRE
(Founded 1975)
Box 9640; Seattle, WA 98109-0640; (206) 443-0807; Web http://www.sct.org
Deborah Frockt, *Dramaturg/Literary Manager*

Submission procedure: accepts unsolicited scripts for Drama School Summerstages only; professional recommendation or agent submission for all others. **Types of material:** full-length plays for young audiences, including translations, adaptations, musicals, solo pieces. **Special interests:** sophisticated works for young audiences that also appeal to adults. **Facilities:** Charlotte Martin Theatre, 485 seats, proscenium stage; Eve Alvord Theatre, 280 seats, black box. **Best submission time:** year-round. **Response time:** 8 months. **Special programs:** Drama School Summerstages: one-act plays, 30–60 minutes long for student performance; must have roles for 12–18 actors, ages 8–19; submit script with SASE for response to Don Fleming; Program Director; *deadline:* 1 Dec 1999.

SEATTLE REPERTORY THEATRE
(Founded 1963)
155 Mercer St; Seattle, WA 98109; (206) 443-2210
Christine Sumption, *Artistic Associate*

Submission procedure: no unsolicited scripts; synopsis, 10-page dialogue sample and letter of inquiry. **Types of material:** full-length plays, translations, adaptations, solo pieces. **Facilities:** Bagley Wright Theatre, 856 seats, proscenium stage; Leo K. Theatre, 284 seats, proscenium stage. **Best submission time:** year-round. **Response time:** 1 month letter; 4–6 months script. **Special programs:** New Plays in Process: annual workshop production program.

SECOND STAGE THEATRE
(Founded 1979)
Box 1807, Ansonia Station; New York, NY 10023; (212) 787-8302,
    FAX 877-9886
Christopher Burney, *Literary Manager/Dramaturg*

Submission procedure: no unsolicited scripts; synopsis, 5–10-page dialogue sample, resume and letter of inquiry. **Types of material:** full-length plays, adaptations, musicals. **Special interests:** new and previously produced American plays (include production history with script); "heightened" realism; sociopolitical issues; plays by women and minority writers. **Facilities:** Midtown Theatre, 296 seats, proscenium stage; McGinn/Cazale Theatre, 108 seats, endstage. **Best submission time:** year-round. **Response time:** 1 month letter; 4–6 months script.

Special programs: annual series of 4–6 readings of new and previously produced plays.

SEVEN ANGELS THEATRE
(Founded 1991)
Box 3358; Waterbury, CT 06705; (203) 591-8223, FAX 591-8223
Semina De Laurentis, *Artistic Director*

Submission procedure: no unsolicited scripts; professional recommendation. **Types of material:** full-length plays, musicals. **Facilities:** Seven Angels Theatre, 350 seats, proscenium stage. **Production considerations:** cast limit of 10; prefers unit set; no fly space. **Best submission time:** year-round. **Response time:** 3–6 months letter; 3–6 months script.

7 STAGES
(Founded 1979)
1105 Euclid Ave NE; Atlanta, GA 30307; (404) 522-0911;
      Web http://www.7stages.w1.com
Del Hamilton, *Artistic Director*

Submission procedure: no unsolicited scripts, direct solicitation to playwright or agent. **Types of material:** full-length plays, translations, adaptations, performance art. **Special interests:** nonrealistic plays and performance texts focusing on social, political or spiritual themes. **Facilities:** 7 Stages, 250 seats, thrust stage; Back Door, 100 seats, flexible stage.

SHADOW LIGHT PRODUCTIONS
(Founded 1994)
22 Chattanooga St; San Francisco, CA 94114; (415) 648-4461, FAX 641-9734;
      E-mail info@shadowlight.com; Web http://www.shadowlight.com
Kate Sheehan, *Managing Director*

Submission procedure: no unsolicited scripts; synopsis and letter of inquiry with SASE for response. **Types of material:** full-length plays, one-acts, translations, adaptations, plays for young audiences, musicals, solo pieces, cabaret/revues. **Special interests:** plays suitable for shadow theatre only, utilizing puppets as well as live actors; scripts dealing with mythological or historical figures; adaptations of stories or novels. **Facilities:** no permanent facility. **Production considerations:** cast limit of 15. **Best submission time:** year-round. **Response time:** 1 month letter; 1 month script.

SHAKESPEARE & COMPANY

(Founded 1978)
The Mount; Box 865; Lenox, MA 01240; (413) 637-1199, FAX 637-4274;
E-mail training@shakespeare.org; Web http://www.shakespeare.org
Ariel Bock, *Artistic Associate for Submissions*

Submission procedure: no unsolicited scripts; synopsis, 4-page dialogue sample and letter of inquiry. **Types of material:** full-length and one-act adaptations. **Special interests:** plays based on or adapted from works by Edith Wharton and other women or Henry James. **Facilities:** Mainstage Theatre, 600 seats, outdoor amphitheatre; Duffin Theatre, 500 seats, proscenium stage; Oxford Court, 200 seats, outdoor amphitheatre; Stables Theatre, 108 seats, thrust stage; Salon Theatre, 90 seats, endstage. **Production considerations:** minimal set pieces only; small casts; most theatre spaces part of historic estate (former home of Edith Wharton). **Best submission time:** fall–winter. **Response time:** 6 months letter (if interested); 6 months script.

SHAKESPEARE SANTA CRUZ

(Founded 1981)
Performing Arts Complex; University of California–Santa Cruz;
1156 High St; Santa Cruz, CA 95064; (831) 459-5109, FAX 459-3316;
E-mail karin_magaldi-unger@macmail.ucsc.edu
Karin Magaldi-Unger, *Literary Manager*

Submission procedure: no unsolicited scripts; synopsis, resume and letter of inquiry; prefers professional recommendation. **Types of material:** full-length plays, one-acts, plays for young audiences. **Special interests:** Shakespearean spinoffs, i.e., plays that use Shakespeare's characters or plots. **Facilities:** Sinsheimer-Stanley Glen, 500–800 seats, outdoor amphitheatre; Performing Arts Theater, 500 seats, thrust stage. **Production considerations:** small cast; minimal set. **Best submission time:** fall–winter. **Response time:** 1 month letter; 1 month script.

THE SHAKESPEARE THEATRE

(Founded 1986)
516 8th St; Washington, DC 20003-3808; (202) 547-3230, FAX 547-0226;
E-mail smazzola@shakespearedc.org; Web http://www.shakespearedc.org
Steven Scott Mazzola, *Assistant to the Artistic Director*

Submission procedure: no unsolicited scripts; professional recommendation. **Types of material:** translations, adaptations. **Special interests:** translations and adaptations of classics only. **Facilities:** The Shakespeare Theatre, 449 seats, proscenium stage. **Best submission time:** summer. **Response time:** 2 months.

SIGNATURE THEATRE

(Founded 1990)
3806 South Four Mile Run Dr; Arlington, VA 22206; (703) 820-9771
Marcia Gardner, *Literary Manager*

Submission procedure: no unsolicited scripts; agent submission. **Types of material:** full-length plays, adaptations, musicals. **Special interests:** work not previously professionally produced only; social issues; comedies. **Facilities:** Signature Theatre, 126 seats, black box. **Production considerations:** prefers cast limit of 10; no fly space. **Best submission time:** Sep–May. **Response time:** 6 months. **Special programs:** Stages: staged readings of new plays-in-process; scripts selected through theatre's normal submission procedure; On the Edge Series: full production of 1 new play a year.

SIGNATURE THEATRE COMPANY, INC.

(Founded 1991)
534 West 42nd St, 2nd Floor; New York, NY 10036-6809; (212) 967-1913,
    FAX 967-2957
James Houghton, *Founding Artistic Director*

Submission procedure: no unsolicited scripts; direct solicitation to playwright or agent. **Types of material:** full-length plays, one-acts. **Special interests:** playwrights with substantial body of work to be produced over course of season. **Facilities:** Signature Theatre, 160 seats, endstage.

SOCIETY HILL PLAYHOUSE

(Founded 1959)
507 South 8th St; Philadelphia, PA 19147; (215) 923-0210, FAX 923-1789;
    E-mail shpcerols.com; Web http://www.erols.com/shp
Walter Vail, *Literary Manager*

Submission procedure: no unsolicited scripts; synopsis and letter of inquiry with SASE for response. **Types of material:** full-length plays, musicals. **Special interests:** musicals and comedies with casts of 5–7. **Facilities:** Society Hill Playhouse, 223 seats, proscenium stage; Second Space, 90 seats, flexible stage. **Production considerations:** prefers small cast. **Best submission time:** year-round. **Response time:** 1 month letter; 6 months script.

SOHO REPERTORY THEATRE

(Founded 1975)
46 Walker St; New York, NY 10013; (212) 941-8632, FAX 941-7148
Alexandra Conley, *Executive Director*

Submission procedure: no unsolicited scripts; direct solicitation to playwright or agent. **Types of material:** full-length plays, one-acts, solo pieces. **Facilities:** Soho Rep, 99 seats, black box.

SOURCE THEATRE COMPANY
(Founded 1978)
1835 14th St NW; Washington, DC 20009; (202) 462-1073
Keith Parker, *Literary Manager*

Submission procedure: accepts unsolicited scripts that have not been professionally produced with synopsis, resume and letter-size SASE for response (scripts not returned); accepts synopsis and reviews for scripts previously produced once. **Types of material:** full-length plays, one-acts, musicals, solo pieces. **Facilities:** Source Theatre Company, 98–150 seats, thrust stage. **Best submission time:** before 15 Jan 2000 only. **Response time:** 15 Feb 2000 letter; 15 May 2000 script. **Special programs:** 20th Annual Washington Theatre Festival: new-play workshop productions; *deadline:* 15 Jan 2000; *dates:* 12 Jul–12 Aug 2000. Source Theatre Company 2000 Literary Prize (see Prizes).

SOUTH COAST REPERTORY
(Founded 1964)
Box 2197; Costa Mesa, CA 92628-2197; (714) 957-2602
Jerry Patch, *Dramaturg*
John Glore, *Literary Manager*

Submission procedure: no unsolicited scripts; synopsis, dialogue sample and letter of inquiry. **Types of material:** full-length plays, one-acts, translations, adaptations, musicals. **Facilities:** Mainstage, 507 seats, modified thrust stage; Second Stage, 161 seats, thrust stage. **Best submission time:** year-round. **Response time:** 1–3 weeks letter; 2–4 months script. **Special programs:** COLAB (Collaboration Laboratory) New Play Program: developmental program culminating in readings, staged readings, workshop productions and full productions; playwright receives grant, commission and/or royalties depending on nature of project. Pacific Playwrights Festival: annual 3-week developmental program for playwrights from across the nation culminating in staged readings, workshop productions and full productions performed for the public and theatre colleagues; plays are chosen through theatre's normal submission procedure and by invitation; not-for-profit theatres are also welcome to submit work; *dates:* Jun 2000.

SPOKANE INTERPLAYERS ENSEMBLE
(Founded 1981)
Box 1961; Spokane, WA 99210; (509) 455-7529, FAX 624-9348;
    E-mail interplayers@interplayers.com; Web http://www.interplayers.com
Robert A. Welch, *Managing Director*

Submission procedure: no unsolicited scripts; synopsis with cast list, set requirements, play's production history and reviews (if any), dialogue sample and letter of inquiry. **Types of material:** full-length plays. **Facilities:** Spokane Interplayers Ensemble, 256 seats, thrust stage. **Production considerations:** prefers cast limit of 8; 1 set. **Best submission time:** year-round. **Response time:** 3 months letter (if interested); 3–6 months script.

ST. LOUIS BLACK REPERTORY COMPANY
(Founded 1977)
634 North Grand Blvd, Suite 10-F; St. Louis, MO 63103; (314) 534-3807,
FAX 533-3345
Ronald J. Himes, *Producing Director*

Submission procedure: no unsolicited scripts; synopsis, 3–5-page dialogue sample, resume and letter of inquiry. **Types of material:** full-length plays, plays for young audiences, musicals. **Special interests:** works by African-American and Third World playwrights. **Facilities:** Grandel Theatre, 470 seats, thrust stage. **Best submission time:** Jun–Aug. **Response time:** 2 months letter; 2 months script. **Special programs:** touring company presenting works for young audiences.

STAGE ONE: THE LOUISVILLE CHILDREN'S THEATRE
(Founded 1946)
5 Riverfront Plaza; Louisville, KY 40202-2957; (502) 589-5946, FAX 588-5910;
E-mail kystageone@aol.com; Web http://www.stageone.org
Moses Goldberg, *Producing Director*

Submission procedure: accepts unsolicited scripts. **Types of material:** plays for young audiences. **Special interests:** plays about young people in the real world; good, honest treatments of familiar titles. **Facilities:** Moritz von Bomard Theater, 610 seats, thrust stage; Louisville Gardens, 300 seats, arena stage. **Production considerations:** prefers cast limit of 12; some productions tour. **Best submission time:** Oct–Dec. **Response time:** 3 months. **Special programs:** Tomorrow's Playwrights: annual one-act competition open to high school students throughout KY region; 3 finalists receive staged readings and prepare rewrite to determine placement; cash awards for winners and sponsoring schools; submit play through school; *deadline:* 1 Mar 2000.

STAGE WEST
(Founded 1979)
3055 South University Dr; Fort Worth, TX 76109-5608; (817) 924-9454,
FAX 926-8650; E-mail stgwest@ix.netcom.com;
Web http://www.stagewest.org
Jim Covault, *Artistic Director*

Submission procedure: no unsolicited scripts; synopsis and letter of inquiry. **Types of material:** full-length plays, translations, adaptations, solo pieces. **Special interests:** Hispanic plays; contemporary issues. **Facilities:** Stage West, 190 seats, arena stage. **Production considerations:** prefers cast limit of 9. **Best submission time:** Jan–Mar. **Response time:** 1 month letter; 3 months script.

STAGES

(Founded 1982)
1540 North McCadden Place; Hollywood, CA 90028; (323) 463-5356;
FAX 463-3904; E-mail ask@stageshollywood.com;
Web http://www.stageshollywood.com
Dramaturg

Submission procedure: no unsolicited scripts; direct solicitation to playwright or agent. **Types of material:** full-length plays, one-acts, translations, adaptations. **Special interests:** plays by foreign writers both in original language and in translation; theatre regularly produces plays in Spanish, French and English but can also find actors fluent in other languages; challenging, experimental work. **Facilities:** Amphitheatre, 99 seats, outdoor flexible stage; Mainstage, 49 seats, proscenium stage; Lab, 25 seats, classroom.

STAGES REPERTORY THEATRE

(Founded 1978)
3201 Allen Prkwy, #101; Houston, TX 77019; (713) 527-0220, FAX 527-8669
Rob Bundy, *Artistic Director*

Submission procedure: accepts unsolicited scripts. **Types of material:** full-length plays, plays for young audiences. **Special interests:** nonrealistic, edgy works. **Facilities:** Stages Repertory Theatre, 235 seats, arena stage; Stages Repertory Theatre, 180 seats, thrust stage. **Production considerations:** cast limit of 6; maximum 1 hour running time for children's shows. **Best submission time:** year-round. **Response time:** 9 months. **Special programs:** Southwest Festival for New Plays (see Development).

STAMFORD THEATRE WORKS

(Founded 1988)
95 Atlantic St; Stamford, CT 06901; (203) 359-4414, FAX 356-1846
Jane Desy, *Literary Manager*

Submission procedure: no unsolicited scripts; synopsis, dialogue sample and letter of inquiry; include cassette for musicals. **Types of material:** full-length plays, translations, adaptations, musicals. **Special interests:** plays that are contemporary, innovative and thought-provoking; socially and culturally relevant; challenging and entertaining. **Facilities:** Center Stage, 150 seats, modified thrust stage. **Production considerations:** prefers small cast; unit set. **Best submission time:** year-round. **Response time:** 2 months letter; 6 months script. **Special programs:** Windows on the Work: developmental workshop for 3 new plays, each play receives rehearsals, staged readings and audience discussions; scripts selected through theatre's normal submission procedure; plays not professionally produced only; *dates:* Feb–Mar.

STATE THEATER COMPANY
(Formerly Live Oak Theatre)
(Founded 1982)
719 Congress Ave; Austin, TX 78701; (512) 472-5143, FAX 472-7199;
    E-mail admin@statetheatrecompany.com;
    Web http://www.statetheatercompany.com

Submission procedure: accepts unsolicited scripts or synopsis, dialogue sample and letter of inquiry. **Types of material:** full-length plays, adaptations, solo pieces. **Special interests:** work not professionally produced only; Texas plays; comedies. Facilities: State Theater, 350 seats, proscenium stage. **Best submission time:** 1 Feb–1 Jun only. **Response time:** scripts chosen in summer of year after submission.

STEPPENWOLF THEATRE COMPANY
(Founded 1976)
1650 North Halsted; Chicago, IL 60614; (312) 335-1888, FAX 335-0808
Michele Volansky, *Dramaturg/Literary Manager*

Submission procedure: no unsolicited scripts; synopsis, 10-page dialogue sample and letter of inquiry. **Types of material:** full-length plays. **Special interests:** ensemble pieces with dynamic acting roles. **Facilities:** Mainstage, 510 seats, proscenium stage; Studio, 50–300 seats, flexible stage. **Best submission time:** year-round. **Response time:** 1–2 months letter; 3–6 months script.

STRATFORD FESTIVAL THEATER
(Founded 1996)
1850 Elm St; Stratford, CT 06615; (203) 378-1200, (FAX) 378-9777
L.D. Pietig, *Resident Director*

Submission procedure: no unsolicited scripts; synopsis and letter of inquiry with SASE for response. **Types of material:** full-length plays, plays for young audiences, musicals, cabaret/revues. **Facilities:** Festival Stage, 1500 seats, proscenium stage; Barn Theater, 499 seats, proscenium stage. **Best submission time:** year-round. **Response time:** 2 months letter; 6 months script. **Special programs:** The Play's the Thing: monthly readings of 4–6 new plays each season by celebrity actors; scripts chosen through theatre's normal selection process.

STRAWDOG THEATRE COMPANY
(Founded 1988)
3829 North Broadway; Chicago, IL 60613; (773) 528-9889, FAX 528-7238;
    E-mail strawdogtc@aol.com
David Warren, *Literary Manager*

Submission procedure: no unsolicited scripts; first 10 pages of script and letter of inquiry with SASE for response (include optional SASP for acknowledgment of receipt). **Types of material:** full-length plays, one-acts, translations, adaptations. **Special interests:** scripts suitable for ensemble aged 25–35; "off-the-wall," dark comedies. **Facilities:** Mainstage, 74 seats, black box. **Production considerations:** no fly or wing space. **Best submission time:** year-round. **Response time:** 3–8 weeks letter; 3–8 weeks script.

STUDIO ARENA THEATRE
(Founded 1965)
710 Main St; Buffalo, NY 14202-1990; (716) 856-8025, FAX 856-3415;
    Web http://www.studioarena.org
Gavin Cameron-Webb, *Artistic Director*

Submission procedure: no unsolicited scripts; agent submission. **Types of material:** full-length plays, translations, adaptations. **Special interests:** plays of local interest; plays of a theatrical nature; American history and culture; ethnic cultures, including plays about minorities. **Facilities:** Studio Arena Theatre, 637 seats, thrust stage. **Production considerations:** cast limit of 12; prefers smaller cast; no fly system and limited wing space. **Best submission time:** year-round. **Response time:** 6 months.

THE STUDIO THEATRE
(Founded 1979)
1333 P St NW; Washington, DC 20005; (202) 232-7267, FAX 588-5262;
    E-mail studio@studiotheatre.org; Web http://studiotheatre.org
Serge Seiden, *Literary Manager*

Submission procedure: no unsolicited scripts; direct solicitation to playwright or agent. **Types of material:** full-length plays, translations, adaptations, musicals, solo pieces. **Special interests:** American lyric realism; ethnic American themes; translations of new European and Asian plays. **Facilities:** Mead Theatre, 200 seats, thrust stage; Milton Theatre, 200 seats, thrust stage; Secondstage, 50 seats, flexible stage. **Response time:** 1 month.

SWINE PALACE PRODUCTIONS
(Founded 1991)
Box 18699; Baton Rouge, LA 70893; (225) 388-3533, FAX 388-4135;
    E-mail swinepal@aol.com
Lucy Maycock, *Dramaturg*

Submission procedure: accepts unsolicited scripts. **Types of material:** full-length plays, musicals. **Special interests:** works that explore issues pertinent to Louisiana. **Facilities:** Reilly Theatre, 500 seats, arena stage. **Best submission time:** summer. **Response time:** 1 month.

SYRACUSE STAGE

(Founded 1973)

820 East Genesee St; Syracuse, NY 13210-1508; (315) 443-4008, FAX 443-9846;
    E-mail geisler@syr.edu; Web http://web.syr.edu/~syrstage

Garrett Eisler, *Literary Manager*

Submission procedure: accepts unsolicited scripts. **Types of material:** full-length plays. **Facilities:** John D. Archbold Theatre, 499 seats, proscenium stage. **Production considerations:** prefers small cast. **Best submission time:** year-round. **Response time:** 6 months.

TACOMA ACTORS GUILD

(Founded 1978)

901 Broadway, 6th Floor; Tacoma, WA 98402-4404; (253) 272-3107,
    FAX 272-3358

(Mr.) Pat Patton, *Producing Artistic Director*

Submission procedure: no unsolicited scripts; synopsis and letter of inquiry. **Types of material:** full-length plays, translations, adaptations, musicals. **Facilities:** Theatre on the Square, 302 seats, proscenium stage. **Production considerations:** prefers small cast; 1 set or unit set. **Best submission time:** spring–summer. **Response time:** 1–2 months letter; 8–12 months script.

TADA!

(Founded 1984)

120 West 28th St, 2nd Floor; New York, NY 10001; (212) 627-1732,
    FAX 243-6736; E-mail tada@tadatheater.com;
    Web http://www.tadatheater.com

Janine Nina Trevens, *Artistic Director*

Submission procedure: accepts unsolicited scripts. **Types of material:** one-acts, plays for young audiences, musicals. **Special interests:** work to be performed by children and teenagers. **Facilities:** Mainstage, 98 seats, black box. **Production considerations:** modest production demands. **Best submission time:** year-round. **Response time:** 6 months. **Special programs:** TADA! One-Act Playwriting Competition (see Prizes).

TAPROOT THEATRE

(Founded 1976)

Box 30946; Seattle, WA 98103-0946; (206) 781-9705;
    E-mail taproot@taproottheatre.org; Web http://www.taproot.org/taproot

Sean Gaffney, *Managing Director*

Submission procedure: accepts unsolicited scripts. **Types of material:** full-length plays, plays for young audiences, musicals. **Special interests:** social issue plays for children suitable for touring; plays of hope. **Facilities:** Taproot Theatre, 224 seats, thrust stage. **Production considerations:** cast limit of 12–15 for mainstage shows; cast limit of 5 for touring shows; no fly space. **Best submission time:** year-round.

Response time: 3–6 months. Special programs: readings of 8–10 new plays each year; participation by invitation.

TENNESSEE REPERTORY THEATRE

(Founded 1985)
427 Chestnut St; Nashville, TN 37203-4826; (615) 244-4878, FAX 244-1232;
     E-mail tnrep@isdn.net
Todd Olson, *Associate Artistic Director*

Submission procedure: no unsolicited scripts; synopsis, dialogue sample and letter of inquiry; include cassette for musicals. Types of material: full-length plays, musicals, musical solo pieces. Facilities: Polk Theatre, 1050 seats, proscenium stage; Johnson Theatre, 100 seats, black box. Best submission time: Jun–Sep. Response time: 4–6 weeks letter; 9–12 months script.

THALIA SPANISH THEATRE

(Founded 1977)
Box 4368; Sunnyside, NY 11104; (718) 729-3880, FAX 729-3388;
     E-mail thaliaspan@aol.com;
     Web http://www.queensnewyork.com/cultural/thalia
Silvia Brito, *Artistic/Executive Director*

Submission procedure: accepts unsolicited scripts. Types of material: full-length plays, translations, adaptations. Special interests: plays in Spanish only. Facilities: Thalia Spanish Theatre, 74 seats, proscenium stage. Production considerations: cast limit of 6; 1 set. Best submission time: Dec–Jan. Response time: 3 months.

THEATER AT LIME KILN

(Founded 1984)
Lime Kiln Arts; Box 663; Lexington, VA 24450; (540) 463-7088, FAX 463-1082;
     E-mail limekiln@cfw.com
Jim Connors, *Artistic Director*

Submission procedure: no unsolicited scripts; direct solicitation to playwright or agent. Types of material: full-length plays, adaptations, musicals. Special interests: work not professionally produced only; issues, language and music indigenous to VA and region; nontraditional staging. Facilities: The Kiln, 299 seats, outdoor amphitheatre. Production considerations: prefers cast limit of 9. Response time: 3 months.

THE THEATER AT MONMOUTH

(Founded 1970)

Box 385; Monmouth, ME 04259-0385; (207) 933-2952, FAX 933-2952;
  E-mail tamoffice@theateratmonmouth.org;
  Web http://www.theateratmonmouth.org
David Greenham, *Managing Director*

Submission procedure: no unsolicited scripts; synopsis and letter of inquiry. **Types of material:** adaptations, plays for young audiences. **Special interests:** large-cast adaptations of classic literature for young audiences. **Facilities:** Cumston Hall, 275 seats, thrust stage. **Production considerations:** simple set. **Best submission time:** Sep. **Response time:** 4–6 weeks letter; 4–6 months script.

THEATER BY THE BLIND

(Founded 1979)

306 West 18th St; New York, NY 10011; (212) 243-4337, FAX 243-4337;
  E-mail ashiotis@panix.com; Web http://www.onisland.com/tbtb
Ike Schambelan, *Artistic Director*

Submission procedure: accepts unsolicited scripts. **Types of material:** full-length plays, one-acts, musicals. **Special interests:** work by and about the blind. **Facilities:** no permanent facility; company performs in various 99-seat venues. **Best submission time:** year-round. **Response time:** 2 months.

THEATRE DE LA JEUNE LUNE

(Founded 1979)

105 First St N; Minneapolis, MN 55401; (612) 332-3968, FAX 332-0048
Barbara Berlovitz, *Co-Artistic Director*

Submission procedure: no unsolicited scripts; synopsis and letter of inquiry. **Types of material:** full-length plays, translations, adaptations, musicals, cabaret/revues. **Special interests:** large-cast plays dealing with universal themes. **Facilities:** Theatre de la Jeune Lune, 500 seats, flexible stage. **Best submission time:** year-round. **Response time:** 8–10 weeks letter; 4 months script.

THEATER EMORY

(Founded 1985)

Rich Building, Room 230; Emory University; Atlanta, GA 30322; (404) 727-3465,
  FAX 727-6253; E-mail vmurphy@emory.edu;
  Web http://www.emory.edu/arts/
Vincent Murphy, *Artistic Producing Director*

Submission procedure: accepts unsolicited scripts through members of Southeast Playwrights Project, Atlanta, GA, only; professional recommendation from artistic director for all others. **Types of material:** full-length plays, one-acts, translations, adaptations. **Special interests:** adaptations and translations of literary and classic works. **Facilities:** MGM-I, 200 seats, thrust stage; MGM-II, 70 seats, flexible stage; Annex Studio, 60 seats, flexible stage. **Production considerations:** cast limit of 20;

no fly or wing space. **Best submission time:** year-round. **Response time:** 2 months letter; 4 months script. **Special programs:** Brave New Works: biennial staged reading marathon of new plays in conjunction with the Southeast Playwrights Project; scripts chosen through regular submission procedure; *deadline:* fall 2000; *dates:* spring 2001. The Playwriting Center of Theater Emory: biennial 5–13 week residency of major playwright to develop new work and teach playwriting workshop; remuneration: $25,000; residency during 2000–01 academic year.

THEATRE FOR A NEW AUDIENCE
(Founded 1979)
154 Christopher St, Suite 3D; New York, NY 10014-2839; (212) 229-2819

Submission procedure: no unsolicited scripts; direct solicitation to playwright or agent. **Types of material:** translations or adaptations of classic texts only. **Facilities:** American Place Theatre, 299 seats, thrust stage.

THEATER FOR THE NEW CITY
(Founded 1970)
155-57 First Ave; New York, NY 10003-2906; (212) 254-1109
Crystal Field, *Executive Artistic Director*

Submission procedure: accepts unsolicited scripts with SASE for response. **Types of material:** full-length plays. **Special interests:** plays with no previous mainstage production; experimental American works; plays with poetry, music and dance; social issues. **Facilities:** Joyce and Seward Johnson Theater, 200 seats, flexible space; 2nd theatre, 75 seats, flexible space; 3rd theatre, 100 seats, flexible space; cabaret space. **Best submission time:** summer. **Response time:** 9–12 months.

THEATRE IV
(Founded 1975)
114 West Broad St; Richmond, VA 23220; (804) 783-1688, FAX 775-2325;
       E-mail millertiv@aol.com
Bruce Miller, *Artistic Director*

Submission procedure: no unsolicited scripts; synopsis and letter of inquiry. **Types of material:** plays for young audiences only, including full-length plays, translations and adaptations. **Special interests:** scripts adaptable for touring with cast of 3–5. **Facilities:** Empire Theatre, 604 seats, proscenium stage; Little Theatre, 84 seats, flexible space. **Best submission time:** year-round. **Response time:** 2 months letter; 2 years script.

THEATRE IV ARTREACH

(Founded 1976)

3567 Edwards Rd, #5; Cincinnati, OH 45208; (513) 871-2300, FAX 533-1295;
    E-mail artreach@zoomtown.com

Kelly Germain, *Associate Artistic Director*

Submission procedure: no unsolicited scripts; synopsis and letter of inquiry. **Types of material:** plays for young audiences only. **Facilities:** no permanent facility; touring company. **Production considerations:** cast limit of 3–5; suitable for touring. **Best submission time:** year-round. **Response time:** 2 months letter; 6 months script.

THEATRE GAEL

(Founded 1984)

Box 77156; Atlanta, GA 30357; (404) 876-1138, FAX 876-1141;
    E-mail theatregael@mindspring.com

John Stephens, *Artistic Director*

Submission procedure: no unsolicited scripts; synopsis and letter of inquiry. **Types of material:** full-length plays, translations, adaptations, plays for young audiences, solo pieces. **Special interests:** plays depicting life in Ireland, Scotland, Wales; plays about Americans of Celtic heritage; plays that compare different cultural backgrounds, e.g., the African-American versus Irish-American experiences. **Facilities:** 14th Street Playhouse, 100–200 seats, flexible stage; company tours to 80–330-seat flexible-stage theatres. **Production considerations:** productions tour to local schools, festivals and churches. **Best submission time:** year-round. **Response time:** 1 month letter; 3 months script. **Special programs:** Worldsong Children's Theatre: company tours to local schools, recreational areas and libraries.

THEATRE IN THE SQUARE

(Founded 1982)

11 Whitlock Ave; Marietta, GA 30064; (770) 422-8369, FAX 424-2637

Literary Manager

Submission procedure: no unsolicited scripts; synopsis and letter of inquiry. **Types of material:** full-length plays, one-acts, translations, musicals. **Special interests:** world and southeastern premieres. **Facilities:** Mainstage, 225 seats, proscenium stage; Alley Stage, up to 120 seats, flexible stage. **Production considerations:** cast limit of 9; unit set; no fly space. **Best submission time:** Dec–Feb. **Response time:** 1 month letter (if interested); 6 months script.

THEATER OF THE FIRST AMENDMENT
(Founded 1990)
MS 3E6; George Mason University; Fairfax, VA 22030-4444; (703) 993-2195, FAX 993-2191;
E-mail rdavi4@gmu.edu
Rick Davis, *Artistic Director*

Submission procedure: no unsolicited scripts; synopsis, sample pages, resume and letter of inquiry. **Types of material:** full-length plays, one-acts, translations, adaptations, plays for young audiences, solo pieces. **Special interests:** sophisticated plays for younger audiences; "cultural history made dramatic as opposed to history dramatized; large battles joined; hard questions asked; word and image stretched." **Facilities:** TheaterSpace, 150–200 seats, flexible space. **Production considerations:** roles for younger actors welcome as TFA works with training program. **Best submission time:** Aug–Jan. **Response time:** 2 weeks letter; 6 months script. **Special programs:** readings, workshops and other development activities tailored to work that is under serious consideration for production.

THEATRE ON THE SQUARE
(Founded 1982)
450 Post St; San Francisco, CA 94102; (415) 433-6461, FAX 433-2910;
E-mail tots@wenet.net
Jonathan Reinis, *Owner*

Submission procedure: no unsolicited scripts; synopsis and letter of inquiry. **Types of material:** full-length plays, musicals. **Facilities:** Theatre on the Square, 750 seats, proscenium/thrust stage. **Production considerations:** no fly space. **Best submission time:** year-round. **Response time:** 6 months letter; 12 months script.

THE THEATRE OUTLET
(Founded 1988)
29 North 9th St; Allentown, PA 18101-1102; (610) 820-9270, FAX 820-9130;
E-mail theatero@aol.com; Web http://www.theatreoutlet.org
George Miller, *Artistic Director*

Submission procedure: no unsolicited scripts; synopsis and letter of inquiry. **Types of material:** full-length plays, one-acts, translations, adaptations, solo pieces. **Special interests:** historical material relevant to eastern Pennsylvania; plays dealing with the Irish/Scotch/Welsh experience; topical work; work exploring cultural diversity. **Facilities:** Mainstage, 100 seats, black box. **Production considerations:** limited fly and wing space. **Best submission time:** summer. **Response time:** 1 month letter; 2 months script. **Special programs:** The Counter-Culture Monday Cafe Series: 3 10-week reading series of new plays and performance art.

THEATRE PREVIEWS AT DUKE
(Founded 1986)
Box 90680; 209 Bivins Building; Durham, NC 27708-0680; (919) 660-3347,
    FAX 684-8906; E-mail zannie@duke.edu
Zannie Giraud Voss, *Managing Director*

Submission procedure: no unsolicited scripts; synopsis and letter of inquiry. **Types of material:** full-length plays, tranlations, adaptations, musicals. **Facilities:** Reynolds Theatre, 600 seats, proscenium stage; Sheafer Theatre, 110 seats, black box. **Best submission time:** spring. **Response time:** 2 months letter; 2–6 months script.

THEATRE RHINOCEROS
(Founded 1977)
2926 16th St; San Francisco, CA 94103; (415) 552-4100, FAX 558-9044;
    Web http://www.therhino.org
Doug Holsclaw, *Literary Manager*

Submission procedure: accepts unsolicited scripts with SASE only. **Types of material:** full-length plays, one-acts, solo pieces. **Special interests:** gay and lesbian works only. **Facilities:** Theatre Rhinoceros, 112 seats, proscenium stage; The Studio at Theatre Rhinoceros, 60 seats, studio. **Best submission time:** year-round. **Response time:** 4–6 months.

THEATRE THREE
(Founded 1969)
Box 512; Port Jefferson, NY 11777-0512; (516) 928-9202, FAX 928-9120
Jeffrey Sanzel, *Artistic Director*

Submission procedure: no unsolicited scripts; synopsis, resume and letter of inquiry with SASE for response. **Types of material:** one-acts. **Special interests:** previously unproduced work only. **Facilities:** Second Stage, 80–100 seats, black box. **Production considerations:** prefers cast limit of 2–6; 1 set; minimal production demands. **Best submission time:** year-round. **Response time:** 1 month letter; 6 months script. **Special programs:** Annual Festival of One-Act Plays: fully staged productions; send SASE to theatre for guidelines; *deadline:* 30 Sep 1999; *notification:* 30 Dec 1999; *dates:* Feb–Mar 2000.

THEATRE THREE, INC.
(Founded 1961)
2800 Routh St; Dallas, TX 75201; (214) 871-2933, FAX 871-3139;
    E-mail theatre3@airmail.net; Web http://www.vline.net/theatre3/
Jac Alder, *Executive Producer/Director*

Submission procedure: no unsolicited scripts; synopsis and letter of inquiry. **Types of material:** full-length plays, musicals. **Special interests:** musicals; sophisticated comedies with socially relevant themes. **Facilities:** Theatre Three, 242 seats, arena stage. **Production considerations:** cast limit of 6–15; modest production demands.

Best submission time: year-round; prefers Sep–Dec. **Response time:** 3 months letter; 3–6 months script.

THEATRE WEST

(Founded 1962)
3333 Cahuenga Blvd W; Los Angeles, CA 90068; (323) 851-4839, FAX 851-5286
Arden Lewis and Doug Haverty, *Workshop Moderators*

Submission procedure: no unsolicited scripts; scripts developed in weekly workshops open to member playwrights only; submit script, resume and letter of inquiry; dues of $40 per month upon acceptance. **Types of material:** full-length plays, one-acts, translations, adaptations, plays for young audiences, musicals. **Facilities:** Theatre West, 180 seats, proscenium stage. **Best submission time:** year-round. **Response time:** 4 months.

THEATRE X

(Founded 1969)
158 North Broadway; Milwaukee, WI 53202; (414) 278-0555
Michael Ramach, *Producing Director*

Submission procedure: accepts unsolicited scripts with SASE for response. **Types of material:** full-length plays, solo pieces. **Special interests:** work with no previous professional production; contemporary plays. **Facilities:** Black Box, 99 seats, flexible stage. **Best submission time:** year-round. **Response time:** 6 months.

THEATREVIRGINIA

(Founded 1955)
2800 Grove Ave; Richmond, VA 23221-2466; (804) 353-6100
George Black, *Producing Artistic Director*

Submission procedure: no unsolicited scripts; agent submission. **Types of material:** full-length plays, musicals. **Facilities:** Main Stage, 500 seats, proscenium stage. **Best submission time:** year-round. **Response time:** 3–8 months. **Special programs:** New Voices for the Theatre: playwriting competition open to VA students grades 5–12; winners grades 9–12 attend 3-week summer residency program and receive dramaturgical assistance and professional staged reading; contact Education and Outreach Department for more information; *deadline:* 1 Feb 2000.

THEATREWORKS

(Founded 1969)
1100 Hamilton Ct; Menlo Park, CA 94025; (650) 463-7126;
      E-mail jeannie@theatreworks.org
Jeannie Barroga, *Literary Manager*

Submission procedure: accepts unsolicited full-length plays and musicals; for translations and adaptations, send only letter of inquiry with SASP for response. **Types of material:** full-length plays, translations, adaptations, musicals. **Special**

interests: works offering opportunities for multiethnic casting. **Facilities:** Mountain View Center, 625 seats, proscenium stage; Stage II, 117 seats, thrust stage. **Best submission time:** Jul–Nov. **Response time:** 1 month letter; 4 months script. **Special programs:** New Works Forum: developmental reading series for plays, musicals and music-theatre pieces.

THEATERWORKS

(Founded 1985)
1 Gold St; Hartford, CT 06103; (860) 727-4027, FAX 525-0758
Andrea Blose, *General Manager*

Submission procedure: no unsolicited scripts; synopsis, dialogue sample and letter of inquiry. **Types of material:** full-length plays, solo pieces. **Facilities:** Hutensky Theater, 200 seats, thrust stage. **Production considerations:** cast limit of 6; simple set. **Best submission time:** year-round. **Response time:** 2 months letter; 3 months script.

THEATREWORKS/USA

(Founded 1961)
151 West 26th St, 7th Floor; New York, NY 10001; (212) 647-1100,
     FAX 924-5377; E-mail info@theatreworksusa.org
Barbara Pasternack, *Associate Artistic Director*

Submission procedure: accepts unsolicited scripts; prefers synopsis, sample scene(s) and songs (include cassette and lyric sheet) and letter of inquiry. **Types of material:** plays and musicals for young audiences. **Special interests:** literary adaptations; historical/biographical themes; fairy tales; contemporary issues. **Facilities:** Promenade Theatre, 398 seats, proscenium stage; also tours. **Production considerations:** cast limit of 5 (can play multiple roles); sets suitable for touring. **Best submission time:** summer. **Response time:** 1 month letter; 6 months script. **Special programs:** Theatreworks/USA Commissioning Program (see Development).

THEATRICAL OUTFIT

(Founded 1976)
Box 1555; Atlanta, GA 30301; (404) 577-5257, FAX 577-5259;
     E-mail katewarner@theatricaloutfit.org; Web http://www.theatricaloutfit.org
Kate Warner, *Managing Director/Artistic Associate*

Submission procedure: no unsolicited scripts; 1-page synopsis and letter of inquiry with SASP for reply. **Types of material:** full-length plays, adaptations, solo pieces. **Facilities:** Theatrical Outfit, 800 seats, proscenium stage. **Best submission time:** Apr–Jun. **Response time:** 2 months letter; 2 months script.

TOTEM POLE PLAYHOUSE
(Founded 1950)
Box 603; Fayetteville, PA 17222; (717) 352-2164, FAX 352-8870
Carl Schurr, *Producing Artistic Director*

Submission procedure: no unsolicited scripts; synopsis, sample pages and letter of inquiry. **Types of material:** full-length plays, one-acts, musicals. **Special interests:** light comedies and musicals that appeal to a general audience. **Facilities:** Mainstage, 453 seats, proscenium stage. **Best submission time:** year-round. **Response time:** 1–2 months letter; 6 months script.

TOUCHSTONE THEATRE
(Founded 1981)
321 East 4th St; Bethlehem, PA 18015; (610) 867-1689, FAX 867-0561;
    E-mail touchstone@nni.com; Web http://www.touchstone.org
Mark McKenna, *Artistic Director*

Submission procedure: no unsolicited scripts; letter of inquiry. **Types of material:** proposals for works to be created in collaboration with company's ensemble only. **Facilities:** Touchstone Theatre, 74 seats, black box. **Production considerations:** 18' x 21' playing area. **Best submission time:** year-round. **Response time:** 1 month.

TRINITY REPERTORY COMPANY
(Founded 1964)
201 Washington St; Providence, RI 02903; (401) 521-1100; FAX 521-0447;
    Web http://www.trinityrep.com
Craig Watson, *Literary Manager*

Submission procedure: no unsolicited scripts; synopsis, dialogue sample and letter of inquiry. **Types of material:** full-length plays, translations, adaptations, musicals, solo pieces. **Facilities:** Upstairs Theatre, 500 seats, thrust stage; Downstairs Theatre, 297 seats, thrust stage. **Best submission time:** year-round. **Response time:** 2 months letter; 3 months script.

TRUSTUS THEATRE
(Founded 1985)
Box 11721; Columbia, SC 29211-1721; (803) 254-9732, (FAX) 771-9153;
    E-mail trustus88@aol.com; Web http://www.trustus.org
Jon Tuttle, *Literary Manager*

Submission procedure: accepts unsolicited one-acts only. **Types of material:** one-acts. **Special interests:** experimental, hard-hitting, off-the-wall comedies or "dramadies" for Late-Night series. **Facilities:** Mainstage, 100 seats, flexible proscenium stage. **Production considerations:** small cast; moderate production demands. **Best submission time:** Aug–Dec. **Response time:** 3–4 months. **Special programs:** Trustus Playwrights' Festival (see Prizes).

TURNIP THEATRE COMPANY

(Founded 1991)
145 West 46th St; New York, NY 10036; (212) 768-4016
Literary Committee

Submission procedure: no unsolicited scripts; professional recommendation.
Types of material: full-length plays. **Special interests:** New York-area playwrights.
Facilities: The Studio, 74–90 seats, black box. **Production considerations:** cast limit
of 4–10; simple set. **Best submission time:** Aug–Nov. **Response time:** 2 months.
Special programs: 15 Minute Play Festival: annual one-act play contest and
festival; cash prizes offered in 4 categories; send SASE for guidelines by 1 Sep
1999; *deadline:* 1 Nov 1999; *notification:* 15 Dec 1999; *dates:* spring 2000.

TWO RIVER THEATRE COMPANY

(Founded 1994)
Box 8035; Red Bank, NJ 07702; (732) 345-1400, FAX 345-1414;
E-mail info@tworivertheatre.org
Jonathan Fox, *Artistic Director*

Submission procedure: no unsolicited scripts; synopsis, first 10 pages of script and
letter of inquiry with SASE for response. **Types of material:** full-length plays,
adaptations. **Facilities:** Algonquin Arts Theatre, 500 seats, proscenium stage.
Production considerations: cast limit of 10. **Best submission time:** year-round.
Response time: 1 month letter; 8–10 months script.

UBU REPERTORY THEATER

(Founded 1982)
95 Wall St, 21st Floor; New York, NY 10005; (212) 509-1455, FAX 509-1635;
E mail uburep@spacelab.net
Françoise Kourilsky, *Artistic Director*

Submission procedure: no unsolicited scripts; synopsis and letter of inquiry. **Types
of material:** full-length plays, one-acts, translations. **Special interests:** French-
language plays or their translations only; contemporary plays from French-
speaking countries and regions. **Facilities:** no permanent facility. **Production
considerations:** cast limit of 7; 1 set or simple sets. **Best submission time:** year-
round. **Response time:** 2 months letter; 6 months script. (See entry in Membership and Service Organizations.)

UNICORN THEATRE

(Founded 1974)
3828 Main St; Kansas City, MO 64111; (816) 531-7529, ext 18, FAX 531-0421
Herman Wilson, *Literary Assistant*

Submission procedure: accepts unsolicited scripts. **Types of material:** full-length
plays. **Special interests:** contemporary social issues. **Facilities:** Unicorn Theatre,
180 seats, thrust stage. **Best submission time:** Sep–Apr. **Response time:** 4–6

months. **Special programs:** Unicorn Theatre National Playwrights' Award (see Prizes).

URBAN STAGES

(Founded 1985)
17 West 47th St; New York, NY 10017; (212) 421-1380, FAX 421-1387;
E-mail urbanstages@aol.com; Web http://www.mint.net/urbanstages
Frances Hill, *Artistic Director*

Submission procedure: accepts unsolicited scripts. **Types of material:** full-length plays. **Special interest:** multicultural/multiethnic material dealing with contemporary issues. **Facilities:** no permanent facility. **Best submission time:** Jun–Aug. **Response time:** 4 months. **Special programs:** outreach program that tours throughout NYC library system.

UTAH SHAKESPEAREAN FESTIVAL

(Founded 1961)
351 West Center St; Cedar City, UT 84720-2498; (435) 586-7880,
FAX 865-8003; E-mail phillips@suu.edu; Web http://www.bard.org
Douglas N. Cook, *Producing Artistic Director*

Submission procedure: no unsolicited scripts; professional recommendation. **Types of material:** full-length plays. **Special interest:** plays with no previous mainstage production only; plays by writers from western intermountain region; plays with western themes; plays with classical themes; plays about minorities or the underserved. **Facilities:** Downtown Cinema Theatre, 150 seats, proscenium stage. **Production considerations:** cast limit of 10–12; no sets, minimal props and costumes; 5-rehearsal limit per production. **Best submission time:** Sep–Dec. **Response time:** 3 months.

VERMONT STAGE COMPANY

(Founded 1994)
Box 874; Burlington, VT 05402; (802) 656-4351, FAX 656-0349
Blake Robison, *Producing Artistic Director*

Submission procedure: no unsolicited scripts; direct solicitation to playwright or agent. **Types of material:** full-length plays. **Facilities:** Royall Tyler Theatre, 300 seats, thrust stage. **Special programs:** Vermont Young Playwrights Project: educational program staffed by Vermont-based playwrights serving VT secondary schools.

VICTORY GARDENS THEATER

(Founded 1974)
2257 North Lincoln Ave; Chicago, IL 60614; (773) 549-5788, FAX 549-2779
Sandy Shinner, *Associate Artistic Director*

Submission procedure: accepts unsolicited scripts from Chicago-area writers only; others send synopsis, 10-page dialogue sample and letter of inquiry with SASE for response. **Types of material:** full-length plays, adaptations, musicals. **Special interests:** Chicago and Midwest playwrights; plays by women and writers of color. **Facilities:** Mainstage One, 195 seats, modified thrust stage; Mainstage Two, 200 seats, thrust stage; 2 studio theaters, 70 seats each, black box. **Production considerations:** prefers cast limit of 10; simple set; small-cast musicals only. **Best submission time:** Mar–Jun. **Response time:** 2 months letter; 9 months script. **Special programs:** Victory Gardens Playwrights Ensemble: core group of twelve resident writers; Readers Theater: staged readings of works-in-progress by area writers twice a month; Artist Development Workshop: playwriting class offered throughout the year that brings people with and without disabilities together in a creative environment.

THE VICTORY THEATRE
(Founded 1979)
3326 West Victory Blvd; Burbank, CA 91505; (818) 841-4404, FAX 841-6328;
    E-mail thevictory@mindspring.com
Tom Ormeny, *Artistic Director*

Submission procedure: no unsolicited scripts; synopsis, first 15 pages of script, resume and letter of inquiry. **Types of material:** full-length plays, adaptations. **Special interests:** plays involving social and political issues; "well-made, but cutting-edge" plays. **Facilities:** The Victory Theatre, 91 seats, arena stage; The Little Victory, 48 seats, arena stage. **Production considerations:** prefers cast limit of 12; maximum 2 simple sets; no fly space. **Best submission time:** year-round. **Response time:** 2 months letter; 3 months script.

THE VINEYARD PLAYHOUSE
(Founded 1982)
Box 2452, 24 Church St; Vineyard Haven, MA 02568; (508) 693-6450
Jon Lipsky, *Associate Artistic Director & Literary Manager*

Submission procedure: no unsolicited scripts; direct solicitation to playwright or agent. **Types of material:** full-length plays, translations, adaptations, plays for young audiences, solo pieces. **Special interests:** contemporary American works; culturally diverse plays; plays that address social issues. **Facilities:** The Vineyard Playhouse, 120 seats, black box. **Production considerations:** prefers cast limit of 10; simple sets.

VINEYARD THEATRE
(Founded 1981)
108 East 15th St; New York, NY 10003-9689; (212) 353-3366, FAX 353-3803
Douglas Aibel, *Artistic Director*

Submission procedure: no unsolicited scripts; synopsis, 10-page dialogue sample, project description and letter of inquiry; include cassette for musicals. **Types of material:** full-length plays, musicals. **Special interests:** plays that incorporate music in a unique way; musicals with strong narrative; "nervy, eccentric theatrical forms." **Facilities:** Vineyard Dimson Theatre, 120 seats, flexible stage; Vineyard 26th Street Theatre, 71 seats, thrust stage. **Best submission time:** year-round.

Response time: 6 months letter; 6 months script. **Special programs:** New Works at the Vineyard: developmental lab productions for new plays and musicals.

VIRGINIA STAGE COMPANY
(Founded 1979)
Box 3770; Norfolk, VA 23514; (757) 627-6988, FAX 628-5958

Submission procedure: no unsolicited scripts; synopsis and letter of inquiry. **Types of material:** full-length plays, musicals. **Special interests:** world premieres; plays by VA writers; work about "twenty-somethings" and youth culture; poetic drama and comedy; hard-hitting, issue-oriented plays. **Facilities:** main stage, 700 seats, proscenium stage; laboratory theatre, 99 seats, flexible space. **Best submission time:** year-round. **Response time:** 1 month letter; 6 months script.

VOICE & VISION
(Founded 1990)
161 Sixth Ave, 14th Floor; New York, NY 10013; (212) 633-9903,
    FAX 255-2053; E-mail vandv@mindspring.com
Marya Mazor, *Artistic Director*

Submission procedure: accepts unsolicited scripts. **Types of material:** full-length plays, one-acts, translations, adaptations, plays for young audiences, musicals, performance art, dance-theatre. **Special interests:** culturally diverse works written by or about women; culturally diverse works for young audiences; multidisciplinary collaborations. **Facilities:** no permanent facility. **Best submission time:** year-round. **Response time:** 12 months. **Special programs:** Play with Your Food: dinner-and-a-play reading series; Dramatic Action: educational program for young women.

THE WALNUT STREET THEATRE COMPANY
(Founded 1809)
825 Walnut St; Philadelphia, PA 19107-5107; (215) 574-3550, FAX 574-3598
Beverly Elliott, *Literary Manager*

Submission procedure: no unsolicited scripts; synopsis, cast list, 10–20-page dialogue sample and letter of inquiry with SASE for response from Dramatist Guild members only; include professional-quality cassette for musicals. **Types of material:** full-length plays, musicals. **Special interests:** original, socially relevant musicals with uplifting themes; commercially viable works for Main Stage; meaningful comedies and dramas with some broad social relevance for Studio 3. **Facilities:** Main Stage, 1050 seats, proscenium stage; Studio 3, 80 seats, flexible stage. **Production considerations:** cast limit of 4 for Studio 3. **Response time:** 3 months letter; 6 months script.

WATERTOWER THEATRE, INC.
(Founded 1976)
15650 Addison Rd; Addison, TX 75001; (972) 450-6220, FAX 450-6244
Gayle Pearson, *Producing Director*

Submission procedure: accepts unsolicited scripts. **Types of material:** full-length plays, plays for young audiences, musicals, solo pieces. **Special interests:** plays that make creative use of flexible space. **Facilities:** Addison Conference & Theatre Centre, 100–300 seats, flexible stage. **Response time:** 2 months. **Special programs:** Stone Cottage New Works Festival: readings of full-length plays or musicals; scripts chosen through theatre's normal submission procedure; *deadline:* 15 Mar 2000; *notification:* 1 Apr 2000; *dates:* July 2000.

WEISSBERGER THEATER GROUP
(Founded 1992)
909 Third Ave, 27th Floor; New York, NY 10022-9998; (212) 339-5529,
    FAX 486-8996
Jay Harris, *Producer*

Submission procedure: no unsolicited scripts; synopsis and letter of inquiry. **Types of material:** full-length plays. **Special interests:** topical issue-oriented plays. **Facilities:** no permanent facility. **Production considerations:** cast limit of 7. **Best submission time:** year-round. **Response time:** 1 month letter; 2 months script.

WEST COAST ENSEMBLE
(Founded 1982)
Box 38728; Los Angeles, CA 90038; (323) 876-9337, FAX 876-8916
Les Hanson, *Artistic Director*

Submission procedure: accepts unsolicited scripts. **Types of material:** full-length plays, one-acts, translations, adaptations, musicals. **Special interests:** plays not previously produced in Southern CA only; musicals; short plays. **Facilities:** main stage, 85 seats, proscenium stage. **Production considerations:** simple set; no fly space. **Best submission time:** Jun–Dec. **Response time:** 6 months. **Special programs:** staged readings of new plays. West Coast Ensemble Contests (see Prizes).

WESTBETH THEATRE CENTER
(Founded 1977)
151 Bank St; New York, NY 10014; (212) 691-2272, FAX 924-7185
Arnold Engelman, *Producing Director*

Submission procedure: no unsolicited scripts; synopsis and letter of inquiry with SASE for response. **Types of material:** full-length plays, one-acts, musicals, solo pieces. **Facilities:** Music Hall, 100–200 seats, proscenium; Big Room, 99 seats, black box; Studio Theatre, 85 seats, black box. **Production considerations:** cast limit of 10; modest technical demands. **Best submission time:** year-round.

Response time: 3 months letter; 4 months script. **Special programs:** Westbeth Playwright Program (see Development).

THE WESTERN STAGE
(Founded 1974)
156 Homestead Ave; Salinas, CA 93901; (831) 755-6990, FAX 755-6954
Michael Roddy, *Literary Manager*

Submission procedure: no unsolicited scripts; synopsis and letter of inquiry; include cassette for musicals; for adaptations of work not in public domain, enclose copy of letter granting rights. **Types of material:** full-length plays, adaptations, plays for young audiences, musicals, cabaret/revues. **Special interests:** adaptations of works of literary significance; large-cast plays. **Facilities:** Mainstage, 500 seats, proscenium stage; Cabaret, 250 seats, proscenium stage; Studio, 100 seats, thrust stage. **Best submission time:** year-round. **Response time:** 4–6 weeks letter; 3 months script.

WILL GEER THEATRICUM BOTANICUM
(Founded 1973)
Box 1222; Topanga, CA 90290; (310) 455-2322; FAX 455-3724;
    E-mail theatricum@aol.com
Ellen Geer, *Artistic Director*

Submission procedure: no unsolicited scripts; synopsis, dialogue sample and letter of inquiry; include cassette for musicals. **Types of material:** full-length plays, musicals. **Special interests:** work suitable for large outdoor playing space. **Facilities:** Will Geer Theatricum Botanicum, 300 seats, outdoor amphitheatre. **Production considerations:** cast limit of 4–10; simple sets. **Best submission time:** Sep. **Response time:** 3 weeks letter; 6 months script.

WILLIAMSTOWN THEATRE FESTIVAL
(Founded 1955)
Sep–May: 100 East 17th St, 3rd Floor; New York, NY 10003; (212) 228-2286,
    FAX 228-9091; Web http://www.wtfestival.org
Jun–Aug: Box 517; Williamstown, MA 01267-0517; (413) 458-3200,
    FAX 458-3147
Michael Ritchie, *Producer*

Submission procedure: no unsolicited scripts; agent submission only. **Types of material:** full-length plays, adaptations, musicals, solo pieces. **Facilities:** Main Stage, 521 seats, proscenium stage; 2nd stage, 96 seats, thrust stage. **Best submission time:** 1 Oct–15 Feb. **Response time:** several months. **Special programs:** New Play Staged Readings Series.

WILLOWS THEATRE COMPANY
(Founded 1977)
1975 Diamond Blvd, Suite B-230; Concord, CA 94520; (925) 798-1300,
　　FAX 676-5726; E-mail willowsth@aol.com
Richard H. Elliott, *Artistic Director*

Submission procedure: no unsolicited scripts; synopsis, character breakdown and letter of inquiry. **Types of material:** full-length plays, translations, adaptations, musicals. **Special interests:** small-scale plays, musicals and revues with an edge and commercial potential that will appeal to both urban and suburban audiences. **Facilities:** Willows Theatre, 203 seats, proscenium stage. **Production considerations:** cast limit of 15; prefers simple set, unit set or environmental staging which uses theatre space as setting. **Best submission time:** 1 Apr–1 Jul. **Response time:** 3 months letter; 6–12 months script. **Special programs:** staged readings and workshop productions.

THE WILMA THEATER
(Founded 1972)
265 South Broad St; Philadelphia, PA 19107; (215) 893-9456, FAX 893-0895;
　　E-mail info@wilmatheater.org; Web http://www.wilmatheater.org
Literary Manager/Dramaturg

Submission procedure: no unsolicited scripts; professional recommendation. **Types of material:** full-length plays, translations, adaptations, musicals. **Special interests:** new translations and adaptations from the international repertoire with emphasis on innovative, bold staging; world premieres; ensemble works; works with poetic dimension; plays with music; multimedia works; social issues. **Facilities:** Wilma Theater, 300 seats, flexible/proscenium stage. **Production considerations:** prefers cast limit of 12; stage 44′ x 46′. **Best submission time:** year-round. **Response time:** 9–12 months.

WINGS THEATRE COMPANY, INC.
(Founded 1986)
154 Christopher St; New York, NY 10014; (212) 627-2960, (FAX) 462-0024;
　　E-mail ejeffer@brainlink.com; Web http://www.brainlink.com/~cjeffer/
Tricia Gilbert, *Literary Manager*

Submission procedure: accepts unsolicited scripts. **Types of material:** full-length plays, musicals. **Special interests:** new musicals or gay-themed plays only. **Facilities:** Wings Theatre, 74 seats, proscenium stage. **Best submission time:** year-round. **Response time:** plays received by 1 May receive response in Sep of that year; plays received after 1 May must wait until Sep of following year.

WOMEN'S PROJECT & PRODUCTIONS
(Founded 1978)
55 West End Ave; New York, NY 10023; (212) 765-1706, FAX 765-2024
Lisa McNulty, *Literary Manager*

Submission procedure: no unsolicited scripts; synopsis, 10-page dialogue sample and letter of inquiry with SASE for response. **Types of material:** full-length plays, solo pieces. **Special interests:** plays by women only. **Facilities:** Theatre Four, 199 seats, proscenium stage. **Best submission time:** year-round. **Response time:** 6 weeks letter; 6 months script. **Special programs:** Playwrights Lab and Directors Forum: developmental program including play readings and work-in-progress presentations; participation by invitation only. Commissioning program.

WOOLLY MAMMOTH THEATRE COMPANY
(Founded 1981)
1401 Church St NW; Washington, DC 20005; (202) 234-6130
Mary Resing, *Literary Manager*

Submission procedure: no unsolicited scripts; professional recommendation. **Types of material:** full-length plays, translations, adaptations, solo pieces. **Special interests:** theatrical, provocative and exciting plays which combine elevated language with edgy situations and complex characters. **Facilities:** MainStage, 132 seats, thrust stage. **Production considerations:** prefers cast limit of 6; minimal staging requirements. **Best submission time:** Jun. **Response time:** 12 months. **Special programs:** Foreplay: reading series of 5–6 plays each year under consideration for MainStage production.

THE WOOSTER GROUP
(Founded 1969)
Box 654, Canal Street Station; New York, NY 10013; (212) 966-9796,
    FAX 226-6576; E-mail woostergrp@aol.com;
    Web http://www.thewoostergroup.org
Kim Whitener, *Managing Director*

Submission procedure: no unsolicited scripts (company customarily collaborates on its own original work). **Types of material:** full-length plays. **Special interests:** experimental works. **Facilities:** The Performing Garage, 99 seats, black box.

WORCESTER FOOTHILLS THEATRE COMPANY
(Founded 1974)
100 Front St, Suite 137; Worcester, MA 01608; (508) 754-3314, FAX 767-0676
Michael Walker, *Executive Producer/Artistic Director*

Submission procedure: no unsolicited scripts; synopsis and letter of inquiry. **Types of material:** full-length plays, translations, adaptations, musicals. **Special interests:** plays suited to multigenerational audiences. **Facilities:** Worcester Foothills Theatre, 349 seats, proscenium stage. **Production considerations:** prefers cast limit of 10, simple set; small-scale musicals only. **Best submission time:** year-round. **Response time:** 3 months letter; 4 months script.

WRITERS' THEATRE CHICAGO

(Founded 1992)
c/o Books on Vernon; 664 Vernon Ave; Glencoe, IL 60022; (847) 835-7366,
    FAX 835-5332; E-mail halbermole@aol.com
Marilyn Campbell, *Artistic Associate*

Submission procedure: accepts unsolicited scripts with professional recommendation if possible. **Types of material:** full-length plays, translations, adaptations. **Special interests:** highly literary plays by or about great writers and writing. **Facilities:** Nicholas Pennell Theatre, 50 seats, thrust stage. **Production considerations:** small cast; small space; minimal production demands. **Best submission time:** year-round. **Response time:** 3 months.

YALE REPERTORY THEATRE

(Founded 1965)
Box 208244, Yale Station; New Haven, CT 06520-8244; (203) 432-1560,
    FAX 432-1550; E-mail catherine.sheehy@yale.edu
Catherine Sheehy, *Resident Dramaturg*

Submission procedure: no unsolicited scripts; synopsis and letter of inquiry. **Types of material:** full-length plays, translations, adaptations, solo pieces. **Special interests:** new work; new translations of classics; contemporary foreign plays. **Facilities:** Yale Repertory Theatre, 487 seats, modified thrust stage; University Theatre, 654 seats, proscenium stage. **Best submission time:** year-round. **Response time:** 6 weeks letter; 3 months script.

THE YORK THEATRE COMPANY

(Founded 1968)
The Theatre at St Peter's Church; Citicorp Center; 619 Lexington Ave;
    New York, NY 10022-4610; (212) 935-5820, FAX 832-0037
Literary Department

Submission procedure: no unsolicited scripts; synopsis and letter of inquiry with SASE for response. **Types of material:** musicals, cabaret/revues. **Special interests:** small-cast musicals. **Facilities:** The Theatre at Saint Peter's Church, 147 seats, flexible. **Best submission time:** year-round. **Response time:** 1–2 months letter; 6–8 months script.

YOUNG PLAYWRIGHTS INC.

See Young Playwrights Festival in Prizes and Young Playwrights Inc. in Membership and Service Organizations.

ZACHARY SCOTT THEATRE CENTER (ZACH)
(Founded 1933)
1510 Toomey Rd; Austin, TX 78704-1078; (512) 476-0594, FAX 476-0314;
      E-mail zach@io.com; Web http://www.zachscott.com
Dave Steakley, *Producing Artistic Director*

Submission procedure: no unsolicited scripts; direct solicitation to playwright or agent. **Types of material:** full-length plays, plays for young audiences. **Facilities:** Mainstage 1, 200 seats, thrust stage; Mainstage 2, 130 seats, arena stage. **Production considerations:** plays for young audiences tour. **Best submission time:** Jan. **Response time:** 6 months.

Prizes

What competitions are included here?

All the playwriting contests we know of that offer prizes of at least $200 or, in the case of awards to playwrights 19 or under, the equivalent in production or publication. Most awards for which the playwright cannot apply— the Joseph Kesselring Award, the Pulitzer Prize—are not listed. Exceptions are made when, as with the Susan Smith Blackburn Prize, the nominating process allows playwrights to encourage nomination of their work by theatre professionals.

How can I give myself the best chance of winning?

Send your script in well before the deadline, when the readers are fresh and enthusiastic rather than buried by an avalanche of submissions. Assume the deadline is the date your script must be received (not the postmark date). Make sure you don't mistake a notification date for the submission deadline. If a listing specifies "write for guidelines," be sure to follow this instruction. It usually means that we don't have space in our brief listing to give you all the information you need; also contests may change their rules or their deadlines after this book has been published. Always send an SASE with your submission, if you expect your materials to be returned.

Should I enter contests that charge entry fees?

It's true that a number of listings require a fee. Many contest sponsors are unable to secure sufficient funding to cover their costs, which are considerable. We have not included those listings with unusually high fees. Some playwrights will not pay fees as a matter of principle, others consider it part of doing business. It's up to you.

How can I find out about new prizes and updates throughout the year?

Write for guidelines to ensure that you have the most recent rules. Also refer to the Membership and Service Organizations and Useful Publications sections in this book for those groups that publish newsletters listing current contest news.

A couple of *Sourcebook* reminders:

"Full-length play" means a full-length, original work without a score or libretto. One-acts, musicals, adaptations, translations, plays for young audiences and solo pieces are listed separately.

Sourcebook entries are alphabetized by first word (excluding "the") even if the title starts with a proper name. So, for instance, you'll find the Harold Morton Landon Translation Award under H. In the index, you will also find this prize cross-listed under L. We've included listings of biennial prizes with deadlines after the dates of this *Sourcebook* (September 1999–August 2000), so please read the deadlines carefully—don't mistake a March 2001 deadline for 2000!

AMERICAN SKETCHES CONTEST
Florida Studio Theatre; 1241 North Palm Ave; Sarasota, FL 34236

Types of material: short plays and cabaret sketches. **Frequency:** annual. **Remuneration:** $500; production for winning script and up to 12 others as part of evening of short works. **Guidelines:** sketch of 5 pages or less on specified theme TBA; write for guidelines. **Submission procedure:** script only. **Deadline:** 30 Mar 2000. (See Florida Studio Theatre in Production.)

AMERICAN TRANSLATORS ASSOCIATION AWARDS

1800 Diagonal Rd, Suite 220; Alexandria, VA 22134-2840; FAX (703) 683-6122;
    E-mail ata@atanet.org
Courtney Searls-Ridge, *Chair, ATA Honors and Awards*

German Literary Translation Prize

Types of material: translations of full-length plays and one-acts. **Frequency:** biennial. **Remuneration:** $1000; up to $500 expenses to attend ATA (see Membership and Service Organizations) annual conference. **Guidelines:** translation from German published in U.S. by American publisher during 2 years before deadline as single volume or in collection. **Submission procedure:** no submission by translator; publisher nominates translation and submits 2 copies of book plus 10 consecutive pages of German original, extra jacket and any advertising copy; brief vita of translator. **Deadline:** 15 May 2001. **Notification:** fall 2001.

Lewis Galantiere Literary Translation Prize

Types of material: translations of full-length plays and one-acts. **Frequency:** biennial. **Remuneration:** $1000; up to $500 expenses to attend ATA (see Membership and Service Organizations) annual conference. **Guidelines:** translation from any language except German published in U.S. by American publisher during 2 years before deadline as single volume or in collection. **Submission procedure:** no submission by translator; publisher nominates translation and submits 2 copies of book plus 10 consecutive pages of original, extra jacket and any advertising copy; brief vita of translator. **Deadline:** 30 Mar 2000. **Notification:** fall 2000.

ANNA ZORNIO MEMORIAL CHILDREN'S THEATRE PLAYWRITING AWARD

Department of Theatre and Dance; University of New Hampshire;
    Paul Creative Arts Center; 30 College Rd; Durham, NH 03824-3538;
    (603) 862-3044, FAX 862-0298
Julie Brinker, *Director of Theatre Education*

Types of material: plays and musicals for young audiences. **Frequency:** every 4 years. **Remuneration:** $1000; production by UNH Theatre in Education Program in May 2002. **Guidelines:** U.S. or Canadian resident; unpublished work not produced professionally and not more than 1 hour long; prefers single or unit set; 2-submission limit; write for guidelines. **Submission procedure:** script with brief synopsis, character breakdown and statement of design/technical considerations; SASP for acknowledgment of receipt; include cassette for musical. **Deadline:** 1 Sep 2001. **Notification:** May 2002 (exact date TBA).

The Annual Blank Theatre Company
Young Playwrights Festival

1301 Lucile Ave; Los Angeles, CA 90026-1519; (323) 662-7734;
E-mail btc@primenet.com; Web http://www.primenet.com/~portal/
Christopher Steele, *Producer*

Types of material: full-length plays, one-acts, plays for young audiences, musicals, solo pieces, operas. **Frequency:** annual. **Remuneration:** workshop production for approximately 9 playwrights; some winning scripts subsequently receive full production. **Guidelines:** playwright 19 years of age or younger as of deadline date; original play of any length on any subject; send SASE in late Jan 2000 for guidelines. **Submission procedure:** script with cover sheet containing name, date of birth, home address, phone number and name of school (if any). **Deadline:** Apr 2000 (exact date TBA). **Notification:** May 2000.

ASF Translation Prize

The American-Scandinavian Foundation; 15 East 65th St; New York, NY 10021;
(212) 879-9779, FAX 249-3444; E-mail agyongy@amscan.org
Publishing Office

Types of material: translations. **Frequency:** annual. **Remuneration:** $2000; publication of excerpt in *Scandinavian Review*; $500 for runner-up. **Guidelines:** unpublished translation from a Scandinavian language into English of work written by a Scandinavian author after 1800; manuscript must be at least 50 pages long if prose drama, 25 pages if verse drama, and must be conceived as part of a book; write for guidelines. **Submission procedure:** 4 copies of translation, 1 of original; permission letter from copyright holder. **Deadline:** 1 Jun 2000. **Notification:** fall 2000.

Attic Theatre Ensemble's One-Act Marathon

Attic Theatre Centre; 6562½ Santa Monica Blvd; Hollywood, CA 90038;
(323) 469-3786, FAX 463-9571
James Carey, *Producing Artistic Director*

Types of material: one-acts. **Frequency:** annual. **Remumeration:** 1st prize $250; 2nd prize $100; 3rd prize $50; 12 finalists get productions. **Guidelines:** previously unproduced one-act no longer than 45 minutes; no adaptations. **Submission procedure:** send SASE for application and guidelines. **Deadline:** 1 Sep 1999. **Notification:** Jan 2000. **Dates:** Jun 2000. (See entry in Production.)

Aurand Harris Memorial Playwriting Award

The New England Theatre Conference; c/o Department of Theatre;
Northeastern University; 306 Huntington Ave; Boston, MA 02115;
(617) 424-9275, FAX 424-1057; E-mail netc@world.com

Types of material: plays for young audiences. **Frequency:** annual. **Remuneration:** $1000 1st prize, $500 2nd prize. **Guidelines:** resident of CT, MA, ME, NH, RI, VT or member of The New England Theatre Conference (NETC) (see Membership and Service Organizations); 1 unpublished, not professionally produced submission per playwright. **Submission procedure:** bound script, synopsis, character breakdown and statement that play has not been published or professionally produced and is not under consideration for publication or production prior to 1 Sep 1999; $20 fee (fee is waived for NETC members); send SASP for acknowledgment of receipt; script will not be returned. **Deadline:** 15 Apr 2000. **Notification:** Sep 2000 (winners only).

AURICLE AWARD

Plays on Tape; Box 5789; Bend, OR 97708-5789; (541) 923-6246,
    FAX 923-9679; E-mail theatre@playsontape.com;
    Web http://www.playsontape.com
Silvia Gonzalez, *Literary Manager*

Types of material: full-length plays, long one-acts. **Frequency:** annual. **Remuneration:** $500 and 10 audio copies if play is produced as audio recording; $100 prize to winner if cost of producing audio recording is prohibitively expensive, i.e., too large a cast, too complicated sound effects, etc. **Guidelines:** any play that has not been audio-produced; running time approximately 74 minutes; prefers 2–5 character play; special interest in plays by women and minorities. **Submission procedure:** script, synopis and $3 fee per script with 2 letter-size SASE. **Deadline:** 31 Dec 1999. **Notification:** 1 Feb 2000.

BAKER'S PLAYS HIGH SCHOOL PLAYWRITING CONTEST

Baker's Plays; Box 699222; Quincy, MA 02269-9222; (617) 745-0805,
    FAX 745-9891; E-mail raypape@hotmail.com;
    Web http://www.bakersplays.com
Ray Pape, *Associate Editor*

Types of material: full-length plays, one-acts, plays for young audiences, musicals. **Frequency:** annual. **Remuneration:** 1st prize $500 and publication; 2nd prize $250; 3rd prize $100. **Guidelines:** high school student, sponsored by high school drama or English teacher; prefers play which has been produced or given public reading; write for guidelines. **Submission procedure:** script with signature of sponsoring teacher. **Deadline:** 31 Jan 2000. **Notification:** May 2000.

BEVERLY HILLS THEATRE GUILD AWARDS

2815 North Beachwood Dr; Los Angeles, CA 90068-1923; (213) 465-2703
Marcella Meharg, *Coordinator*

Julie Harris Playwright Award

Types of material: full-length plays. **Frequency:** annual. **Remuneration:** $5000 1st prize; $2000 2nd prize; $1000 3rd prize. **Guidelines:** U.S. citizen; 1 submission, not previously submitted, published, produced or optioned or winner of major competition; send SASE for guidelines. **Submission procedure:** completed entry form and script; script will not be returned. **Deadline:** 1 Nov 1999. **Notification:** Jun 2000.

The Marilyn Hall Award

Types of material: plays for young audiences. **Frequency:** annual. **Remuneration:** $750 1st prize; $250 2nd prize. **Guidelines:** play appropriate for audiences aged 7–14 by U.S. citizen; 1 submission 40–60 minutes long, not previously submitted, published, produced, optioned or winner of major competition; send SASE for guidelines. **Submission procedure:** script; script will not be returned. **Deadline:** 29 Feb 2000; no submission postmarked before 15 Jan 2000. **Notification:** Jun 2000.

BIENNIAL PROMISING PLAYWRIGHT AWARD
Colonial Players, Inc; 108 East St; Annapolis, MD 21401
Frances Marchand, *Contest Coordinator*

Types of material: full-length plays, adaptations. **Frequency:** biennial. **Remuneration:** $750; production (playwright must be available to attend rehearsals). **Guidelines:** resident of CT, DC, DE, GA, MA, MD, NC, NH, NJ, NY, PA, RI, SC, VA or WV; play not produced professionally, suitable for arena stage; between 90–120 minutes; 2-set limit; cast limit of 10; only adaptation of material in public domain; send SASE for guidelines. **Submission procedure:** script and SASP for acknowledgment of receipt. **Deadline:** 31 Dec 2000; no submission before 1 Sep 2000. **Notification:** Jun 2001.

CALIFORNIA YOUNG PLAYWRIGHTS CONTEST
Playwrights Project; 450 B St, Suite 1020; San Diego, CA 92101-8002;
    (619) 239-8222, FAX 239-8225; E-mail youth@playwright.com;
    Web http://www.playwrightsproject.com
Deborah Salzer, *Director*

Types of material: full-length plays, one-acts, musicals, solo pieces. **Frequency:** annual. **Remuneration:** $100, production or staged reading, travel and housing to attend rehearsals to each of several winners (4 in 1998); all entrants receive written evaluation of work. **Guidelines:** CA writer or collaborating writers under 19 years of age as of deadline date; work at least 10 pages long; previous submissions ineligible; write for guidelines. **Submission procedure:** 2 copies of script, brief bio and cover letter; script will not be returned. **Deadline:** 1 Apr 2000. **Notification:** late fall 2000.

CENTER THEATER INTERNATIONAL PLAYWRIGHTING CONTEST
1346 West Devon Ave; Chicago, IL 60660; (773) 508-0200
Dale Calandra, *Literary Manager*

Types of material: full-length plays, solo pieces. **Frequency:** annual. **Remuneration:** $300; possible production. **Guidelines:** unpublished play, not produced or optioned; cast limit of 8, minimal technical requirements; send SASE for guidelines. **Submission procedure:** script, completed entry form, 1-page synopsis, character breakdown, resume, $15 fee per submission and SASE for response; script will not be returned. **Deadline:** TBA (15 Aug in 1999). (See entry in Production.)

CHICANO/LATINO LITERARY CONTEST
Department of Spanish and Portuguese; University of California at Irvine;
Irvine, CA 92697-5275; (949) 824-5443, -6901; E-mail ruby@uci.edu;
Web http://www.hnet.uci.edu/spanishandportuguese/contest.html
Alejandro Morales, *Director*

Types of material: full-length plays. **Frequency:** every 4 years. **Remuneration:** $1000 1st prize, publication, travel to attend award ceremony; $500 2nd prize; $250 3rd prize. **Guidelines:** U.S. citizen or resident; unpublished play written in Spanish or English; 1-submission limit; send SASE for guidelines. **Submission procedure:** 3 copies of bound script, minimum 110 typed, double-spaced pages. **Deadline:** 15 May 2002. **Notification:** Oct 2002.

CLAUDER COMPETITION FOR EXCELLENCE IN PLAYWRITING
Box 383259; Cambridge, MA 02238-3259; (781) 322-3187;
E-mail betsy@email.com
Betsy Carpenter, *Director*

Types of material: full-length plays. **Frequency:** biennial. **Remuneration:** $3000 1st prize; production by Portland Stage; $500 prize and staged reading for several runners-up. **Guidelines:** resident of or student attending school or college in CT, MA, ME, NH, RI or VT; play not produced professionally and minimum 45 minutes long; write for guidelines. **Submission procedure:** script and production history, if any. **Deadline:** Sep 1999; exact date TBA. **Notification:** TBA.

COE COLLEGE NEW WORKS FOR THE STAGE COMPETITION
Department of Theatre Arts; 1220 First Ave NE; Cedar Rapids, IA 52402;
(319) 399-8689, FAX 399-8557; E-mail swolvert@coe.edu
Susan Wolverton, *Chair, Playwriting Festival*

Types of material: full-length plays, plays for young audiences. **Frequency:** biennial, contingent on funding. **Remuneration:** $325; staged reading; travel, room and board for 1-week residency during Jan term. **Guidelines:** unproduced, unpublished play dealing with theme of Playwriting Festival and Symposia; theme for 2001 is "Radicals and Revolutionaries"; festival includes workshops and public discussions; no translations, adaptations or musicals; send SASE for guidelines. **Submission procedure:** script only. **Deadline:** 1 Jun 2000. **Notification:** 1 Sep 2000. **Dates:** Jan 2001.

COLUMBUS SCREENPLAY DISCOVERY AWARDS
Christopher Columbus Society; 433 North Camden Dr, Suite 600;
Beverly Hills, CA 90210; (310) 288-1881, FAX 288-0257;
E-mail writing@screenwriters.com; Web http://screenwriters.com
Carlos de Abreu and Janice Pennington, *Co-Founders*

Types of material: screenplays. **Frequency:** annual. **Remuneration:** Discovery of the Month Award: up to 3 scripts a month selected for development and may be referred to industry professionals; all winners become eligible for Discovery of the

Year Award: up to 3 scripts a year optioned by society for up to $10,000. **Guidelines:** unproduced feature screenplay not under current option; write for guidelines. **Submission procedure:** screenplay, completed application, release form and $45 fee; screenplay will not be returned. **Deadline:** last day of each month for monthly selection; 1 Dec each year for annual cycle.

THE CUNNINGHAM PRIZE FOR PLAYWRITING

The Theatre School; DePaul University; 2135 North Kenmore;
    Chicago, IL 60614-4111; (773) 325-7938, FAX 325-7920;
    E-mail lgoetsch@wppost.depaul.edu;
    Web http://theatreschool.depaul.edu/prize.htm
Lara Goetsch, *Director of Marketing and Public Relations*

Types of material: full-length plays, plays for young audiences, musicals, solo pieces. **Frequency:** annual. **Remuneration:** $5000. **Guidelines:** Chicago-area playwright; play which "affirms the centrality of religion, broadly defined, and the human quest for meaning, truth and community"; write for guidelines. **Submission procedure:** script and brief statement making connection to purpose of prize. **Deadline:** 1 Dec 1999. **Notification:** 1 Mar 2000.

DAYTON PLAYHOUSE FUTUREFEST

1301 East Siebenthaler Ave, Box 1958; Dayton, OH 45414; (937) 277-0144,
    FAX 277-9539
Don Warrick, *Managing Director*

Types of material: full-length plays, solo pieces. **Frequency:** annual. **Remuneration:** $1000 1st prize, 5 $500 runners-up; 3 plays receive full productions, 3 plays receive reading at Jul 2000 FutureFest weekend; travel and housing to attend production. **Guidelines:** unproduced, unpublished play; send SASE or fax number for guidelines. **Submission procedure:** script and resume. **Deadline:** 30 Sep 1999. **Notification:** Apr 2000.

DEEP SOUTH WRITERS CONFERENCE

c/o English Department; Box 44691; University of Southwestern Louisiana;
    Lafayette, LA 70504-4691; FAX (318) 482-5071; E-mail jlm8047@usl.edu;
    Web http://www.cacs.usl.edu/departments/english/index.html
Jerry McGuire, *Director*

James H. Wilson Full-Length Play Award

Types of material: full-length plays, solo pieces. **Frequency:** annual. **Remuneration:** $300 1st prize, $100 2nd prize. **Guidelines:** original, unpublished play (no adaptations or musicals), not produced commercially. **Submission procedure:** send SASE for guidelines. **Deadline:** 15 Jul 2000. **Notification:** Sep 2000.

Paul T. Nolan One-Act Play Award

Types of material: one-acts, solo pieces. **Frequency:** annual. **Remuneration:** $200 1st prize, $100 2nd prize; possible publication in DSWC *Chapbook*. **Guidelines:**

original, unpublished play (no adaptations or musicals) less than 50 pages long, not produced commercially; publication rights to winning plays reserved until 1 Jun 2001. **Submission procedure:** send SASE for guidelines. **Deadline:** 15 Jul 2000. **Notification:** Sep 2000.

DOROTHY SILVER PLAYWRITING COMPETITION
Jewish Community Center of Cleveland; 3505 Mayfield Rd;
     Cleveland Heights, OH 44118; (216) 382-4000, ext 275, FAX 382-5401
Lisa Kollins, *Managing Director*

Types of material: full-length plays. **Frequency:** annual. **Remuneration:** $1000 (including $500 to cover residency expenses); staged reading; possible production. **Guidelines:** unproduced play that provides fresh and significant perspective on the range of Jewish experience. **Submission procedure:** script only. **Deadline:** 15 Dec 1999. **Notification:** Aug 2000.

DRAMARAMA
The Playwrights' Center of San Francisco; Box 460466;
     San Francisco, CA 94146-0466; (415) 626-4603, FAX 863-0901;
     E-mail playctrsf@aol.com; Web http://www.playwrights.org
Sheppard Kominars, *Chairman*

Long Play Contest

Types of material: full-length plays, solo pieces. **Frequency:** annual. **Remuneration:** up to 4 scripts given 4–5 rehearsals and staged readings at fall festival; $500 prize awarded on basis of readings. **Guidelines:** unproduced play minimum 60 minutes; send SASE for guidelines and application. **Submission procedure:** write for guidelines; $25 fee. **Deadline:** 15 Mar 2000. **Notification:** 15 Aug 2000. **Dates:** Oct 2000.

Short Play Contest

Types of material: one-acts, solo pieces. **Frequency:** annual. **Remuneration:** up to 4 scripts given 4–5 rehearsals and staged readings at fall festival; $500 prize awarded on basis of readings. **Guidelines:** unproduced play maximum 60 minutes; send SASE for guidelines and application. **Submission procedure:** write for guidelines; $25 fee. **Deadline:** 15 Mar 2000. **Notification:** 15 Aug 2000. **Dates:** Oct 2000.

DRURY COLLEGE ONE-ACT PLAY COMPETITION
Drury College; 900 North Benton Ave; Springfield, MO 65802; (417) 873-7430
Sandy Asher, *Writer-in-Residence*

Types of material: one-acts. **Frequency:** biennial. **Remuneration:** $300 1st prize, 2 runners-up receive $150; possible production; winners recommended to The Open Eye Theater (see entry in Production). **Guidelines:** unproduced, unpublished play 20–45 minutes long; prefers small cast, 1 set; 1-submission limit; send SASE for guidelines. **Submission procedure:** script only. **Deadline:** 1 Dec 2000. **Notification:** 1 Apr 2001.

DUBUQUE FINE ARTS PLAYERS
NATIONAL ONE-ACT PLAYWRITING CONTEST
330 Clarke Dr; Dubuque, IA 52001; (319) 588-0646
Jennie G. Stabenow, *Coordinator*

Types of material: one-acts, one-act adaptations. **Frequency:** annual. **Remuneration:** $600 1st prize, $300 2nd prize, $200 3rd prize; possible production for all 3 plays. **Guidelines:** unproduced, unpublished play maximum 35 pages and 40 minutes long; prefers cast limit of 5, 1 set; no submission limit; only adaptations of material in public domain; send SASE for guidelines. **Submission procedure:** completed entry form, 2 copies of script, 1-paragraph synopsis and $10 fee per submission; optional SASE for critique and optional SASP for acknowledgment of receipt. **Deadline:** 31 Jan 2000; no submission before 1 Nov 1999. **Notification:** 30 Jun 2000.

EAST WEST PLAYERS NEW VOICES PLAYWRITING COMPETITION
East West Players; 244 South San Pedro St; Suite 301; Los Angeles, CA 90012;
    (213) 625-7000, FAX 625-7111; E-mail info@eastwestplayers.com
    Web http://www.eastwestplayers.com
Ken Narasaki, *Literary Manager*

Types of material: full-length plays, plays for young audiences, musicals. **Frequency:** annual. **Remumeration:** 1st prize $1000, reading, possible workshop or production; 2nd prize $500, reading, possible workshop or production. **Guidelines:** English-language play not produced professionally; prefers Asian-Pacific writers and works with Asian-Pacific themes and cast; send SASE for guidelines after 31 Aug 1999. **Submission procedure:** 2 copies of script, character breakdown, cover letter and SASP for acknowledgement of receipt. **Deadline:** TBA (1 Apr in 1999). **Notification:** TBA (1 Jul in 1999).

EMERGING PLAYWRIGHT AWARD

Urban Stages; 17 East 47th St; New York, NY 10017; (212) 421-1380,
    FAX 421-1387; E-mail urbanstage@aol.com;
    Web http://www.mint.net/urbanstages
Frances Hill, *Artistic Director*

Types of material: full-length plays. **Frequency:** annual. **Remuneration:** $500,
production, travel to attend rehearsals. **Guidelines:** play unproduced in New York;
submissions from minority playwrights and plays with ethnically diverse casts
encouraged. **Submission procedure:** script, production history (if any) and bio.
Deadline: ongoing; best submission time Jul–Aug.

EMPIRE SCREENPLAY CONTEST

Empire Productions; 12358 Ventura Blvd, #602; Studio City, CA 91604-2508;
    (800) 997-3988; FAX (818) 506-1207; E-mail empiresc@aol.com
Michael J. Farrand, *Contest Administrator*

Types of material: narrative screenplays. **Frequency:** annual. **Remuneration:** 2
$3,000 prizes; staged reading for 1 winner. **Guidelines:** scripts evaluated in 2
categories: "Hollywood or Bust" for films with large casts and expensive sets,
props, costumes or special effects; "High Value" for films with contemporary
settings, small casts, minimal locations and inexpensive props and costumes; no
submission limit. **Submission procedure:** completed application, first 20 pages and
last 10 pages of script, 2-page synopsis, contest award notification letters (if any),
resume, cover letter and $45 fee per submission; send SASE for guidelines and
application. **Deadline:** 6 Sep 1999. **Notification:** early 2000, exact date TBA.

THE FESTIVAL OF EMERGING AMERICAN THEATRE (FEAT) COMPETITION

The Phoenix Theatre; 749 North Park Ave; Indianapolis, IN 46202;
    (317) 635-7529, FAX 635-0010; E-mail phoenixt@oaktree.net;
    Web http://www.phoenixtheatre.org
Bryan Fonseca, *Producing Director*

Types of material: full-length plays, one-acts, solo pieces. **Frequency:** annual.
Remuneration: $750 for full-length play, $375 for one-act; full production of
either a full-length play or a bill of one-acts; housing to attend rehearsals.
Guidelines: unpublished play not professionally produced and suitable for theatre
with 150-seat house; contemporary, thought-provoking, challenging works;
moderate cast size and production demands; prefers playwright available for
rehearsals; 1-submission limit. **Submission procedure:** script, production history,
1- or 2-page synopsis, bio and $5 entry fee; optional SASE for critique. **Deadline:**
29 Feb 2000. **Notification:** Aug/Sep 2000. (See The Phoenix Theatre in
Production.)

FESTIVAL OF FIRSTS PLAYWRITING COMPETITION

Sunset Center; Box 1950; Carmel, CA 93921; (831) 624-3996
Director

Types of material: full-length plays. **Frequency:** annual. **Remuneration:** up to $1000; possible production. **Guidelines:** unproduced play; send SASE for guidelines. **Submission procedure:** completed entry form, script, character breakdown, synopsis and $15 entry fee. **Deadline:** 31 Aug 2000; no submission before 15 Jun 2000. **Notification:** Sep 2001.

FESTIVAL OF NEW AMERICAN THEATRE

Essential Theatre; 995 Greenwood Ave, #6; Atlanta, GA 30306; (404) 876-8471
Peter Hardy, *Producing Artistic Director*

Types of material: full-length plays. **Frequency:** annual. **Remuneration:** $300; full production. **Guidelines:** resident of GA; unproduced play. **Submission procedure:** script with SASE for response. **Deadline:** 15 May 2000. **Notification:** 1 Sep 2000. **Dates:** Jan–Feb 2001.

THE FRANCESCA PRIMUS PRIZE

Denver Center Theatre Company; 1050 13th St; Denver, CO 80204;
    (303) 446-4856, FAX 825-2117
Bruce K. Sevy, *Associate Artistic Director/New Play Development*

Types of material: full-length plays. **Frequency:** annual. **Remuneration:** $2000–3000; workshop; reading as part of Denver Center Theatre Company U S WEST Theatre Fest (see Development); travel and housing to attend rehearsals; possible full production. **Guidelines:** plays by women only; send SASE for guidelines. **Submission procedure:** script, cover letter and SASE for response. **Deadline:** 1 Jan 2000. **Notification:** Mar–Apr 2000. (See Denver Center Theatre Company in Production.)

GEORGE HOUSTON BASS PLAY-RITES FESTIVAL

Rites & Reason Theatre/Brown University; Box 1148; Providence, RI 02912;
    (401) 863-3558, FAX 863-3559
Elmo Terry-Morgan, *Artistic Director*

Types of material: one-acts. **Frequency:** annual. **Remuneration:** up to 4 awards of $250; staged reading; transportation and lodging to attend rehearsals and festival; 1 play chosen as "Best of Fest" may receive $1000 developmental contract and workshop production. **Guidelines:** unproduced, unpublished play, not more than 90 minutes long, exploring sexual orientation, race, religion, disabilities or women's issues in an innovative way; 1-submission limit; write for guidelines. **Submission procedure:** script, synopsis and resume. **Deadline:** 1 Apr 2000. **Notification:** Jun 2000.

GEORGE R. KERNODLE PLAYWRITING CONTEST

Department of Drama; 619 Kimpel Hall; University of Arkansas;
Fayetteville, AR 72701; (501) 575-2953, FAX 575-7602
Director

Types of material: one-acts. **Frequency:** annual. **Remuneration:** $300 1st prize, $200 2nd prize, $100 3rd prize; possible staged reading or production. **Guidelines:** U.S. or Canadian playwright; unproduced, unpublished play, not more than 1 hour long; cast limit of 8; 3-submission limit; write for guidelines. **Submission procedure:** script with statement that play has not received full production, $3 fee per submission and optional SASE or SASP for acknowledgment of receipt. **Deadline:** 1 Jun 2000; no submission before 1 Jan 2000. **Notification:** 1 Nov 2000.

GILMAN AND GONZALEZ-FALLA THEATRE FOUNDATION MUSICAL THEATRE AWARD

109 East 64th St; New York, NY 10021; (212) 734-8011, FAX 734-9606;
E-mail soncel@aol.com
Ariel Nazryan, *Coordinator*

Types of material: musicals. **Frequency:** annual. **Remuneration:** $25,000. **Guidelines:** writer(s) must have had a musical produced by commercial or not-for-profit theatre; write for guidelines. **Submission procedure:** write for guidelines. **Deadline:** 31 Dec 1999.

GOSHEN COLLEGE PEACE PLAYWRITING CONTEST

Goshen College; 1700 South Main St; Goshen, IN 46526; (219) 535-7393,
FAX 535-7660; E-mail douglc@goshen.edu
Douglas Caskey, *Director of Theatre*

Types of material: one-acts. **Frequency:** biennial. **Remuneration:** $500; production; room and board to attend rehearsals and/or production. **Guidelines:** 1 unproduced submission, 30–50 minutes long, exploring a contemporary peace theme. **Submission procedure:** script, 1-paragraph synopsis and resume. **Deadline:** 31 Dec 1999. **Notification:** 1 May 2000.

GREAT PLAINS PLAY CONTEST

University Theatre; 317 Murphy Hall; University of Kansas;
Lawrence, KS 66045; (785) 864-3381, FAX 864-5251
Delbert Unruh, *Director*

Types of material: full-length plays, musicals and operas for adult and young audiences. **Frequency:** annual. **Remuneration:** $2000 1st prize, production, $500 to cover travel and housing; $500 2nd prize. **Guidelines:** play not previously professionally produced dealing with any historical or contemporary aspect of the Great Plains; 2nd prize gives theatre option to produce work. **Submission procedure:** script only. **Deadline:** 1 Sep 1999. **Notification:** 15 Jan 2000.

GREAT PLATTE RIVER PLAYWRIGHTS' FESTIVAL

University of Nebraska-Kearney Theatre; Kearney, NE 68849-5260;
    (308) 865-8406, FAX 865-8806; E-mail greenj@unk.edu
Jeffrey Green, *Artistic Director*

Types of material: full-length plays, one-acts, plays for young audiences, musicals. **Frequency:** annual. **Remuneration:** $500 1st prize, $300 2nd prize, $200 3rd prize; production; travel and housing to attend rehearsals. **Guidelines:** unproduced, unpublished original work; submission of works-in-progress for possible development encouraged. **Submission procedure:** script; resume and cover letter; include cassette for musical. **Deadline:** 1 Apr 2000. **Notification:** 31 Jul 2000.

THE GREGORY KOLOVAKOS AWARD

PEN American Center; 568 Broadway; New York, NY 10012; (212) 334-1660,
    FAX 334-2181; E-mail jm@pen.org
John Morrone, *Awards Coordinator*

Types of material: translations. **Frequency:** biennial. **Remuneration:** $2000. **Guidelines:** award to U.S. writer, critic or translator whose work has made a sustained contribution over time to the cause of Latin American literature, as well as their Iberian counterparts, in English; primarily recognizes work from Spanish but contributions from other Hispanic languages also considered; candidate must be nominated by editor or colleague; write for guidelines. **Submission procedure:** letter from nominator documenting candidate's qualifications with particular attention to depth and vision of his or her work; candidate's vita; supporting materials may be requested from finalists. **Deadline:** 1 Dec 1999. **Notification:** finalists mid-Dec 1999; winner mid-May 2000. (See PEN American Center in Membership and Service Organizations, and two PEN prizes in this chapter.)

HAROLD MORTON LANDON TRANSLATION AWARD

The Academy of American Poets; 584 Broadway, Suite 1208;
    New York, NY 10012; (212) 274-0343, FAX 274-9427;
    E-mail poets@artswire.org; Web http://www.poets.org
India Amos, *Awards Administrator*

Types of material: translations. **Frequency:** annual. **Remuneration:** $1000. **Guidelines:** U.S. citizen; published translation of verse, including verse drama, from any language into English verse; book published in 1999. **Submission procedure:** 3 copies of book (no manuscripts). **Deadline:** 31 Dec 1999.

HENRICO THEATRE COMPANY ONE-ACT PLAYWRITING COMPETITION

The County of Henrico; Division of Recreation and Parks; Box 27032;
    Richmond, VA 23273; (804) 501-5138, FAX 501-5284;
    E-mail per22@co.henrico.va.us
Amy A. Perdue, *Cultural Arts Coordinator*

Types of material: one-acts, musicals and solo pieces. **Frequency:** annual. **Remuneration:** $250 and production 1st prize; $125, possible production and video for runner-up. **Guidelines:** unproduced, unpublished work; no controversial themes; prefers small cast, simple set; write for guidelines. **Submission procedure:** 2 copies of script. **Deadline:** 1 Jul 2000. **Notification:** 31 Dec 2000.

HRC's ANNUAL PLAYWRITING CONTEST
Hudson River Classics, Inc; Box 940; Hudson, NY 12534; (518) 828-1329
W. Keith Hedrick, *President*

Types of material: full-length plays, one-acts, solo pieces. **Frequency:** annual. **Remuneration:** $500; staged reading; room, board and travel to attend performance. **Guidelines:** 60–90-minute unpublished play by New York State playwright. **Submission procedure:** script and $5 fee. **Deadline:** 1 Jun 2000; no submission before 1 Mar 2000. **Notification:** 15 Nov 2000.

IHT/SRT INTERNATIONAL PLAYWRIGHTING COMPETITION
Singapore Repertory Theatre; Telok Ayer Performing Arts Centre;
    182 Cecil St; Singapore 069547; 65-221-5585, FAX 65-221-1936;
    E-mail singrep@cyberway.com.sg; Web http://www.sing.com.sg
Stephanie Green, *Publicity Manager*

Types of material: full-length plays. **Frequency:** annual. **Remuneration:** $15,000 (U.S. dollars); full production; transportation, lodging and per diem to attend rehearsals and performances. **Guidelines:** playwright of any nationality or ethnicity; professionally unproduced English-language play dealing with some aspect of modern Pan-Asian indentity. **Submission procedure:** script only; 1 submission; script will not be returned. **Deadline:** 1 Dec 1999. **Notification:** May 2000.

JACKIE WHITE MEMORIAL NATIONAL CHILDREN'S PLAYWRITING CONTEST
309 Parkade Blvd; Columbia, MO 65202; (573) 874-5628
Betsy Phillips, *Director*

Types of material: plays and musicals to be performed by young actors. **Frequency:** annual. **Remuneration:** $250; optional production by Columbia Entertainment Company Children's Theatre School; room, board and partial travel to attend performance; all entrants receive written evaluation. **Guidelines:** unpublished original work, 60–90 minutes in length, with 20–30 speaking characters of all ages, at least 10 developed in some detail, to be played by students aged 10–15; send SASE for guidelines. **Submission procedure:** completed entry form, script, character breakdown, act/scene synopsis, resume and $10 fee; include cassette for musical. **Deadline:** 1 Jun 2000. **Notification:** 30 Aug 2000.

JAMES D. PHELAN AWARD IN LITERATURE

Intersection for the Arts/The San Francisco Foundation; 446 Valencia St;
San Francisco, CA 94103; (415) 626-2787, FAX 626-1636;
E-mail intrsect@wenet.net
Awards Coordinator

Types of material: full-length plays, one-acts, plays for young audiences.
Frequency: annual. **Remuneration:** $2000. **Guidelines:** author CA born and aged
20–35 years as of 31 Jan 2000; unpublished play-in-progress. **Submission
procedure:** completed application and script. **Deadline:** 31 Jan 2000; no submission before 15 Nov 1999. **Notification:** 15 Jun 2000.

JANE CHAMBERS PLAYWRITING AWARD

c/o Department of Theatre Arts; Wright State University;
Dayton, OH 45435-0001; (937) 775-4128
Mary Donahoe, *Coordinator*

Types of material: full-length plays, one-acts, solo pieces, performance-art texts.
Frequency: annual. **Remuneration:** $1000; free registration and rehearsed reading
at the Women and Theatre Conference in late July; student submissions eligible
for $250 Student Award. **Guidelines:** work by a woman that reflects a feminist
perspective and contains a majority of roles for women; special interest in works
by and about women from a diversity of positions in respect to race, class, sexual
preference, physical ability, age and geographical region; experimentation with
dramatic form encouraged; 1-submission limit; award administered by the
Association for Theatre in Higher Education (see Membership and Service
Organizations); send SASE for guidelines and application. **Submission procedure:**
completed application form, 2 copies of script, synopsis and resume; if possible,
professional recommendation; optional SASP for acknowledgment of receipt.
Deadline: 15 Feb 2000. **Notification:** 30 Jun 2000.

JEWEL BOX THEATRE PLAYWRIGHTING AWARD

3700 North Walker; Oklahoma City, OK 73118-7099; (405) 521-1786,
FAX 525-6562
Charles Tweed, *Production Director*

Types of material: full-length plays, one-acts, solo pieces. **Frequency:** annual.
Remuneration: $500; possible production. **Guidelines:** unproduced full-length
play or evening-length collection of one-acts of strong ensemble nature with
emphasis on character rather than spectacle; send SASE in Oct for guidelines and
forms. **Submission procedure:** completed entry form, 2 copies of script,
playwright's agreement and $10 fee. **Deadline:** 15 Jan 2000. **Notification:** Apr
2000.

JOHN GASSNER MEMORIAL PLAYWRITING AWARD

The New England Theatre Conference; c/o Department of Theatre;
Northeastern University; 306 Huntington Ave; Boston, MA 02115;
(617) 424-9275, FAX 424-1057; E-mail netc@world.com

Types of material: full-length plays. **Frequency:** annual. **Remuneration:** $1000 1st prize, $500 2nd prize; staged reading; possible publication. **Guidelines:** New England resident or NETC (see Membership and Service Organizations) member; unpublished play that has not had professional full production and is not under consideration for publication or professional production; 1-submission limit. **Submission procedure:** script with cover page, character breakdown, brief synopsis and statement that play has not been published or professionally produced and is not under consideration; SASP for acknowledgment of receipt; $10 fee, except for NETC members; script will not be returned. **Deadline:** 15 Apr 2000. **Notification:** 1 Sep 2000 (winners only).

KENNEDY CENTER AMERICAN COLLEGE THEATER FESTIVAL: MICHAEL KANIN PLAYWRITING AWARDS PROGRAM

The John F. Kennedy Center for the Performing Arts;
Washington, DC 20566-0001; (202) 416-8857, FAX 416-8802
John Lion, *Producing Director*

Anchorage Press Theater for Youth Playwriting Award

Types of material: full-length plays, adaptations, musicals. **Frequency:** annual. **Remuneration:** $1000; $1,250 fellowship to attend either the New Visions/New Voices (see Development) or the National Youth Theatre Symposium (see Waldo M. and Grace C. Bonderman IUPUI/IRT Playwriting Event for Young Audiences in this section); possible publication by Anchorage Press with royalties. **Guidelines:** writer enrolled as full-time student at college or university during year of production or during either of the 2 years preceding the production; play on theme appealing to young people from kindergarten–12th grade produced by an ACTF-participating college or university; write for KC/ACTF brochure. **Submission procedure:** college or university which has entered production of work in ACTF registers work for awards program. **Deadline:** 1 Dec 1999. **Dates:** 17 Apr–25 Apr 2000.

The Fourth Freedom Forum Playwriting Award

Types of material: full-length plays. **Frequency:** annual. **Remuneration:** 1st prize: for playwright, $5000 plus publication by Palmetto Play Service and all-expense-paid 9-day residency at Sundance Theatre Laboratory (see Development), which includes consultation with Sundance directors and dramaturgs and reading by Lab actors; $1500 to producing college or university; 2nd prize: $2500 to playwright; $1000 to producing college or university. **Guidelines:** writer enrolled as full-time student at college or university during year of production or during either of 2 years preceding the production; play on themes of world peace and international disarmament produced by an ACTF-participating college or university; write for KC/ACTF brochure. **Submission procedure:** college or university which has entered production of work in ACTF registers work for awards program. **Deadline:** 1 Dec 1999. **Dates:** 17 Apr–25 Apr 1999.

The Jean Kennedy Smith Playwriting Award

Types of material: full-length plays, adaptations, musicals. **Frequency:** annual. **Remuneration:** $2500 plus Dramatists Guild membership and fellowship to attend a prestigious playwriting program. **Guidelines:** writer enrolled as full-time student at college or university during year of production or during either of 2 years preceding the production; play that explores the human experience of living with disabilities produced by an ACTF-participating college or university; write for KC/ACTF brochure. **Submission procedure:** college or university which has entered production of work in ACTF registers work for awards program. **Deadline:** 1 Dec 1999. **Dates:** 17 Apr–25 Apr 2000.

The KC/ACTF Musical Theater Award

Types of material: musicals. **Frequency:** annual. **Remuneration:** $1000 for lyrics; $1000 for music; $1000 for book; $1000 to producing college or university. **Guidelines:** at least 50% of writing team must be enrolled as full-time student(s) at college or university during year of production or during either of the 2 years preceding the production; original and copyrighted work produced by an ACTF-participating college or university; write for KC/ACTF brochure. **Submission procedure:** college or university which has entered production of work in ACTF registers work for awards program. **Deadline:** 1 Dec 1999. **Dates:** 17 Apr–25 Apr 2000.

The Lorraine Hansberry Playwriting Award

Types of material: full-length plays. **Frequency:** annual. **Remuneration:** 1st prize: for playwright, $2500 plus an internship at the National Playwrights Conference at the O'Neill Theater Center (see Development) and publication of play by The Dramatic Publishing Company (see Publication); $750 to producing college or university; 2nd prize: $1000 to playwright; $500 to producing college or university. **Guidelines:** writer enrolled as full-time student at college or university during year of production or during either of the 2 years preceding the production; play dealing with the black experience produced by an ACTF-participating college or university; write for KC/ACTF brochure. **Submission procedure:** college or university which has entered production of work in ACTF registers work for awards program. **Deadline:** 1 Dec 1999. **Dates:** 17 Apr–25 Apr 2000.

The National AIDS Fund CFDA-Vogue Initiative Award for Playwriting

Types of material: full-length plays, adaptations, musicals. **Frequency:** annual. **Remuneration:** $2500 plus fellowship to attend Bay Area Playwrights Festival (see Development). **Guidelines:** writer enrolled as full-time student at college or university during year of production or during either of the 2 years preceding the production; play concerning personal and social implications of HIV/AIDS produced by an ACTF-participating college or university; write for KC/ACTF brochure. **Submission procedure:** college or university which has entered production of work in ACTF registers work for awards program. **Deadline:** 1 Dec 1999. **Dates:** 17 Apr–25 Apr 2000.

The National Student Playwriting Award

Types of material: full-length plays, adaptations, musicals. **Frequency:** annual. **Remuneration:** for playwright, $2500; production at Kennedy Center during festival; publication by Samuel French (see Publication) with royalties; fellowship to attend Sundance Theatre Laboratory (see Development); Dramatists Guild membership (see Membership and Service Organizations); $1000 to producing college or university. **Guidelines:** writer enrolled as full-time student at college or university during year of production or during either of the 2 years preceding the production; work must be produced by an ACTF-participating college or university; write for KC/ACTF brochure. **Submission procedure:** college or university which has entered production of work in ACTF registers work for awards program. **Deadline:** 1 Dec 1999. **Dates:** 17 Apr–25 Apr 2000.

The Short Play Awards Program

Types of material: one-acts, one-act adaptations. **Frequency:** annual. **Remuneration:** up to 3 awards: $1000; publication by Samuel French (see Publication); Dramatists Guild of America membership (see Membership and Service Organizations). **Guidelines:** writer enrolled as full-time student at college or university during year of production or during either of the 2 years preceding the production; one-act must be produced by an ACTF-participating college or university; simple production demands (minimal setup and strike time); write for KC/ACTF brochure. **Submission procedure:** college or university which has entered production of work in ACTF registers work for awards program. **Deadline:** 1 Dec 1999. **Dates:** 17 Apr–25 Apr 2000.

KUMU KAHUA THEATRE/UHM DEPARTMENT OF THEATRE & DANCE PLAYWRITING CONTEST

Kumu Kahua Theatre; 46 Merchant St; Honolulu, HI 96813; (808) 536-4222, FAX 536-4226
Harry Wong III, *Artistic Director, Kumu Kahua Theatre*

Hawai'i Prize

Types of material: full-length plays. **Frequency:** annual. **Remuneration:** $500. **Guidelines:** play set in HI or dealing with some aspect of HI experience;

unproduced play; previous entries ineligible. **Submission procedure:** write for entry brochure. **Deadline:** 1 Jan 2000. **Notification:** 1 May 2000.

Pacific/Rim Prize

Types of material: full-length plays. **Frequency:** annual. **Remuneration:** $400. **Guidelines:** play set in or dealing with Pacific Islands, Pacific Rim or Pacific/Asian-American experience; unproduced play; previous entries ineligible. **Submission procedure:** write for entry brochure. **Deadline:** 1 Jan 2000. **Notification:** 1 May 2000.

Resident Prize

Types of material: full-length plays, one-acts. **Frequency:** annual. **Remuneration:** $200; reading and/or production if playwright present. **Guidelines:** play on any topic by HI resident; unproduced play; previous entries ineligible. **Submission procedure:** write for entry brochure. **Deadline:** 1 Jan 2000. **Notification:** 1 May 2000.

LAMIA INK! INTERNATIONAL ONE-PAGE PLAY COMPETITION
Box 202; Prince St Station; New York, NY 10012
Cortland Jessup, *Editor*

Types of material: 1-page plays. **Frequency:** annual. **Remuneration:** $200; reading in New York City and publication in magazine (see Lamia Ink! in Publication) for winner and 11 other best plays. **Guidelines:** 3-submission limit; send SASE for guidelines. **Submission procedure:** script, SASE for response and $1 fee per submission. **Deadline:** 15 Mar 2000. **Notification:** 15 May 2000.

THE LEE KORF PLAYWRITING AWARDS
The Original Theatre Works; Burnight Center; Cerritos College; 11110 Alondra
    Blvd; Norwalk, CA 90650-6298; (310) 860-2451, ext 2638, FAX 467-5097
Gloria Manriquez, *Production Coordinator*

Types of material: full-length plays, musicals, theatre pieces, extravaganzas. **Frequency:** annual. **Remuneration:** $750; production. **Guidelines:** special interest in works with multicultural themes. **Submission procedure:** send SASE for guidelines and application. **Deadline:** 1 Sep 1999. **Notification:** 1 Apr 2000.

THE LITTLE THEATRE OF ALEXANDRIA
NATIONAL ONE-ACT PLAYWRITING COMPETITION
Little Theatre of Alexandria; 600 Wolfe St; Alexandria, VA 22314;
    (703) 683-5778, FAX 683-1378; E-mail ltlthtre@erols.com
Chairman, Playwriting Competition

Types of material: one-acts. **Frequency:** annual. **Remuneration:** $350 1st prize, $250 2nd prize, $150 3rd prize; possible production. **Guidelines:** unpublished, unproduced work; prefers plays with running times of 20–60 minutes, few scenes and 1 set; 2-submission limit. **Submission procedure:** script, synopsis, character breakdown and $5 fee; send SASE for guidelines. **Deadline:** 31 May 2000; no submission before 1 Jan 2000. **Notification:** fall 2000.

LOIS AND RICHARD ROSENTHAL NEW PLAY PRIZE
Cincinnati Playhouse in the Park; Box 6537; Cincinnati, OH 45206-0537;
(513) 345-2242
Associate Artistic Director

Types of material: full-length plays, musicals. **Frequency:** annual. **Remuneration:** $10,000; production; travel and housing to attend rehearsals. **Guidelines:** 1 unpublished submission, not produced professionally; no translations or adaptations. **Submission procedure:** no scripts; 5-page dialogue sample, 2-page maximum abstract including synopsis, character breakdown and bio; include cassette for musicals. **Deadline:** 31 Dec 1999. **Notification:** 2 months; 6 months if script is requested. (See Cincinnati Playhouse in the Park in Production.)

LOS ANGELES DESIGNERS' THEATRE COMMISSIONS
Box 1883; Studio City, CA 91614-0883; (323) 650-9600 (voice),
654-2700 (TDD), FAX 654-3260; E-mail ladesigners@juno.com
Richard Niederberg, *Artistic Director*

Types of material: full-length plays, bills of related one-acts, translations, adaptations, plays for young audiences, musicals, solo pieces, operas. **Frequency:** ongoing. **Remuneration:** negotiable commissioning fee; possible travel to attend rehearsals if developmental work is needed. **Guidelines:** commissioning program for work with commercial potential which has not received professional full production, is not under option and is free of commitment to specific director, actors or other personnel; large casts and multiple sets welcome; prefers controversial material. **Submission procedure:** proposal or synopsis and resume; include cassette for musical; materials will not be returned. **Deadline:** ongoing. **Notification:** at least 4 months.

LOVE CREEK ANNUAL SHORT PLAY FESTIVAL
Love Creek Productions; c/o 162 Nesbit St; Weehawken, NJ 07087-6817
Cynthia Granville-Callahan, *Festival Literary Manager/Chair, Reading Committee*

Types of material: one-acts. **Frequency:** annual. **Remuneration:** minimum of 60 finalists receive mini-showcase production in New York City during festival; cash prize for best play of festival. **Guidelines:** unpublished play not produced in NYC area within past year; maximum length of 40 minutes; cast of 2 or more, simple sets and costumes; 2-submission limit; strongly prefers women in major roles and predominantly female cast; mini-festivals centered around specific themes; upcoming themes include "Fear of God: Religion in the '90s," gay and lesbian themes, political plays; send SASE for themes and deadlines. **Submission procedure:** script with letter giving theatre permission to produce play if chosen and specifying whether Equity showcase is acceptable. **Deadline:** ongoing. **Dates:** year-round.

THE MARC A. KLEIN PLAYWRITING AWARD

Department of Theater Arts; Case Western Reserve University;
    10900 Euclid Ave; Cleveland, OH 44106-7077; (216) 368-4868,
    FAX 368-5184; E-mail ksg@po.cwru.edu
John Orlock, *Chair, Reading Committee*

Types of material: full-length plays, bills of related one-acts. **Frequency:** annual. **Remuneration:** $1000 ($500 is used to cover residency expenses); production. **Guidelines:** student currently enrolled at U.S. college or university; work endorsed by faculty member of university theatre department that has not received professional full production or trade-book publication. **Submission procedure:** completed entry form and script. **Deadline:** 15 May 2000. **Notification:** 1 Aug 2000.

MARVIN TAYLOR PLAYWRITING AWARD

Sierra Repertory Theatre; Box 3030; Sonora, CA 95370; (209) 532-3120,
    FAX 532-7270; E-mail srt@mlode.com;
    Web http://www.mlode.com/~nsierra/srt
Dennis Jones, *Producing Director*

Types of material: full-length plays, adaptations, musicals, solo pieces. **Frequency:** annual. **Remuneration:** $500; possible production. **Guidelines:** 1 submission that has received no more than 2 productions or staged readings; cast limit of 15, prefers 6; not more than 2 sets. **Submission procedure:** script only. **Deadline:** 31 Aug 2000. **Notification:** Mar 2001.

MAXIM MAZUMDAR NEW PLAY COMPETITION

Alleyway Theatre; 1 Curtain Up Alley; Buffalo, NY 14202-1911; (716) 852-2600,
    FAX 852-2266; E-mail alleywayth@aol.com
Kevin Stevens, *Literary Manager*

Types of material: full-length plays, one-acts, musicals. **Frequency:** annual. **Remuneration:** $400, production with royalty, and travel and housing to attend rehearsals for full-length play or musical; $100 and production for one-act play or musical. **Guidelines:** unproduced full-length work minimum 90 minutes long with cast limit of 10 and unit set or simple set, or unproduced one-act work less than 40 minutes long with cast limit of 6 and simple set; prefers work with unconventional setting that explores the boundaries of theatricality; 1-submission limit in each category. **Submission procedure:** script, character breakdown and resume; include cassette of complete score for musicals; $5 fee per playwright. **Deadline:** 1 Jul 2000. **Notification:** 1 Oct 2000 for finalists; 1 Feb 2001 for winners.

McLaren Memorial Comedy Playwriting Competition

Midland Community Theatre; 2000 West Wadley Ave; Midland, TX 79705;
(915) 682-2544, FAX 682-6136; Web http://www.mct-cole.org
Coordinator

Types of material: full-length plays, one-acts, translations, adaptations, plays for young audiences, musicals, solo pieces. **Frequency:** annual. **Remuneration:** 4 finalists chosen for staged readings; winner receives $400. **Guidelines:** comedies only; prefers work that has not received professional full production but will consider work with 1 not-for-profit theatre production. **Submission procedure:** script and $5 fee. **Deadline:** 31 Jan 2000; no submission before 1 Dec 1999. **Notification:** May 2000.

Midwest Theatre Network Original Play Competition/ Rochester Playwright Festival

5031 Tongen Ave NW; Rochester, MN 55901; (507) 281-8887
Joan Sween, *Executive Director/Dramaturg*

Types of material: full-length plays, collections of one-acts, plays for young audiences, musicals, full-length solo pieces, satirical revues. **Frequency:** biennial. **Remuneration:** 4–8 awards of $300–1000 each (contingent on individual theatre's funding); full production by cooperating theatres; travel, room and board to attend performance. **Guidelines:** unpublished work that has not received professional production; send SASE for guidelines and entry form. **Submission procedure:** 1 completed entry form with each script; include cassette for musical. **Deadline:** 30 Nov 1999. **Notification:** Jan 2000 for finalists; Mar 2000 for winners.

Mildred and Albert Panowski Playwriting Award

Forest A. Roberts Theatre; Northern Michigan University; Marquette, MI 49855;
(906) 227-2553, FAX 227-2567
James A. Panowski, *Director*

Types of material: full-length plays, adaptations, solo pieces. **Frequency:** annual. **Remuneration:** $2000; production; travel, room and board for 1-week residency. **Guidelines:** 1 unpublished, unproduced submission; rewrites of previous entries ineligible; production will be entered in Kennedy Center American College Theater Festival (see entry in this section) if playwright is eligible; write for guidelines. **Submission procedure:** completed entry form and script. **Deadline:** 21 Nov 1999. **Notification:** Apr 2000.

THE MILL MOUNTAIN THEATRE NEW PLAY COMPETITION: THE NORFOLK SOUTHERN FESTIVAL OF NEW WORKS

1 Market Square SE, 2nd Floor; Roanoke, VA 24011-1437; (540) 342-5730,
FAX 342-5745; E-mail mmtmail@millmountain.org;
Web http://www.millmountain.org
New Play Competition Coordinator

Types of material: full-length plays, one-acts, musicals, solo pieces. **Frequency:** annual. **Remuneration:** $1000; staged reading with possibility of production; travel stipend and housing for limited residency. **Guidelines:** U.S. resident; 1 unproduced, unpublished submission; cast limit of 10; no 10-minute plays; send SASE for guidelines. **Submission procedure:** agent submission or script with professional recommendation by director, literary manager or dramaturg; include cassette for musical. **Deadline:** 1 Jan 2000; no submission before 1 Oct 1999. **Notification:** Aug 2000. (See Mill Mountain Theatre in Prodction.)

MORTON R. SARETT NATIONAL PLAYWRITING COMPETITION

Department of Theatre; University of Nevada, Las Vegas;
4505 Maryland Pkwy, Box 455036; Las Vegas, NV 89154-5036;
(702) 895-3666
Corrine A. Bonate, *Coordinator*

Types of material: full-length plays, musicals. **Frequency:** biennial. **Remuneration:** $3000; production; travel and housing to attend rehearsals and opening performance. **Guidelines:** unpublished, unproduced play or musical; no adaptations; send SASE for guidelines. **Submission procedure:** completed application, 2 bound copies of script and 50-word synopsis. **Deadline:** 15 Dec 1999; no submission before 1 Sep 1999. **Notification:** Jun 2000.

MOVING ARTS PREMIERE ONE-ACT COMPETITION

1822 Hyperion Ave; Los Angeles, CA 90027; (323) 665-8961,
FAX 665-1816; E-mail rrasmussen@movingarts.org;
Web http://www.movingarts.org
Rebecca Rasmussen, *Director of One-Act Competition*

Types of material: one-acts. **Frequency:** annual. **Remuneration:** $200; production. **Guidelines:** play not previously produced in L.A. area; cast limit of 8; single set. **Submission procedure:** script without author's name or address, cover letter and $8 fee. **Deadline:** 29 Feb 2000. **Notification:** Jul 2000.

MRTW SCRIPT CONTEST

Midwest Radio Theatre Workshop; KOPN Radio; 915 East Broadway;
Columbia, MO 65201; (573) 874-5676, FAX 499-1662;
E-mail mrtw@mrtw.org; Web http://www.mrtw.org
Sue Zizza, *Executive Director*

Types of material: short radio plays. **Frequency:** annual. **Remuneration:** $800 to be divided among 2–4 winners; possible radio production for local broadcast and national distribution via satellite and tape sales; scholarship to attend May 2000 Midwest Radio Theatre Workshop (see Development); publication in MRTW Scriptbook. **Guidelines:** original radio play 15–30 minutes long (no adaptations) by established or emerging writer; special interest in plays by women, gay and lesbian writers and writers of color and in issue-oriented plays on contemporary themes; 1-submission limit; write for guidelines; for additional information, call (516) 483-8321. **Submission procedure:** 3 copies of script in radio format and cover letter indicating if play has been produced; $10 fee. **Deadline:** 15 Nov 1999. **Notification:** Apr 2000. (See entries in Membership and Service Organizations and Development.)

NANTUCKET SHORT PLAY FESTIVAL AND COMPETITION
Nantucket Theatrical Productions; Box 2177; Nantucket, MA 02584;
    (508) 228-5002
Jim Patrick, *Literary Manager*

Types of material: one-acts. **Frequency:** annual. **Remuneration:** $200; 1 or more staged readings for winning play and selected additional plays as part of summer festival. **Guidelines:** unpublished play which has not received Equity production; maximum length of 40 pages; simple production demands; send SASE for guidelines. **Submission procedure:** script and $6 fee. **Deadline:** ongoing. **Notification:** ongoing. **Dates:** Jul 2000.

NATIONAL CHILDREN'S THEATRE FESTIVAL
Actors' Playhouse at the Miracle Theatre; 280 Miracle Mile;
    Coral Gables, FL 33134; (305) 444-9293, ext 615, FAX 444-4181
Earl Maulding, *Director of Theatre for Young Audiences*

Types of material: musicals for young audiences. **Frequency:** annual. **Remuneration:** $100–1000 prize plus reading or production, travel and housing to attend festival. **Guidelines:** unpublished musical for young people aged 5–12, 45–60 minutes long, with cast limit of 8 (may play multiple roles) and minimal sets suitable for touring; translations and adaptations eligible only if writer owns copyright to material; special interest in works dealing with social issues including multiculturalism in today's society; write for guidelines. **Submission procedure:** completed entry form, script and $10 fee; include score and cassette for musical. **Deadline:** 1 Aug 2000. **Notification:** Nov 2000. **Dates:** Jan 2001.

NATIONAL HISPANIC PLAYWRITING AWARD
Arizona Theatre Company; Box 1631; Tucson, AZ 85702; (520) 884-8210,
    FAX 628-9129
Elaine Romero, *Contest Director*

Types of material: full-length plays, adaptations. **Frequency:** annual. **Remuneration:** $1000; possible staged reading; travel, room and board to attend rehearsals and performance. **Guidelines:** playwright of Hispanic heritage residing in U.S., U.S. territories or Mexico; 1 unproduced, unpublished submission written in English, Spanish or both languages. **Submission procedure:** script (with English translation if original in Spanish), 1-page cover letter including production history, if any, and bio. **Deadline:** 31 Oct 1999. **Notification:** spring 2000. (See Arizona Theatre Company in Production.)

NATIONAL NEW PLAY AWARD

Department of Theatre Arts; Humboldt State University; Arcata, CA 95521; (707) 826-4606, FAX 826-5494; E-mail mtk3@axe.humboldt.edu; Web http://www.humboldt.edu/~mtk3

Margaret Thomas Kelso, *Assistant Professor of Theatre Arts*

Types of material: full-length plays. **Frequency:** triennial. **Remuneration:** 2 awards of $1000; full production; 2-week residency. **Guidelines:** unproduced, unpublished play. **Submission procedure:** script only; 2-submission limit. **Deadline:** 30 Jan 2002; no submission before 1 Dec 2001. **Notification:** spring 2002.

NATIONAL PLAY AWARD

Box 286; Hollywood, CA 90078; (323) 465-9517, FAX (310) 652-2543; E-mail nrtf@aol.com; Web http://www.nrtf.org

Raul Espinoza, *Chair*

Types of material: full-length plays. **Frequency:** annual. **Remuneration:** 1st prize $5000; $500 each for 4 runners-up. **Guidelines:** original unpublished play, not produced with paid Equity cast, that has not won major award or been previously submitted to NPA. **Submission procedure:** script and $25 fee (check payable to National Repertory Theatre Foundation). **Deadline:** 31 Mar 2000; no submission before 1 Jan 2000. **Notification:** 1 Sep 2000 for finalists; 31 Dec 2000 for winner.

NATIONAL TEN-MINUTE PLAY CONTEST

Actors Theatre of Louisville; 316 West Main St; Louisville, KY 40202-4218; (502) 584-1265, FAX 584-1265; E-mail actors@aye.net

Michael Bigelow Dixon, *Literary Manager*

Amy Wegener, *Assistant Literary Manager*

Types of material: 10-minute plays. **Frequency:** annual. **Remuneration:** Heideman Award of $1000; possible production with royalty. **Guidelines:** U.S. citizen or resident; play 10 pages long or less which has not had Equity production; 1-submission limit; previous entries ineligible; write for guidelines. **Submission procedure:** script only; script will not be returned. **Deadline:** 1 Dec 1999. **Notification:** fall 2000.

NEW AMERICAN COMEDY (NAC) FESTIVAL

Ukiah Players Theatre; 1041 Low Gap Rd; Ukiah, CA 95482; (707) 462-1210, FAX 462-1790

Michael Ducharme, *Executive Director*

Types of material: full-length plays. **Frequency:** biennial. **Remuneration:** $50 per performance for play selected for full production (6 to 8 performances); $25 each per performance for 2 plays chosen as staged readings; up to $400 travel and $25

per diem to attend 1-week workshop. **Guidelines:** playwright must be available to participate in 1-week developmental workshop; unproduced, unpublished comedy; prefers small cast, simple set; write for guidelines. **Submission procedure:** completed application, script with 1-page plot summary, scenic requirements, character breakdown and estimated running time; optional resume. **Deadline:** 30 Nov 1999. **Notification:** Feb 2000. **Dates:** May–Jun 2000.

NEW PROFESSIONAL THEATRE WRITERS FESTIVAL
424 West 42nd St, 3rd Floor; New York, NY 10036;
      (212) 290-8150, FAX 290-8202; E-mail newprof@aol.com
Kenneth Johnson, *Literary Manager*

Types of material: full-length plays. **Frequency:** annual. **Remuneration:** $2000; excerpts performed at Oct gala; seminars and mentoring. **Guidelines:** special interest in African-American women writers. **Submission procedure:** script, resume and SASP for acknowledgment of receipt. **Deadline:** 1 Jun 2000. **Notification:** Sep 2000.

NEW YORK CITY HIGH SCHOOL PLAYWRITING CONTEST
Young Playwrights Inc; 321 West 44th St, Suite 906; New York, NY 10036;
      (212) 307-1140, FAX 307-1454; E-mail writeaplay@aol.com;
      Web http://youngplaywrights.org
Sheri M. Goldhirsch, *Artistic Director*

Types of material: full-length plays, one-acts. **Frequency:** annual. **Remuneration:** varies. **Guidelines:** New York City high school student; writers under 18 years of age automatically entered in Young Playwrights Festival National Playwriting Contest (see listing in this section); write for guidelines. **Submission procedure:** script with playwright's name, date of birth, home address, phone number, school and grade on title page. **Deadline:** 15 Apr 2000. **Notification:** 1 Jun 2000.

OGLEBAY INSTITUTE TOWNGATE THEATRE CONTESTS
Oglebay Institute; Stifel Fine Arts Center; 1330 National Rd;
      Wheeling, WV 26003; (304) 242-7700, FAX 242-7700
Performing Arts Department

Playwriting Contest

Types of material: full-length plays. **Frequency:** annual. **Remuneration:** $300; production; partial travel to attend performances. **Guidelines:** unpublished, unproduced play; simple set. **Submission procedure:** script and resume. **Deadline:** 30 Dec 1999. **Notification:** 1 May 2000.

Playwriting Contest for College Students

Types of material: full-length plays. **Frequency:** annual. **Remuneration:** $100; production. **Guidelines:** unpublished, unproduced play; simple set. **Submission procedure:** script. **Deadline:** 15 Mar 2000. **Notification:** 1 Jun 2000.

PATHWAY PRODUCTIONS' NATIONAL PLAYWRITING CONTEST
Pathway Productions; 9561 East Daines Dr; Temple City, CA 91780;
      (626) 287-4771; E-mail pathwaypro@aol.com
R. Brent Beerman, *Artistic Director*

Types of material: plays for young audiences. **Frequency:** annual. **Remuneration:** $200; production; publication by Pathway Plays. **Guidelines:** full-length plays, musicals or collections of one-acts for and about teenagers; no submission limit. **Submission procedure:** bound script with synopsis and character breakdown; send SASP for acknowledgment of receipt. **Deadline:** 1 May 2000. **Notification:** Jun 2000.

PAUL GREEN PLAYWRIGHTS PRIZE
3501 Highway 54 W; Studio C; Chapel Hill, NC 27516;
      E-mail ncwn@sunsite.unc.edu; Web http://sunsite.unc.edu/ncwriters

Types of material: full-length plays, one-acts, solo pieces. **Frequency:** annual. **Remuneration:** $500. **Guidelines:** unpublished, unproduced play; send SASE for guidelines. **Submission procedure:** 2 copies of script, synopsis and $10 fee for nonmembers or $7.50 fee for members; do not list name on manuscript, include separate cover sheet with title, name and contact information; include SASE for winners list. **Deadline:** 30 Sep 1999. **Notification:** Feb 2000.

PEN CENTER USA WEST LITERARY AWARDS
672 South Lafayette Park Pl, Suite 41; Los Angeles, CA 90057;
      (213) 365-8500, FAX 365-9616; E-mail penwest@tx.netcom.com
Christina Apeles, *Awards Coordinator*

Types of material: full-length plays, screenplays, teleplays. **Frequency:** annual. **Remuneration:** $1000 award in each of several categories, including drama, screenwriting and television writing. **Guidelines:** writer residing west of Mississippi River; only full-length (original or adapted) screenplays and teleplays; script first produced during 1999 calendar year. **Submission procedure:** 4 copies of script, playbill or press materials verifying eligibility and cover letter giving title of work, author's name and state of residence, name of producer and production dates. **Deadline:** 31 Jan 2000.

PEN–BOOK-OF-THE-MONTH CLUB TRANSLATION PRIZE
PEN American Center; 568 Broadway; New York, NY 10012;
      (212) 334-1660, FAX 334-2181; E-mail jm@pen.org
John Morrone, *Program Coordinator*

Types of material: translations. **Frequency:** annual. **Remuneration:** $3000. **Guidelines:** book-length translation from any language into English published in U.S. during current calendar year. **Submission procedure:** 3 copies of book. **Deadline:** 15 Dec 1999. **Notification:** spring 2000. (See entry in Membership and Service Organizations and the next entry of this chapter.)

PEN/LAURA PELS FOUNDATION AWARD FOR DRAMA

PEN American Center; 568 Broadway; New York, NY 10012-3225;
(212) 334-1660, FAX 334-2181; E-mail jm@pen.org
John Morrone, *Literary Awards Manager*

Types of material: full-length plays. **Frequency:** annual. **Remuneration:** $5000. **Guidelines:** mid-career American playwright who has had at least 2 full-length plays professionally produced in theatres 299 seats or larger. **Submission procedure:** playwright must be nominated by a professional colleague through a letter of support accompanied by a list of candidate's produced work. **Deadline:** 3 Jan 2000. **Notification:** spring 2000. (See entry in Membership and Service Organizations and the previous listing in this chapter.)

PERISHABLE THEATRE WOMEN'S PLAYWRITING FESTIVAL

Box 23132; Providence, RI 02903; (401) 331-2695, FAX 331-7811;
E-mail perishable@as220.org; Web http://www.perishable.org
Vanessa Gilbert, *Festival Director*

Types of material: one-act plays. **Frequency:** annual. **Remuneration:** 3 awards of $250; production; publication in anthology. **Guidelines:** unproduced one-act, no more than 40 minutes in length, by woman playwright; 2-submission limit. **Submission procedure:** script, resume and $5 fee. **Deadline:** 31 Dec 1999. **Notification:** 31 Mar 2000.

PETERSON EMERGING PLAYWRIGHT COMPETITION

Theatre Arts Department, Catawba College; 2300 West Innes St;
Salisbury, NC 28144; (704) 637-4771, FAX 637-4207
E-mail jepperso@catawba.edu
James R. Epperson, *Chair, Theatre Arts Department*

Types of material: full-length plays, musicals. **Frequency:** annual. **Remuneration:** $2000; full production; transportation, room and board to attend rehearsals and performances. **Guidelines:** unpublished, unproduced full-length work by an emerging playwright; two one-acts with common theme accepted. **Submission procedure:** script only; send SASP for acknowledgment of receipt. **Deadline:** 15 Mar 2000. **Notification:** 1 May 2000.

PLAYHOUSE ON THE SQUARE NEW PLAY COMPETITION

Playhouse on the Square; 51 South Cooper St; Memphis, TN 38104;
(901) 725-0776, 726-4498
Jackie Nichols, *Executive Director*

Types of material: full-length plays, musicals. **Frequency:** annual. **Remuneration:** $500; production. **Guidelines:** unproduced work; small cast; full arrangement for piano for musical; prefers southern playwrights. **Submission procedure:** script only. **Deadline:** 1 Apr 2000. (See entry in Production.)

PLAYS FOR THE 21ST CENTURY
The Playwrights Theater; Box 803305; Dallas, TX 75380; (972) 980-7390,
FAX 980-7480; E-mail jackmarsh@earthlink.net
Jack Marshall, *Artistic Director*

Types of material: full-length plays. **Frequency:** annual. **Remuneration:** $1500;
reading. **Guidelines:** U.S. citizen; professionally unproduced play. **Submission
procedure:** completed application form, script, synopis, character breakdown, set
requirements and $15 fee. **Deadline:** 31 Jan 2000. **Notification:** 30 Jun 2000.

PLAYWRIGHTS FIRST AWARD
c/o The National Arts Club; 15 Gramercy Park S; New York, NY 10003;
(212) 249-6299

Types of material: full-length plays. **Frequency:** annual. **Remuneration:** $1000 for
best play; reading for selected plays; useful introductions to theatre professionals.
Guidelines: 1 unproduced play written within last 2 years (no translations,
adaptations or musicals). **Submission procedure:** script and resume. **Deadline:** 15
Oct 1999. **Notification:** May 2000.

QRL POETRY SERIES AWARDS
Quarterly Review of Literature; Princeton University; 26 Haslet Ave;
Princeton, NJ 08540
Renée Weiss, *Co-Editor*

Types of material: full-length plays, one-acts, translations. **Frequency:** annual.
Remuneration: $1000; publication in QRL Poetry Series; 100 complimentary
paperback copies. **Guidelines:** up to 6 awards a year for poetry and poetic drama
only; play 50–100 pages in length; send SASE for guidelines. **Submission
procedure:** submissions accepted in Nov and May only; must be accompanied by
$20 subscription for books published in series.

REVA SHINER FULL-LENGTH PLAY CONTEST
Bloomington Playwrights Project; 308 South Washington St;
Bloomington, IN 47401; (812) 334-1188;
E-mail bppwrite@bluemarble.net; Web http://www.newplays.org
John Edward Kinzer, *Artistic Director*

Types of material: full-length plays, musicals. **Frequency:** annual. **Remuneration:**
$500; staged reading; production. **Guidelines:** unpublished, unproduced work
75–150 minutes long, suitable for production in small 65-seat theatre; welcomes
innovative works; small-scale musicals; simple set; write or visit Web for guidelines.
Submission procedure: script, cover letter and $5 fee; include cassette for musical.
Deadline: 15 Jan 2000. **Notification:** Apr 2000.

ROBERT J. PICKERING AWARD FOR PLAYWRITING EXCELLENCE

Coldwater Community Theater; 89 Division St; Coldwater, MI 49036;
(517) 278-2389, FAX 279-8095
J. Richard Colbeck, *Award Chairman*

Types of material: full-length plays, one-acts, adaptations, plays for young audiences, musicals. **Frequency:** annual. **Remuneration:** $200; full production; room and board. **Guidelines:** unproduced play. **Submission procedure:** completed application form and script. **Deadline:** 31 Dec 1999. **Notification:** 15 Jan 2000.

THE ROY BARKER PLAYWRIGHTING PRIZE

The Rocky Mountain Student Theater Project; Box 1626; Telluride, CO 81435;
(970) 728-4052; E-mail playfest@aol.com;
Web http://members.aol.com/PlayFest/RMSTP.html
Owen Perkins, *Executive Director*

Types of material: full-length plays, one-acts, translations, adaptations, plays for young audiences, musicals, solo pieces. **Frequency:** annual. **Remuneration:** $500 1st prize, full production, travel and housing; $250 2nd prize, full production; $100 3rd prize, full production. **Guidelines:** plays by high school students only; prefers one-act plays 30–45 minutes long. **Submission procedure:** script without author's name and address, cover letter and $5 fee. **Deadline:** 1 May 2000. **Notification:** 1 Jun 2000. (See The Rocky Mountain Playwriting Festival in Production.)

SCHOLASTIC WRITING AWARDS

555 Broadway; New York, NY 10012; (212) 343-6892, FAX 343-4885
Writing Awards Coordinator

Types of material: 2 categories: for high school seniors only, portfolios of 3–8 pieces (fiction, poetry, drama, etc.); for students grades 7–12, individual pieces in various categories, including drama (stage, film, television and radio scripts). **Frequency:** annual. **Remuneration:** $5000 scholarship toward college tuition for author of each of 5 best senior portfolios; $1000 merit award, to be applied toward tuition for New York University's Tisch School of the Arts dramatic writing program, for best work in any category by high school senior; cash prizes totaling $175,000 awarded to several top students in each category, including dramatic writing. **Guidelines:** portfolio totaling not more than 50 pages; for dramatic category, unpublished script not more than 30 minutes long; write for further information by 1 Sep 1999. **Submission procedure:** completed application and manuscript. **Deadline:** varies from state to state; many in mid-Jan 2000; exact date TBA. **Notification:** May 2000.

SHORT GRAIN CONTEST

Grain Magazine; Box 1154; Regina, SK S4P 3B4; Canada; (306) 244-2828,
FAX 244-0255; E-mail grain.mag@sk.sympatico.ca;
Web http://www.skwriter.com
Jennifer Still, *Business Manager*

Types of material: monologues. **Frequency:** annual. **Remuneration:** $400 1st prize, $250 2nd prize, $150 3rd prize (Canadian dollars); winners and honorable mentions receive payment for publication in magazine. **Guidelines:** unpublished, unproduced monologue not submitted elsewhere; 500-word maximum; write or E-mail for guidelines. **Submission procedure:** U.S. and international entries: entry form and $22 fee plus $4 U.S. postage for subscription mailing cost; Canadian entries: entry form and $22 fee for first 2 entries ($5 fee for each additional entry); fee includes 1-year subscription. **Deadline:** 31 Jan 2000. **Notification:** 30 Apr 2000.

SHUBERT FENDRICH MEMORIAL PLAYWRITING CONTEST

Pioneer Drama Service; Box 4267; Englewood, CO 80155-4267; (303) 779-4035,
FAX 779-4315; E-mail piodrama@aol.com;
Web http://www.pioneerdrama.com
Beth Somers, *Editor*

Types of material: full-length plays, one-acts, translations, adaptations, plays for young audiences, musicals. **Frequency:** annual. **Remuneration:** publication with $1000 advance on royalties (10% book royalty, 50% performance royalty). **Guidelines:** produced, unpublished work not more than 90 minutes long; subject matter and language appropriate for schools and community theatres; prefers works with a preponderance of female roles; minimal set requirements; all entries considered for publication; send SASE for guidelines. **Submission procedure:** script with proof of production (e.g., program, reviews); include score or cassette for musical. **Deadline:** 1 Mar 2000 (scripts received after deadline will be considered for 2001 contest). **Notification:** 1 Jun 2000. (See Pioneer Drama Service in Publication.)

SIENA COLLEGE INTERNATIONAL PLAYWRIGHTS COMPETITION

Department of Creative Arts; Siena College; 515 Loudon Rd;
Loudonville, NY 12211-1462; (518) 783-2381, FAX 783-4293;
E-mail maciag@siena.edu; Web http://www.siena.edu/theatre
Gary Maciag, *Director of Theatre*

Types of material: full-length plays. **Frequency:** biennial. **Remuneration:** $2000; production; maximum $1000 to cover residency expenses. **Guidelines:** playwright available for 6-week residency in Jan/Feb 2001; play that has had no previous workshop or full production; prefers play suitable for college audience and featuring characters suitable for college-age performers; prefers small cast and unit set or minimal set change. **Submission procedure:** send SASE for application form and guidelines after 1 Nov 1999; completed application and script. **Deadline:** 30 Jun 2000; no submission before 1 Feb 2000. **Notification:** 30 Sep 2000.

SOURCE THEATRE COMPANY 2000 LITERARY PRIZE

1835 14th St NW; Washington, DC 20009; (202) 462-1073
Keith Parker, *Literary Manager*

Types of material: full-length plays, one-acts, musicals, solo pieces. **Frequency:** annual. **Remuneration:** $250; workshop production in Washington Theatre Festival (see Source Theatre's entry in Production). **Guidelines:** work not produced professionally. **Submission procedure:** script, synopsis, resume and letter-size SASE for response; materials will not be returned. **Deadline:** 15 Jan 2000. **Notification:** 15 May 2000.

SOUTH FLORIDA WRITERS CONTEST

South Florida Chapter National Writers Association; Box 570415;
    Miami, FL 33257-0415; (305) 275-8666
Charles Aye, *President*

Types of material: full-length plays, one-acts. **Frequency:** annual. **Remuneration:** $300 1st prize, staged reading; $150 2nd prize, staged reading. **Guidelines:** unpublished, unproduced work. **Submission procedure:** script, cover letter and $12 fee; script will not be returned. **Deadline:** 15 Nov 1999. **Notification:** Feb 2000.

SOUTHEASTERN THEATRE CONFERENCE NEW PLAY PROJECT

Box 9868; Greensboro, NC 27429-0868; (336) 272-3645
Elizabeth Spicer, *Coordinator*

Types of material: full-length plays, collection of related one-acts. **Frequency:** annual. **Remuneration:** $1000; staged reading at SETC Annual Convention; travel, room and board to attend convention; submission of work by SETC to O'Neill Theater Center for favored consideration for National Playwrights Conference (see Development). **Guidelines:** resident of state in SETC region (AL, FL, GA, KY, MS, NC, SC, TN, VA, WV); unproduced work; collection of one-acts bound in 1 cover; limit of 1 full-length submission or collection of one-acts. **Submission procedure:** completed application and script. **Deadline:** 1 Jun 2000. **Notification:** Nov 2000.

SOUTHERN PLAYWRIGHTS COMPETITION

228 Stone Center; Jacksonville State University; Jacksonville, AL 36265;
    (256) 782-5411, FAX 782-5441; E-mail swhitton@jsucc.jsu.edu;
    Web http://www.jsu.edu/depart/english/southpla.htm
Steven J. Whitton, *Coordinator*

Types of material: full-length plays, solo pieces. **Frequency:** annual. **Remuneration:** $1000; production; housing to attend rehearsals. **Guidelines:** native or resident of AL, AR, FL, GA, KY, LA, MS, NC, SC, TN, TX, VA or WV; 1 unpublished, original submission that deals with the Southern experience and has not received Equity production; write for guidelines after Sep 1999. **Submission**

procedure: completed entry form, script and synopsis. **Deadline:** 15 Feb 2000. **Notification:** 1 May 2000.

THE STANLEY DRAMA AWARD

Wagner College Theatre; 1 Campus Rd; Staten Island, NY 10301;
    (718) 390-3325, FAX 390-3323; E-mail lterry@wagner.edu
Liz Terry, *Director*

Types of material: full-length plays, one-acts, plays for young audiences, musicals. **Frequency:** annual. **Remuneration:** $2000; production; travel to attend rehearsals and room and board during performances. **Guidelines:** unpublished, unproduced play or collection of one-acts; 1-submission limit. **Submission procedure:** completed application, script, cassette for musicals and $20 fee. **Deadline:** 1 Oct 1999. **Notification:** Mar 2000.

SUMMERFIELD G. ROBERTS AWARD

The Sons of the Republic of Texas; 1717 8th St; Bay City, TX 77414;
    (409) 245-6644, FAX 245-6644
Melinda Williams

Types of material: full-length plays. **Frequency:** annual. **Remuneration:** $2500 given to work from 1 of several genres, including playwriting. **Guidelines:** play about living in the Republic of Texas, completed during calendar year preceding deadline. **Submission procedure:** 5 copies of script; scripts will not be returned. **Deadline:** 15 Jan 2000. **Notification:** early Apr 2000.

THE SUSAN SMITH BLACKBURN PRIZE

3239 Avalon Place; Houston, TX 77019; (713) 308-2842, FAX 654-8184
Emilie S. Kilgore, *Board of Directors*

Types of material: full-length plays. **Frequency:** annual. **Remuneration:** $5000 1st prize plus signed Willem de Kooning print, made especially for Blackburn Prize; $2000 2nd prize; $500 to each of 8–10 other finalists. **Guidelines:** woman playwright of any nationality writing in English; unproduced play or play produced within one year of deadline; previous first-prize winners are not eligible. **Submission procedure:** no submission by playwright; professional artistic directors of specified theatres are invited to nominate play and submit 2 copies of script; playwright may bring script to attention of eligible nominator; send 55¢-postage SASE for guidelines and list of theatres eligible to nominate. **Deadline:** 20 Sep 1999. **Notification:** Jan 2000 for finalists; Feb 2000 for winners.

SWTA NATIONAL NEW PLAY CONTEST

Southwest Theatre Association, Inc.; University of Texas at Arlington;
    Theatre Arts Dept; 700 West 2nd St; Box 19103;
    Arlington, TX 76019-0103; (817) 272-3141, -5708;
    E-mail gaupp@exchange.uta.edu
    E-mail dmmaher@uta.edu
Andrew Gaupp and Dennis Maher, *New Plays Committee Co-Chairs*

Types of material: full-length plays, one-acts. **Frequency:** annual. **Remuneration:** $200 1st prize; reading at SWTA convention in Nov 2000; possible excerpt publication in SWTA journal, *Theatre Southwest.* **Guidelines:** U.S. resident; unproduced, unpublished play; 1-submission limit. **Submission procedure:** script, 1-page synopsis and $10 fee (check payable to SWTA); letter of recommendation helpful. **Deadline:** 15 Mar 2000.

TADA! ONE-ACT PLAYWRITING COMPETITION

(Formerly TADA! Spring Staged Reading Series/New Play Project)
120 West 28th St; New York, NY 10001; (212) 627-1732, FAX 243-6736;
    E-mail tada@tadatheater.com; Web http://www.tadatheater.com
John Foster, *Project Coordinator*

Types of material: one-acts for young audiences. **Frequency:** annual. **Remuneration:** 5 awards of $200 and staged reading. **Guidelines:** unproduced, unpublished one-act by professional or student playwright dealing with current teen topic; prefers plays not more than 1 hour long; no more than 3 adult characters, majority of roles must be for child actors; prefers works with human characters, as opposed to "animal" plays. **Submission procedure:** 2 copies of script and character breakdown. **Deadline:** 1 Aug 2000. **Notification:** 1 Feb 2001. **Dates:** spring 2001. (See entry in Production.)

TENNESSEE WILLIAMS/NEW ORLEANS LITERARY FESTIVAL
ONE-ACT PLAY COMPETITION

c/o Creative Writing Workshop; University of New Orleans; New Orleans, LA
    70148; (504) 581-1144, FAX 529-2430; E-mail twfest@gnofn.org

Types of material: one-acts. **Frequency:** annual. **Remuneration:** $1000; reading in spring 2000 festival; production in spring 2001 festival. **Guidelines:** unpublished play, not more than 1 hour long and not produced professionally. **Submission procedure:** script and $15 fee (check payable to Tennessee Williams Festival); script will not be returned; write for guidelines before submitting work. **Deadline:** 1 Dec 1999. **Dates:** 22–26 Mar 1999.

THEATRE CONSPIRACY ANNUAL NEW PLAY CONTEST
Theatre Conspiracy, Inc; 10091 McGregor Blvd; Ft. Myers, FL 33919;
(941) 936-3239
Bill Taylor, *Artistic Director*

Types of material: full-length plays. **Frequency:** annual. **Remuneration:** $500; production. **Guidelines:** play not previously produced; cast limit of 8; simple production demands. **Submission procedure:** script, 1-page synopsis, character breakdown, technical requirements, bio and $10 fee. **Deadline:** 14 Jan 2000. **Notification:** Apr 2000. **Dates:** late Jul–early Aug 2000.

THEATREFEST REGIONAL PLAYWRITING CONTEST
Montclair State University; Upper Montclair, NJ 07043; (973) 655-7496,
FAX 655-5335; Web http://www.montclair.edu
John Wooten, *Artistic Director*

Types of material: full-length plays. **Frequency:** annual. **Remuneration:** $500; full production; housing. **Guidelines:** playwright resident of CT, NJ or NY; unproduced, unpublished work exploring contemporary issues; experimental works; cast limit of 8. **Submission procedure:** 1–5 page synopsis, 5-page sample dialogue and SASE for response. **Deadline:** 1 Jan 2000. **Notification:** 1 Feb 2000.

THEODORE WARD PRIZE FOR AFRICAN-AMERICAN PLAYWRIGHTS
Columbia College Chicago Theater/Music Center; 72 East 11th St;
Chicago, IL 60605; (312) 344-6136, FAX 344-8077;
E-mail chigochuck@aol.com
Chuck Smith, *Facilitator*

Types of material: full-length plays, translations, adaptations, full-length solo pieces. **Frequency:** annual. **Remuneration:** $2000 1st prize, production, travel and housing to attend rehearsals; $500 2nd prize, staged reading; 3rd prize, staged reading at Goodman Theatre. **Guidelines:** African-American U.S. resident; 1 full-length submission not professionally produced; translations and adaptations of material in public domain only; write for guidelines. **Submission procedure:** script, short synopsis, production history and brief resume. **Deadline:** 1 Jul 2000; no submission before 1 Apr 2000. **Notification:** Nov 2000.

TOWNGATE THEATRE PLAYWRITING CONTEST
Oglebay Institute; Stifel Fine Arts Center; 1330 National Rd;
Wheeling, WV 26003, (304) 242-7700, FAX 242-7767

Types of material: full-length plays. **Frequency:** annual. **Remuneration:** $300; production; partial travel expenses. **Guidelines:** unproduced, unpublished play; no musicals; no submission limit. **Submission procedure:** script only. **Deadline:** 1 Jan 2000. **Notification:** 1 May 2000.

TOWSON UNIVERSITY PRIZE FOR LITERATURE
Towson University; Towson, MD 21252; (410) 830-2128
Dean, College of Liberal Arts

Types of material: book or book-length manuscript; all literary genres eligible, including plays. **Frequency:** annual. **Remuneration:** $1500. **Guidelines:** work published within 3 years prior to submission or scheduled for publication within the year; author no more than 40 years of age, MD resident for 3 years and at time prize awarded. **Submission procedure:** publisher or playwright submits completed application and 5 copies of work; write for guidelines. **Deadline:** 15 May 2000. **Notification:** 1 Dec 2000.

TRUSTUS PLAYWRIGHTS' FESTIVAL
(Formerly South Carolina Playwrights' Festival)
Trustus Theatre; Box 11721; Columbia, SC 29211-1721; (803) 254-9732,
 FAX 771-9153; E-mail Trustus88@aol.com; Web http://www.trustus.org
John Tuttle, *Literary Manager*

Types of material: full-length plays. **Frequency:** annual. **Remuneration:** $500 1st prize, full production with travel and housing to attend opening; $250 2nd prize, staged reading. **Guidelines:** professionally unproduced play; cast limit of 8; no musicals or plays for young audiences; send SASE for guidelines and application. **Submission procedure:** completed application, 2 copies of synopsis and resume. **Deadline:** 1 Mar 2000; no submission before 1 Jan 2000. **Notification:** 1 Jun 2000. (See entry in Production.)

UNICORN THEATRE NATIONAL PLAYWRIGHTS' AWARD
3828 Main St; Kansas City, MO 64111; (816) 531-7529, ext 18, FAX 531-0421
Herman Wilson, *Literary Assistant*

Types of material: full-length plays. **Frequency:** no set dates. **Remuneration:** $1000; production; possible travel and residency. **Guidelines:** unpublished play not produced professionally; special interest in social issues; contemporary (post-1950) themes and settings only; no musicals; cast limit of 10; 2-submission limit. **Submission procedure:** no scripts; send synopsis, at least 10 pages of dialogue, character breakdown, resume, cover letter and SASE for response. **Deadline:** ongoing. **Notification:** 4 weeks; 4–6 months if script is requested. (See entry in Production.)

UNIVERSITY OF LOUISVILLE GRAWEMEYER AWARD
FOR MUSIC COMPOSITION
Grawemeyer Music Award Committee; School of Music; University of Louisville;
 Louisville, KY 40292; (502) 852-6907, FAX 852-0520;
 E-mail grawemeyer@hotmail.com
Paul Brink, *Chair*

Types of material: works in major musical genres, including music-theatre works and operas. **Frequency:** annual. **Remuneration:** $150,000 (paid in 5 annual installments of $30,000). **Guidelines:** work premiered during previous 5 years; entry must be sponsored by professional music organization or individual; write for guidelines. **Submission procedure:** completed application, score, cassette, supporting materials and $40 fee submitted jointly by composer and sponsor. **Deadline:** 31 Jan 2000. **Notification:** TBA.

VERMONT PLAYWRIGHTS AWARD

The Valley Players; Box 441; Waitsfield, VT 05673-0441; (802) 496-3751
Jennifer Howard, *Coordinator*

Types of material: full-length plays. **Frequency:** annual. **Remuneration:** $1000; probable production. **Guidelines:** resident of ME, NH or VT; unproduced, unpublished play, suitable for community group, that has not won playwriting competition; moderate production demands; send SASE for guidelines. **Submission procedure:** completed entry form and 2 copies of script. **Deadline:** 1 Feb 2000.

VSA PLAYWRIGHT DISCOVERY PROGRAM

(Formerly Very Special Arts Playwright Discovery Program)
Education Office; The John F. Kennedy Center for the Performing Arts;
    Washington, DC 20566; (800) 933-8721 (voice), (202) 737-0645 (TTY),
    FAX (202) 737-0725; E-mail playwright@vsarts.org;
    Web http://www.vsarts.org
Elena Widder, *Program Manager, Program Development*

Types of material: one-acts. **Frequency:** annual. **Remuneration:** awards in 2 categories: $2500 for playwright 22 years of age or older, $500 for playwright 21 years of age or younger; professional production at Kennedy Center; travel, room and board to attend performance. **Guidelines:** play dealing with some aspect of disability by writer with a disability; write for guidelines. **Submission procedure:** 2 copies of script and short bio. **Deadline:** Apr 2000; exact date TBA.

WALDO M. AND GRACE C. BONDERMAN
IUPUI/IRT PLAYWRITING EVENT FOR YOUNG AUDIENCES

IUPUI University Theatre; 425 University Blvd, Suite 309;
    Indianapolis, IN 46202; (317) 274-2095, FAX 278-1025;
    E-mail dwebb@iupui.edu
Director, Bonderman Event

Types of material: plays for young audiences. **Frequency:** biennial. **Remuneration:** 4 prizes of $1000; 1 week of developmental work culminating in showcase reading at National Youth Theatre Playwriting Symposium; travel from within continental U.S. and housing during residency. **Guidelines:** writer must be available for weeklong developmental residency; unpublished play at least 45 minutes long with strong storyline, compelling characters and careful attention to language not previously produced by Equity company. **Submission procedure:** send SASE for entry form and guidelines. **Deadline:** 1 Sep 2000. **Notification:** Dec 2000. **Dates:** Apr–May 2001.

WAREHOUSE THEATRE COMPANY ONE-ACT COMPETITION

Stephens College; Columbia, MO 65215; (314) 876-7194
Artistic Director

Types of material: one-acts. **Frequency:** annual. **Remuneration:** $200; production as part of company's Evening of One-Acts. **Guidelines:** unpublished, unproduced script by undergraduate or graduate student; special interest in scripts by, for or about women; write for guidelines. **Submission procedure:** script and $10 fee. **Deadline:** 31 Dec 1999. **Notification:** 1 Feb 2000.

WE DON'T NEED NO STINKIN' DRAMAS

Mixed Blood Theatre Company; 1501 South 4th St; Minneapolis, MN 55454;
(612) 338-0937
David Kunz, *Script Czar*

Types of material: full-length comedies, musical comedies. **Frequency:** annual. **Remuneration:** $2000 if theatre chooses to produce play; $1000 if not. **Guidelines:** unproduced, unpublished work by U.S. citizen who has had at least 1 work produced or workshopped professionally or by educational institution; 2-submission limit (dual entries must be sent under separate cover); plays minimum 65 pages long about race issues, sports or with a political edge; write for guidelines. If interested in MBTC but not sure if work is suitable, send brief cover letter and 1-page-maximum synopsis to MBTC. **Submission procedure:** script; resume optional. **Deadline:** 1 Feb 2000. **Notification:** fall 2000. (See entry in Production.)

WEST COAST ENSEMBLE CONTESTS

Box 38728; Los Angeles, CA 90038; (310) 876-9337, FAX (323) 876-8916
Les Hanson, *Artistic Director*
(Also see entry in Production)

West Coast Ensemble Full-Length Play Competition

Types of material: full-length plays. **Frequency:** annual. **Remuneration:** $500; production; royalty on any performances beyond 8-week run. **Guidelines:** 1 submission not produced in southern CA; cast limit of 12. **Submission procedure:** script with SASE or SASP for acknowledgment of receipt. **Deadline:** 31 Dec 1999. **Notification:** within 6 months of deadline.

West Coast Ensemble Musical Stairs

Types of material: musical theatre works. **Frequency:** annual. **Remuneration:** $500; production; royalty on any performances beyond 8-week run. **Guidelines:** 1 unpublished musical submission not produced in southern CA; all genres and styles eligible, including pop, rock, country and western, etc.; cast limit of 12. **Submission procedure:** script, cassette of music (include score and lead sheets if available). **Deadline:** 30 Jun 2000. **Notification:** within 6 months of deadline.

WHITE BIRD PLAYWRITING CONTEST

White Bird Productions, Inc.; 27 Prospect Park SW; Brooklyn, NY 11215;
(718) 369-3308, FAX 369-3308
Kathryn Dickinson, *Artistic Director*
John Istel, *Literary Manager*

Types of material: full-length plays. **Frequency:** annual. **Remuneration:** $200; staged reading; possible travel to attend rehearsals. **Guidelines:** play with theme, plot and/or central idea that deals in a general or specific way with the environment; 2-submission limit. **Submission procedure:** script and resume. **Deadline:** 15 Feb 2000. **Notification:** Oct 2000.

WICHITA STATE UNIVERSITY PLAYWRITING CONTEST

University Theatre; Wichita State University; 1845 Fairmount;
Wichita, KS 67260-0153; (316) 978-3368, FAX 978-3951
Leroy Clark, *Contest Director*

Types of material: full-length plays, bills of related one-acts. **Frequency:** annual. **Remuneration:** production; expenses for playwright to attend production. **Guidelines:** unpublished, unproduced work at least 90 minutes long by student currently enrolled at U.S. college or university; no musicals or plays for young audiences; write for guidelines. **Submission procedure:** bound script with unbound cover sheet containing author's name, address and phone number (no author's name on script); send SASP for acknowlegment of receipt. **Deadline:** 15 Feb 2000. **Notification:** 15 Apr 2000.

WRITER'S DIGEST WRITING COMPETITION

1507 Dana Ave; Cincinnati, OH 45207-1005; (513) 531-2690, ext 328,
FAX 531-1843; E-mail competitions@fwpubs.com
Competition Coordinator

Types of materials: full-length plays, screenplays, teleplays. **Frequency:** annual. **Remuneration:** $1500 Grand Prize, expenses-paid trip to New York City to meet with editors and agents; $750 1st prize, $350 2nd prize, $250 3rd prize, each with $100 worth of Writer's Digest books; $100 4th prize with current *Writer's Market* and 1-year subscription to *Writer's Digest* magazine; $25 5th prize with current *Writer's Market* and 1-year subscription to *Writer's Digest* magazine. **Guidelines:** unproduced, unpublished work, not accepted by publisher or producer at time of submission; previous entries ineligible; send SASE for guidelines. **Submission procedure:** completed entry form, first 15 pages of script, 1-page synopsis, indication of projected market for work and $10 fee. **Deadline:** 30 May 2000. **Notification:** fall 2000.

YEAR-END-SERIES (Y.E.S.) NEW PLAY FESTIVAL
Department of Theatre; Northern Kentucky University; Highland Heights, KY
    41099; (606) 572-6362, FAX 572-6057; E-mail forman@nku.edu
Sandra Forman, *Project Director*

Types of material: full-length plays, adaptations, musicals. **Frequency:** biennial.
Remuneration: 4 awards of $400; production; travel and expenses to attend late
rehearsals and performance. **Guidelines:** unproduced work in which majority of
roles can be handled by students; small orchestra for musicals; 1-submission limit.
Submission procedure: completed application and script. **Deadline:** 31 Oct 2000.
Notification: Jan 2001. **Dates:** 15–25 Apr 2001.

YOUNG CONNECTICUT PLAYWRIGHTS FESTIVAL
Maxwell Anderson Playwrights Series; Box 671; West Redding, CT 06896;
    (203) 938-2770
Bruce Post, *Dramaturg*

Types of material: full-length plays, one-acts, musicals, translations, adaptations,
plays for young audiences, solo pieces. **Frequency:** annual. **Remuneration:** staged
reading in May festival; certificate. **Guidelines:** CT resident playwright age 12–19
only; script maximum 60 pages in length; send SASE for guidelines. **Submission
procedure:** bound, typed script with playwright's name, date of birth, home
address, phone number and name of school on title page. **Deadline:** 27 Mar 2000.
Notification: May 2000. **Dates:** May 2000.

YOUNG PLAYWRIGHTS FESTIVAL NATIONAL PLAYWRITING CONTEST
Young Playwrights Inc.; 321 West 44th St, Suite 906; New York, NY 10036;
    (212) 307-1140; E-mail writeaplay@aol.com;
    Web http://youngplaywrights.org
Sheri M. Goldhirsch, *Artistic Director*

Types of material: full-length plays, one-acts. **Frequency:** annual. **Remuneration:**
staged reading or production with royalty; travel and residency; 1-year Dramatists
Guild membership (see Membership and Service Organizations). **Guidelines:**
playwright 18 years of age or younger as of 1 Dec 1999; submissions from
playwrights of all backgrounds encouraged; write for guidelines. **Submission
procedure:** script with playwright's name, date of birth, home address and phone
number on title page. **Deadline:** 1 Dec 1999.

Publication

What is listed in this section?

Those who are primarily or exclusively play publishers and who consider work of unpublished writers. In addition, we list literary magazines and other small presses which have indicated they publish plays.

Online publishers and Web site zines that post new plays are increasing in number. We have included information on some sites in our Online Resources chapter, rather than here in Publications, since online publishing is such a new field with many questions regarding copyright and royalty issues.

How can I determine the best places to submit my play?

Think of these publishers as highly individual people looking for very particular kinds of material, which means you should find out as much as possible about their operations before submitting scripts. One of the best ways to do research is by contacting the Council of Literary Magazines and Presses: 154 Christopher St, Suite 3C; New York, NY 10014-2839; (212) 741-9110. Ask for *The 1999 Directory of Literary Magazines* ($13.00 paper, plus $3.00 for 1st-class postage and handling), a descriptive listing of hundreds of magazines, including many which say they publish plays. You may be able to look at copies of some of these in a local library or bookstore. Other leads may be found in the *1999–00 International Directory of Little Magazines and Small Presses* (Dustbooks; Box 100; Paradise, CA 95967; (530) 877-6110; $35.95 paper, $55.00 cloth, plus $6.00 shipping and handling). You can also write to individual publishers listed here and ask for style sheets, catalogs, sample copies, etc. Don't forget that when publishers say they accept unsolicited scripts, they *always* require you to enclose an SASE for return of the manuscript.

ALABAMA LITERARY REVIEW

272 Smith Hall; Troy State University; Troy, AL 36082; (334) 670-3971
FAX 670-3519
Ed Hicks, *Chief Editor*

Types of material: full-length plays, one-acts, translations, adaptations, solo pieces. **Remuneration:** 3 complimentary copies (more on request); $5–10 a page when funds are available. **Guidelines:** annual literary journal publishing 2–3 plays a year; plays less than 50 pages long, less than 30 pages preferred. **Submission procedure:** accepts unsolicited scripts. **Response time:** 2–3 months.

AMELIA MAGAZINE

329 "E" St; Bakersfield, CA 93304; (661) 323-4064, FAX 323-5326;
E-mail amelia@lightspeed.net
Frederick A. Raborg, Jr., *Editor*

Types of material: one-acts, including translations and solo pieces. **Remuneration:** $150 prize; 10 complimentary copies. **Guidelines:** winner of annual Frank McClure One-Act Play Award published in magazine; unpublished play maximum 45 minutes long. **Submission procedure:** submit script, including note of any productions, and $15 fee; sample copy $9.95. **Deadline:** 15 May 2000. **Notification:** 15 Sep 2000.

AMERICAN THEATRE

Theatre Communications Group; 355 Lexington Ave; New York, NY 10017-0217;
(212) 697-5230; E-mail atm@tcg.org; Web http://www.tcg.org
Jim O'Quinn, *Editor in Chief*

Types of material: full-length plays, one-acts, translations, adaptations, plays for young audiences; solo pieces. **Remuneration:** fee for one-time serial rights; 25 complimentary copies. **Guidelines:** national magazine publishing 5 plays a year; previously produced works from the contemporary world theatre. **Submission procedure:** no unsolicited scripts; submissions at magazine's request only. (See entry in Useful Publications; see Theatre Communications Group in Membership and Service Organizations and Fellowships and Grants.)

AMERICAN WRITING: A MAGAZINE

4343 Manayunk Ave; Philadelphia, PA 19128
Alexandra Grilikhes, *Editor*

Types of material: translations, solo pieces, short experimental theatre pieces, performance pieces, performance artists' in-process notes and diaries. **Remuneration:** 3 complimentary copies. **Guidelines:** biannual literary/arts journal publishing 1 or 2 theatrical works a year; seeks new writing that takes risks and explores new forms; special interest in works exploring themes of androgyny, "the voice of the loner," "artist as shaman," "myth in urban life"; 4000-word maximum. **Submission procedure:** accepts unsolicited scripts. **Response time:** 3–6 months.

ANCHORAGE PRESS

Box 8067; New Orleans, LA 70182; (504) 283-8868, FAX 866-0502
Orlin Corey, *Editor*

Types of material: works for young audiences, including full-length plays, one-acts, translations, adaptations and musicals. **Remuneration:** negotiated royalty. **Guidelines:** specialty house publishing quality works for young audiences only; works produced a minimum of 3 times. **Submission procedure:** accepts unsolicited scripts with proof of production. **Response time:** 2–3 months.

ARTE PÚBLICO PRESS

University of Houston; Houston, TX 77204-2090; (713) 743-2841, FAX 743-2847
Nicolás Kanellos, *Publisher*

Types of material: full-length plays, one-acts, adaptations, plays for young audiences, musicals. **Remuneration:** negotiated royalty; complimentary copies. **Guidelines:** unpublished works in English or Spanish by Hispanic writers only. **Submission procedure:** accepts unsolicited scripts. **Response time:** 6 months.

ASIAN PACIFIC AMERICAN JOURNAL

37 Saint Marks Pl, Suite B; New York, NY 10003-7801; (212) 228-6718,
     FAX 228-7718; E-mail aaww@panix.com;
     Web http://www.panix.com./~aaww
Editors

Types of material: one-acts. **Remuneration:** 2 complimentary copies. **Guidelines:** biannual literary journal publishing work by and/or of interest to Asian-Americans; plays maximum 4000 words. **Submission procedure:** accepts unsolicited scripts; send 2 copies of script. **Response time:** 3 months.

AUDREY SKIRBALL-KENIS PLAY COLLECTION
630 West 5th St; Los Angeles, CA 90071; (213) 228-7327, FAX 228-7339;
   Web http://www./ap/.org
Tom Harris, *Project Director*

Types of material: full-length plays, one-acts, translations, adaptations, plays for young audiences, musicals, solo pieces, performance-art texts. **Remuneration:** descriptive listing of work in Southern California Unpublished Plays Collection, catalog of plays housed in Central Library in downtown Los Angeles. **Guidelines:** unpublished and professionally produced plays in Southern California only. **Submission procedure:** accepts unsolicited scripts.

BAKER'S PLAYS
Box 699222; Quincy, MA 02269-699222; (617) 745-0805, FAX 745-9891;
   E-mail raypape@hotmail.com; Web http://www.bakersplays.com
Ray Pape, *Associate Editor*

Types of material: full-length plays, one-acts, plays for young audiences, musicals, chancel dramas. **Remuneration:** negotiated book and production royalty. **Guidelines:** prefers produced plays; prefers plays suitable for high school, community and regional theatres; "Plays from Young Authors" division features plays by high school playwrights. **Submission procedure:** accepts unsolicited scripts with resume; include press clippings if play has been produced. **Response time:** 2–6 months. **Special programs:** Baker's Plays High School Playwriting Contest (see Prizes).

THE BELLINGHAM REVIEW
The Signpost Press; Mail Stop 9053; Western Washington University;
   Bellingham, WA 98225; Web http://www.wwu.edu/~bhreview/
Robin Hemley, *Editor*

Types of material: one-acts, solo pieces. **Remuneration:** 1 complimentary copy; 1-year subscription. **Guidelines:** biannual small-press periodical featuring short plays, fiction, poetry and creative nonfiction; unpublished plays less than 10,000 words long. **Submission procedure:** accepts unsolicited scripts; submit 1 Oct–1 May only. **Response time:** 4 months.

BROADWAY PLAY PUBLISHING, INC.
56 East 81st St; New York, NY 10028-0202; (212) 772-8334, FAX 772-8358;
   E-mail BroadwayPl@aol.com; Web http://www.broadwayplaypubl.com

Types of material: full-length plays. **Remuneration:** 10% book royalty, 80% amateur royalty, 90% stock royalty; 10 complimentary copies. **Guidelines:** major interest is in original, innovative work by American playwrights; no historical or autobiographical plays. **Submission procedure:** no unsolicited scripts; letter of inquiry. **Response time:** 2 months letter; 4 months script.

CALLALOO

322 Bryan Hall; Department of English; University of Virginia;
    Charlottesville, VA 22903; (804) 924-6637, FAX 924-6472;
    E-mail callaloo@virginia.edu; Web http://muse.jhu.edu/journals/cal
Charles H. Rowell, *Editor*

Types of material: one-acts, including translations. **Remuneration:** complimentary copies and offprints. **Guidelines:** journal of African-American and African arts and letters published by Johns Hopkins University Press. **Submission procedure:** accepts unsolicited scripts. **Response time:** 6 months.

COLLAGES & BRICOLAGES

Box 360; Shippenville, PA 16254; E-mail cb@penn.com
Marie-José Fortis, *Editor*

Types of material: one-acts. **Remuneration:** 2 complimentary copies. **Guidelines:** annual journal of international writing publishing poetry, fiction, drama and criticism, including 1–5 plays a year; minimalist plays; avant-garde and feminist work; innovative plays less than 30 pages long; plays must relate to issue theme (1999 theme was Racial and Cultural Tensions); write or e-mail for 2000 theme. **Submission procedure:** accepts unsolicited scripts; no simultaneous submissions; submit 15 Aug–15 Dec only. **Response time:** 2 weeks–3 months.

CONFRONTATION

English Department; C.W. Post College of Long Island University;
    Greenvale, NY 11548; (516) 299-2391, FAX 299-2735;
    E-mail mtucker@eagle.liunet.edu
Martin Tucker, *Editor*

Types of material: one-acts. **Remuneration:** $15–75; 1 complimentary copy. **Guidelines:** general magazine for "literate" audience; unpublished plays. **Submission procedure:** accepts unsolicited scripts. **Response time:** 8–10 weeks.

CONTEMPORARY DRAMA SERVICE

Meriwether Publishing, Ltd; 885 Elkton Dr; Colorado Springs, CO 80907
    (719) 594-4422, FAX 594-9916
Theodore Zapel, *Executive Editor*

Types of material: one-acts, adaptations, plays for young audiences, musicals, readers' theatre, monologues. **Remuneration:** book royalties or payment for amateur and professional performance rights. **Guidelines:** publishes works suitable for teenage, high school and college market, as well as collections of scenes and practical books on theatre arts; prefers comedies; prefers produced works; special interest in adaptations. **Submission procedure:** accepts unsolicited scripts; send $2 for sample catalog and guidelines. **Response time:** 2 months.

DESCANT

Box 314, Station P; Toronto, Ontario; Canada M5S 2S8; (416) 593-2557
Michelle Maynes, *Managing Editor*

Types of material: full-length plays, one-acts, performance-art texts. **Remuneration:** $100 honorarium; 1 complimentary copy (40% discount on additional copies). **Guidelines:** quarterly literary magazine publishing an average of 2 plays a year; unpublished plays. **Submission procedure:** accepts unsolicited scripts. **Response time:** 6 months.

THE DRAMATIC PUBLISHING COMPANY

311 Washington St; Box 129; Woodstock, IL 60098; (815) 338-7170,
    FAX 338-8981; E-mail plays@dramaticpublishing.com;
    Web http://www.dramaticpublishing.com
Linda Habjan, *Editor*

Types of material: full-length plays, one-acts, translations, adaptations, plays for young audiences, musicals. **Remuneration:** standard royalty; 10 complimentary copies (33% discount on additional copies). **Guidelines:** works for professional, stock and amateur markets; at least 10 minutes long; prefers produced plays. **Submission procedure:** accepts unsolicited scripts. **Response time:** 4–8 months.

DRAMATICS MAGAZINE

2343 Auburn Ave; Cincinnati, OH 45219; (513) 421-3900, FAX 421-7077;
    E-mail dcorathers@etassoc.org
Don Corathers, *Editor*

Types of material: full-length plays, one-acts and solo pieces for young performers. **Remuneration:** payment for 1-time publication rights; complimentary copies. **Guidelines:** educational theatre magazine; plays suitable for high school production; prefers produced plays. **Submission procedure:** accepts unsolicited scripts. **Response time:** 2–3 months.

DRAMATISTS PLAY SERVICE

440 Park Ave South; New York, NY 10016; (212) 683-8960, FAX 213-1539;
    E-mail postmaster@dramatists.com;
    Web http://www.dramatists.com/dramatists
Stephen Sultan, *President*

Types of material: full-length plays, one-acts, translations, adaptations, plays for young audiences, musicals. **Remuneration:** possible advance against royalties; 10% book royalty, 80% amateur royalty, 90% stock royalty; 10 complimentary copies (40% discount on additional copies). **Guidelines:** works for stock and amateur market; prefers works produced in New York City. **Submission procedure:** no unsolicited scripts; letter of inquiry. **Response time:** 3–5 months letter; 2–4 months script.

ELDRIDGE PUBLISHING COMPANY

Box 1595; Venice, FL 34284-1595; (800) HI-STAGE; E-mail info@histage.com;
    Web http://www.histage.com
Nancy S. Vorhis, *Editor*

Types of material: full-length plays, one-acts, musicals. **Remuneration:** outright purchase of religious material only; all other works, 10% book royalty, 50% amateur and educational royalty; complimentary copies (50% discount on additional copies). **Guidelines:** publishes 50–75 plays and musicals a year for school, church and community theatre; comedies, mysteries or serious drama. **Submission procedure:** accepts unsolicited scripts; if possible, include cassette for musicals. **Response time:** 2 months.

ENCORE PERFORMANCE PUBLISHING

Box 692; Orem, UT 84057; (801) 225-0605
Michael C. Perry, *President*

Types of material: full-length plays, one-acts, translations, adaptations, plays for young audiences, musicals, solo pieces. **Remuneration:** 10% book royalty, 50% performance royalty; 10 complimentary copies (discount on additional copies). **Guidelines:** publishes 10–30 plays and musicals a year; works must have had a minimum of 2 amateur or professional productions; special interest in works with strong family or Judeo-Christian message and in Christmas, Halloween and other holiday plays. **Submission procedure:** no unsolicited scripts; synopsis, production information and letter of inquiry; best submission time May–Aug. **Response time:** 2–4 weeks letter; 2–3 months script.

FREELANCE PRESS

Box 548; Dover, MA 02030; (508) 785-8250, FAX 785-8291
Narcissa Campion, *Managing Editor*

Types of material: musicals. **Remuneration:** 10% book royalty, 70% performance royalty; 1 complimentary copy. **Guidelines:** unpublished issue-oriented musicals and musical adaptations of classics; approximately 1 hour long; suitable for performing by young people only. **Submission procedure:** accepts unsolicited scripts. **Response time:** 3 months.

HEUER PUBLISHING COMPANY

Box 248; Cedar Rapids, IA 52406; (319) 364-6311, FAX 364-1771;
    E-mail editor@hitplays.com; Web http://www.hitplays.com
C. Emmett McMullen, *Editor and Publisher*

Types of material: works for young audiences, including full-length plays, one-acts and musicals. **Remuneration:** outright purchase or performance royalty; complimentary copies. **Guidelines:** works suitable for middle school and junior and senior high school markets. **Submission procedure:** accepts unsolicited scripts. **Response time:** 1–2 months.

I. E. Clark Publications
Box 246; Schulenburg, TX 78956-0246; (409) 743-3232
Donna Cozzaglio, *Editorial Department*

Types of material: full-length plays, one-acts, translations, adaptations, plays for young audiences, musicals. **Remuneration:** book and performance royalties. **Guidelines:** publishes for worldwide professional, amateur and educational market; prefers produced works. **Submission procedure:** accepts unsolicited scripts; cassette or videotape must accompany musical; include proof of production with reviews and photos for produced works; send $3 for catalogue; send SASE for submission guidelines. **Response time:** 2–6 months.

International Readers' Theatre (IRT)
Publish-on-Demand Script Service
Blizzard Publishing; 73 Furby St; Winnipeg; Canada MB R3C 2A2
(204) 775-2923, (800) 694-9256, FAX (204) 775-2947;
E-mail irt@blizzard.mb.ca; Web http://www.blizzard.mb.ca/catalog
David Fuller, *Production Coordinator*

Types of material: full-length plays, one-acts, plays for young audiences, monologues. **Remuneration:** 10% book royalty. **Guidelines:** publishes more than sixty plays a year in chapbook format; submissions also considered for Blizzard Publishing trade paperback publishing program; work must have been previously produced; write for submission guidelines and forms. **Submission procedure:** accepts unsolicited scripts with submission forms and SASE for response. **Response time:** 4–6 months.

Kalliope, a Journal of Women's Literature & Art
Florida Community College; 3939 Roosevelt Blvd; Jacksonville, FL 32205
Mary Sue Koeppel, *Editor*

Types of material: one-acts, including solo pieces. **Remuneration:** 3 complimentary copies or free 1-year subscription. **Guidelines:** triannual journal of women's art publishing short fiction, poetry, artwork, photography, interviews, reviews and an average of 1 play a year; unpublished plays, less than 25 pages long, by women only; "no trite themes or erotica." **Submission procedure:** accepts unsolicited scripts. **Response time:** 3–6 months.

The Kenyon Review
Kenyon College; Gambier, OH 43022; (740) 427-5202, FAX 427-5417;
E-mail kenyonreview@kenyon.edu; Web http://www.kenyonreview.com
David H. Lynn, *Editor*

Types of material: one-acts, solo pieces, excerpts from full-length plays. **Remuneration:** cash payment; 2 complimentary copies. **Guidelines:** literary journal publishing an average of 2 plays a year; unproduced, unpublished works maximum 30 pages long. **Submission procedure:** no submissions until Oct 2000.

KIMBALL & MORASKE LTD./K & M MUSICALS
88 Sherwood Place; Greenwich, CT 06830; (203) 661-4325
Dan Moraske, *Co-President*

Types of material: full-length plays, one-acts, adaptations, plays for young audiences, musicals. **Remuneration:** royalty; 1 complimentary copy (additional copies available at discount). **Guidelines:** publishes 30–60 plays a year; special interest in educational theatre and musicals suitable for intermediate and high schools. **Submission procedure:** no unsolicited scripts; synopsis and letter of inquiry with $5 fee. **Response time:** 2 weeks.

LAMIA INK!
Box 202; Prince St Station; New York, NY 10012
Cortland Jessup, *Editor*

Types of material: very short monologues and performance pieces; 1-page plays for contest (see below). **Remuneration:** 4 complimentary copies. **Guidelines:** biannual "art rag" magazine; experimental theatre pieces maximum 5 pages long, prefers 2–3 pages; special interest in Japanese, Pacific Rim and Native American writers, and poets' theatre, performance poems, theatre manifestos and essays. **Submission procedure:** accepts unsolicited scripts with SASE for response. **Response time:** 2–3 weeks minimum. **Special programs:** Lamia Ink! International One-Page Play Competition (see Prizes).

LILLENAS DRAMA RESOURCES
Lillenas Publishing Company; Box 419527; Kansas City, MO 64141;
(816) 931-1900, (800) 877-0700, FAX 412-8390
Kimberly R. Messer, *Consultant/Editor*

Types of material: full-length plays, one-acts, musicals, collections of sketches, playlets, recitations. **Remuneration:** outright purchase or royalty. **Guidelines:** unpublished "creatively conceived and practically producible scripts and outlines that provide church and school with an opportunity to glorify God and his creation in drama." **Submission procedure:** accepts unsolicited scripts; send SASE for guidelines and current need letter. **Response time:** 3 months.

NEW PLAYS
Box 5074; Charlottesville, VA 22905; (804) 979-2777, FAX 984-2230;
E-mail patwhitton@aol.com; Web http://www.newplaysforchildren.com
Patricia Whitton, *Publisher*

Types of material: plays for young audiences. **Remuneration:** 10% book royalty, 50% performance royalty. **Guidelines:** innovative material not duplicated by other sources of plays for young audiences; produced plays, directed by someone other than author. **Submission procedure:** accepts unsolicited scripts. **Response time:** 1–2 months minimum.

PACIFIC REVIEW

English Department; California State University; 5500 University Pkwy;
　　San Bernardino, CA 92407-2397; (909) 880-5894
James Brown and Juan Delgado, *Faculty Editors*

Types of material: one-acts, including solo pieces. **Remuneration:** 2 complimentary copies. **Guidelines:** annual literary journal; plays maximum 25 pages long. **Submission procedure:** accepts unsolicited scripts; 2-submission limit; submit 1 Sep–1 Feb only. **Response time:** 3 months.

PAJ BOOKS

Box 260; Village Station; New York, NY 10014-0260; (212) 243-3885,
　　FAX 243-3885; E-mail pajpub@aol.com
Bonnie Marranca and Gautam Dasgupta, *Editors*

Types of material: full-length plays, one-acts, translations, solo pieces. **Remuneration:** royalty and/or fee. **Guidelines:** contemporary plays and critical literature on international performance, drama, video, music and film published by Johns Hopkins University Press; special interest in translations. **Submission procedure:** no unsolicited scripts; synopsis and letter of inquiry. **Response time:** 1–2 months letter; 1–2 months script.

PERFORMING ARTS JOURNAL

Box 260; Village Station; New York, NY 10014-0260; (212) 243-3885,
　　FAX 243-3885; E-mail pajpub@aol.com
Bonnie Marranca and Gautam Dasgupta, *Co-Publishers and Editors*

Types of material: short full-length plays, one-acts, translations, solo pieces. **Remuneration:** fee. **Guidelines:** publishes plays and critical essays on international performance, drama, video, music, film and photography; special interest in translations; plays less than 40 pages long. **Submission procedure:** no unsolicited scripts; synopsis and letter of inquiry. **Response time:** 1–2 months letter; 1–2 months script.

PIONEER DRAMA SERVICE

Box 4267; Englewood, CO 80155-4267; (303) 779-4035, FAX 779-4315;
　　E-mail piodrama@aol.com; Web http://www.pioneerdrama.com

Types of material: full-length plays, one-acts, plays for young audiences, musicals. **Remuneration:** royalty. **Guidelines:** produced work suitable for educational theatre, including melodramas and Christmas plays. **Submission procedure:** accepts unsolicited scripts; prefers synopsis and letter of inquiry. **Response time:** 2 weeks letter; 3–4 months script. **Special programs:** Shubert Fendrich Memorial Playwriting Contest (see Prizes).

PLAYERS PRESS

Box 1132; Studio City, CA 91614-0132; (818) 789-4980
Robert W. Gordon, *Senior Editor*

Types of material: full-length plays, one-acts, translations, adaptations, plays for young audiences, musicals, solo pieces, monologues, scenes, teleplays, screenplays. **Remuneration:** cash option and/or outright purchase or royalty; complimentary copies (additional copies at 20% discount). **Guidelines:** theatre press publishing technical and reference books and scripts; produced works for professional, amateur and educational markets. **Submission procedure:** accepts unsolicited scripts with proof of production, resume and 2 business-size SASEs; prefers synopsis, proof of production, resume and letter of inquiry with SASE for response. **Response time:** 1–6 weeks letter; 1–6 months script.

PLAYS ON TAPE

Box 5789; Bend, OR 97708-5789; (541) 923-6246, FAX 923-9679;
    E-mail theatre@playsontape.com; Web http://www.playsontape.com
Silvia Gonzalez S., *Literary Manager*

Types of material: full-length plays, one-acts, adaptations. **Remuneration:** negotiable fee and royalty; 10 complimentary copies of audiotape or CD. **Guidelines:** audiobook company marketing primarily to theatre gift bookstores; "works that do not diminish in quality due to restrictions of audiotape" only; special interest in works by women and minorities; maximum 74 minutes for adaptations. **Submission procedure:** accepts unsolicited scripts; prefers synopsis, letter of inquiry and up to 10 pages of dialogue with SASE or e-mail address for response; accepts scripts and synopses via e-mail; send SASE for guidelines. **Response time:** 3 months letter; 5–6 months script.

PLAYS, THE DRAMA MAGAZINE FOR YOUNG PEOPLE

120 Boylston St; Boston, MA 02116-4615; (617) 423-3157,
    FAX (no submissions) 423-2168; E-mail writer@user1.channel1.com;
    Web http://www.channel1.com/plays
Elizabeth Preston, *Managing Editor*

Types of material: one-act plays for young audiences, including adaptations of material in the public domain. **Remuneration:** payment on acceptance. **Guidelines:** publishes 70 plays and programs a year; prefers work 20–30 minutes long for junior and senior high school, 15–20 minutes for middle grades, 8–15 minutes for lower grades; no religious plays. **Submission procedure:** accepts unsolicited original scripts; letter of inquiry for adaptations; prefers format used in magazine (send SASE for style sheet). **Response time:** 1 week letter; 2–3 weeks script.

POEMS & PLAYS

English Department; Middle Tennessee State University; Murfreesboro, TN 37132;
(615) 898-2712, FAX 898-5098;
Web http://www.mtsu.edu/~english/poemplay.html
Gaylord Brewer, *Editor*

Types of material: one-acts and short plays, including solo pieces. **Remuneration:** 1 complimentary copy. **Guidelines:** annual magazine of poetry and short plays published Apr, includes an average of 2–3 plays in each issue; unpublished works; prefers produced works not more than 10–12 pages long. **Submission procedure:** accepts unsolicited scripts 1 Oct–15 Jan only; sample issue $6. **Response time:** 1–2 months. **Special programs:** Tennessee Chapbook Prize: annual award for either a one-act play or collection of short plays, maximum manuscript length 24–30 pages; winning script published as interior chapbook in magazine; playwright receives 50 complimentary copies; submit script and $10 for reading fee and copy of next issue; *deadline:* 15 Jan 2000; no submissions before 1 Oct 1999.

PRISM INTERNATIONAL

Creative Writing Program; University of British Columbia;
Buch E462–1866 Main Mall; Vancouver, BC; Canada V6T 1Z1;
(604) 822-2514, FAX 822-3616; E-mail prism@interchange.ubc.ca;
Web http://www.arts.ubc.ca/prism
Jennica Harper and Kiera Miller, *Co-Editors*

Types of material: one-acts (including translations and solo pieces), excerpts from full-length plays. **Remuneration:** $20–30 per printed page; 1-year subscription. **Guidelines:** quarterly literary magazine; unpublished plays, maximum 40 pages long; send SASE for guidelines. **Submission procedure:** accepts unsolicited scripts, include copy or original with translations. **Response time:** 3–6 months. **Special programs:** Page to the Stage: forthcoming 2000 playwriting award; call for guidelines.

PROVINCETOWN ARTS/PROVINCETOWN ARTS PRESS

650 Commercial St; Provincetown, MA 02657; (508) 487-3167, FAX 487-8634;
E-mail press@capecodaccess.com
Christopher Busa, *Founder and Director*

Types of material: one-acts, translations, solo pieces, performance-art texts. **Remuneration:** $50–100; 2 complimentary copies. **Guidelines:** annual magazine focuses broadly on artists and writers who inhabit or visit the tip of Cape Cod, publishes an average of 1 play a year; also small press publishing 1 play or collection of plays a year; unpublished plays not more than 30 pages long; especially interested in performance-art texts. **Submission procedure:** accepts unsolicited scripts; submissions read Sep–Mar. **Response time:** 6 months.

RAG MAG

Box 12; Goodhue, MN 55027; (612) 923-4590
Beverly Voldseth, *Editor and Publisher*

Types of material: full-length plays, one-acts, solo pieces. **Remuneration:** 1 complimentary copy. **Guidelines:** biannual small-press literary magazine publishing artwork, prose and poetry, with interest in innovative character plays; prefers short one-acts but will consider longer plays with a view to publishing extracts or scenes. **Submission procedure:** accepts unsolicited short one-acts; send maximum 10-page sample, bio and letter of inquiry for longer plays; send SASE for guidelines. **Response time:** 1–2 months.

RESOURCE PUBLICATIONS, INC.

160 East Virginia St, #290; San Jose, CA 95112-5848; (408) 286-8505,
   FAX 287-8748; E-mail Kguentert@rpinet.com;
   Web http://www.rpinet.com
Ken Guentert, *Editor*

Types of material: plays 7–15 minutes long. **Remuneration:** royalty. **Guidelines:** collection of skits suitable for middle school or high school students. **Submission procedure:** accepts unsolicited scripts. **Response time:** 2 months.

ROCKFORD REVIEW

Box 858; Rockford, IL 61105; E-mail dragonldy@prodigy.net;
   Web http://members.tripod.com/~rwguild
David Ross, *Editor*

Types of material: one-acts, including solo pieces. **Remuneration:** one-acts selected for publication eligible for quarterly "Editor's Choice" prize of $25 (winner invited to reading and reception as guest of honor in Jun); 1 complimentary copy. **Guidelines:** quarterly journal publishing poetry, fiction, satire, artwork and an average of 4–5 plays a year; one-acts not more than 10 pages long, preferably of a satirical nature; interested in work that provides new insight into the human dilemma ("to cope or not to cope"). **Submission procedure:** accepts unsolicited scripts; sample copy $5. **Response time:** 1–2 months.

SAMUEL FRENCH

45 West 25th St; New York, NY 10010-2751; (212) 206-8990, FAX 206-1429
Lawrence Harbison, *Editor*

Types of material: full-length plays, one-acts, plays for young audiences, musicals, solo pieces. **Remuneration:** 10% book royalty; 10 complimentary copies (40% discount on additional copies). **Guidelines:** "Many of our publications have never been produced in New York; these are generally comprised of light comedies, mysteries, mystery-comedies, a handful of one-acts and plays for young audiences, and plays with a preponderance of female roles; however, do not hesitate to send in your future Pulitzer Prize Winner." **Submission procedure:** accepts unsolicited scripts. **Response time:** 2–4 months minimum.

SCRIPTS AND SCRIBBLES
141 Wooster St; New York, NY 10012-3163; (212) 473-6695, FAX 473-6695
Daryl Chin, *Consulting Editor*

Types of material: full-length plays, one-acts, solo pieces, performance-art texts or scenarios. **Remuneration:** 25 complimentary copies. **Guidelines:** series initiated to publish texts for nontraditional theatre work and works produced outside New York City. **Submission procedure:** no unsolicited scripts; synopsis and letter of inquiry. **Response time:** 1 month letter; 6 months script.

SINISTER WISDOM
Box 3252; Berkeley, CA 94703; E-mail sinister@serious.com
Margo Mercedes Rivera, *Editor*

Types of material: one-acts, excerpts from full-length plays (3000 words maximum). **Remuneration:** 2 complimentary copies. **Guidelines:** lesbian quarterly of art and literature; works by lesbians reflecting the diversity of lesbians; no heterosexual themes; send SASE for current themes. **Submission procedure:** accepts unsolicited scripts. **Response time:** 2–9 months.

SMITH AND KRAUS
Box 127; Lyme, NH 03768; (603) 643-6431, FAX 643-1831;
    E-mail sandk@sover.net
Marisa Smith, *President*

Types of material: full-length plays, one-acts, translations, adaptations, plays for young audiences, solo pieces, monologues. **Remuneration:** usually fee or royalty; at least 10 complimentary copies. **Guidelines:** theatre press publishing works of interest to theatrical community, especially to actors, including collections of monologues and an average of 50 full-length plays a year. **Submission procedure:** no unsolicited scripts; synopsis and letter of inquiry. **Response time:** 2–3 weeks letter; 2–4 months script.

SUN & MOON PRESS
6026 Wilshire Blvd; Los Angeles, CA 90036; (323) 857-1115;
    E-mail djmess@sunmoon.com; Web www.sunmoon.com
American Theater and Literature Program (ATL)

Types of material: full-length plays, one-acts, translations. **Remuneration:** royalty; 10 complimentary copies. **Guidelines:** press publishing average of 10 single-play volumes a year; unpublished plays. **Submission procedure:** accepts unsolicited scripts. **Response time:** 2–6 months.

THEATER

222 York St; New Haven, CT 06520; (203) 432-1568, FAX 432-8336;
   E-mail theater.magazine@yale.edu;
   Web http://www.yale.edu/drama/publications/theater
Erika Munk, *Editor*

Types of material: full-length plays, one-acts, translations, adaptations, solo pieces. **Remuneration:** maximum fee of $150; complimentary copies. **Guidelines:** triannual theatre journal publishing an average of 2 plays in each issue; special interest in experimental, innovative work; "no standard psychological realism or TV-script clones." **Submission procedure:** accepts unsolicited scripts with resume. **Response time:** 3–6 months.

THEATREFORUM

Theatre & Dance Department 0344; University of California–San Diego;
   9500 Gilman Dr; La Jolla, CA 92093-0344; (619) 534-6598,
   FAX 534-1080; E-mail TheatreForum@ucsd.edu;
   Web http://www-theatre.ucsd.edu/TF/
Jim Carmody, Adele Edling Shank and Theodore Shank, *Editors*

Types of material: full-length plays, translations, adaptations. **Remuneration:** $200; 10 complimentary copies; discount for additional copies. **Guidelines:** biannual international journal focusing on innovative work, publishing 2 scripts in each issue, plus articles, interviews and photographs; professionally produced, unpublished plays. **Submission procedure:** no unsolicited scripts; professional recommendation. **Response time:** 3 months.

THIS MONTH ON STAGE

Box 62; Hewlett, NY 11557-0062; (800) 536-0099; E-mail tmosmail@aol.com
Editorial Department

Types of material: full-length plays, one-acts, translations, adaptations, libretti, solo pieces. **Remuneration:** $1; 2 complimentary copies. **Guidelines:** monthly theatre magazine; special interest in short plays and one-acts; accepted scripts must be available in electronic form. **Submission procedure:** accepts unsolicited scripts with resume, cover letter and SASE for response; send SASE for guidelines. **Response time:** 12–18 months.

UBU REPERTORY THEATER PUBLICATIONS

See Membership and Service Organizations.

UNITED ARTS

141 Wooster St; New York, NY 10012-3163; (212) 473-6695, FAX 473-6695
Daryl Chin, *Editor*

Types of material: one-acts, translations, solo pieces, performance-art texts, scenarios, manifestos. **Remuneration:** complimentary copies. **Guidelines:** journal of analysis and opinion covering visual arts, film, video, theatre and dance, published 3–4 times a year by University Arts Resources; nontraditional, avant-garde plays. **Submission procedure:** accepts unsolicited scripts; prefers synopsis and letter of inquiry. **Response time:** 1 month letter; 6 months script.

Development

What's in this section?

Conferences, festivals, workshops and programs whose primary purpose is to develop plays and playwrights. Also listed are some playwright groups and membership organizations whose main activity is play development. Developmental organizations such as New Dramatists whose many programs cannot be adequately described in the brief format used in this section are listed in Membership and Service Organizations. Some programs listed in Prizes also include a developmental element. Note: Some programs provide writers with stipends or living situations, etc. Others require a small fee. Read the "financial arrangement" section carefully.

How can I get into these programs?

Keep applying to those for which you are convinced your work is suited. If you're turned down one year, you may be accepted the next on the strength of your latest piece. If you're required to submit a script with your application, don't forget your SASE!

ABINGDON THEATRE COMPANY
432 West 42nd St, 4th Floor; New York, NY 10036; (212) 736-6604,
FAX 736-6608; E-mail atcnyc@aol.com; Web http://www.abingdon-nyc.org
Cynthia Ohanian, *Literary Manager*

Open to: playwrights. **Description:** year-round workshop for approximately 8 writers; biweekly in-house readings; 10 plays receive 12 hours of rehearsal and staged readings; of those, 4 plays selected for workshop production; of those, 2 plays selected for mainstage production. **Financial arrangement:** stipend for workshops and mainstage production. **Guidelines:** play unproduced in New York. **Application procedure:** script only. **Deadline:** ongoing. **Notification:** 6 months. **Dates:** year-round.

ACT/HEDGEBROOK WOMEN PLAYWRIGHTS FESTIVAL
A Contemporary Theatre; The Eagles Building, 700 Union St;
Seattle, WA 98101-2330; (206) 292-7660, FAX 292-7670;
Web http://www.acttheatre.org
Gordon Edelstein, *Artistic Director*

Open to: playwrights. **Description:** 6 playwrights chosen for reading of play with audience feedback; playwright then goes to Hedgebrook (see Colonies) for a week to work on any revisions that come out of reading. **Financial arrangement:** $500 stipend, travel and lodging. **Guidelines:** woman playwright; unproduced play. **Application procedure:** professional nomination only; theatre panel selects finalists. **Deadline:** fall 1999. **Notification:** Feb 2000. **Dates:** May 2000. (See A Contemporary Theatre in Production.)

ALCAZAR SCRIPTS IN PROGRESS
650 Geary St; San Francisco, CA 94102; (415) 441-6655, FAX 441-9567
Alan Ramos, *Script Supervisor*

Open to: playwrights, composers, solo performers, screenwriters. **Description:** 1 play developed through 3-month process, including 2 staged readings; possible full production with 4 weeks of rehearsal. **Financial arrangement:** room and board; royalties, if produced. **Guidelines:** unproduced play. **Application procedure:** synopsis, sample dialogue and letter of inquiry with SASE for response. **Deadline:** 31 Dec 1999. **Notification:** 31 Mar 2000. **Dates:** Jun–Sep 2000.

ANNUAL BACKDOOR THEATRE NEW PLAY PROJECT
Wichita Falls Backdoor Players, Inc; Box 896; Wichita Falls, TX 76307;
(940) 322-5000, FAX 322-8167; E-mail backdoor@wf.net
Gare Brundidge, *Artistic Director*

Open to: playwrights. **Description:** 1 play each Sep receives five weeks of rehearsal and workshop production with a minimum of 6 performances. **Financial arrangement:** $500 honorarium; travel and housing. **Guidelines:** special interest in playwrights from Texas and surrounding region; full-length plays which have not received professional production. **Application procedure:** script, brief synopsis, resume and SASP for acknowledgment of receipt. **Deadline:** 15 Mar 2000. **Notification:** Jul 2000. **Dates:** Sep 2000.

ASCAP MUSICAL THEATRE WORKSHOP
1 Lincoln Plaza; New York, NY 10023; (212) 621-6234
Michael A. Kerker, *Director of Musical Theatre*

Open to: composers, lyricists. **Description:** 10-session workshop under the direction of Stephen Schwartz; works presented to panels of musical theatre professionals. **Financial arrangement:** $500 Bernice Cohen Musical Theatre Fund Award given to most promising participating individual or team. **Guidelines:** write for guidelines and dates. **Application procedure:** resume and cassette of 4 theatrical songs (no pop songs). **Deadline:** exact date TBA (15 Mar in 1999). **Notification:** exact date TBA. **Dates:** exact dates TBA.

ASHLAND NEW PLAYS FESTIVAL
ArtWork Enterprises, Inc.; Box 453; Ashland, OR 97520; (541) 858-7164

Open to: playwrights. **Description:** up to 6 new works given 16–20 hours of rehearsal with actors, director and dramaturg, culminating in 2 public readings. **Financial arrangement:** $500 stipend; travel (within Ashland only) and housing. **Guidelines:** U.S. resident; previously unproduced full-length play; cast limit of 8; 1-submission limit. **Application procedure:** script and double-spaced, 1-page maximum synopsis. **Deadline:** 15 Mar 2000. **Notification:** 1 Aug 2000. **Dates:** Oct 2000.

ASIAN AMERICAN THEATER COMPANY EMERGING ARTISTS PROJECT
1840 Sutter St, Suite 207; San Francisco, CA 94115; (415) 440-5545,
    FAX 440-5597; E-mail aatc@wenet.net; Web http://www.wenet.net/~aatc
Pamela A. Wu, *Producing Director*

Open to: playwrights. **Description:** developmental workshop for 2–4 plays, leading to staged reading or production; plays not selected for workshop considered for inclusion in series of 8–10 readings presented each season. **Financial arrangement:** free. **Guidelines:** American playwright of Asian-Pacific descent writing in English; prefers plays depicting Asian-Pacific–American perspective. **Application procedure:** script, synopsis and character breakdown. **Deadline:** ongoing. **Notification:** 1–6 months. **Dates:** exact dates TBA.

A.S.K. THEATER PROJECTS
11845 West Olympic Blvd, Suite 1250 West; Los Angeles, CA 90064;
    (310) 478-3200, FAX 478-5300; E-mail askplay@primenet.com;
    Web http://www.askplay.org
Mead K. Hunter, *Director of Literary Programs*

Open to: playwrights. **Description:** approximately 15 playwrights either receive public rehearsed reading of play or participate in private writer's retreat; 2–3 plays receive workshop production. **Financial arrangement:** playwright receives

$150 for rehearsed reading, $500 for retreat participation, $1000 for workshop production. **Guidelines:** full-length play-in-progress not produced or scheduled for production. **Application procedure:** script submissions accepted only from agents or by professional recommendation; playwrights may submit sample pages and resume. **Deadline:** ongoing. **Notification:** 4–6 months. (See entry in Membership and Service Organizations.)

BALTIMORE PLAYWRIGHTS FESTIVAL
251 South Ann St; Baltimore, MD 21231; (410) 276-2153
Rodney Bonds, *President*

Open to: playwrights, composers, librettists, lyricists. **Description:** selected plays receive 3–5 developmental readings Sep–Mar; from these, participating theatres choose scripts for full production in summer festival. **Financial arrangement:** $100 honorarium for produced scripts. **Guidelines:** past or current resident of MD; unproduced play. **Application procedure:** 3 copies of script and letter of inquiry with $5 fee; send SASE for guidelines. **Deadline:** 30 Sep 1999. **Notification:** 15 Apr 2000. **Dates:** summer 2000.

BAY AREA PLAYWRIGHTS FESTIVAL
The Playwrights Foundation; Box 460357; San Francisco, CA 94106;
   (415) 263-3986; E-mail playwrights_fdn@hotmail.com
Jayne Wenger, *Artistic Director*

Open to: playwrights. **Description:** 6–9 scripts given dramaturgical attention and 2 rehearsed readings separated by 5–6 days for rewrites during 2-week festival; mandatory prefestival weekend retreat for initial brainstorming with directors and dramaturgs. **Financial arrangement:** small stipend, travel. **Guidelines:** unproduced full-length play only. **Application procedure:** script and resume. **Deadline:** 15 Feb 2000. **Notification:** Jun 2000. **Dates:** prefestival weekend Aug 2000; festival Sep or Oct 2000. (See The Playwrights Foundation in Membership and Service Organizations.)

BMI–LEHMAN ENGEL MUSICAL THEATRE WORKSHOP
Broadcast Music, Inc.; 320 West 57th St; New York, NY 10019; (212) 830-2508,
   FAX 262-2824; E-mail jbanks@bmi.com
Jean Banks, *Senior Director, Musical Theatre*

Open to: composers, librettists, lyricists. **Description:** 2-year program of weekly workshop meetings; ongoing advanced group for invited alums of Workshop; showcase presentations to invited members of entertainment industry. **Financial arrangement:** free. **Application procedure:** completed application and work samples. **Deadline:** 1 May 2000 for librettists; 1 Aug 2000 for composers and lyricists. **Notification:** Sep 2000. (See entry in Membership and Service Organizations.)

BROADWAY TOMORROW

191 Claremont Ave, Suite 53; New York, NY 10027; (212) 531-2447,
FAX 531-2447; E-mail solight@worldnet.att.net;
Web http://home.att.net/~solight
Elyse Curtis, *Artistic Director*

Open to: composers, librettists, lyricists. **Description:** new musicals presented in concert with writers' involvement. **Financial arrangement:** participant pays $50 annual membership fee. **Guidelines:** resident of NY metropolitan area. **Application procedure:** cassette of 3 songs with description of 3 scenes in which they occur, synopsis, resume, reviews if available and SASE for response. **Deadline:** 31 Aug 2000. **Notification:** 3–6 months. **Dates:** year-round.

C. BERNARD JACKSON READERS THEATRE

(Formerly Inner City Cultural Center Competition)
Box 272; Los Angeles, CA 90028; (213) 627-7670, FAX 622-5881

Open to: playwrights, translators. **Description:** cold reading series held first Monday of every month followed by critique. **Financial arrangement:** free. **Guidelines:** play maximum 90 minutes; special interest in international, multicultural work. **Application procedure:** synopsis and letter of inquiry; write for guidelines. **Deadline:** ongoing. **Dates:** year-round.

CAC PLAYWRIGHT'S UNIT

Contemporary Arts Center; Box 30498; New Orleans, LA 70190; (504) 528-3805,
FAX 528-3828
Emory White, *Theatre Coordinator*

Open to: playwrights. **Description:** 9-month workshop for 8–10 writers; participants' works developed and given staged readings. **Financial arrangement:** write or call for information. **Guidelines:** writer living in New Orleans area. **Application procedure:** call for information. **Deadline:** ongoing. **Dates:** Sep–May.

CARNEGIE MELLON DRAMA'S SUMMER NEW PLAYS PROJECT

(Formerly Carnegie Mellon Drama's Showcase of New Plays)
Carnegie Mellon Drama; College of Fine Arts; Pittsburgh, PA 15213;
(412) 268-3284, FAX 621-0281
Peter Frisch, Milan Stitt and Gregory Lehane, *Artistic Directors*

Open to: playwrights, translators, solo performers. **Description:** 4 playwrights each brought in for 2 weeks to work on play with director and Equity company of actors, culminating in 2 public script-in-hand performances. **Financial arrangement:** $1000 stipend, travel and housing. **Guidelines:** full-length play or bill of related one-acts already under development by established professional regional theatre. **Application procedure:** no submission by playwright; CMU approaches theatre for possible co-production. **Dates:** Jul–Aug 2000.

CHARLOTTE FESTIVAL/NEW PLAYS IN AMERICA
Charlotte Repertory Theatre; 129 West Trade St; Charlotte, NC 28244;
   (704) 333-8587
Claudia Carter Covington, *Literary Manager*
Carol Bellamy, *Literary Associate*

Open to: playrights, translators. **Description:** 4 plays each given 12–16 hours of rehearsal with Equity company, culminating in 2 public staged readings, during week-long festival; some scripts subsequently receive full production as part of theatre's regular season. **Financial arrangement:** honorarium, travel, housing. **Guidelines:** only full-length plays and translations that have not received professional production. **Application procedure:** script only. **Deadline:** ongoing. **Dates:** 8–13 Feb 2000.

THE CHESTERFIELD FILM COMPANY/WRITER'S FILM PROJECT
1158 26th St, Box 544; Santa Monica, CA 90403; (213) 683-3977,
   FAX (310) 260-6116; Web http://www.chesterfield-co.com

Open to: playwrights, screenwriters. **Description:** up to 5 writers annually chosen for year-long screenwriting workshop meeting 3–5 times a week; writer creates 2 feature-length screenplays; company intends to produce best of year's work. **Financial arrangement:** $20,000 stipend. **Guidelines:** current and former writing-program students encouraged to apply; write or call for information. **Application procedure:** 2 copies of completed application, writing samples and $39.50 fee. **Deadline:** 9 Nov 1999. **Dates:** Apr 2000–Mar 2001.

CORNERSTONE DRAMATURGY AND DEVELOPMENT PROJECT
Penumbra Theatre Company; 270 North Kent St; St. Paul, MN 55102-1794;
   (651) 224-4601, FAX 224-7074
Lou Bellamy, *Artistic Director*

Open to: playwrights. **Description:** 1 playwright a year offered mainstage production with possible 3–4 week residency; 1 playwright offered 4-week workshop-residency culminating in staged reading. **Financial arrangement:** varies according to needs of project. **Guidelines:** full-length play dealing with the African-American and/or Pan-African experience which has not received professional full production; one-acts considered; write for guidelines. **Application procedure:** script and resume. **Deadline:** ongoing. (See Penumbra Theatre Company in Production.)

DAVID HENRY HWANG WRITERS INSTITUTE
East West Players; 244 South San Pedro St, Suite 301; Los Angeles, CA 90012;
   (213) 625-7000, FAX 625-7111; E-mail info@eastwestplayers.com
Ken Narasaki, *Literary Manager*

Open to: playwrights, screenwriters. **Description:** 2 20-week workshops each year culminating in a public staged reading. **Financial arrangement:** $350 fee; 1 scholarship available. **Application procedure:** completed application form and work sample with $25 nonrefundable deposit. **Deadline:** 15 Dec 1999. **Notification:** 5 Jan 2000.

Denver Center Theatre Company U S West Theatre Fest

1050 13th St; Denver, CO 80204; (303) 446-4856
Bruce K. Sevy, *Associate Artistic Director/New Play Development*

Open to: playwrights. **Description:** new plays receive workshops and rehearsed readings during spring festival; most plays given 15–30 hours of rehearsal, culminating in 1 public presentation. **Financial arrangement:** stipend, travel, housing. **Application procedure:** send SASE for guidelines. **Deadline:** 1 Jan 2000. **Dates:** late May–early Jun. (See entry in Production.)

Diamond Head Theatre Originals

520 Makapuu Ave; Honolulu, HI 96816; (808) 734-8763, FAX 735-1250
John Rampage, *Artistic Director*

Open to: playwrights. **Description:** ongoing playwrights' workshops in which playwrights meet regularly to develop their scripts through reading and discussion; occasional public readings of works-in-progress. **Financial arrangement:** participant pays $5 a session. **Application procedure:** attend workshop session; check date and time of sessions.

Drama League New Directors–New Works Series

The Drama League of New York; 165 West 46th St, Suite 601;
New York, NY 10036; (212) 302-2100, FAX 302-2254;
E-mail dlny@echonyc.com; Web http://www.echonyc.com/~dlny

Open to: playwright-director teams. **Description:** 3 projects each summer receive up to 4 weeks of rehearsal space in New York City; development ranges from exploratory rehearsals to workshop production according to needs of collaborative team. **Financial arrangement:** $1000 for each team. **Application procedure:** proposal describing project submitted jointly by director and playwright; bios; write, call or visit Web site for guidelines. **Deadline:** 15 Feb 2000. **Notification:** 1 May 2000.

Drama West Productions

Box 5022-127; Lake Forest, CA 92630
Catherine Stanley, *Artistic Director*

Open to: playwrights. **Description:** 5–6 plays each month given staged reading, followed by audience feedback. **Financial arrangement:** free. **Guidelines:** one-acts appropriate for a general audience which have not received professional production. **Application procedure:** script only. **Deadline:** ongoing. **Notification:** 2 weeks, if script is accepted.

FIRST STAGE

Box 38280; Los Angeles, CA 90038; (323) 850-6271, FAX 850-6295
Dennis Safren, *Literary Manager*

Open to: playwrights, solo performers, screenwriters. **Description:** organization providing year-round developmental services using professional actors, directors and dramaturgs; weekly staged readings of plays and screenplays followed by discussions; bimonthly playwriting and screenwriting workshops; periodic dramaturgy workshops; annual short-play marathon; annual One-Act Play Contest with $100 first prize, $50 second and third prizes and videotaped staged reading for all winners, *deadline:* 1 Jul 2000 (send SASE for guidelines), *notification:* 1 Nov 2000. **Financial arrangement:** subscription of $120 a year or $35 a quarter for resident of Los Angeles, Orange or Ventura counties; $58 annual subscription for nonresident; nonmember may submit script for reading. **Application procedure:** script only. **Deadline:** ongoing. **Notification:** 2–6 months. **Dates:** year-round.

FLORIDA PLAYWRIGHTS' PROCESS

(Formerly West Central Florida Playwrights' Process)
PACT Institute for the Performing Arts at Ruth Eckerd Hall;
    1111 McMullen-Booth Rd; Clearwater, FL 33759;
    (727) 791-7060, ext 354, FAX 791-7449; E-mail ensignsp@gte.net;
    Web http://www.rutheckerdhall.net
Elizabeth Brincklow, *Program Director*

Open to: playwrights. **Description:** 3 plays (2 by playwright 19 or younger) receive 5–6 weeks of workshopping, rehearsal and staged reading, culminating in workshop production. **Financial arrangement:** $400 and maximum travel stipend of $250. **Guidelines:** FL playwright; unproduced and unpublished full-length play; cast limit of 6; maximum running time 2 hours; simple props and set. **Application procedure:** send or call for guidelines. **Deadline:** 1 Dec 1999. **Notification:** 31 Jan 2000. **Dates:** exact dates TBA.

THE 42ND STREET WORKSHOP

432 West 42nd St, 5th Floor; New York, NY 10036; (212) 695-4173,
    FAX 695-3384
Sheila Walsh, *Literary Manager*

Open to: playwrights, screenwriters. **Description:** writers meet weekly to develop scripts through in-house readings and critique; approximately 30 works a year receive staged readings; 3–4 works receive showcase productions. **Financial arrangement:** $25 monthly fee. **Application procedure:** script and letter of reference from company member. **Deadline:** ongoing. **Notification:** 1 Dec 1999. **Dates:** year-round.

THE FRANK SILVERA WRITERS' WORKSHOP

Box 1791; Manhattanville Station; New York, NY 10027; (212) 281-8832,
    FAX 281-8839 (call first); E-mail playrite@artswire.org;
    Web http://www.artswire.org/~playrite
Garland Lee Thompson, *Founding Executive Director*

Open to: playwrights. **Description:** upper Manhattan- and Harlem-based program which includes Monday series of readings of new plays by new and established writers, followed by critiques; Saturday seminars conducted by master playwrights; staged readings and 2–3 showcase and readers' theatre productions a year. **Financial arrangement:** $35 annual fee plus $10 per Saturday class; Monday-night readings free. **Guidelines:** interested in new plays by writers of all colors and backgrounds. **Application procedure:** attend Sep open house; submitting script and attending a Monday-night session encouraged; call for information.

FREDERICK DOUGLASS CREATIVE ARTS CENTER
WRITING WORKSHOPS

270 West 96th St; New York, NY 10025; (212) 864-3375,
    FAX 864-3474 (call first); E-mail fdcac@aol.com;
    Web http://www.fdcac.org
Fred Hudson, *Artistic Director*

Open to: playwrights, screenwriters, television writers. **Description:** 4 cycles a year of 8-week workshops; beginning and advanced playwriting; latter includes readings and possible productions; also film and television writing workshops; weekly meetings. **Financial arrangement:** $150 fee per workshop; author of play given staged reading receives $50, author of produced play receives $500. **Application procedure:** contact FDCAC for information. **Deadline:** Sep 1999 for 1st cycle; Jan 2000 for 2nd cycle; May 2000 for 3rd cycle; Jul 2000 for 4th cycle; call for exact dates. **Dates:** Oct–Dec 1999; Jan–Mar 2000; Apr–Jun 2000; Jul–Sep 2000.

FREE PLAY READING SERIES AND PLAYWRIGHT DEVELOPMENT WORKSHOP

American Renaissance Theatre of Dramatic Arts; 10 West 15th St, Suite 325;
    New York, NY 10011; (212) 924-6862
Rich Stone, *Artistic Director*

Open to: playwrights. **Description:** up to 5 plays-in-progress given 2 rehearsals and a public reading, followed by audience critique; some scripts may subsequently receive full production; playwright also attends workshop addressing each of the plays and the "business" of playwriting. **Financial arrangement:** free. **Guidelines:** unproduced play; resident of New York city area. **Application procedure:** synopsis, 10-page dialogue sample and SASE for response. **Deadline:** 31 Jan 2000. **Notification:** 30 Mar 2000. **Dates:** June 2000; exact dates TBA.

THE GENESIUS GUILD PROGRAMS
FOR THE DEVELOPMENT OF NEW PLAYS & MUSICALS
Box 2213; New York, NY 10108; E-mail literary@genesiusguild.org;
    Web http://www.genesiusguild.org
William Whitefield, *Artistic Director*

Open to: playwrights, translators, composers, librettists, lyricists, solo performers.
Description: program offering range of developmental services including in-house
readings; staged readings; workshop and showcase productions; development
process varies according to needs of script. **Financial arrangement:** free.
Guidelines: emerging or established playwright. **Application procedure:** 1- or 2-
page synopsis, scene breakdown, cast requirements, production needs, cassette for
musical and bio or resume. **Deadline:** ongoing. **Dates:** Sep–May.

HAROLD PRINCE MUSICAL THEATRE PROGRAM
The Directors Company; 311 West 43rd St, Suite 307; New York, NY 10036;
    (212) 246-5877, FAX 246-5882
HPMTP Selection Committee

Open to: playwrights, composers, librettists, lyricists. **Description:** program
supports creation, development and production of new musicals; writers and
composers work collaboratively with director under guidance of program's artistic
directors and Harold Prince; process includes monthly meetings, readings and
presentation for invited audience in New York City. **Financial arrangement:**
commissioning and optioning fees available. **Guidelines:** musicals in any stage of
development. **Application procedure:** full scripts accepted from agent or with
professional recommendation; all others submit synopsis, 15-page dialogue sample
and 6-song cassette or CD; call for specific guidelines. **Deadline:** ongoing.
Notification: 3–6 months.

HEDGEROW HORIZONS
146 West Rose Valley Rd; Wallingford, PA 19086; (610) 565-4211
Walt Vail, *Literary Manager*

Open to: playwrights. **Description:** 5 full-length plays and 2 one-acts each given
2 rehearsals and 1 public reading. **Financial arrangement:** free. **Guidelines:**
playwright must be resident of DE, PA or NJ; play not professionally produced.
Application procedure: send SASE for guidelines. **Deadline:** 29 Feb 2000.
Notification: 30 Apr 2000. **Dates:** 30 May 2000.

HISPANIC PLAYWRIGHTS PROJECT
South Coast Repertory; Box 2197; Costa Mesa, CA 92628-2197;
    (714) 708-5500, ext 5405
Juliette Carrillo, *Project Director*

Open to: playwrights. **Description:** up to 3 scripts given 1–3 week workshop with
director, dramaturg and professional cast, culminating in public reading or
workshop production and discussion; playwright meets with director and

dramaturg prior to workshop. **Financial arrangement:** honorarium, travel, housing. **Guidelines:** Hispanic-American playwright; unproduced play preferred but produced play which would benefit from further development will be considered; play must not be written entirely in Spanish; no musicals. **Application procedure:** script, synopsis and bio. **Deadline:** Jan 2000. **Notification:** Mar 2000. **Dates:** Jun 2000.

THE ISIDORA AGUIRRE PLAYWRIGHTING LAB

El Teatro de la Esperanza; Box 40578; San Francisco, CA 94140-0578;
(415) 255-2320, FAX 255-8031
Program Manager

Open to: playwrights. **Description:** 6–9 plays developed through individual sessions and weekly seminars with professional dramaturg over 3-month period. **Financial arrangement:** stipend. **Guidelines:** Chicano/Latino playwright residing in the Bay Area; full-length play-in-progress reflective of or adaptable to the Latino experience; prefers bilingual plays, but accepts monolingual plays in Spanish or English; prefers cast limit of 7 (doubling allowed); write for guidelines. **Application procedure:** 2 copies of script and resume (material will not be returned). **Deadline:** ongoing. **Notification:** 2 months. **Dates:** summer 2000.

KEY WEST THEATRE FESTIVAL

Box 992; Key West, FL 33041; (305) 292-3725, FAX 293-0845;
E-mail theatrekw@ibm.net
Joan McGillis, *Artistic Director*

Open to: playwrights, translators, solo performers. **Description:** up to 8 plays given staged readings and 5 plays given full productions during 10-day festival, which also includes workshops and seminars. **Financial arrangement:** travel and housing. **Guidelines:** unproduced full-length play, one-act, musical, work for young audiences. **Application procedure:** script, resume and 2 letters of recommendation. **Deadline:** ongoing. **Notification:** Aug 2000. **Dates:** Oct 2000.

L. A. BLACK PLAYWRIGHTS

5926 5th Ave; Los Angeles, CA 90043; (323) 292-9438
James Graham Bronson, *President*

Open to: playwrights, librettists, lyricists. **Description:** group meets every second Sunday for guest speakers, private and public readings, and showcases. **Financial arrangement:** free. **Guidelines:** resident of Los Angeles area; members mainly but not exclusively African-American; prefers produced playwright. **Application procedure:** submit full-length play. **Deadline:** ongoing. **Dates:** year-round.

The Lehman Engel Musical Theatre Workshop

335 North Brand Blvd; Glendale, CA 91203; (818) 502-3309, FAX 502-3365;
    E-mail jsparksco@aol.com
John Sparks, *Artistic Director*

Open to: composers, librettists, lyricists. **Description:** Sep–Jun workshop; in-house staged readings; skeletal productions (Equity contract). **Financial arrangement:** 1st-year workshop members pay dues of $500, which include nonrefundable application fee (see below); in subsequent years, members pay dues of $300. **Application procedure:** completed application; 1-page resume; cassette of 3 songs or equivalent for composer; 3 lyrics for lyricist; short scene for librettist; nonrefundable $50 fee. **Deadline:** 15 Aug 2000. **Notification:** Sep 2000. **Dates:** Sep 2000–Jun 2001.

Manhattan Playwrights Unit

338 West 19th St, #6B; New York, NY 10011-3982; (212) 989-0948
Saul Zachary, *Artistic Director*

Open to: playwrights, screenwriters. **Description:** developmental workshop meeting weekly for in-house readings and discussions of members' works-in-progress; end-of-season series of staged readings of new plays. **Financial arrangement:** free. **Guidelines:** produced or published writer. **Application procedure:** letter of inquiry, resume and SASE for response. **Deadline:** ongoing.

Mark Taper Forum Developmental Programs

135 North Grand Ave; Los Angeles, CA 90012; (213) 972-8033
Pier Carlo Talenti, *Literary Manager*
    (Also see entry in Production)

Asian Theatre Workshop (ATW)

Open to: playwrights, solo performers. **Description:** ongoing developmental program including Asian Pacific American Friends of Center Theatre Group (APAF) Reading Series; discussions with outside theatre artists; workshop productions. **Financial arrangement:** honorarium. **Guidelines:** Asian-Pacific playwright. **Application procedure:** script and resume. **Deadline:** ongoing.

Blacksmyths

Open to: playwrights, solo performers. **Description:** ongoing developmental program including writers' group, staged readings and workshops. **Financial arrangement:** honorarium. **Guidelines:** African-American playwright; resident of Los Angeles area. **Application procedure:** script and resume. **Deadline:** ongoing.

Latino Theatre Initiative (LTI)

Open to: playwrights, solo performers. **Description:** ongoing developmental program including staged readings and workshops. **Financial arrangement:** remuneration varies. **Guidelines:** Latino playwright. **Application procedure:** script and resume. **Deadline:** ongoing.

New Work Festival

Open to: playwrights, solo performers. **Description:** 16–18 plays given workshops (2 weeks of rehearsal, 2 public presentations) or rehearsed readings. **Financial arrangement:** remuneration varies. **Guidelines:** unproduced, unpublished play. **Application procedure:** brief synopsis, 5–10 sample pages and resume. **Deadline:** 30 Apr 2000.

Other Voices Project

Open to: playwrights, solo performers. **Description:** ongoing developmental program including community and professional development; staged readings; workshops; Summer Chautauqua: biennial week-long seminar. **Financial arrangement:** remuneration varies. **Guidelines:** disabled playwright writing about disability; program designed to increase presence of disabled community in mainstream theatre. **Application procedure:** script and resume; call for guidelines for Summer Chautauqua. **Deadline:** call for information.

THE MAXWELL ANDERSON PLAYWRIGHTS SERIES
Box 671; West Redding, CT 06896; (203) 938-2770
Bruce Post, *Dramaturg*

Open to: playwrights. **Description:** 10 new plays a year each given staged reading with professional director and actors, followed by audience discussion. **Financial arrangement:** stipend. **Guidelines:** unproduced play. **Application procedure:** letter of inquiry. **Deadline:** ongoing.

MIDWEST RADIO THEATRE WORKSHOP
KOPN Radio; 915 East Broadway; Columbia, MO 65201; (573) 874-5676,
    FAX 499-1662; E-mail mrtw@mrtw.org; Web http://www.mrtw.org
Sue Zizza, *Executive Director*

Open to: playwrights, radio writers. **Description:** annual program of 6-day radio-theatre workshops for writers, actors, directors and sound designers: 55 participants of all disciplines take workshops in production, direction, acting, writing and engineering; commissioned plays or scripts selected through MRTW Script Contest (see Prizes) produced for radio broadcast and live performance with audience. **Financial arrangement:** $300–400 fee for each workshop; some partial and full scholarships available based on financial need and experience, with priority given to women and people of color; possibility of free housing in community. **Application procedure:** completed registration form with deposit; write or call for additional information: (516) 483-8321. **Deadline:** 1 Apr 2000 for scholarship applications; most workshops filled at least 1 month before starting date. **Dates:** May–Jun 2000. (See entries in Prizes and Membership and Service Organizations.)

MUSICAL THEATRE WORKS
440 Lafayette St; New York, NY 10003; (212) 677-0040, FAX 598-0105
Lonny Price, *Artistic Director*

Open to: composers, librettists, lyricists. **Description:** new composers, librettists and lyricists work with established musical theatre professionals to develop projects through labs, readings and workshop productions. **Financial arrangement:** free. **Guidelines:** completed unproduced work. **Application procedure:** send SASE for guidelines. **Deadline:** ongoing.

NATIONAL MUSIC THEATER CONFERENCE
O'Neill Theater Center; 234 West 44th St, Suite 901; New York, NY 10036-3909;
    (212) 382-2790, FAX 921-5538
Paulette Haupt, *Artistic Director*
Michael E. Nassar, *Associate Director*

Open to: composers, librettists, lyricists. **Description:** development period of 2–4 weeks at O'Neill Theater Center, Waterford, CT for new music theatre works of all genres, traditional and nontraditional; some works developed privately, others presented as staged readings. **Financial arrangement:** stipend, round-trip travel from NYC, room and board. **Guidelines:** U.S. citizen; unproduced work; adaptations acceptable if rights have been obtained. **Application procedure:** send SASE for guidelines and application form after 15 Sep 1999. **Deadline:** 1 Mar 2000; no submission before 1 Nov 1999. **Dates:** Aug 2000.

NATIONAL MUSIC THEATER NETWORK/BROADWAY USA
1697 Broadway, Suite 902; New York, NY 10019; (212) 664-0979,
    FAX 664-0978; E-mail info@broadwayusa.org;
    Web http://www.broadwayusa.org
Tim Jerome, *President*

Open to: composers, librettists, lyricists. **Description:** national evaluation of submitted musical theatre works; written critiques sent to all writers; descriptive listings of recommended works published in Web catalogue and 6 of these works annually selected for promotional public staged readings by Broadway USA in New York City and in regional affiliated venues. **Financial arrangement:** free. **Guidelines:** completed work with original music which has not received a major production. **Application procedure:** completed application and $45 fee; write, call or e-mail for details. **Deadline:** ongoing.

NATIONAL PLAYWRIGHTS CONFERENCE
O'Neill Theater Center; 234 West 44th St, Suite 901; New York, NY 10036-3909;
    (212) 382-2790, FAX 921-5538
James Houghton, *Artistic Director*
Mary F. McCabe, *Managing Director*

Open to: playwrights, screenwriters, television writers. **Description:** 4-week conference at O'Neill Theater Center, Waterford, CT; 9–12 plays developed and presented as staged readings; 1–3 screenplays/teleplays developed and read; preconference weekend for initial reading and planning. **Financial arrangement:** stipend, travel, room and board. **Guidelines:** U.S. citizen or resident; unoptioned and unproduced work; no adaptations or translations. **Application procedure:** send SASE for guidelines after 15 Sep 1999. **Deadline:** 1 Dec 1999. **Notification:** Apr 2000. **Dates:** preconference weekend TBA; conference Jul 2000.

THE NEW HARMONY PROJECT LABORATORY

613 North East St; Indianapolis, IN 46202; (317) 464-9405, FAX 635-4201
Jeffrey L. Sparks, *Executive Director*

Open to: playwrights, composers, librettists, screenwriters, television writers. **Description:** 4–6 scripts given up to 2 weeks of intensive development with professional community of directors, actors, producers, dramaturgs and musical directors. **Financial arrangement:** $400 stipend; travel, room and board. **Guidelines:** narrative works that "emphasize the dignity of the human spirit and the worth of the human experience." **Application procedure:** 10-page writing sample, project proposal and statement of artistic purpose. **Deadline:** 15 Nov 1999. **Notification:** 15 Mar 2000. **Dates:** May–Jun 2000.

NEW PERSPECTIVES NEW PLAY DEVELOPMENT PROGRAM

New Perspectives Theatre Company; 750 Eighth Ave, #601;
New York, NY 10036; (212) 730-2030, FAX 730-2030
Melody Brooks, *Artistic Director*

Open to: playwright. **Description:** 5–10 plays chosen each year for range of developmental services from rehearsed staged readings with audience feedback to full workshop productions; devlopment process varies according to needs of script; special interest in works by women and minority writers or with a multicultural focus; annual staged reading series in May. **Financial arrangement:** free. **Guidelines:** full-length play. **Application procedure:** 15-page dialogue sample, synopsis and character breakdown. **Deadline:** ongoing. **Notification:** 2–6 months from submission date. **Dates:** year-round.

NEW VISIONS/NEW VOICES

The Kennedy Center–Youth and Family Programs; 2700 F Street NW;
Washington, DC 20566; (202) 416-8880, FAX 416-8297;
E-mail yfp@mail.kennedy-center.org
Kim Peter Kovac, *Senior Program Manager*

Open to: playwrights. **Description:** biennial program; up to 8 plays given rehearsals and staged readings. **Guidelines:** previously unproduced plays for young and family audiences; playwright must be sponsored by theatre; call for information and application. **Financial arrangement:** small stipend. **Application procedure:** sponsoring theatre submits completed application and supporting materials. **Deadline:** 1 Oct 1999. **Notification:** 15 Jan 2000. **Dates:** May 2000.

New Voices Play Development Program

Plowshares Theatre Company; 2870 East Grand Blvd, Suite 600;
Detroit, MI 48202-3146; (313) 872-0279, FAX 872-0067;
E-mail ga@plowshares.org; Web http://www.plowshares.org
Gary Anderson, *Producing Artistic Director*

Open to: playwrights, translators, solo performers. **Description:** up to 6 plays-in-progress given 2 weeks of rehearsal with professional company of actors, directors and dramaturgs, culminating in 2 staged readings followed by audience discussion; program provides marketing assistance following development; possible future full production. **Financial arrangement:** $1000 cash gift to play chosen best of festival; some travel stipends available. **Guidelines:** African-American playwright; unproduced play addressing the African-American experience. **Application procedure:** completed application, synopsis and resume. **Deadline:** 31 Oct 1999. **Notification:** Mar 2000. **Dates:** Jul 2000.

New Works for a New World

c/o Department of Theater; University of Massachusetts; 112 Fine Arts Center;
Amherst, MA 01003; (413) 545-3490; E-mail lmburns@english.umass.edu
Lucy Burns, *Literary Manager*

Open to: playwrights, composers, librettists, lyricists, solo performers. **Description:** 4 plays developed over 2-week residency with actors, director and dramaturg, culminating in staged reading. **Guidelines:** special interest in works by writers of color and plays that "reflect the diversity of American culture." **Financial arrangement:** $1500 stipend; travel and housing. **Application procedure:** send SASE for guidelines. **Deadline:** Sep 1999; exact date TBA. **Notification:** spring 2000. **Dates:** Jul 2000.

New York Foundation for the Arts Sponsorship Program

155 Avenue of the Americas, 14th Floor; New York, NY 10013-1507;
(212) 366-6900, ext 225, FAX 366-1778; E-mail sponsor@nyfa.org
Sarah Jarkon, *Senior Program Officer, Sponsorship*

Open to: playwrights, translators, composers, librettists, lyricists, solo performers, screenwriters, television and radio writers. **Description:** program provides fiscal sponsorship, financial services and technical assistance to collaborating not-for-profit organizations and individuals or organizations without not-for-profit status so that they can seek funds from foundations, corporations and individuals that require not-for-profit status in order to contribute funds. The program has two categories: Artists' Projects (individual artists or collaborating artists); and Emerging Organizations (emerging arts organizations in the process of obtaining not-for-profit status). Program does not offer grants or provide funding. **Financial arrangement:** as a service fee, NYFA retains a percentage of grants and contributions it receives on behalf of a project; $50–100 one-time processing fee payable on signing. **Guidelines:** selection based on artistic excellence, uniqueness and fundability of project, and on artist's previous work and proven ability to complete proposed work. **Application procedure:** write for application form and guidelines. **Deadline:** Nov 1999; Mar 2000; Jul 2000; contact NYFA for exact dates. **Notification:** 6 weeks.

NEWGATE THEATRE NEW PLAY DEVELOPMENT
134 Mathewson St; Providence, RI 02906;
    Web http://www.oso.com/community/groups/newgate
New Works Coordinator

Open to: playwrights, solo performers. **Description:** organization providing year-round developmental services; 3–4 scripts each season receive staged reading, in some cases leads to workshop production. Test Tube Theatre: workshop productions held Jan–Feb for playwrights interested in deeper rehearsal involvement. **Financial arrangement:** small stipend and possible housing. **Guidelines:** resident of southern New England; full-length plays in need of development. **Application procedure:** script, resume and SASE for response. **Deadline:** 15 Oct 1999 for Test Tube; 1 Feb 2000 for regular program. **Dates:** year-round.

THE NEXT STAGE
The Cleveland Play House; 8500 Euclid Ave; Cleveland, OH 44106-0189;
    (216) 795-7010, ext 207, FAX 795-7005
Scott Kanoff, *Literary Manager/Resident Director*

Open to: playwrights. **Description:** 3-tier developmental program: The Playwrights Unit, ongoing workshop for Cleveland-area playwrights; new plays developed through discussion and readings; Next Stage Festival: in Jan, 4–8 plays each given 2–3 days of rehearsal with Play House company, culminating in public readings. Premiere Series: at least 1 play developed in Playwrights Unit or Next Stage Festival offered main stage production each season. **Financial arrangement:** for Playwrights Unit: access to administrative resources and reimbursement for professional expenses; for Next Stage Festival: stipend, travel and housing; for Premiere Series: varies. **Guidelines:** for Playwrights Unit: resident of Northern Ohio area, produced or unproduced full-length play; for Next Stage Festival: unproduced full-length play. **Application procedure:** script, resume and letter of inquiry. **Deadline:** for Playwrights Unit: 30 Apr 2000, no submission before 1 Apr 2000; for Next Stage Festival: 30 Jun 2000, no submission before 15 May 2000. (See The Cleveland Play House in Production.)

OFF-OFF BROADWAY ORIGINAL SHORT PLAY FESTIVAL
45 West 25th St; New York, NY 10010-2751; (212) 206-8990, FAX 206-1429
William Talbot, *Festival Coordinator*

Open to: playwrights. **Description:** festival production hosted by Love Creek Productions on Theatre Row in New York City; possible publication by Samuel French. **Financial arrangement:** free. **Guidelines:** one-acts or segments of full-length plays less than 40 minutes long only; play must have been developed and produced by theatre, professional school or college that has playwriting program; send SASE for application after Jan 2000. **Application procedure:** no submission by playwright; completed application submitted by organization producing work. **Deadline:** Feb–Mar 2000; exact date TBA. **Notification:** within 2 weeks. **Dates:** late spring 2000.

OLD PUEBLO PLAYWRIGHTS
Box 767; Tucson, AZ 85702; (520) 743-0940, FAX 887-6741;
  E-mail 4stern@92starnet.com
Chris Stern, *Member*

Open to: playwrights, translators, screenwriters, television and radio writers. **Description:** members meet weekly to develop scripts; staged readings at annual New Play Festival in Jan. **Financial arrangement:** $36 annual dues. **Application procedure:** submit writing sample at weekly meeting. **Deadline:** ongoing. **Dates:** ongoing.

ONE ACTS IN PERFORMANCE
Polaris North, c/o Diane Martella; 1265 Broadway, Room 803;
  New York, NY 10001; (212) 684-1985
Diane Martella, *Treasurer/Co-sponsor*

Open to: playwrights. **Description:** approximately every 2 months, 3–5 plays given brief rehearsal period, culminating in workshop production followed by informal audience discussion. **Guidelines:** unproduced one-act play not more than 30 minutes long; 4-character maximum; single set. **Financial arrangement:** free. **Application procedure:** script only. **Deadline:** ongoing. **Notification:** 2–6 weeks. **Dates:** year-round.

ORANGE COUNTY PLAYWRIGHTS' ALLIANCE
DEVELOPMENTAL WORKSHOP
Box 6927; Fullerton, CA 92834; (714) 738-3841, (818) 345-3064,
  FAX (714) 738-7833; Web http://www.ocpaplaywrights.org
Eric Eberwein, *Co-Director*

Open to: playwrights. **Description:** ongoing developmental workshop meeting bimonthly; up to 12 scripts each year receive staged reading or production; annual Page to Stage Contest for one-acts by California writers with $100 first prize, $50 second prize and $25 third prize and workshop production for all winners, *deadline:* 1 Jul 2000 (send script with character breakdown and $5 fee), *notification:* Feb 2001. **Financial arrangement:** $80 annual membership fee. **Guidelines:** residents of Orange County and greater Los Angeles area only. **Application procedure:** work sample and resume. **Deadline:** ongoing. **Notification:** 2 months.

THE PLAY PEN
The Asylum; Box 70267; Las Vegas, NV 89170; (702) 893-8980
Maggie Winn-Jones, *Artistic Director*

Open to: playwrights. **Description:** up to 12 plays-in-progress given 1 week of rehearsal each with resident company culminating in 2 public staged readings followed by audience discussion. **Financial arrangement:** $50 stipend and housing. **Guidelines:** U.S. citizen or permanent resident; professionally unproduced play. **Application procedure:** script only. **Deadline:** 31 Jul 2000. **Notification:** 31 Dec 2000. **Dates:** Feb 2001; Oct–Nov 2001.

PLAYFORMERS
20 Waterside Plaza, Apt 11G; New York, NY 10010; (212) 213-9835
John Fritz, *Executive Director*

Open to: playwrights. **Description:** playwrights' support group meetings once a month Sep–Jun for readings of works-in-progress and critiques. **Financial arrangement:** $15 initiation fee on acceptance; $75 annual dues. **Guidelines:** playwright invited to attend meetings as guest before applying for membership. **Application procedure:** script and resume. **Deadline:** ongoing.

PLAYLABS
The Playwrights' Center; 2301 Franklin Ave; Minneapolis, MN 55406-1099;
        (612) 332-7481; E-mail pwcenter@mtn.org; Web http://www.pwcenter.org
Megan Monaghan, *PlayLabs Artistic Director*

Open to: playwrights, solo performers. **Description:** 4–6 new works given 2 weeks of development with playwright's choice of professional director, dramaturg and Twin Cities actors, culminating in staged reading followed by audience discussion. **Financial arrangement:** travel, housing and per diem. **Guidelines:** U.S. citizen or permanent resident; unproduced, unpublished play, solo performance piece or mixed-media piece; full-length works preferred; writer must be available to attend entire conference and preconference weekend. **Application procedure:** completed application and script; send SASE for application after 15 Oct 1999. **Deadline:** 15 Dec 1999. **Notification:** 1 May 2000. **Dates:** preconference weekend May/June 2000; exact dates TBA; conference 23 Jul–5 Aug 2000.

PLAYS-IN-PROGRESS FESTIVALS OF NEW WORKS
615 4th St; Eureka, CA 95501; (707) 443-3724
Susan Bigelow-Marsh, *Executive Director*

Open to: playwrights. **Description:** 5 scripts each given full production and 8–10 scripts each given 3–4 weeks of development with actors and directors, culminating in staged reading followed by discussion, in spring or fall festival of new work; ongoing development and Monday night reading series for local writers. **Financial arrangement:** negotiable; housing. **Guidelines:** primarily CA writers; 1 out-of-state writer selected for each festival; unproduced, unpublished play. **Application procedure:** script and resume. **Deadline:** 1 Mar 2000; 1 Jul 2000. **Dates:** Sep 2000; May 2001.

PLAYWRIGHTS' CENTER OF SAN FRANCISCO STAGED READINGS
Box 460466; San Francisco, CA 94146-0466; (415) 626-4603, FAX 863-0901;
E-mail playctrsf@aol.com; Web http://www.playwrights.org
Sheppard B. Kominers, *Chairman of the Board*

Open to: playwrights. **Description:** developmental program meeting weekly for 1 staged reading, monthly for reading and discussion of works-in-progress. **Financial arrangement:** $45 annual membership fee; some scholarships available for students. **Application procedure:** completed application. **Deadline:** ongoing.

PLAYWRIGHTS CIRCLE
Pulse Ensemble Theatre; 432 West 42nd St; New York, NY 10036;
(212) 695-1596, FAX 736-1255
Lezzey Steele, *Director, Playwrights Circle*

Open to: playwrights, solo performers, screenwriters. **Description:** 3-month workshop meeting weekly culminating in public staged reading or workshop production in either Open Pulse Arts Lab (OPAL) for one-acts or the Studio Series for full-length plays. **Guidelines:** experienced playwrights residing in NY area only. **Financial arrangement:** $150 fee. **Application procedure:** completed application and professional recommendation. **Deadline:** ongoing. **Notification:** ongoing. **Dates:** year-round.

PLAYWRIGHTS FORUM
Box 5322; Rockville, MD 20848; (301) 816-0569; E-mail pforum@erols.com;
Web http://www.erols.com/pforum/welcome.htm
Ernest Joselovitz, *President*

Open to: playwrights. **Description:** ongoing developmental program including 3-tier range of membership options: Forum 1, workshop program offering three 3-month sessions a year for apprentice playwrights; Forum 2, professional playwriting groups meeting biweekly; and Associate membership offering participation in many of Forum's auxiliary programs but not in workshops; depending on type of membership, members variously eligible for in-house and public readings, Musical Theatre Wing, mentorships, special classes, including Rewrites and Screenwriting, production observerships, free theatre tickets, internet activities, semiannual conference, organization's newsletter and handbook, and new published series of members' scripts. **Financial arrangement:** for Forum 1, $90 per 15-week session; for Forum 2, $90 every 4 months; Associate membership $25 a year; financial aid available. **Guidelines:** resident of mid-Atlantic area only; for Forum 2, prefers produced playwright or former Forum 1 participant, willing to make long-term commitment; send SASE or visit Web site for further information. **Application procedure:** for Forum 1, send SASE or call for information; for Forum 2, script and bio; for Associate membership, send annual fee. **Deadline:**

for Forum 1, 10 Sep 1999, 10 Jan 2000, 10 May 2000; for Forum 2, ongoing. **Notification:** 4 weeks.

PLAYWRIGHTS GALLERY

Abraham Goodman House: Theatre Wing; 129 West 67th St;
New York, NY 10023; (212) 595-4597, FAX 595-6129;
E-mail savadge@juno.com
Deborah Savadge, *Coordinator*

Open to: playwrights, solo performers, screenwriters. **Description:** developmental workshop meeting bimonthly Sep–Jun; plays receive staged readings at 3-day festivals in Jan and Jun. **Financial arrangement:** playwrights share cost of space rental. **Application procedure:** completed application form and 15–20 page work sample. **Deadline:** 10 Sep 1999. **Notification:** 1 Oct 1999.

PLAYWRIGHTS' KITCHEN ENSEMBLE

c/o Coronet Theatre; 368 North La Cienega; Los Angeles, CA 90048;
FAX (310) 652-6401
Dan Lauria, *Artistic Director*

Open to: playwrights. **Description:** 1 play per week given staged reading by celebrity actors and directors for audience including theatre, film and TV professionals. **Financial arrangement:** free. **Guidelines:** play unproduced in Los Angeles. **Application procedure:** script only. **Deadline:** 31 Dec 1999; no submission before 1 Sep 1999. **Notification:** 31 Mar 2000.

PLAYWRIGHTS' PLATFORM

164 Brayton Rd; Boston, MA 02135; (617) 630-9704; E-mail ghorton@tiac.net;
Web http://www.tiac.net/users/ghorton/playplat.html
Beverly Creasey, *President*

Open to: playwrights. **Description:** ongoing developmental program including weekly workshop held at Massachusetts College of Art, staged readings, summer festival of full productions, dramaturgical and referral services. **Financial arrangement:** playwright receives percentage of gate for festival productions; participants encouraged to become members of organization ($35 annual dues). **Guidelines:** MA resident only available for regular meetings; unpublished, unproduced play; write for membership information. **Application procedure:** letter of inquiry only. **Deadline:** ongoing.

PLAYWRIGHTS PROJECT

Henry Street Settlement/Abrons Arts Center; 466 Grand St;
New York, NY 10002-4804; (212) 598-0400, FAX 505-8329
Jonathon Ward, *Director of Drama Program*

Open to: playwrights. **Description:** 5–6 plays developed during two 5-week programs, culminating in workshop production. **Financial arrangement:** $500 production budget. **Guidelines:** playwrights from New York City area only.

Application procedure: first act or first 10 pages of script, synopsis, character breakdown, resume or brief bio; finalists will be interviewed. **Deadline:** ongoing. **Notification:** 5 weeks. **Dates:** year-round.

PLAYWRIGHTS THEATRE OF NEW JERSEY
NEW PLAY DEVELOPMENT PROGRAM
33 Green Village Rd; Madison, NJ 07940; (973) 514-1787
Peter Hays, *Literary Manager*

Open to: playwrights. **Description:** new plays developed through sit-down readings, staged readings and productions; liaison with other producing theatres provided. **Financial arrangement:** playwright receives royalty. **Guidelines:** American playwright; previously unproduced play; send SASE for guidelines. **Application procedure:** 10-page dialogue sample, developmental history, if any, resume and SASP for acknowledgment of receipt. **Deadline:** 30 Apr 2000; no submission before 1 Sep 1999. **Notification:** 8 months. **Dates:** year-round. (See entry in Membership and Service Organizations.)

PLAYWRIGHTS WEEK
The Lark Theatre Company; 939 Eighth Ave, Suite 301; New York, NY 10019;
(212) 246-2676, FAX 246-2609; E-mail larkco@aol.com;
Web http://www.larktheatre.org
Literary Department

Open to: playwrights. **Description:** 8 plays-in-progress given 10 hours of rehearsal, culminating in staged reading followed by optional audience discussion or critique; scripts may receive subsequent "BareBones" workshop production. **Financial arrangement:** possible travel and housing. **Guidelines:** 1-submission limit. **Application procedure:** script and $15 fee. **Deadline:** 1 Dec 1999. **Notification:** 15 Mar 2000. **Dates:** 4–12 Jun 2000.

PUERTO RICAN TRAVELING THEATRE PLAYWRIGHTS' WORKSHOP
141 West 94th St; New York, NY 10025; (212) 354-1293, FAX 307-6769
Allen Davis III, *Director*

Open to: playwrights, solo performers. **Description:** 7–9-month workshops comprised of 2 units, 1 for professional playwrights, 1 for beginners; weekly meetings; spring staged reading series; City "In Sight" showcase production series. **Financial arrangement:** $100 fee per workshop cycle. **Guidelines:** resident of New York City area; Latino or other minority playwright or playwright interested in multicultural theatre. **Application procedure:** for professional unit, submit full-length play; beginners contact director. **Deadline:** 30 Sep 1999. **Notification:** within 2 weeks. **Dates:** Oct 1999–Jul 2000.

Remembrance Through the Performing Arts
New Play Development
3300 Bee Caves Rd, Suite 650; Austin, TX 78746; (512) 329-9118,
    FAX 329-9118
Marla Macdonald, *Director of New Play Development*

Open to: playwrights, solo performers. **Description:** 8 playwrights chosen annually for summer developmental workshops, culminating in work-in-progress productions in fall; plays subsequently given referral to nationally recognized theatres for world premieres. **Financial arrangement:** free. **Guidelines:** resident of central TX; full-length play that has not received Equity production. **Application procedure:** script, synopsis, SASE and resume. **Deadline:** ongoing.

The Richard Rodgers Awards
American Academy of Arts and Letters; 633 West 155th St;
    New York, NY 10032-7599; (212) 368-5900, FAX 491-4615
Richard Rodgers Awards

Open to: playwrights, composers, librettists, lyricists. **Description:** 1 or more works a year given full production, studio/lab production or staged reading by not-for-profit theatre in New York City; writer(s) participate in rehearsal process. **Financial arrangement:** free. **Guidelines:** U.S. citizen or permanent resident; new work by writer/composer not already established in musical theatre; innovative, experimental material encouraged; 1 submission; previous submissions ineligible. **Application procedure:** send SASE for application and information. **Deadline:** 1 Nov 1999. **Notification:** Mar 2000.

The Schoolhouse
Owens Rd; Croton Falls, NY 10519; (914) 234-7232, FAX 234-4196
Douglas Michael, *Literary Manager*

Open to: playwrights. **Description:** about 6 plays a year receive development with director and actors, culminating in public reading and possible full production; ongoing weekly writer's group. **Financial arrangement:** small fee to help offset costs. **Guidelines:** resident of Westchester or Putnam counties, NY or Fairfield County, CT, who can participate in program; prefers full-length plays. **Application procedure:** script or excerpt (at least 10 pages) and letter of inquiry. **Deadline:** ongoing. **Notification:** 1 month.

The Scripteasers
3404 Hawk St; San Diego, CA 92103-3862; (619) 295-4040, FAX 299-2084
Jonathan Dunn-Rankin, *Corresponding Secretary*

Open to: playwrights, screenwriters, television writers. **Description:** writers, directors and actors meet every other Friday evening in private home for cold readings of new scripts, followed by period of constructive criticism; 1 or 2 rehearsed staged readings a year presented at local theatres as showcases. **Financial arrangement:** donations of $1 accepted at each reading. **Guidelines:**

membership by invitation only; guest writer must attend at least 2 readings before submitting script; unproduced script by new or established writer who is resident of San Diego County; write or call for guidelines. **Submission procedure:** write or call for guidelines. **Deadline:** ongoing.

7TH ANNUAL WOMEN AT THE DOOR STAGED READING SERIES

Famous Door Theatre Company; Box 57029; Chicago, IL 60657;
  (773) 404-8283, FAX 404-8292; E-mail theatre@famousdoortheatre.org;
  Web http://www.famousdoortheatre.org
Laura T. Fisher, *Artistic Producer*

Open to: playwrights. **Description:** 3–5 plays receive 3–4 rehearsals for professional staged readings; plays considered for subsequent workshop and/or mainstage production. **Guidelines:** woman playwright; previously unproduced full-length play; 1-submission limit; no musicals or adaptations. **Financial arrangement:** possible housing. **Application procedure:** 1-page synopsis, first scene or first 10 pages of play, resume and $10 fee. **Deadline:** 15 Oct 1999. **Notification:** finalists 1 Dec 1999; winners 1 Apr 2000. **Dates:** May–Jun 2000.

SHENANDOAH INTERNATIONAL PLAYWRIGHTS RETREAT

ShenanArts; Rt 5, Box 167-F; Staunton, VA 24401; (540) 248-1868,
  FAX 248-7728; E-mail shenarts@cfw.com
Robert Graham Small, *Director*
Kathleen Tosco, *Managing Director*

Open to: playwrights, screenwriters. **Description:** 4-week retreat for 4–6 American writers and 4 international writers at Pennyroyal farm in Shenandoah Valley; program geared to facilitate major rewrite or new draft of existing script; personal writing balanced by workshops and staged readings with professional company of dramaturgs, directors and actors. **Financial arrangement:** travel, room and board. **Guidelines:** competitive admission based on submitted work. **Application procedure:** 2 copies of completed draft of script to be worked on at retreat; personal statement of applicant's background as a writer; SASP for acknowledgment of receipt; write or call for guidelines. **Deadline:** 1 Feb 2000. **Notification:** after 10 Jun 2000. **Dates:** Jul–Aug 2000.

SOUTHERN APPALACHIAN PLAYWRIGHTS' CONFERENCE

Southern Appalachian Repertory Theatre; Box 1720; Mars Hill, NC 28754;
  (704) 689-1384, FAX 689-1211; E-mail sart@mhc.edu
Dianne J. Chapman, *Managing Director*

Open to: playwrights. **Description:** up to 5 writers selected to participate in annual 3-day conference at which 1 work by each writer is given informal reading and critiqued by panel of theatre professionals; 1 work may be selected for production as part of summer 2000 season. **Financial arrangement:** room and board; writer of work selected for production receives $500 honorarium. **Guidelines:** unproduced, unpublished play. **Application procedure:** script with synopsis, character breakdown and resume. **Deadline:** 31 Oct 1999. **Dates:** Apr 2000.

SOUTHWEST FESTIVAL FOR NEW PLAYS

Stages Repertory Theatre; 3201 Allen Pkwy, #101; Houston, TX 77019;
   (713) 527-0240, FAX 527-8669
Rob Bundy, *Artistic Director*
   (Also see entry in Production)

Children's Theatre Playwright Festival

Open to: playwrights. **Description:** 3 plays chosen for development with actors and director over period of 1 week, culminating in presentation of scenes; 1 play chosen for full reading. **Financial arrangement:** stipend, contingent on funding. **Guidelines:** play for 4–10-year-old audience to be performed by adult actors; maximum 50 minutes long; cast limit of 8. **Application procedure:** script only. **Deadline:** 14 Feb 2000; no submission before 1 Oct 1999. **Notification:** May 2000. **Dates:** Jun 2000.

Latino Playwrights' Festival

(Formerly Hispanic Playwrights' Festival)

Open to: playwrights. **Description:** 3 plays chosen for development with professional actors and director over period of 1 week, culminating in presentation of scenes; 1 play chosen for full reading. **Financial arrangement:** stipend, contingent on funding. **Guidelines:** Latino playwright; plays written in Spanish must be sent with English translation. **Application procedure:** script only. **Deadline:** 14 Feb 2000; no submission before 1 Oct 1999. **Notification:** May 2000. **Dates:** early Jun 2000.

Texas Playwrights' Festival

Open to: playwrights. **Description:** 4 plays chosen for development with dramaturg, director and actors over period of 1 week, culminating in staged readings. **Financial arrangement:** stipend, contingent on funding. **Guidelines:** TX native or resident or non-TX playwright writing on TX theme; play not produced professionally; prefers small cast. **Application procedure:** script only. **Deadline:** 14 Feb 2000; no submission before 31 Oct 1999. **Notification:** May 2000. **Dates:** Jun 2000.

Women's Repertory Project

Open to: playwrights. **Description:** 6 plays chosen for development with professional actors and director over period of 1 week, culminating in presentation of scenes. **Financial arrangement:** stipend, contingent on funding. **Guidelines:** woman playwright. **Application procedure:** script only. **Deadline:** 14 Feb 2000; no submission before 1 Oct 1999. **Notification:** May 2000. **Dates:** Jun 2000.

STREISAND FESTIVAL OF NEW JEWISH PLAYS

Lawrence Family JCC; 4126 Executive Dr; La Jolla, CA 92037;
 (619) 457-3161, ext 149, FAX 457-2422; E-mail lfjccla@aol.com
Lynette Allen, *Director of Cultural Arts*

Open to: playwrights, composers, librettists, lyricists. **Description:** 4 plays receive 2½ days of rehearsal, culminating in staged reading followed by audience discussion; possible future full production. **Financial arrangement:** travel and housing. **Guidelines:** plays and musicals with Jewish content. **Application procedure:** 3 copies of script and resume. **Deadline:** 15 Jan 2000. **Notification:** Apr 2000. **Dates:** Jun 2000.

SUMMERNITE, NEW PLAY STUDIO

School of Theatre Arts, Stevens Bldg; Northern Illinois University;
 DeKalb, IL 60115-2854; (815) 753-8253, FAX 753-8415
Christopher Markle, *Artistic Director*

Open to: playwrights. **Description:** up to 10 plays receive staged readings during 15-week program; 2 plays chosen for subsequent full production. **Financial arrangement:** royalties for plays chosen for production. **Guidelines:** special interest in large-cast full-length plays or translations not previously produced in Chicago area. **Application procedure:** synopsis and letter of inquiry. **Deadline:** 1 Sep 1999. **Notification:** 1 Dec 1999. **Dates:** May–Aug 2000.

THE SUN VALLEY FESTIVAL OF NEW WESTERN DRAMA

Box 2950; Ketchum, ID 83340; (208) 726-8849
Ed LaGrande, *Coordinator*

Open to: playwrights. **Description:** 2-week festival; 4 plays-in-progress receive 1 week of rehearsal, culminating in staged reading of excerpt of play; 2 plays receive 3 weeks of rehearsal and full production; plays-in-progress considered for future full production. **Financial arrangement:** for play-in-progress: travel, room and board; for full production: negotiable. **Guidelines:** unproduced full-length or one-act with American Western setting, theme and voice; adaptations accepted; one-acts not considered for full production. **Application procedure:** script, letter of inquiry and SASE for acknowledgment of receipt; scripts are not returned. **Deadline:** 15 Mar 2001. **Notification:** 15 Apr 2001. **Dates:** mid-Jun 2001.

THE SUNDANCE INSTITUTE FEATURE FILM PROGRAM

225 Santa Monica Blvd, 8th Floor; Santa Monica, CA 90401;
 (310) 394-4662, FAX 394-8353; Web http://www.sundance.org

Open to: playwrights, screenwriters, filmmaking teams (e.g., writer/director). **Description:** program includes 5-day Screenwriters Labs each Jan and Jun offering participants one-on-one problem-solving sessions with professional screenwriters; 3-week Filmmakers Lab in Jun in which projects are explored through work with directors, writers, actors, cinematographers, producers, editors and other resource personnel; network/advisory service offers practical and creative assistance to selected projects. **Financial arrangement:** travel, room and board for at least 1 writer/filmmaker per project; possible room and board for additional members of team. **Guidelines:** "compelling, original narrative feature film scripts (they can be based on a true story or be adaptations of plays, novels, short stories, etc.) which represent the unique vision of the writer and/or director"; special interest in supporting new talent and artists in transition (e.g., theatre artist who wants to work in film, writer who wants to direct); send SASE for guidelines. **Submission procedure:** completed application, cover letter, first 5 pages of screenplay, synopsis, bios of project participants and $30 fee; after review process, applicants who pass 1st round of selection will be asked to send full screenplay. **Deadline:** May 2000; exact date TBA for all 2001 programs. **Notification:** July 2000.

THE SUNDANCE THEATRE LABORATORY
225 Santa Monica Blvd, 8th Floor; Santa Monica, CA 90401; (310) 394-4662,
    FAX 394-4863; E-mail philip_himberg@sundance.org;
    Web http://www.sundance.org
Philip Himberg, *Producing Director*
Beth Nathanson, *Lab Producer*

Open to: playwright-director teams. **Description:** 8–12 scripts workshopped for 10–20 days. **Financial arrangement:** travel, room and board. **Guidelines:** full-length play, new adaptation and/or translation of classic material, one-act, musical, solo piece; play can be for young or adult audiences. **Application procedure:** send SASE for guidelines and application. **Deadline:** 10 Dec 1999. **Notification:** Apr 2000. **Dates:** Jul 2000.

THE TEN-MINUTE MUSICALS PROJECT
Box 461194; West Hollywood, CA 90046; (323) 651-4899
Michael Koppy, *Producer*

Open to: composers, librettists, lyricists, solo performers. **Description:** up to 10 brief pieces selected during annual cycle for possible inclusion in full-length anthology-musicals to be produced at Equity theatres in U.S. and Canada; occasionally some pieces workshopped using professional actors and director. **Financial arrangement:** $250 royalty advance with equal share of licensing royalties when produced. **Guidelines:** complete work with a definite beginning, middle and end, 7–14 minutes long, in any musical style or genre; adaptations of strongly structured material in the public domain, or for which rights have been obtained, are encouraged; cast of 2–10, prefers 6–10; write for guidelines. **Application procedure:** script, lead sheets and cassette of sung material. **Deadline:** 31 Aug 2000. **Notification:** 30 Nov 2000.

THEATREWORKS/USA COMMISSIONING PROGRAM
Theatreworks/USA; 151 West 26th St, 7th Floor; New York, NY 10001;
(212) 647-1100, FAX 924-5377; E-mail info@theatreworksusa.org
Barbara Pasternack, *Associate Artistic Director*

Open to: composers, librettists, lyricists. **Description:** step commissioning process, possibly leading to 2-week developmental workshop and production. **Financial arrangement:** free. **Guidelines:** works dealing with issues relevant to target audiences; special interest in historical/biographical subject matter and musical adaptations of fairy tales and traditional or contemporary classics; 1 hour long; cast of 5 actors, set suitable for touring. **Application procedure:** prefers treatment with sample scenes, lyric sheets and cassette of music; will accept script only. **Deadline:** ongoing. **Notification:** 6 months. (See entry in Production.)

THE TUESDAY GROUP
404 East 88th St, Apt 6A; New York, NY 10128; (212) 462-9135
Larry Kunofsky, *Coordinator*

Open to: playwrights. **Description:** group meets every 2 weeks to read and discuss members' works; some plays workshopped with resident directors and ensemble; members' work showcased in annual *Caught in Our Acts* festival. **Financial arrangement:** $60 fee per trimester. **Guidelines:** New York City playwright. **Application procedure:** writing sample and letter of inquiry with SASE for response. **Deadline:** ongoing. **Notification:** 2 months.

UNIVERSITY OF ALABAMA NEW PLAYWRIGHTS' PROGRAM
Department of Theatre and Dance; University of Alabama; Box 870239;
Tuscaloosa, AL 35487-0239; (205) 348-9032, FAX 348-9048;
E-mail pcastagn@woodsquad.as.ua.edu;
Web http://www.as.ua.edu/theatre/npp.htm
Paul C. Castagno, *Director and Dramaturg*

Open to: playwrights, composers, librettists, lyricists, solo performers. **Description:** opportunity for writer to develop unproduced script or to pursue further development of produced work, culminating in full production; writer may visit campus several times during rehearsal process and is required to offer limited playwriting workshops during visit(s); recent MFA playwrights encouraged to apply; production considered for entry in the Kennedy Center American College Theater Festival (see Prizes). **Financial arrangement:** substantial stipend, travel and expenses. **Guidelines:** writer with some previous experience and script that has had some development; special interest in works with Southern themes. **Application procedure:** script or synopsis and letter of inquiry. **Deadline:** submit Aug–Mar only. **Notification:** 6 months. **Dates:** fall–spring. **Other programs:** department will also consider one-acts for festival by its directing students and writers' proposals for workshops with its playwriting and acting students.

THE WATERFRONT ENSEMBLE, INC.
Box 1486; Hoboken, NJ 07030; (201) 963-2235;
Web http://www.waterfrontensemble.org/homep.htm
Jason Grote, *Literary Manager*

Open to: playwrights, translators, solo performers. **Description:** ongoing developmental workshop meeting weekly; 30 one-acts and 2 full-length plays receive production each year. **Financial arrangement:** $75 membership fee per year; $40 for 3 months; playwright may try out group for 1 month for no fee. **Guidelines:** NJ-area playwright. **Application procedure:** script or sample of writing from any genre (including screenplays) and letter of recommendation. **Deadline:** ongoing. **Notification:** 6 months. **Dates:** year-round. **Other programs:** New Jersey All Ages Playwright Festival: open to teenage, adult and senior NJ residents; 2-week summer festival of workshop productions; *deadline:* 1 May 2000; *dates:* Jul 2000; contact theatre after 1 Sep 1999 for more information.

WESTBETH PLAYWRIGHT PROGRAM
Westbeth Theatre Center; 151 Bank St; New York, NY 10014; (212) 691-2272

Open to: playwrights, solo performers. **Description:** program to develop full-length plays through critiques, story conferences and staged readings; possible production by Westbeth Theatre Center or through referral to other producing organizations. **Financial arrangement:** free. **Guidelines:** contemporary themes; cast limit of 8, minimal set; welcomes work by minority playwrights; send SASE for guidelines. **Application procedure:** synopsis and resume. **Deadline:** ongoing. **Notification:** 4–6 months. (See entry in Production.)

WILLIAMSTOWN THEATRE FESTIVAL
100 East 17th St., 3rd Floor; New York, NY 10003; (212) 228-2286,
FAX 228-9091; Web http://www.wtfestival.org
Michael Ritchie, *Producer*

Open to: playwrights, composers, librettists, lyricists. **Description:** 4 plays each season given public reading. **Financial arrangement:** stipend, travel and housing. **Guidelines:** American playwright; play not professionally produced. **Application procedure:** agent submission only. **Deadline:** 15 Feb 2000; no submission before 1 Oct 1999.

WOMEN OF COLOR PRODUCTIONS
163 East 104th St, Suite 4E; New York, NY 10029; (212) 501-3842
Jacqueline Wade, *Executive Producer*

Open to: playwrights, composers, librettists, lyricists, solo performers. **Description:** monthly reading series; possible inclusion in Through Her Eyes: Women of Color Arts Festival (see below). **Financial arrangement:** $10 fee per reading. **Guidelines:** prefers woman playwright of color or any writer whose work features female characters of color; special interest in one-acts. **Application procedure:** completed application, 2 copies of script, 1-page synopsis, professional recommendation, character breakdown, resume with SASE for reading series; write for application and guidelines. **Deadline:** ongoing. **Dates:** Sep 1999–Jun 2000 for reading series. **Special programs:** Through Her Eyes: Women of Color Arts Festival: annual 3-week festival held at various venues throughout New York City; 2 producing levels: Tier 1, 10 guest artists receive $300–600 honorarium, rehearsal space, technical staff and marketing support; Tier 2, 40 playwrights contribute to production cost, receive percentage of ticket sales, marketing support and 10–15 hours rehearsal time; completed application, professional recommendation, resume and $35 fee for Festival; write for application and guidelines; *deadline:* 1 Nov 1999; *notification:* Jan 2000; *dates:* Mar 2000.

WOMEN PLAYWRIGHTS PROJECT

Centenary Stage Company; 400 Jefferson St; Hackettstown, NJ 07840;
(908) 979-0900, FAX 813-1984
Catherine Rust, *Project Director*

Open to: playwrights. **Description:** 1 play given 1 week of rehearsal with professional actors and director, followed by staged reading and possible main stage production. **Financial arrangement:** $200 honorarium; travel, room and board. **Guidelines:** woman playwright; full-length play preferred. **Application procedure:** script only. **Deadline:** 1 Nov 1999. **Notification:** 1 Jan 2000. **Dates:** Mar 2000.

WOMEN'S WORK PROJECT

New Perspectives Theatre Company; 750 Eighth Ave, Suite 601;
New York, NY 10036; (212) 730-2030, FAX 730-2030
Celia Braxton, *Women's Work Director*

Open to: playwrights. **Description:** 2 playwrights chosen for 6–9 month residency to develop full-length play. **Financial arrangement:** free. **Guidelines:** woman playwright; special interest in works by writers of color; previously unproduced full-length play; call for application and guidelines. **Application procedure:** completed application and script. **Deadline:** 1 Jun 2000. **Notification:** 1 Aug 2000. **Dates:** year-round.

WORKING STAGES

Colorado Shakespeare Festival; Campus Box 460; Boulder, CO 80309-0460;
(303) 544-0134; E-mail gretchen.haley@colorado.edu
Gretchen Haley, *Dramaturg*

Open to: playwrights. **Description:** 3 plays chosen for 1–2 week workshops culminating in a staged reading. **Financial arrangement:** travel and housing provided. **Guidelines:** resident of AZ, southern CA, CO, NM, northern TX or UT; professionally unproduced play. **Application procedure:** 2 copies of script, synopsis, character breakdown, resume and letter of inquiry with SASE for response. **Deadline:** 7 Jan 2000. **Notification:** 1 Apr 2000. **Dates:** Jul–Aug 2000.

Career
Opportunities

- Agents
- Fellowships and Grants
- Emergency Funds
- State Arts Agencies
- Colonies and Residencies
- Membership and Service Organizations

Agents

I'm wondering whether or not I should have an agent. Where can I get information to help me decide?

Write to the Association of Authors' Representatives at 10 Astor Pl, 3rd Floor; New York, NY 10003. Send a check or money order for $7 and a 55¢ SASE to receive the AAR's brochure describing the role of the literary agent and how to find an agent, and its membership list and canon of ethics. AAR's member list may be found at their Web site (http://www.AAR-online.org). See Useful Publications for books you can consult on the subject. Ask fellow playwrights what they think. Look at copies of scripts for the names of agents representing specific playwrights; see what kinds of plays agents handle and make an intelligent guess as to whether they would be interested in representing your work.

How do I select the names of appropriate agents to contact?

All of the agents listed here represent playwrights. The Dramatists Guild also has a list of agents available to its members, and provides advice on relationships with agents (see Membership and Service Organizations). You may come across names that appear on none of these lists, but be wary, especially if someone tries to charge you a fee to read your script.

How do I approach an agent?

Do not telephone, do not drop in, do not send manuscripts. Write a brief letter describing your work and asking if the agent would like to see a script. Enclose your professional resume; it should show that you have had work produced or published and make clear that you look at writing as an ongoing career, not an occasional hobby. If you're a beginning writer who's just finished your first play, you'd probably do better to work on getting a production rather than an agent.

THE AGENCY
1800 Ave of the Stars, Suite 400; Los Angeles, CA 90067; (310) 551-3000
Nick Mechanic, Steve Whitney, Jerome Zeitman, *Agents*

AGENCY FOR THE PERFORMING ARTS
888 Seventh Ave, Suite 602; New York, NY 10106; (212) 582-1500
Leo Bookman, *Agent*

ALAN BRODIE REPRESENTATION LTD.
211 Piccadilly; London W1V 9LD; England; 44-171-917-2871
Alan Brodie, Sarah McNair, *Agents*

ok! ## ANN ELMO AGENCY — 2/11
60 East 42nd St; New York, NY 10165; (212) 661-2880
Mari Cronin, Letti Lee, *Agents*

NO ## THE BARBARA HOGENSON AGENCY, INC. 2/23
165 West End Ave, Suite 19C; New York, NY 10023; (212) 874-8084
Barbara Hogenson, *Agent*

NO ## BERMAN, BOALS & FLYNN 2/11
208 West 30th St, Suite 401; New York, NY 10001; (212) 868-1068
Judy Boals, Jim Flynn, *Agents*

THE BETHEL AGENCY 2/23
311 West 43rd St, Suite 602; New York, NY 10036; (212) 664-0455
Lewis Chambers, *Agent*

BRET ADAMS LTD.
448 West 44th St; New York, NY 10036; (212) 765-5630
Bret Adams, Bruce Ostler, *Agents*

NO ## CURTIS BROWN, LTD. 2/14
10 Astor Pl; New York, NY 10003; (212) 473-5400
Ginger Knowlton, Perry Knowlton, Timothy Knowlton, *Agents*

DON BUCHWALD & ASSOCIATES 2/14
10 East 44th St; New York, NY 10017; (212) 867-1200
Tina Friedman, *Agent*

THE DRAMATIC PUBLISHING COMPANY
311 Washington St; Box 129; Woodstock, IL 60098; (815) 338-7170
Linda Habjan, Dana Wolworth (musicals), *Agents*

DUVA-FLACK ASSOCIATES, INC. 2/15
200 West 57th St, Suite 1008; New York, NY 10019; (212) 957-9600
Robert Duva, *Agent*

ELISABETH MARTON AGENCY
1 Union Square, Room 612; New York, NY 10003-3303; (212) 255-1908
Tonda Marton, *Agent*

NO **FIFI OSCARD ASSOCIATES** 2/15
24 West 40th St, 17th Floor; New York, NY 10018; (212) 764-1100
Carolyn French, Carmen LaVia, Kevin McShane,
Fifi Oscard, Peter Sawyer, *Agents*

FLORA ROBERTS
157 West 57th St; New York, NY 10019; (212) 355-4165
Sarah Douglas, *Agent*

FREIDA FISHBEIN ASSOCIATES
Box 723; Bedford, NY 10506; (914) 234-7232
Douglas Michael, *Agent*

GAGE GROUP
9255 Sunset Blvd, Suite 515; Los Angeles, CA 90069; (310) 859-8777
Martin Gage, *Agent*

THE GERSH AGENCY 2/17
130 West 42nd St, Suite 2400; New York, NY 10036; (212) 997-1818
John Buzzetti, Peter Hagan, Scott Yoselow, *Agents*

GRAHAM AGENCY
311 West 43rd St; New York, NY 10036; (212) 489-7730
Earl Graham, *Agent*

HARDEN-CURTIS ASSOCIATES
850 Seventh Ave, Suite 405; New York, NY 10019; (212) 977-8502
Mary Harden, *Agent*

HAROLD MATSON COMPANY, INC. 2/16
276 Fifth Ave; New York, NY 10001; (212) 679-4490
Ben Camardi, Jonathan Matson, *Agents*

HELEN MERRILL, LTD. 2/16
425 West 23rd St, Suite 1F; New York, NY 10011; (212) 691-5326
Beth Blickers, Patrick Herold, Morgan Jenness, *Agents*

INTERNATIONAL CREATIVE MANAGEMENT
40 West 57th St; New York, NY 10019; (212) 556-5600
Bridget Aschenberg, Mitch Douglas, *Agents*

THE JOY HARRIS LITERARY AGENCY
156 Fifth Ave, Suite 617; New York, NY 10010; (212) 924-6269
Joy Harris, *Agent*

THE JOYCE KETAY AGENCY
1501 Broadway, Suite 1908; New York, NY 10036; (212) 354-6825
Joyce P. Ketay, Carl Mulert, Wendy Streeter, *Agents*

THE KOPALOFF COMPANY
6399 Wilshire, Suite 414; Los Angeles, CA 90048; (323) 782-1854
Don Kopaloff, Arnold Soloway, *Agents*

LANTZ AGENCY 2/21
888 Seventh Ave, Suite 3001; New York, NY 10106; (212) 586-0200
Robert Lantz, *Agent*

PARAMUSE ARTISTS ASSOCIATES, INC.
25 Central Park W; New York, NY 10023; (212) 315-0640
Mike Sbabo

PEREGRINE WHITTLESEY AGENCY
345 East 80th St, #31F; New York, NY 10021; (212) 737-0153
Peregrine Whittlesey, *Agent*

PINDER LANE & GARON-BROOKE ASSOCIATES
159 West 53rd St; New York, NY 10019; (212) 489-0880
Nancy Coffey, Dick Duane, Robert Thixton, *Agents*

ROBERT A. FREEDMAN DRAMATIC AGENCY
1501 Broadway, Suite 2310; New York, NY 10036; (212) 840-5760
Robert A. Freedman, Selma Luttinger, *Agents*

ROSENSTONE/WENDER
3 East 48th St, 4th Floor; New York, NY 10017; (212) 832-8330
Ronald Gwiazda, Howard Rosenstone, Phyllis Wender, *Agents*

SAMUEL FRENCH
45 West 25th St; New York, NY 10010-2751; (212) 206-8990
Lawrence Harbison, *Editor*

SHUKAT COMPANY, LTD.
340 West 55th St, Suite 1A; New York, NY 10019; (212) 582-7614
Scott Shukat, Patricia McLaughlin, *Agents*

STEPHEN PEVNER, INC.
248 West 73rd St, 2nd Floor; New York, NY 10023; (212) 496-0474
Stephen Pevner, *Agent*

THE SUSAN GURMAN AGENCY
865 West End Ave, #15A; New York, NY 10025; (212) 749-4618
Gail Eisenberg, Susan Gurman, *Agents*

SUSAN SCHULMAN A LITERARY AGENCY
2 Bryan Plaza; Washington Depot, CT 06794; (212) 713-1633,
(860) 868-3700

THE TANTLEFF OFFICE
375 Greenwich St, Suite 603; New York, NY 10013; (212) 941-3939
Charmaine Ferenczi, Jack Tantleff, *Agents*

WILLIAM MORRIS AGENCY
1325 Ave of the Americas; New York, NY 10019; (212) 586-5100
Peter Franklin, David Kalodner, George Lane, Owen Laster, Biff Liff,
Gilbert Parker, Susan Weaving, *Agents*

WRITERS & ARTISTS AGENCY
19 West 44th St, Suite 1000; New York, NY 10036; (212) 391-1112
Jeff Berger, William Craver, Greg Wagner, *Agents*

Fellowships and Grants

Can I apply directly to all the programs listed in this section?

No. A number of the grant programs we list must be applied to by a producing or presenting organization. However, you should be aware that these programs are listed so that you can bring them to the attention of organizations with which you have a working relationship. All or most of the funds disbursed directly benefit the individual artist since they go to cover commissioning fees, residencies and other expenses related to the creation of new works.

How can I enhance my chances of winning an award?

Apply for as many awards for which you qualify; once you have written the first grant proposal, you can often, with little additional work, adapt it to fit other guidelines. Start early. This is so important that we give full listings to the increasing number of awards offered in alternate years, even when the deadline falls outside the period this *Sourcebook* covers. Use the Submission Calendar in the back of this book to help you plan your campaign. In the case of all awards for which you can apply directly, write for guidelines and application forms months ahead. Study the guidelines carefully and follow them meticulously. Don't hesitate to ask for advice and assistance from the organization to which you are applying. Submit a well-thought-out, excellently written, neatly typed application—and make sure it arrives in the organization's office by the deadline. (Never assume, without checking, that the deadline is the postmark date.)

THE ALFRED HODDER FELLOWSHIP

The Council of the Humanities; 122 East Pyne; Princeton University; Princeton, NJ 08544-5264; (609) 258-4717, FAX 258-2783; Web http://www.princeton.edu/~humcounc/

Open to: playwrights, translators. **Frequency:** annual. **Remuneration:** $45,000 (approx) fellowship. **Guidelines:** emerging artist; writer spends academic year at Princeton pursuing independent project; prefers writer outside of academia. **Application procedure:** maximum 10-page work sample, 2–3 page project proposal and resume; send SASE for guidelines. **Deadline:** 1 Nov 1999.

THE AMERICAN-SCANDINAVIAN FOUNDATION

15 East 65th St; New York, NY 10021; (212) 879-9779, FAX 249-3444; E-mail grants@amscan.org; Web http://www.amscan.org
Fellowships and Grants Division

Open to: playwrights, translators, composers, librettists, lyricists. **Frequency:** annual. **Remuneration:** $3000–15,000. **Guidelines:** grants and fellowships for research and study in Scandinavian countries; U.S. citizen or permanent resident with undergraduate degree. **Application procedure:** completed application, supplementary materials and $10 fee. **Deadline:** 1 Nov 1999. **Notification:** Mar 1999.

ARIZONA COMMISSION ON THE ARTS PERFORMING ARTS FELLOWSHIP

417 West Roosevelt St; Phoenix, AZ 85003; (602) 255-5882, FAX 256-0282; E-mail general@arizonaarts.org; Web http://az.arts.asu.edu/artscomm
Claire West, *Performing Arts Director*

Open to: playwrights, composers. **Frequency:** award rotates triennially among disciplines. **Remuneration:** $5000 fellowship. **Guidelines:** AZ resident 18 years of age or older who is not enrolled for more than 3 credit hours at college or university; send SASE for guidelines and application. **Application procedure:** completed application and work sample. **Deadline:** Sep 2000 for composers; Sep 2001 for playwrights. **Notification:** Mar 2001 for composers; Mar 2002 for playwrights.

ARTIST TRUST

1402 Third Ave, Suite 404; Seattle, WA 98101-2118; (206) 467-8734, FAX 467-9633; E-mail info@artisttrust.org
Heather Dwyer, *Program Director*

Fellowships

Open to: playwrights, composers, librettists, lyricists, screenwriters, radio and television writers. **Frequency:** award rotates among disciplines. **Remuneration:** $5500 award. **Guidelines:** WA resident only; practicing professional artist of exceptional talent and demonstrated ability; award based on creative excellence and continuing dedication to an artistic discipline; send SASE for guidelines. **Application procedure:** completed application and work sample. **Deadline:** late spring 2000 for playwrights; exact date TBA (12 Jun in 1998); late spring 2001 for composers, librettists, lyricists, screenwriters, radio and television writers; exact date TBA (18 Jun in 1999).

GAP (Grants for Artist Projects)

Open to: playwrights, composers, librettists, lyricists, screenwriters, radio and television writers. **Frequency:** annual. **Remuneration:** grant up to $1200. **Guidelines:** WA resident only; grant for the initiation, continuation or completion of specific creative project undertaken by individual artist; award based on quality of work as represented by supporting material and on creativity and feasibility of proposed project; write for guidelines. **Application procedure:** completed application and work sample. **Deadline:** late Feb 2000; exact date TBA.

ARTISTS-IN-BERLIN PROGRAMME

To obtain application only: German Academic Exchange Service (DAAD);
    950 Third Ave, 19th Floor; New York, NY 10022; (212) 758-3223,
    FAX 755-5780; E-mail daadny@daad.org; Web http://www.daad.org
All applications and inquiries to: German Academic Exchange Service (DAAD);
    Jaegerstr 23; D-10117 Berlin, Germany; 49-30-202-2080;
    E-mail bkp.berlin@daad.de; Web http://www.daad.de/e-info-foreign/artists
    -in-berlin_programme.shtml

Open to: playwrights, composers. **Frequency:** annual. **Remuneration:** monthly grant to cover living costs and rent during 1-year Berlin residency (6 months in special cases); workspace provided; travel for writer and members of immediate family staying in Berlin for residency; health and accident insurance; optional subsidized projects such as readings or publications. **Guidelines:** to enable 15–20 internationally known, qualified, young artists to pursue work while participating in city's cultural life and making contact with local artists; must reside in Berlin for period of grant; German nationals and foreign writers who are resident in Germany ineligible; write for guidelines. **Application procedure:** completed application; samples of published work (no manuscripts), preferably in German, otherwise in English or French, for playwrights; scores, records, tapes or published work for composers. **Deadline:** 31 Dec 1999. **Notification:** May 2000. **Dates:** residency begins between 1 Jan and 30 Jun 2001.

ARTS INTERNATIONAL

Institute of International Education; 809 United Nations Plaza;
    New York, NY 10017-3580; (212) 984-5370, FAX 984-5574;
    E-mail thefund@iie.org/ai

Cintas
Linda Walton, *Program Officer*

This fellowship program is open to individuals of Cuban descent or citizenship living outside Cuba. Award rotates among disciplines; discipline for 2000–2001 fellowship TBA; call after Dec 1999 for information. **Deadline:** Mar 2000; exact date TBA.

The Fund for U.S. Artists at International Festivals and Exhibitions
(see National Endowment for the Arts International Partnerships in this section)
Linda Walton, *Program Officer*

Open to: performing artists and organizations. **Frequency:** triannual. **Remuneration:** grants of up to $25,000 (most grants $500–10,000) to cover expenses related to festival participation including travel, lodging, artists' fees and per diem. **Guidelines:** U.S. citizen or permanent resident who has been invited to international festival. **Application procedure:** completed application; letter of proposal; copy of invitation from festival; full budget showing all costs of participation in festival and festival's contribution to these costs; work sample and bio. **Deadline:** Sep 1999 (exact date TBA); Jan 2000 (exact date TBA); May 2000 (exact date TBA). Notification: 2 months.

Inroads
Cheryl Katz, *Program Officer*
E-mail aiinternational@iie.org

Open to: performing artists and organizations. **Frequency:** annual. **Remuneration:** grants of $20,000–30,000. **Guidelines:** funds to be used for short-term planning residencies for partnership between artists in different disciplines; 1 artist must be U.S. resident, 1 must be resident of Africa, Asia, Latin America, the Middle East, the Pacific Islands or the Caribbean; project must be under umbrella of U.S. host organization. **Application procedure:** write for guidelines and application. **Deadline:** TBA; call for information.

ASIAN CULTURAL COUNCIL
437 Madison Ave, 37th Floor; New York, NY 10022; (212) 812-4300,
FAX 812-4299; E-mail acc@accny.org;
Web http://www.asianculturalcouncil.org

ACC Residency Program in Asia

Open to: playwrights, composers, librettists, lyricists. **Frequency:** annual. **Remuneration:** amount varies. **Guidelines:** to support American artists, scholars, and specialists undertaking collaborative research, teaching or creative residencies at cultural and educational institutions in East and Southeast Asia. **Application procedure:** write for application, include project description. **Deadline:** 1 Feb 2000.

Japan-United States Arts Program

Open to: playwrights, composers, librettists, lyricists. **Frequency:** annual. **Remuneration:** amount varies. **Guidelines:** to support residencies in Japan for American artists for a variety of purposes, including creative activities (other than performances), research projects, professional observation tours and specialized training. **Application procedure:** write for application, include project description. **Deadline:** 1 Feb 2000.

ATLANTA BUREAU OF CULTURAL AFFAIRS

675 Ponce de Leon Ave; Atlanta, GA 30308; (404) 817-6815, FAX 817-6827;
    E-mail culturalaffairs@mindspring.com; Web http://www.bcaatlanta.org
Camille Russell Love, *Director*

Artists Project

Open to: playwrights, composers, librettists, lyricists. **Frequency:** annual. **Remuneration:** grant up to $3000. **Guidelines:** practicing professional artist resident in city of Atlanta for at least 1 year prior to deadline. **Application procedure:** write for guidelines and application. **Deadline:** Dec 1999 (exact date TBA). **Notification:** 3 months.

Mayor's Fellowships in the Arts

Open to: playwrights, composers, librettists, lyricists. **Frequency:** award rotates among disciplines. **Remuneration:** $5000 award. **Guidelines:** practicing professional artist resident in city of Atlanta for at least 3 consecutive years prior to deadline; playwright may apply under literary or theatre arts; composer, librettist, lyricist apply under music. **Application procedure:** write for guidelines and application. **Deadline:** Dec 1999 for playwrights (exact date TBA); Dec 2000 for composers, librettists, lyricists (exact date TBA). **Notification:** 3 months.

AURAND HARRIS CHILDREN'S THEATRE GRANTS AND FELLOWSHIPS

The Children's Theatre Foundation of America; Box 8067;
    New Orleans, LA 70182; (504) 283-8868, FAX 866-0502
Orlin Corey, *President*
    (Also see entry in Membership and Service Organizations)

Fellowships

Open to: playwrights. **Frequency:** annual. **Remuneration:** $2500 maximum award. **Guidelines:** U.S. resident; funds to be used for specific projects or professional development of theatre artists who work in the area of children's theatre. **Application procedure:** write for guidelines. **Deadline:** 1 May 2000. **Notification:** 1 Sep 2000.

Grants

Open to: not-for-profit theatres. **Frequency:** annual. **Remuneration:** grant up to $3000. **Guidelines:** grant to assist in production costs of premiere of new play for children including expenses to enable playwright to participate in rehearsals and attend performances. **Application procedure:** write for guidelines. **Deadline:** 1 May 2000. **Notification:** 1 Sep 2000.

BRODY ARTS FUND

California Community Foundation; 606 South Olive St, Suite 2400;
Los Angeles, CA 90014-1526; (213) 413-4130; Web http://www.calfund.org
Program Secretary

Open to: playwrights, composers, librettists, lyricists, solo performers, screenwriters, radio and television writers. **Frequency:** award rotates among disciplines. **Remuneration:** fellowship of $5000. **Guidelines:** L.A. county resident; emerging artist in "expansion arts" field (minority, inner-city, rural and tribal arts); write for guidelines; application available in spring of application year. **Application procedure:** completed application and supporting materials. **Deadline:** Mar 2000 (exact date TBA). **Notification:** Jun 2000.

BUNTING FELLOWSHIP PROGRAM

The Mary Ingraham Bunting Institute of Radcliffe College; 34 Concord Ave;
Cambridge, MA 02138; (617) 495-8212, FAX 495-8136;
Web http://www.radcliffe.edu/bunting
Paula Soares, *Fellowships Coordinator*

Open to: playwrights, composers, librettists. **Frequency:** annual. **Remuneration:** $36,500 1-year fellowship. **Guidelines:** to provide opportunity and support for professionals of demonstrated accomplishment and exceptional promise to complete substantial project in their field; full-time appointment; fellow required to reside in Boston area and expected to present work-in-progress in public colloquia during year; office or studio space, auditing privileges and access to libraries and other resources of Radcliffe and Harvard provided; call or write for guidelines and application. **Application procedure:** completed application with $45 fee. **Deadline:** 1 Oct 1999. **Notification:** Apr 2000. **Dates:** 15 Sep 2000–15 Aug 2001.

BUSH ARTIST FELLOWS PROGRAM

The Bush Foundation; E-900 First National Bank Bldg; 332 Minnesota St;
St. Paul, MN 55101; (651) 227-5222
Julie Dalgleish, *Program Director*

Open to: playwrights, composers, screenwriters. **Frequency:** award rotates biennially among disciplines. **Remuneration:** $40,000 in equal monthly installments for 12–18 months. **Guidelines:** MN, ND, SD or western WI resident at least 25 years old who is not a student; playwright must have had at least 1 play given full production or workshop production for which admission was charged; screenwriter must have had 1 public staged reading or workshop production for which admission was charged, or screenplay sale or option. **Application procedure:** write for guidelines and application. **Deadline:** next deadline for playwrights, composers and screenwriters Oct 2000 (exact date TBA). **Notification:** Apr 2001.

DOBIE-PAISANO FELLOWSHIP
University of Texas at Austin; J. Frank Dobie House; 702 East Dean Keeton St;
   Austin, TX 78705; (512) 471-8542, FAX 471-9997;
   E-mail aslate@mail.utexas.edu
Audrey Slate, *Coordinator*

Open to: playwrights. **Frequency:** annual. **Remuneration:** living allowance to cover 6-month residency at 265-acre ranch; free housing; families welcome. **Guidelines:** native Texan, or playwright who has lived in TX for at least 2 years or has published work about TX; ordinarily 2 writers selected each year. **Application procedure:** write for application after 1 Oct 1999. **Deadline:** 21 Jan 2000. **Notification:** May 2000.

THE DON AND GEE NICHOLL FELLOWSHIPS IN SCREENWRITING
Academy of Motion Picture Arts and Sciences; 8949 Wilshire Blvd;
   Beverly Hills, CA 90211-1972; (310) 247-3059;
   Web http://www.oscars.org/nicholl
Greg Beal, *Program Coordinator*

Open to: playwrights, screenwriters. **Frequency:** annual. **Remuneration:** up to 5 fellowships of $25,000. **Guidelines:** playwright, screenwriter or fiction writer who has not worked as a professional screenwriter for theatrical films or television or sold screen or television rights to any original story, treatment, stage play, screenplay or teleplay; 1st-round selection based on submission of original screenplay or screen adaptation of writer's own original work, 100–130 pages, written in standard screenplay format; send SASE for guidelines after 1 Jan 2000; application may be obtained from Web. **Application procedure:** completed application, screenplay and $30 application fee. **Deadline:** 1 May 2000. **Notification:** 1st-round selection Aug 2000; winners late Oct 2000.

ELECTRONIC ARTS GRANT PROGRAM
Experimental Television Center; 109 Lower Fairfield Rd; Newark Valley, NY
   13811; (607) 687-4341, FAX 687-4341; E-mail etc@servtech.com;
   Web http://www.experimentaltvcenter.org
Sherry Miller Hocking, *Program Director*

Finishing Funds

Open to: media artists, including writers and composers, involved in creation of film, audio, video or computer-generated time-based works. **Frequency:** annual. **Remuneration:** up to $1000. **Guidelines:** resident of NY State; funds to be used to assist completion of work which is time-based in conception and execution and is to be presented as tape or installation; work must be completed before 30 Sep 2000; write for guidelines. **Application procedure:** 3 copies of completed application, project description, work samples and resume. **Deadline:** 15 Mar 2000. **Notification:** 6–8 weeks.

Presentation Funds

Open to: not-for-profit organizations presenting audio, film, video or computer-generated time-based works. **Frequency:** ongoing. **Remuneration:** grant of up to $750 to assist presentation of work and artist's involvement in activities related to presentation. **Guidelines:** NY State organization; event must be open to public and should emphasize work of NY State artist(s); write for guidelines. **Application procedure:** individual may not apply; completed application and supporting materials submitted by organization well in advance of event. **Deadline:** ongoing. **Notification:** 15th of month following month of submission.

FULBRIGHT SENIOR SCHOLAR AWARDS
FOR FACULTY AND PROFESSIONALS

Council for International Exchange of Scholars (CIES); 3007 Tilden St NW,
    Suite 5L; Washington, DC 20008-3009; (202) 686-7877, FAX 362-3442;
    E-mail apprequest@cies.iie.org; Web http://www.cies.org

Open to: scholars and professionals in all areas of theatre and the arts, including playwrights, translators, composers, librettists and lyricists. **Frequency:** annual. **Remuneration:** grant for university lecturing or research in one of more than 125 countries for 2–9 months; amount varies with country of award; travel; maintenance allowance for living costs of grantee and possibly family. **Guidelines:** U.S. citizen; Ph.D., MFA or comparable professional qualifications; university or college teaching experience for lecturing awards; for selected countries, proficiency in a foreign language; application may be obtained from Web. **Application procedure:** completed application. **Deadline:** 1 Aug 2000. **Notification:** up to 11 months, depending on country.

GEORGE BENNETT FELLOWSHIP

Phillips Exeter Academy; Exeter, NH 03833-1104; Web http://www.exeter.edu
Charles Pratt, *Coordinator, Selection Committee*

Open to: playwrights. **Frequency:** annual. **Remuneration:** academic-year stipend of $6000; room and board for fellow and family. **Guidelines:** individual who is seriously contemplating or pursuing a career as a writer and who needs time and freedom from material considerations to complete a project in progress; committee favors writers who have not yet been produced commercially or at a major not-for-profit theatre; fellow expected to make self and talents available in informal and unofficial way to students interested in writing; send SASE for guidelines and application or visit Web (no phone inquiries). **Application procedure:** completed application, work sample, statement concerning work-in-progress, names of 2 references and $5 fee. **Deadline:** 1 Dec 1999. **Notification:** 15 Mar 2000. **Dates:** Sep 2000–Jun 2001.

THE JAPAN FOUNDATION
152 West 57th St, 39th Floor; New York, NY 10019; (212) 489-0299,
      FAX 489-0409; Web http://www.jfny.org/jfny/index.html
Artists Fellowship Program

Open to: specialists in the fields of fine arts, performing arts, music, journalism and creative writing, including playwrights, composers, librettists, lyricists and screenwriters. **Frequency:** annual. **Remuneration:** monthly stipend of ¥370,000 (about $3050) or ¥430,000 (about $3550), depending on grantee's professional career; travel; other allowances. **Guidelines:** U.S. citizen or permanent resident; fellowship of 2–6 months, not to be held concurrently with another major grant, to support project substantially related to Japan. **Application procedure:** write for guidelines and application, stating theme of project, present position and citizenship. **Deadline:** 1 Dec 1999. **Notification:** early-mid Apr 2000. **Dates:** residency begins between 1 Apr 2000 and 31 Mar 2001.

JOHN SIMON GUGGENHEIM MEMORIAL FOUNDATION
90 Park Ave; New York, NY 10016; (212) 687-4470, FAX 697-3248;
      E-mail fellowships@gf.org; Web http://www.gf.org

Open to: playwrights, composers. **Frequency:** annual. **Remuneration:** 1-year fellowship (in 1998, 168 fellowships with average grant of $32,000). **Guidelines:** citizen or permanent resident of U.S. or Canada; recipient must demonstrate exceptional creative ability; grant to support research in any field of knowledge or creation in any of the arts under the freest possible conditions. **Application procedure:** write for guidelines. **Deadline:** 1 Oct 1999. **Notification:** Mar 2000.

THE KENNEDY CENTER FUND FOR NEW AMERICAN PLAYS
The John F. Kennedy Center for the Performing Arts; 2700 F St NW;
      Washington, DC 20566; (202) 416-8024, FAX 416-8205;
      E-mail mawoodward@mail.kennedy-center.org;
      Web http://kennedy-center.org/newwork/fnap
Max Woodward, *Director*

Open to: not-for-profit professional theatres. **Frequency:** annual. **Remuneration:** $10,000 grant to playwright whose work theatre is producing, plus grant (amount dependent on quality of proposal and need) to theatre (3 in 1998); occasional $5000 award to most promising comedy writer; occasional $2,500 Roger L. Stevens award to playwright whose work shows "extraordinary promise" (2 in 1998). **Guidelines:** grant to theatre covers living and travel expenses for playwright during minimum 4 weeks of rehearsal and during any necessary additional rehearsals and rewrites in course of run; grant also covers expenses exceeding theatre's budget allocation for hiring of director, designer and guest actors; limit of 1 proposal per theatre; translations and musicals ineligible; write or visit Web for guidelines after 15 Jan 2000. **Application procedure:** playwright may not apply; proposal and supporting materials submitted by theatre. **Deadline:** May 2000 (exact date TBA).

THE KLEBAN AWARD

c/o Stein & Stein; 270 Madison Ave, Suite 1410; New York, NY 10016;
    (212) 683-5320, FAX 686-2182
Alan J. Stein, *Secretary*

Open to: librettists and/or lyricists (TBA). **Frequency:** annual. **Remuneration:** TBA ($100,000 each to lyricist and librettist, paid in installments of $50,000 a year, in 1998–99). **Guidelines:** applicant whose work has received a full or workshop production, or who has been a member or associate of a professional musical workshop or theatre group (e.g., ASCAP or BMI workshop; see the Development and Membership and Service Organizations chapters); writer whose work has been performed on the Broadway stage for a cumulative period of 2 years ineligible; write for guidelines. **Application procedure:** completed application and work sample. **Deadline:** TBA (Sep in 1998).

MANHATTAN THEATRE CLUB PLAYWRITING FELLOWSHIPS

311 West 43rd St, 8th Floor; New York, NY 10036; (212) 399-3000,
    FAX 399-4329; Web http://www.mtc-nyc.org
Maggie Malone, *Literary Assistant*

Open to: playwrights. **Frequency:** annual. **Remuneration:** $10,000 fellowship. **Guidelines:** New York-based playwright who has completed formal education and can demonstrate financial need; writers from diverse cultural groups encouraged to apply; fellowship includes commission for new play, production assistantship, 1-year residency at MTC; send SASE for guidelines or vist Web. **Application procedure:** sample script, resume, statement of purpose and letter of recommendation from theatre professional or professor. **Deadline:** 31 Dec 1999. (See entry in Production.)

MARY FLAGLER CARY CHARITABLE TRUST COMMISSIONING PROGRAM

122 East 42nd St, Room 3505; New York, NY 10168; (212) 953-7705,
    FAX 953-7720; E-mail gmorgan@carytrust.org
Gayle Morgan, *Music Program Director*

Open to: performance institutions including theatre and opera companies. **Frequency:** biennial. **Remuneration:** grant to help not-for-profit professional organization commission new musical work from established or emerging composer; amount varies (total of $300,000 available for 1999 grants). **Guidelines:** New York City organization only; funds to be used to compensate composer and librettist for creative work and to cover copying costs; write for guidelines. **Application procedure:** individual may not apply; letter of application and representative audiotape of composer's music submitted by organization. **Deadline:** 30 Jun 2001.

MATURE WOMAN SCHOLARSHIP AWARD

The National League of American Pen Women; 1300 17th St NW;
   Washington, DC 20036-1973; (202) 785-1997
Mary Jane Hillery, *National Scholarship Chairman*
All inquiries to 66 Willow Rd; Sudbury, MA 01776-2663

Open to: playwrights, composers, librettists, lyricists. **Frequency:** biennial. **Remuneration:** $1000 grant. **Guidelines:** American woman age 35 and over; 3 awards (1 in art, 1 in music, 1 in letters) to further creative goals of women at age when encouragement can lead to realization of long-term purposes; present and past NLAPW members ineligible; send SASE for guidelines. **Application procedure:** work sample; statement of purpose for which money will be used; statement that applicant is over age 35 and not a member of NLAPW (see Membership and Service Organizations) and $8 fee. **Deadline:** 15 Jan 2000. **Notification:** 15 Mar 2000.

THE MCKNIGHT INTERDISCIPLINARY FELLOWSHIP GRANT

Intermedia Arts, Minnesota; 2822 Lyndale Ave S; Minneapolis, MN 55408;
   (612) 871-4444, FAX 871-6927; E-mail allstaff@intermediaarts.org;
   Web http://www.intermediaarts.org
Sandy Agustin, *Community Programs Manager*

Minnesota Fellowship

Open to: interdisciplinary artists. **Frequency:** annual. **Remuneration:** $12,000 fellowship; $2000 in travel expenses. **Guidelines:** resident of MN for 1 year before application; mid-career interdisciplinary artists; fellowship and technical support to pursue educational/presentational activity during 18-month fellowship period; send SASE for guidelines after Oct 1999. **Application procedure:** completed application, 1-page maximum artist statement, 10-page maximum work sample, resume and optional SASP for acknowledgment of receipt. **Deadline:** 14 Jan 2000. **Notification:** spring 2001.

National McKnight Interdisciplinary Fellow in Residence

Open to: interdisciplinary artists. **Frequency:** biennial. **Remuneration:** $10,000 artist's fee; up to $4000 in travel expenses. **Guidelines:** artists with accomplished body of work; must have teaching and/or mentoring experience; must be in Minneapolis for at least 4 weeks (not necessarily consecutive) during 2002; send SASE for guidelines. **Application procedure:** letter of intent no more than 2 pages in length describing artist's body of interdisciplinary work, teaching and/or mentoring experience and previous residency experience. **Deadline:** 1 Feb 2001 intent to apply; Apr 2001 application (exact date TBA). **Notification:** Jun 2001.

MEET THE COMPOSER GRANT PROGRAMS
2112 Broadway, Suite 505; New York, NY 10023; (212) 787-3601,
    FAX 787-3745
    (Also see Membership and Service Organizations)

Meet The Composer/Arts Endowment Commissioning Music/USA
Kelly Rauch, *Program Manager*

Open to: opera, theatre and music-theatre companies; arts presenters; musical organizations; TV production companies; radio stations; soloists and performing ensembles of all kinds (jazz, chamber and new music). **Frequency:** annual. **Remuneration:** commissioning grant up to $30,000 to cover composer, librettist, TV writer and/or radio writer fees for opera or music-theatre work (amount dependent on scope and length of work). **Guidelines:** organizations that have been producing or presenting for at least 3 years; application may be from single organization for grants up to $10,000, or from consortium of organizations for grants up to $30,000; plans must involve full production of work and at least 4 performances for a single organization, or at least 6 for a consortium; write for guidelines. **Application procedure:** individual may not apply; 1 host organization submits completed application and supporting materials. **Deadline:** TBA. **Notification:** TBA.

New Residencies
Pablo Martínez, *Vice President for Programs*

Open to: opera, theatre and music-theatre companies, arts presenters and musical organizations. **Frequency:** annual. **Remuneration:** grant for composer's salary ($40,000 per annum for 2 years; $20,000 toward 3rd-year salary, to be matched by host organizations); $15,000 toward institutional partnership building activities; possible $1500 for composer's relocation costs. **Guidelines:** 3–5 organizations, including at least 2 producing or presenting organizations and at least 1 human service or community-based organization, form Residency Partnership to sponsor 3-year composer residency; composer writes pieces for all host organizations and works at least 60 hours per month "making music a positive force in community life" through teaching, organizing cultural events, recruiting other composers to community work, etc; host organizations produce residency works, provide office space and logistical support and provide health insurance; write for guidelines. **Application procedure:** individual may not apply; performing organizations in Residency Partnership apply on behalf of composer. **Deadline:** TBA.

NATIONAL ENDOWMENT FOR THE ARTS INTERNATIONAL PARTNERSHIPS
1100 Pennsylvania Ave NW, Room 704; Washington, DC 20506;
(202) 682-5429, FAX 682-5602; Web http://arts.endow.gov
Pennie Ojeda, *International Coordinator*

ArtsLink Collaborative Projects
All applications and inquiries to: CEC International Partners; 12 West 31st St;
New York, NY 10001-4415; (212) 643-1985, FAX 643-1996;
E-mail artslink@cecip.org

Open to: creative, interpretive and traditional artists, including playwrights, translators, composers, librettists, lyricists and solo performers. **Frequency:** annual. **Remuneration:** grant up to $6000 (most grants $1500–3500). **Guidelines:** U.S. citizen or permanent resident; to enable individual artists or groups of up to 5 artists to work with their counterparts in Central or Eastern Europe, the former Soviet Union or the Baltics; mutually beneficial collaborative project that will enrich artists' work and/or create new work that draws inspiration from knowledge and experience gained in country visited; write for guidelines. **Application procedure:** completed application and supporting materials. **Deadline:** 18 Jan 2000. **Notification:** Apr 2000.

The Fund for U.S. Artists at International Festivals and Exhibitions
(see Arts International in this section)
All applications and inquiries to: Arts International; Institute of International
Education; 809 United Nations Plaza; New York, NY 10017-3580;
(212) 984-5370, FAX 984-5564; E-mail thefund@iie.org/ai

Open to: performing artists and organizations. **Frequency:** triannual. **Remuneration:** grants up to $25,000 (most grants $500–10,000) to cover expenses related to festival participation including travel, housing, artists' fees and per diem. **Guidelines:** U.S. citizen or permanent resident who has been invited to international festival. **Application procedure:** completed application; letter of proprosal; copy of invitation from festival; full budget showing all costs of participation in festival and festival's contribution to these costs; work sample and bio. **Deadline:** Sep 1999 (exact date TBA); Jan 2000 (exact date TBA); May 2000 (exact date TBA). **Notification:** 2 months after deadline.

United States/Japan Creative Artists' Fellowships
All applications and inquiries to: Japan/U.S. Friendship Commission;
1120 Vermont Ave NW, Suite 925; Washington, DC 20005;
(202) 275-7712; E-mail jusfc@compuserve.com;
Web http://www2.dgsys.com/~jusfc/

Open to: creative, interpretive or traditional artists, including playwrights, translators, composers, librettists and lyricists. **Frequency:** annual. **Remuneration:** monthly stipend to cover housing, living expenses and modest professional support services; roundtrip transportation for artist and family members; stipend to study Japanese language in U.S. if necessary. **Guidelines:** U.S. citizen or permanent resident; to enable established artist to pursue discipline in Japan for 6 consecutive months; artist who has spent more than 3 months in Japan ineligible. **Application procedure:** write or call for guidelines and application materials. **Deadline:** 26 Jun 2000. **Notification:** Sep 2000.

NATIONAL ENDOWMENT FOR THE ARTS LITERATURE PROGRAM
1100 Pennsylvania Ave NW, Room 720; Washington, DC 20506;
(202) 682-5428; Web http://arts.endow.gov
Amy Stolls, *Literature Specialist*

Fellowships for Translators

Open to: translators. **Frequency:** annual. **Remuneration:** $20,000 fellowship. **Guidelines:** 2001 fellowship for translators of verse drama only; previously published translators of exceptional talent. **Application procedure:** write for guidelines and application. **Deadline:** 14 Mar 2000.

NATIONAL ENDOWMENT FOR THE HUMANITIES PUBLIC PROGRAMS
1100 Pennsylvania Ave NW; Washington, DC 20506; (202) 606-8269,
FAX 606-8557
Nancy Rogers, *Director*

Humanities Projects in Media
James J. Dougherty, *Assistant Director* (202) 606-8280

Open to: independent producers, radio and television writers. **Frequency:** annual. **Remuneration:** varies. **Guidelines:** support for planning, writing and/or production of, as well as collaboration on, television and radio projects focused on subjects and issues central to the humanities, and aimed at a national adult or broad regional audience; no adaptations of literary works; write for guidelines. **Application procedure:** submit draft proposal before making formal application. **Deadline:** 13 Sep 1999 and 17 May 2000 for collaboration grants; 1 Nov 1999 for planning grants; 1 Feb 2000 for planning, research and scripting, and production grants. **Notification:** Nov 1999 for Sep deadline; Mar 2000 for Nov deadline; Jul 2000 for Feb and May deadlines.

NATIONAL ENDOWMENT FOR THE HUMANITIES RESEARCH AND EDUCATION PROGRAMS
1100 Pennsylvania Ave NW; Washington, DC 20506; (202) 606-8200
James Herbert, *Director*

Collaborative Research
Margot Backas, *Senior Academic Advisor*; (202) 606-8209;
E-mail mbackas@neh.gov

Open to: translators. **Frequency:** annual. **Remuneration:** amount varies according to project. **Guidelines:** U.S. citizen or resident for 3 years; money to support collaborative projects to translate into English works that provide insight into the history, literature, philosophy and artistic achievements of other cultures and that make available to scholars, students, teachers and the public the thought and learning of those civilizations. **Application procedure:** completed application and supporting materials; write for guidelines. **Deadline:** 1 Sep 1999. **Notification:** Apr 2000.

NEW PLAY COMMISSIONS IN JEWISH THEATRE

National Foundation for Jewish Culture; 330 Seventh Ave, 21st Floor;
    New York, NY 10001; (212) 629-0500, ext 205, FAX 629-0508;
    E-mail nfjc@jewishculture.org; Web http://www.jewishculture.org
Rebecca Metzger, *Grants Administrator*

Open to: North American not-for-profit theatres. **Frequency:** annual. **Remuneration:** grant of $1000–5000. **Guidelines:** approximately 5 awards a year to theatres that have completed at least 2 seasons of public performances and are commissioning either new full-length play, adaptation, work for young audiences, musical or opera dealing substantively with issues of Jewish history, tradition, values or contemporary life; theatre must commit to presenting at least a public workshop production and/or staged reading of work, followed by discussion with audience; funds may be applied to commissioning fee, playwright's residency expenses or workshop costs; write, call or e-mail for guidelines. **Application procedure:** completed proposal, cover sheet and supporting materials, submitted by theatre. **Deadline:** 1 Oct 1999. **Notification:** Dec 1999.

NEW YORK FOUNDATION FOR THE ARTS (NYFA)

155 Ave of the Americas, 14th Floor; New York, NY 10013-1507;
    (212) 366-6900, FAX 366-1778; E-mail nyfaafp@artswire.org;
    Web http://nyfa.org
Penelope Dannenberg, *Director of Programs*

Artists' Fellowships

Open to: playwrights, composers, librettists, screenwriters. **Frequency:** award alternates biennially among disciplines. **Remuneration:** $7000 fellowship. **Guidelines:** NY State resident for 2 years prior to deadline; students ineligible. **Application procedure:** completed application and supporting materials; application seminars held each Sep. **Deadline:** next deadline for playwrights, composers, librettists and screenwriters Oct 1999 (exact date TBA).

Artists in the School Community
(Formerly Artists in Residence Program)

Open to: schools. **Description:** matching grant to assist schools that bring in artists, including playwrights, composers, librettists and lyricists, for residencies of 12 days–10 months; residency activities include artist-conducted student, teacher or parent workshops, lecture-demonstrations, readings and performances. **Financial arrangement:** artist is paid by school; recommended minimum fee of $250 a day. **Guidelines:** artist must be NY state resident. **Application procedure:** completed application from school; individual artist may not apply but is encouraged to write for guidelines and to collaborate with eligible sponsors to set up residencies; artist may also contact program for information and for help in finding sponsors. **Deadline:** 2 Apr 2000; subsidiary deadlines for smaller grants in Oct, Nov, Feb and Jun each year. **Notification:** Jul 2000. **Dates:** Sep 2000–Jun 2001.

NEW YORK THEATRE WORKSHOP PLAYWRITING FELLOWSHIP
(Formerly Van Lier Playwriting Fellowship)
New York Theatre Workshop; 79 East 4th St; New York, NY 10003;
    (212) 780-9037; FAX 460-8996
Chiori Miyagawa, *Artistic Associate*

Open to: playwrights. **Frequency:** annual. **Remuneration:** commission; amount of award varies. **Guidelines:** writer of color under 30 years of age and resident of New York City; must be available to attend monthly group meetings and 1-week summer retreat. **Application procedure:** script, artistic statement, resume and cover letter. **Deadline:** 15 Mar 2000. (See entry in Production.)

PEW FELLOWSHIPS IN THE ARTS
The University of the Arts; 230 South Broad St, Suite 1003;
    Philadelphia, PA 19102; (215) 875-2285, FAX 875-2276;
    Web http://www.pewarts.org
Melissa Franklin, *Director*

Open to: playwrights, composers, screenwriters. **Frequency:** annual; award rotates among disciplines. **Remuneration:** up to 12 $50,000 fellowships. **Guidelines:** to give artists living in Southeastern PA the opportunity to dedicate themselves wholly to the development of their work for up to 2 years; students not eligible; call or write for application and guidelines. **Application procedure:** completed application and work sample. **Deadline:** TBA. **Notification:** Jun 2000.

PILGRIM PROJECT
156 Fifth Ave, Suite 400; New York, NY 10010; (212) 627-2288, FAX 627-2184
Davida Goldman, *Secretary*

Open to: playwrights, solo performers, individual producers and theatre companies. **Frequency:** ongoing. **Remuneration:** grant of $1000–7000. **Guidelines:** grant toward cost of reading, workshop production or full production of play that deals with questions of moral significance; write for further information. **Application procedure:** script only. **Deadline:** ongoing.

THE PLAYWRIGHTS' CENTER GRANT PROGRAMS

2301 Franklin Ave East; Minneapolis, MN 55406-1099; (612) 332-7481;
    E-mail pwcenter@mtn.org; Web http://www.pwcenter.org
Carlo Cuesta, *Executive Director*
    (Also see Membership and Service Organizations)

Jerome Playwright-in-Residence Fellowships

Open to: playwrights, solo performers. **Frequency:** annual. **Remuneration:** 5 1-year fellowships of $7200. **Guidelines:** U.S. citizen or permanent resident; emerging playwright whose work has not received more than 2 professional full productions; fellow must spend year in residence at Center, where fellow has access to developmental workshops, readings and other services; send SASE for guidelines. **Application procedure:** completed application and supporting materials. **Deadline:** 15 Sep 1999. **Notification:** 15 Jan 2000. **Dates:** 1 Jul 2000–30 Jun 2001.

Many Voices Multicultural Collaboration Grants

Open to: playwrights, translators, composers, librettists, solo performers, screenwriters. **Frequency:** annual, contingent on funding. **Remuneration:** $200–2000 grant each to 2–4 teams. **Guidelines:** team of 2 or more artists of differing cultural backgrounds with commitment from MN organization to produce proposed collaborative work; team's lead artist must be MN playwright of color. **Application procedure:** send SASE for guidelines. **Deadline:** 1 Jul 2000. **Notification:** 1 Aug 2000. **Dates:** 1 Oct 2000–30 Jun 2001.

Many Voices Playwriting Residency Awards

Open to: playwrights, solo performers. **Frequency:** annual, contingent on funding. **Remuneration:** 8 awards: $1250 stipend, playwriting class scholarship, 1-year Playwrights' Center membership, opportunity to participate in playwriting roundtables, dramaturgical assistance, workshop and public reading. **Guidelines:** MN resident of color. **Application procedure:** send SASE for guidelines. **Deadline:** 1 Jul 2000. **Notification:** 1 Aug 2000. **Dates:** 1 Oct 2000–30 Jun 2001.

McKnight Advancement Grants

Open to: playwrights, solo performers. **Frequency:** annual. **Remuneration:** 3 grants of $8500; up to $1500 per fellow for workshops and staged readings using Center's developmental program or for allocation to partner organization for joint development and/or production. **Guidelines:** U.S. citizen or permanent resident and legal MN resident since 1 May 1998; playwright of exceptional merit and potential who has had at least 2 plays fully produced by professional theatres; funds intended to significantly advance fellow's art and/or career and may be used to cover a variety of expenses, including writing time, residency at theatre or other arts organization, travel/study, production or presentation; fellow must designate 2 months of grant year during which he or she plans to participate actively in Center's programs, including weekly attendance at and critical participation in readings and workshops of other members' work; send SASE for guidelines after 1 Dec 1999. **Application procedure:** completed application and supporting materials. **Deadline:** 1 Feb 2000. **Notification:** 1 May 2000. **Dates:** 1 Jul 2000–30 Jun 2001.

McKnight Fellowships

Open to: playwrights, solo performers. **Frequency:** annual. **Remuneration:** 2 fellowships of $10,000; up to $2000 program allocation to cover reading/ workshop expenses; possible partial travel and living expenses for fellows living outside 150-mile radius of Twin Cities. **Guidelines:** U.S. citizen or permanent resident whose work has made significant impact on contemporary theatre and who has had at least 2 plays fully produced by professional theatres; fellow must spend 1 month in residence at Center, where fellow has access to developmental workshops, readings and other services; fellowship is by nomination only. **Application procedure:** nomination by a theatre professional; completed application and supporting materials. **Deadline:** 1 Feb 2000. **Notification:** 15 Apr 2000. **Dates:** 1 Jul 2000–30 Jun 2001.

PRINCESS GRACE AWARDS: PLAYWRIGHT FELLOWSHIP

Princess Grace Foundation–USA; 150 East 58th St, 21st Floor;
    New York, NY 10155; (212) 317-1470, FAX 317-1473;
    E-mail pgfusa@pgfusa.com; Web http://www.pgfusa.com
(Ms.) Toby Boshak, *Executive Director*

Open to: playwrights. **Frequency:** annual. **Remuneration:** $7500 grant; 10-week residency with travel at New Dramatists, New York City (see listing in Membership and Service Organizations); inclusion of submitted script in New Dramatists' lending library and in its ScriptShare national script-distribution program for 1 year. **Guidelines:** U.S. citizen or permanent resident; under ordinary circumstances, playwright not more than 30 years of age at time of application; award based primarily on artistic quality of submitted play and potential of fellowship to assist writer's growth; send SASE for guidelines and application. **Application procedures:** completed application; unproduced, unpublished play (no adaptations); letter of recommendation and resume. **Deadline:** 31 Mar 2000.

TCG ARTISTIC PROGRAMS

Theatre Communications Group; 355 Lexington Ave;
    New York, NY 10017-0217; (212) 697-5230, FAX 983-4847;
    E-mail grants@tcg.org; Web http://www.tcg.org
Emilya Cachapero, *Director of Artistic Programs*
    (Also see Membership and Service Organizations, Publication and Useful Publications)

Extended Collaboration Grants

Open to: not-for-profit theatres, in collaboration with playwrights. **Frequency:** annual, contingent on funding. **Remuneration:** grant of $5000 (5 awarded in 1998-99). **Guidelines:** augments normal development resources of TCG Constituent theatre by enabling playwright to develop work over an extended period of time in collaboration with director, designer, choreographer, composer and/or artist from another discipline; period of collaboration must exceed that which theatre would normally support; funds cover inter-city transportation within the U.S. and Canada and other expenses related to research and meetings among the collaborators. **Application procedure:** playwright may not apply; completed application submitted by artistic leader of TCG constituent theatre. **Deadline:** late fall 1999, spring 2000 (both contingent on funding; exact dates TBA).

National Theatre Artist Residency Program

Category I: Residency Grants

Open to: playwrights, translators, composers, librettists, lyricists and other theatre artists in association with not-for-profit professional theatres. **Frequency:** annual (contingent on funding). **Remuneration:** approximately 10–14 grants of $50,000 or $100,000. **Guidelines:** experienced theatre artists who have created significant body of work and theatres with high artistic standards and organizational capacity to provide substantial support services to artists; funds cover compensation and residency expenses of 1 or 2 resident artists, working singly or in collaboration, during discrete periods used exclusively for residency-related activities that total at least 6 full months over 2-year period; proposals must be developed jointly by artists and institutions; theatres applying for $100,000 grant must have minimum operating budget of $500,000 in most recently completed fiscal year; theatres applying for $50,000 grant must have minimum operating budget of $250,000 in most recently completed fiscal year; write for guidelines. **Application procedure:** 2 copies of completed application and supporting materials. **Deadline:** 1 Dec 1999 intent to apply; 15 Dec 1999 application. **Notification:** 10 Mar 2000.

Category II: Matching Grants

Open to: playwrights, translators, composers, librettists, lyricists and other theatre artists in association with not-for-profit professional theatres. **Frequency:** annual, contingent on funding. **Remuneration:** up to $50,000 in matching funds. **Guidelines:** matching funds to support the continuation of particularly fruitful partnerships; to be considered, applicants must meet Category I eligibility requirements. **Application procedure:** 2 copies of completed application and supporting materials. **Deadline:** 1 Dec 1999 intent to apply; 15 Dec 1999 application. **Notification:** 10 Mar 2000.

Travel Grants

Open to: artistic leaders of theatres with budgets between $250,000 and $3 million that have not participated in the National Theatre Artists Residency Program. **Frequency:** quarterly. **Remuneration:** $2500. **Guidelines:** travel grant to allow artistic leaders of eligible theatres to meet with and/or see the work of artist(s) who have not previously participated in the National Theatre Artist Residency Program; funds cover transportation and out-of-town living expenses for theatre exploring a possible Residency Program proposal. **Application procedure:** 2 copies of completed application and supporting materials. **Deadlines:** 15 Sep 1999; 15 Dec 1999; 15 Mar 2000; 15 Jun 2000. **Notification:** 6 weeks.

NEA/TCG Theatre Residency Program for Playwrights

Open to: playwrights in association with not-for-profit professional theatres. **Frequency:** annual (contingent on funding). **Remuneration:** grant of $25,000 (12 awarded in 1998). **Guidelines:** playwrights must be citizens or permanent residents of U.S. at the time of application and have had at least one play published or produced within the last 5 years; theatres must have history of developing new work, high artistic standards and a minimum operating budget of $150,000 in the most recently completed fiscal year; a total of 6 months (not necessarily consecutive) must be dedicated to the development of a new work with the host theatre; call or write for application and guidelines. **Application procedure:** intent to apply card, followed by completed application and supporting materials. **Deadline:** write, call or E-mail for 2000 deadlines.

THE THANKS BE TO GRANDMOTHER WINIFRED FOUNDATION
Box 1449; Wainscott, NY 11975-1449; (516) 725-0323
Deborah Ann Light, *President, Board of Trustees*

Open to: playwrights, translators, composers, librettists, lyricists, TV and radio writers, solo performers. **Frequency:** biannual. **Remuneration:** grants of $500–5000. **Guidelines:** U.S. citizen; woman 54 years of age or older; grant must be applied to a project designed to enrich or empower the lives of adult women 21 years of age or older only; projects designed for children or adolescents not eligible. **Application procedure:** project discription; write or call for guidelines. **Deadline:** 21 Sep 1999; 21 Mar 2000. **Notification:** 1 Nov 1999 for Sep deadline; 1 May 2000 for Mar deadline.

TRAVEL AND STUDY GRANT PROGRAM
c/o Jerome Foundation; 125 Park Square Ct; 400 Sibley St;
St. Paul, MN 55101; (612) 224-9431, FAX 224-3439
Cynthia Gehrig, *President*

Open to: theatre artists and not-for-profit theatre administrators, including playwrights, composers, librettists and lyricists. **Frequency:** annual. **Remuneration:** grant up to $5000 for foreign or domestic travel. **Guidelines:** resident of Minnesota; program funded by Dayton-Hudson, General Mills and Jerome Foundation to support period of significant professional development through travel and study for independent professional artist or staff member of not-for-profit organization; write for guidelines. **Application procedure:** completed application, work sample and resume. **Deadline:** Feb 2000 (exact date TBA).

USIA FULBRIGHT STUDENT PROGRAM AT THE INSTITUTE OF INTERNATIONAL EDUCATION
(Formerly Institute of International Education)
809 United Nations Plaza; New York, NY 10017-3580; (212) 984-5330;
Web http://www.iie.org/fulbright
U.S. Student Programs Division

Open to: playwrights, translators, composers, librettists, lyricists. **Frequency:** annual. **Remuneration:** fellowship or grant; amount varies with country of award. **Guidelines:** specific opportunities for study abroad in the arts; write for brochure. **Application procedure:** completed application and supporting materials. **Deadline:** 25 Oct 1999. **Notification:** Jan 2000.

U.S.-MEXICO FUND FOR CULTURE
Londres 16 P.B.; Col. Juárez México, DF; Mexico 06600; 52-5-592-5386,
FAX 52-5-208-8943; E-mail usmexcult@laneta.apc.org;
Web http://www.laneta.apc.org/usmexcult/intro.html
Beatriz Nava Rivera, *Program Officer*

Open to: playwrights, translators, librettists, lyricists, screenwriters, TV and radio writers, and producing organizations. **Frequency:** annual. **Remuneration:** grants of $2000-25,000. **Guidelines:** Mexican and North American artists and cultural institutions; program sponsored by Bancomer Cultural Foundation, the Rockefeller Foundation and Mexico's National Fund for Culture and the Arts to fund performing arts projects of excellence that reflect artistic and cultural diversity of Mexico and U.S. and encourage mutual collaboration between artists of both countries; media arts, script translation and adaptation of fiction, drama and poetry also considered; for brochure and application materials, send $1.01 postage 8 1/2 x 11 SASE to U.S. Mexico Fund for Culture, c/o Benjamin Franklin Library, Laredo, TX 78044-3087. **Application procedure:** write for guidelines and application or visit Web. **Deadline:** 31 Mar 2000; no application before 15 Jan 2000. **Notification:** Aug 2000.

THE WALT DISNEY STUDIOS FELLOWSHIP PROGRAM
500 South Buena Vista St; Burbank, CA 91521-0705; (818) 560-6894,
FAX 557-6702; Web http://www.members.tripod.com/disfel
Troy Nethercott, *Program Director*

Open to: playwrights, screenwriters, television writers. **Frequency:** annual. **Remuneration:** 1-year salary of $33,000 for up to 10 writers; travel and 1 month's housing for fellows from outside Los Angeles area. **Guidelines:** to enable writers to work full-time at developing their craft in Disney Studios features or television division; no previous film or TV writing experience necessary; writer with Writers Guild of America credits eligible but should apply through the Guild's Employment Access at (213) 782-4648; call or visit Web for guidelines. **Application procedure:** completed application and notarized standard letter agreement with resume and writing sample (for feature division: screenplay approximately 120 pages long or full-length play; for TV division: 30-minute TV script approximately

45 pages long, full-length play, or one-act more than 24 pages long). **Deadline:** 24 Apr 2000; no submission before 3 Apr 2000. **Notification:** Sep 2000. **Dates:** fellowship year begins Oct 2000.

WISCONSIN ARTS BOARD ARTIST FELLOWSHIP AWARDS
101 East Wilson St, 1st Floor; Madison, WI 53702; (608) 264-8191,
    FAX 267-0380; E-mail mark.fraire@arts.state.wi.us;
    Web http://arts.state.wi.us
Mark Fraire, *Grant Programs and Services Specialist*

Open to: playwrights, composers. **Frequency:** biennial. **Remuneration:** $8000 fellowship. **Guidelines:** WI resident for at least 1 year at time of application; artist must produce 1 public presentation of work as part of fellowship; send SASE for guidelines and application. **Application procedure:** completed application and work sample. **Deadline:** 15 Sep 2000. **Notification:** Jan 2001.

Emergency Funds

How do emergency funds differ from other sources of financial aid?

Emergency funds are for writers in *severe temporary* financial difficulties. Some funds give outright grants, others make interest-free loans. For support for anything other than a genuine emergency, turn to Fellowships and Grants.

THE AUTHORS LEAGUE FUND
330 West 42nd St, 29th Floor; New York, NY 10036; (212) 268-1208,
FAX 564-8363
Susan Drury, *Administrator*

Open to: playwrights. **Type of assistance:** interest-free loan; request should be limited to immediate needs. **Guidelines:** published or produced working professional; must demonstrate real need. **Application procedure:** completed application and supporting materials. **Notification:** 2–4 weeks.

CARNEGIE FUND FOR AUTHORS
1 Old Country Rd, Suite 113; Carle Place, NY 11514

Open to: playwrights. **Type of assistance:** emergency grant. **Guidelines:** playwright who has had at least 1 play or collection of plays published commercially in book form (anthologies excluded); emergency which has placed applicant in substantial verifiable financial need. **Application procedure:** write for application form.

THE DRAMATISTS GUILD FUND
330 West 42nd St, 29th Floor; New York, NY 10036; (212) 268-1208
        FAX 564-8363
Susan Drury, *Administrator*

Open to: playwrights, composers, librettists, lyricists. **Type of assistance:** interest-free loan; request should be limited to immediate needs. **Guidelines:** published or produced working professional; must demonstrate real need. **Application procedure:** completed application and supporting materials. **Notification:** 2–4 weeks.

PEN FUND FOR WRITERS & EDITORS WITH AIDS
PEN American Center; 568 Broadway; New York, NY 10012; (212) 334-1660,
        FAX 334-2181; E-mail pen@pen.org
Victoria Vinton, *Program Coordinator*

Open to: playwrights, translators, librettists, lyricists, screenwriters, television writers, radio writers. **Type of assistance:** grant or interest-free loan of up to $1000. **Guidelines:** emergency assistance for published and/or produced writer who is HIV-positive and having financial difficulties. **Application procedure:** completed application, work sample, documentation of financial emergency and resume. **Notification:** 6–8 weeks. (See Membership and Service Organizations, and PEN awards in Prizes.)

PEN WRITERS FUND
PEN American Center; 568 Broadway; New York, NY 10012; (212) 334-1660,
        FAX 334-2181; E-mail pen@pen.org
Victoria Vinton, *Program Coordinator*

Open to: playwrights, translators, librettists, lyricists, screenwriters, television writers, radio writers. **Type of assistance:** grant or interest-free loan of up to $500. **Guidelines:** emergency assistance for published and/or produced writer in financial difficulties. **Application procedure:** completed application, work sample, documentation of financial emergency and resume. **Notification:** 6–8 weeks. (See Membership and Service Organizations, and PEN awards in Prizes.)

State Arts Agencies

What can my state arts agency do for me?

Possibly quite a bit—ask your agency for guidelines and study them carefully. State programs vary greatly and change frequently. Most have some sort of residency requirement, but eligibility is not always restricted to current residents, and may include people who were born in, raised in, attended school in or had some other association with the state in question.

What if my state doesn't give grants to individual artists?

A number of state arts agencies are restricted in this way. However, those with such restrictions, by and large, are eager to help artists locate not-for-profit organizations that channel funds to individuals, and you should ask specifically about this.

The New York State Council on the Arts, for example, is prohibited from funding individuals directly, and must contract with a sponsoring not-for-profit organization when it awards grants to individual artists. Yet NYSCA has a number of ways of supporting the work of theatre writers. The Literature Program funds translations and writers' residencies in communities. The Individual Artists Program assists, in alternate years, not-for-profit organizations in commissioning new theatre works. Moreover, NYSCA subgrants funds to the New York Foundation for the Arts, which in turn provides funds and project development assistance for individual artists (see New York Foundation for the Arts in Fellowships and Grants and their Sponsorship Program in Development).

At the least, every state has some kind of Artist-in-Education program; if you are able and willing to function in an educational setting you should certainly investigate this possibility.

ALABAMA STATE COUNCIL ON THE ARTS

201 Monroe St; Montgomery, AL 36130-1800; (334) 242-4076, FAX 240-3269; E-mail staff@arts.state.al.us; Web http://www.arts.state.al.us/
Al Head, *Executive Director*

ALASKA STATE COUNCIL ON THE ARTS

411 West 4th Ave, Suite 1E; Anchorage, AK 99501-2343; (907) 269-6610, FAX 269-6601; E-mail asca@alaska.net; Web http://www.aksca.org/
Helen Howarth, *Executive Director*

AMERICAN SAMOA COUNCIL ON CULTURE, ARTS AND HUMANITIES

Box 1540; Office of the Governor; Pago Pago, AS 96799; 011-684-633-4347, FAX 011-684-633-2059;
Web http://www.nasaa-arts.org/new/nasaa/gateway/AS.html
(Mrs.) Fa'ailoilo Lauvao, *Executive Director*

ARIZONA COMMISSION ON THE ARTS

417 West Roosevelt St; Phoenix, AZ 85003; (602) 255-5882, FAX 256-0282; E-mail general@ArizonaArts.org;
Web http://az.arts.asu.edu/artscomm/
Shelley Cohn, *Executive Director*

ARKANSAS ARTS COUNCIL

1500 Tower Bldg; 323 Center St; Little Rock, AR 72201; (501) 324-9766, FAX 324-9154; E-mail info@dah.state.ar.us;
Web http://www.heritage.state.ar.us/aac/
Jim Mitchell, *Executive Director*

CALIFORNIA ARTS COUNCIL

1300 I St, Suite 930; Sacramento, CA 95814; (916) 322-6555, FAX 322-6575; E-mail cac@cwo.com; Web http://www.cac.ca.gov/
Barbara Pieper, *Executive Director*

COLORADO COUNCIL ON THE ARTS

750 Pennsylvania St; Denver, CO 80203; (303) 894-2617, FAX 894-2615; E-mail coloarts@state.co.us; Web http://www.state.co.us/gov_dir/arts/
Fran Holden, *Executive Director*

CONNECTICUT COMMISSION ON THE ARTS
1 Financial Plaza; 755 Main St; Hartford, CT 06103;
(860) 566-4770, FAX 566-6462; E-mail kdemo@cslib.org;
Web http://www.cslnet.ctstateu.edu/cca/
John Ostrout, *Executive Director*

DELAWARE DIVISION OF THE ARTS
Carvel State Office Bldg; 820 North French St, 5th Floor;
Wilmington, DE 19801; (302) 577-8278, FAX 577-6561;
E-mail delarts@artswire.org; Web http://www.artsdel.org/
Peggy Amsterdam, *Director*

DISTRICT OF COLUMBIA (DC) COMMISSION
ON THE ARTS AND HUMANITIES
415 12th St NW, Suite 804; Washington, DC 20004;
(202) 724-5613, FAX 727-4135; E-mail dcah@erols.com;
Web http://www.capaccess.org/ane/dccah/
Anthony Gittens, *Executive Director*

FLORIDA DIVISION OF CULTURAL AFFAIRS
Department of State, The Capitol; Tallahassee, FL 32399-0250;
(850) 487-2980, FAX 922-5259; E-mail secretary@mail.dos.state.fl.us;
Web http://www.dos.state.fl.us/
Peggy Richardson, *Executive Director*

GEORGIA COUNCIL FOR THE ARTS
260 14th St NW, Suite 401; Atlanta, GA 30318; (404) 685-ARTS (2787),
FAX 685-2788; E-mail info@arts-ga.com; Web http://www.ganet.org/georgia-arts/
Caroline Ballard Leake, *Executive Director*

GUAM COUNCIL ON THE ARTS & HUMANITIES AGENCY
Box 2950; Agana, GU 96910; (671) 475-CAHA (2242/3), FAX 472-ART1 (2781);
Web http://www.nasaa-arts.org/new/nasaa/gateway/Guam.html/
Deborah Bordallo, *Executive Director*

STATE FOUNDATION ON CULTURE AND THE ARTS (HAWAII)
44 Merchant St; Honolulu, HI 96813; (808) 586-0300, FAX 586-0308
E-mail sfca@sfca.state.hi.us; Web http://www.state.hi.us/sfca/
Holly Richards, *Executive Director*

IDAHO COMMISSION ON THE ARTS
Box 83720; Boise, ID 83720-0008; (208) 334-2119, FAX 334-2488;
E-mail fhebert@ica.state.id.us; Web http://www.state.id.us/arts/
Frederick J. Hebert, *Executive Director*

ILLINOIS ARTS COUNCIL
100 West Randolph St, Suite 10-500; Chicago, IL 60601;
(312) 814-6750, FAX 814-1471; E-mail info@arts.state.il.us;
Web http://www.state.il.us/agency/iac/
Rhoda Pierce, *Executive Director*

INDIANA ARTS COMMISSION
402 West Washington St, Room W072; Indianapolis, IN 46204; (317) 232-1268,
FAX 232-5595; E-mail inartscomm@aol.com; Web http://www.state.in.us/iac/
Dorothy Ilgen, *Executive Director*

IOWA ARTS COUNCIL
Capitol Complex; 600 East Locust; Des Moines, IA 50319;
(515) 281-4451, FAX 242-6498; E-mail dhunter@max.state.ia.us;
Web http://www.state.ia.us/government/idca/iac
Dan Hunter, *Executive Director*

KANSAS ARTS COMMISSION
Jayhawk Tower; 700 Southwest Jackson, Suite 1004;
Topeka, KS 66603-3761; (785) 296-3335, FAX 296-4989;
Web http://www.nasaa-arts.org/new/nasaa/gateway/KS.html
David Wilson, *Executive Director*

KENTUCKY ARTS COUNCIL
31 Fountain Place; Frankfort, KY 40601; (502) 564-3757,
FAX 564-2839; E-mail kyarts@arts.smag.state.ky.us;
Web http://www.state.ky.us/agencies/arts/Kachome.html/
Gerri Combs, *Executive Director*

LOUISIANA DIVISION OF THE ARTS
Box 44247; Baton Rouge, LA 70804; (225) 342-8180, FAX 342-8173;
E-mail arts@crt.state.la.us; Web http://www.crt.state.la.us/arts/index.htm
James Borders, *Executive Director*

MAINE ARTS COMMISSION
55 Capitol St; State House Station 25; Augusta, ME 04333;
(207) 287-2724, FAX 287-2335; E-mail alden.wilson@state.me.us;
Web http://www.mainearts.com/
Alden C. Wilson, *Executive Director*

MARYLAND STATE ARTS COUNCIL
601 North Howard St, 1st Floor; Baltimore, MD 21201; (410) 767-6555,
FAX 333-1062; E-mail jbackas@mdbusiness.state.md.us;
Web http://www.msac.org/
Jim Backas, *Executive Director*

MASSACHUSETTS CULTURAL COUNCIL
120 Boylston St, 2nd Floor; Boston, MA 02116-4600;
(617) 727-3668, FAX 727-0044; E-mail web@art.state.ma.us;
Web http://www.massculturalcouncil.org/
Mary Kelley, *Executive Director*

MICHIGAN COUNCIL FOR THE ARTS & CULTURAL AFFAIRS
G. Mennan Williams Bldg, 3rd Floor; Box 30705; 525 West Ottawa;
Lansing, MI 48909-8205; (517) 241-4011, FAX 241-3979;
E-mail Betty.Boone@cis.state.mi.us; Web http://www.cis.state.mi.us/arts
Betty Boone, *Executive Director*

MINNESOTA STATE ARTS BOARD
Park Square Court; 400 Sibley St, Suite 200;
St. Paul, MN 55102; (651) 215-1600, FAX 215-1602;
E-mail msab@state.mn.us; Web http://www.arts.state.mn.us/
Robert Booker, *Executive Director*

MISSISSIPPI ARTS COMMISSION
239 North Lamar St, 2nd Floor; Jackson, MS 39201; (601) 359-6030, -6040,
FAX 359-6008; E-mail vlindsay@arts.state.ms.us; Web http://www.arts.state.ms.us/
Betsy Bradley, *Executive Director*

MISSOURI ARTS COUNCIL
111 North 7th St, Suite 105; St. Louis, MO 63101; (314) 340-6845,
FAX 340-7215; E-mail cheithau@mail.state.mo.us;
Web http://www.missouriartscouncil.org/
Flora Maria Garcia, *Executive Director*

MONTANA ARTS COUNCIL
City County Bldg; 316 North Park Ave, Room 252;
Helena, MT 59620-2201; (406) 444-6430, FAX 444-6548;
E-mail mac@state.mt.us; Web http://www.arts.state.mt.us/
Arlynn Fishbaugh, *Executive Director*

NEBRASKA ARTS COUNCIL
Joslyn Castle Carriage House; 3838 Davenport; Omaha, NE 68131-2329;
(402) 595-2122, FAX 595-2334; E-mail lindanac@artswire.org;
Web http://www.gps.K12.ne.us/nac_web_site/nac.htm
Jennifer S. Clark, *Executive Director*

NEVADA STATE COUNCIL ON THE ARTS
Capitol Complex; 602 North Curry St; Carson City, NV 89703;
(775) 687-6680, FAX 687-6688; E-mail seboskof@clan.lib.nv.us;
Web http://www.clan.lib.nv.us/ARTS
Susan Boskoff, *Executive Director*

NEW HAMPSHIRE STATE COUNCIL ON THE ARTS
40 North Main St, Phenix Hall; Concord, NH 03301; (603) 271-2789,
FAX 271-3584; E-mail rlawrence@nharts.state.nh.us;
Web http://www.state.nh.us/nharts/
Rebecca Lawrence, *Director*

NEW JERSEY STATE COUNCIL ON THE ARTS
Box 306; Trenton, NJ 08625-0306; (609) 292-6130,
FAX 989-1440; E-mail barbara@arts.sos.state.nj.us;
Web http://www.njartscouncil.org/
Barbara Russo, *Executive Director*

NEW MEXICO ARTS DIVISION
228 East Palace Ave; Santa Fe, NM 87501; (505) 827-6490,
FAX 827-6043; E-mail mbrommelsiek@lvr.state.nm.us;
Web http://www2.nmmnh-abq.mus.nm.us/nmarts/
Margaret Brommelsiek, *Executive Director*

NEW YORK STATE COUNCIL ON THE ARTS
915 Broadway, 8th Floor; New York, NY 10010; (212) 387-7000, FAX 387-7164;
E-mail nclarke@nysca.org; Web http://www.state.nysca.org
Nicolette B. Clarke, *Executive Director*

NORTH CAROLINA ARTS COUNCIL
Department of Cultural Resources; Raleigh, NC 27611; (919) 733-2821,
FAX 733-4834; E-mail mregan@ncacmail.dcr.state.nc.us;
Web http://www.ncarts.org/
Mary Regan, *Executive Director*

NORTH DAKOTA COUNCIL ON THE ARTS
418 East Broadway, Suite 70; Bismarck, ND 58501-4086; (701) 328-3954,
FAX 328-3963; E-mail comserve@pioneer.state.nd.us;
Web http://www.state.nd.us/arts/
Patsy Thompson, *Executive Director*

COMMONWEALTH COUNCIL FOR ARTS AND CULTURE (NORTHERN MARIANA ISLANDS)
Box 5553, CHRB; Saipan, MP 96950; (670) 322-9982, -9983, FAX 322-9028;
Web http://www.nasaa-arts.org/new/nasaa/gateway/NorthernM.html
Robert H. Hunter, *Executive Director*

OHIO ARTS COUNCIL
727 East Main St; Columbus, OH 43205; (614) 466-2613, FAX 466-4494;
E-mail wlawson@www.oac.state.oh.us; Web http://www.oac.state.oh.us/
Wayne Lawson, *Executive Director*

OKLAHOMA ARTS COUNCIL

Jim Thorpe Bldg; Box 52001-2001; Oklahoma City, OK 73152-2001;
(405) 521-2931, FAX 521-6418; E-mail okarts@arts.state.ok.us;
Web http://www.oklaosf.state.ok.us/~arts/
Betty Price, *Executive Director*

OREGON ARTS COMMISSION

775 Summer St, NE; Salem, OR 97310; (503) 986-0087, FAX 986-0260;
E-mail oregon.artscom@state.or.us; Web http://art.econ.state.or.us/
Christine D'Arcy, *Executive Director*

PENNSYLVANIA COUNCIL ON THE ARTS

Finance Bldg, Room 216; Harrisburg, PA 17120; (717) 787-6883, FAX 783-2538;
E-mail phorn@oa.state.pa.us; Web http://artsnet.heinz.cmu.edu/pca/
Philip Horn, *Executive Director*

INSTITUTE OF PUERTO RICAN CULTURE

Box 9024184; San Juan, PR 00902-4184; (787) 725-5137, FAX 724-8393;
Web http://www.nasaa-arts.org/new/nasaa/gateway/PR.html
Dr. José Ramon de la Torre, *Executive Director*

RHODE ISLAND STATE COUNCIL ON THE ARTS

95 Cedar St, Suite 103; Providence, RI 02903-1034; (401) 222-3883,
FAX 521-1351; E-mail info@risca.state.ri.us; Web http://www.risca.state.ri.us/
Randall Rosenbaum, *Executive Director*

SOUTH CAROLINA ARTS COMMISSION

1800 Gervais St; Columbia, SC 29201; (803) 734-8696, FAX 734-8526;
E-mail sukamsu@arts.state.sc.us; Web http://www.state.sc.us/arts/
Suzette Surkamer, *Executive Director*

SOUTH DAKOTA ARTS COUNCIL

Office of the Arts; 800 Governors Dr; Pierre, SD 57501-2294;
(605) 773-3131, FAX 773-6962; E-mail sdac@stlib.state.sd.us;
Web http://www.state.sd.us/state/executive/deca/sdarts.htm
Dennis Holub, *Executive Director*

TENNESSEE ARTS COMMISSION

Citizens Plaza, 401 Charlotte Ave; Nashville, TN 37243-0780;
(615) 741-1701, FAX 741-8559; E-mail btarleton@mail.state.tn.us;
Web http://www.arts.state.tn.us/
Bennett Tarleton, *Executive Director*

TEXAS COMMISSION ON THE ARTS

Box 13406, Capitol Station; Austin, TX 78711; (512) 463-5535, FAX 475-2699;
E-mail frontdesk@arts.state.tx.us; Web http://www.arts.state.tx.us/
John Paul Batiste, *Executive Director*

UTAH ARTS COUNCIL
617 East South Temple St; Salt Lake City, UT 84102; (801) 236-7555,
FAX 236-7556; E-mail bstephen@arts.state.ut.us;
Web http://www.ce.ex.state.ut.us/arts/
Bonnie Stephens, *Executive Director*

VERMONT ARTS COUNCIL
136 State St, Drawer 33; Montpelier, VT 05633-6001; (802) 828-3291,
FAX 828-3363; E-mail info@arts.vca.state.vt.us;
Web http://www.state.vt.us/vermont-arts
Alexander Aldrich, *Executive Director*

VIRGIN ISLANDS COUNCIL ON THE ARTS
Box 103; St. Thomas, VI 00802; (340) 774-5984,
FAX 774-6206; E-mail vicouncil@islands.vi;
Web http://www.nasaa-arts.org/new/nasaa/gateway/VI.html
John Jowers, *Executive Director*

VIRGINIA COMMISSION FOR THE ARTS
223 Governor St, 2nd Floor; Richmond VA 23219; (804) 225-3132,
FAX 225-4327; E-mail vacomm@artswire.org;
Web http://www.arts.wire.org/~vacomm/
Peggy Baggett, *Executive Director*

WASHINGTON STATE ARTS COMMISSION
234 East 8th Ave; Box 42675; Olympia, WA 98504-2675; (360) 753-3860,
FAX 586-5351; E-mail krist@wsac.wa.gov; Web http://www.wa.gov/art
Kristen Tucker, *Executive Director*

WEST VIRGINIA COMMISSION ON THE ARTS
1900 Kanawha Blvd E; Charleston, WV 25305; (304) 558-0240,
FAX 558-2779; E-mail ressmeyr@wvlc.wvnet.edu;
Web http://www.wvlc.wvnet.edu/culture/arts.html
Richard Ressmeyer, *Executive Director*

WISCONSIN ARTS BOARD
101 East Wilson St, 1st Floor; Madison, WI 53702; (608) 266-0190,
FAX 267-0380; E-mail artsboard@arts.state.wi.us;
Web http://www.arts.state.wi.us/
George Tzougros, *Executive Director*

WYOMING ARTS COUNCIL
2320 Capitol Ave; Cheyenne, WY 82002; (307) 777-7742, FAX 777-5499;
E-mail rbovee@missc.state.wy.us; Web http://commerce.state.wy.us/cr/arts
John G. Coe, *Executive Director*

Colonies and Residencies

What entries make up this section?

Though artist colonies that admit theatre writers constitute the majority of the listings, there are other kinds of residencies, such as artist-in-residence positions at universities, listed here as well. You can also find listings in Development and the Fellowships and Grants sections that could be considered residencies. We have also included some "writers' rooms" where playwrights in need of a quiet place for uninterrupted work are welcome. Of course there are hotels and inns throughout the country that would be desirable for an artist seeking refuge or in need of a quiet place to work, but we have chosen to limit our listings to those places set up as retreats for writers or that, in addition to reasonable lodging, provide services to benefit writers.

Note: you should assume that each deadline listed in this section is the date application materials must be *received*, unless stated otherwise.

ALDEN B. DOW CREATIVITY CENTER

Northwood University; 3225 Cook Rd; Midland, MI 48640-2398;
  (517) 837-4478, FAX 837-4468; E-mail creativity@northwood.edu
Carol B. Coppage, *Executive Director*

Open to: playwrights, translators, composers, librettists, lyricists, screenwriters. **Description:** 4 "Creativity Fellowships" each year for individuals working in any field, including the arts; 10-week summer residency at Northwood University, which provides environment for intense independent study; program includes interaction among fellows and formal presentation of work in Aug. **Financial arrangement:** travel, room, board, $750 for personal expenses and project materials. **Guidelines:** projects that are creative, original and have potential for impact on applicant's field; prefers 1 applicant per project; no accommodation for spouses or children. **Application procedure:** completed application, brief project description, work sample, resume and $10 application fee. **Deadline:** 31 Dec 1999. **Notification:** 1 Apr 2000. **Dates:** Jun–Aug 2000.

ALTOS DE CHAVON

c/o Parsons School of Design; 2 West 13th St, Room 707; New York, NY 10011;
  (212) 229-5370, FAX 229-8988; E-mail altos@spacelab.net
Stephen D. Kaplan, *Arts/Education Director*

Open to: playwrights, composers, screenwriters. **Description:** residencies of 3½ months for 15 artists a year, 1–2 of whom may be writers or composers, at nonprofit arts center located in tropical Caribbean surroundings 8 miles from town of La Romana in the Dominican Republic; efficiency studios or apartments with kitchenettes; small individual studios nearby; small visual-arts-oriented library; no typewriters for writers. **Financial arrangement:** $100 nonreturnable reservation fee; resident pays rent of $350 a month and provides own meals (estimated cost $20 a day). **Guidelines:** prefers Spanish-speaking artists who can use talents to benefit community, and whose work relates to Dominican or Latin American context; residents may teach workshops and are expected to contribute to group exhibition/performance at end of stay; write for further information. **Application procedure:** letter explaining applicant's interest in program, work sample and resume. **Deadline:** 15 Jul 2000. **Notification:** 1 Aug 2000. **Dates:** residencies start 1 Feb 2001, 1 Jun 2001, 1 Sep 2001.

APOSTLE ISLANDS NATIONAL LAKESHORE

Route 1, Box 4; Bayfield, WI 54814; (715) 779-3397, FAX 779-3049
Myra Dec, *Chief, Resources Education*

Open to: playwrights, composers, lyricists, solo performers. **Description:** 1 writer, poet, visual artist or choreographer at a time housed for 2–3 weeks on island in national park; cabin near beach and forest; no running water or electricity; resident must bring 2–3 week supply of food. **Financial arrangement:** free housing. **Guidelines:** artist "with accomplishment, artistic integrity" and ability to relate park through their work; must donate 1 work to park and communicate experience of residency through 1 program for public. **Application procedure:** completed application, project description, work sample, resume and cover letter.

Deadline: 15 Jan 2000; no submission before 1 Oct 1999. **Notification:** 1 Mar 2000. **Dates:** Jun–Sep.

ATLANTIC CENTER FOR THE ARTS

1414 Art Center Ave; New Smyrna Beach, FL 32168; (904) 427-6975,
  (800) 393-6975, FAX (904) 427-5669;
  E-mail program@atlantic-centerarts.org;
  Web http://www.atlantic-centerarts.org
Todd Levin, *Executive Director*
Nicholas Conroy, *Program Director*

Open to: playwrights, composers. **Description:** 6 1–3-week workshops each year offering writers; choreographers; media, visual and performing artists opportunity of concentrated study with internationally known Master Artists-in-Residence. **Financial arrangement:** resident pays $100 a week for tuition, $25 a day for private room with bath; scholarships available. **Application procedure:** Master Artist specifies submission materials and selects participants; write or call for brochure. **Deadline:** 3 months before residency. **Notification:** 2 months before residency. **Dates:** TBA; see brochure or Web site.

BLUE MOUNTAIN CENTER

Box 109; Blue Mountain Lake, NY 12812; (518) 352-7391
Harriet Barlow, *Director*

Open to: playwrights, composers, librettists, lyricists, solo performers. **Description:** 4-week residencies for 14 writers, composers and visual artists at center in Adirondack Mountains. **Financial arrangement:** free room and board. **Guidelines:** artist whose work is aimed at a general audience and reflects social concerns. **Application procedure:** send SASE for information. **Deadline:** 1 Feb 2000. **Notification:** early Apr 2000. **Dates:** mid-Jun–late-Oct 2000.

BYRDCLIFFE ART COLONY

The Woodstock Guild; 34 Tinker St; Woodstock, NY 12498; (914) 679-2079,
  FAX 679-4529; E-mail wguild@ulster.net;
  Web http://www.woodstockguild.org
Artists Residency Program

Open to: playwrights, translators, librettists, lyricists, solo performers, screenwriters. **Description:** 4-week residencies for writers, composers and visual artists at historic 300-acre colony in the Catskill Mountains, 1½ miles from Woodstock village center, 90 miles north of New York City; private room and separate individual studio space in Villetta Inn, spacious turn-of-the-century mountain lodge; common dining room and living room; residents provide own meals, using community kitchen. **Financial arrangement:** resident pays fee of $500 per session. **Guidelines:** proof of serious commitment to field of endeavor is major criterion for acceptance; professional recognition helpful but not essential; send SASE for further information. **Application procedure:** completed application, work sample, project description, resume, reviews and articles if available, contact information for 2 references and $5 fee. **Deadline:** 1 Apr 2000 (applications received after deadline considered for space still available). **Notification:** 15 May 2000. **Dates:** Jun–Sep.

CAMARGO FOUNDATION
B.P. 75; 13260 Cassis; France; 33-42-01-1157, -1311
Michael Pretina, *Director*
U.S. Office:
125 Park Square Ct, 400 Sibley St, St. Paul, MN 55101
William Reichard, *U.S. Secretariat*

Open to: playwrights, translators, composers. **Description:** 11 concurrent residencies, most for scholars and teachers pursuing projects relative to Francophone culture, but also including 1 for writer, 1 for composer and 1 for visual artist, at estate in ancient Mediterranean fishing port 30 minutes from Marseilles; furnished apartments; music studio available for composer. **Financial arrangement:** free housing; residents provide own meals. **Guidelines:** resident outlines project to fellow colony members during stay and writes final report; families welcome when space available; write to U.S. office for guidelines. **Application procedure:** completed application, project description, bio and 3 letters of recommendation. **Deadline:** 1 Feb 2000. **Notification:** 5 Apr 2000. **Dates:** Sep–Dec; Jan–May.

CENTRUM CREATIVE RESIDENCIES PROGRAM
(Formerly Centrum Artist-in-Residency Program)
Fort Worden State Park; Box 1158; Port Townsend, WA 98368; (360) 385-3102, FAX 385-2470; Web http://www.centrum.com
Marlene Bennett, *Residency Program Facilitator*

Open to: playwrights, translators, composers, librettists, lyricists, solo performers, screenwriters, television writers. **Description:** creative residencies for writers, composers, poets, visual artists and choreographers at center near Victorian seaport in 440-acre Fort Worden State Park; self-contained cabins near beach and hiking trails; separate studio space. **Financial arrangement:** free; some stipends available. **Guidelines:** artist who has clear direction and substantial accomplishment in field. **Application procedure:** completed application, project description, work sample and resume. **Deadline:** 8 Sep 1999. **Notification:** 31 Oct 1999. **Dates:** Jan–May 2000; Sep–Dec 2000.

DJERASSI RESIDENT ARTISTS PROGRAM
2325 Bear Gulch Rd; Woodside, CA 94062-4405; (650) 747-1250, FAX 747-0105; E-mail drap@djerassi.org; Web http://www.djerassi.org
Dennis O'Leary, *Executive Director*
Judy Freeland, *Residency Coordinator*

Open to: playwrights, translators, composers, librettists, lyricists, solo performers, screenwriters. **Description:** 1-month residencies for writers; choreographers; composers; media, visual and interdisciplinary artists and performers concurrently at 600-acre ranch in Santa Cruz mountains 1 hour south of San Francisco; interdisciplinary projects encouraged; collaborative projects considered. **Financial arrangement:** free room and board. **Guidelines:** emerging or established artist whose work has clear direction; send SASE for application or download from Web. **Application procedure:** completed application, sample of published work or work-in-progress, resume and $25 fee. **Deadline:** 15 Feb 2000 for 2001 residencies. **Notification:** 15 Aug 2000. **Dates:** Apr–Nov.

DORLAND MOUNTAIN ARTS COLONY

Box 6; Temecula, CA 92593; (909) 302-3837; E-mail dorland@ez2.net;
    Web http://www.ez2.net/dorland/
Admissions

Open to: playwrights, composers, lyricists. **Description:** 1-month residencies for 6 writers, composers and visual artists concurrently in individual studios on 300-acre nature preserve 50 miles northeast of San Diego; no electricity. **Financial arrangement:** $50 nonrefundable processing fee upon scheduling, if accepted; resident pays cabin donation of $300 a month. **Guidelines:** artist must demonstrate clear direction and accomplishment in field. **Application procedure:** send SASE for application and information. **Deadline:** 1 Sep 1999; 1 Mar 2000. **Notification:** 2 months. **Dates:** year-round.

DORSET COLONY FOR WRITERS

Box 519; Dorset, VT 05251; (802) 867-2223, FAX 867-0144;
    E-mail theatre@sover.net; Web http://www.theatredirectories.com
John Nassivera, *Executive Director*

Open to: playwrights, composers, librettists, lyricists and collaborative teams. **Description:** residencies of 1 week–1 month at house located in historic village in southern VT. **Financial arrangement:** resident pays fee for housing according to means (suggested fee $120 a week); meals not provided; large, fully equipped kitchen. **Guidelines:** artist must demonstrate seriousness of purpose and have record of professional achievement (readings or productions of works); work sample may be requested from less established artist. **Application procedure:** letter of inquiry with description of proposed project and desired length and dates of stay; resume. **Deadline:** on-going. **Notification:** 2–3 weeks. **Dates:** 10 Sep–30 Nov; 15 Mar–20 May; some winter residencies available in ancillary space. (See entry in Production.)

THE GELL WRITERS CENTER

c/o Writers & Books; 740 University Ave; Rochester, NY 14607; (716) 473-2590,
    FAX 729-0982, 442-9333
Joseph Flaherty, *Executive Director*

Open to: playwrights, translators, librettists, lyricists, solo performers, screenwriters, television writers. **Description:** 2 private bedrooms available in house surrounded by 23 acres of woodlands; workshops on creative writing sometimes available at extra cost; residents provide own meals. **Financial arrangement:**

resident pays $35 a day. **Application procedure:** write or call for application and brochure. **Deadline:** ongoing. **Notification:** 1 week. **Dates:** year-round.

THE HAMBIDGE CENTER FOR CREATIVE ARTS AND SCIENCES

Box 339; Rabun Gap, GA 30568; (706) 746-5718, FAX 746-9933;
E-mail hambidge@rabun.net; Web http://www.rabun.net/~hambidge
Executive Director

Open to: playwrights, translators, composers, librettists, lyricists. **Description:** residencies of 2 weeks–2 months for professionals in all areas of arts and humanities on 600 acres in northeast GA mountains; 8 private cottage with bedroom, kitchen, bathroom and studio/work area; evening meal provided Mon–Fri, May–Oct only; send SASE for guidelines. **Financial arrangement:** resident pays minimum of $125 a week toward total cost. **Application procedure:** completed application, work sample, resume, reviews, 3 letters of recommendation from professionals in applicant's field and $20 fee. **Deadline:** 1 Nov for 1 May–31 Oct residency; 1 May for 1 Nov–30 Apr residency. **Notification:** 2–3 months. **Dates:** year-round.

HAWTHORNDEN CASTLE INTERNATIONAL RETREAT FOR WRITERS

Lasswade, Midlothian; Scotland EH18 1EG; 44-131-440-2180
Administrator

Open to: playwrights. **Description:** residencies of 4 weeks for playwrights, poets and novelists at medieval castle on secluded crag overlooking valley of the River Esk 8 miles south of Edinburgh; 5 writers in residence at any one time; fully furnished study-bedroom; communal breakfast and dinner, lunch brought to writer's room; typewriter rental and use of excellent libraries in Edinburgh can be arranged. **Financial arrangement:** free room and board. **Guidelines:** author of at least 1 published work. **Application procedure:** write for application and further information. **Deadline:** 30 Sep 1999. **Notification:** mid-Jan 2000. **Dates:** Feb–Dec 2000.

HEADLANDS CENTER FOR THE ARTS

944 Fort Barry; Sausalito, CA 94965; (415) 331-2787, FAX 331-3857
Kathryn Reasoner, *Executive Director*

Open to: playwrights, composers, librettists, lyricists, screenwriters, television writers. **Description:** residencies of 1–3 months for artists in all disciplines at center in national park on 13,000 acres of coastal wilderness across the bay from San Francisco; accommodation in 4-bedroom house with communal kitchen; evening meal provided in mess hall Sun–Thur; 11-month "live-out" residencies available for Bay Area artists only, providing studio space, 2 meals a week and access to center's facilities but no housing; all residents encouraged to interact with fellow artists in other media and with the environment. **Financial arrangement:** stipend of $500 a month, travel and free housing for artist from outside Bay Area; $2500 stipend and studio space for Bay Area artist. **Guidelines:** CA, NC or OH residents only; students ineligible. **Application procedure:** call or write for information (applications available Apr 2000). **Deadline:** 2 Jun 2000. **Dates:** Feb–Dec 2001.

HEDGEBROOK

2197 East Millman Rd; Langley, WA 98260; (360) 321-4786
Linda Bowers, *Director*

Open to: playwrights, librettists. **Description:** residencies of 1 week–2 months for women writers of diverse cultural backgrounds working in all literary genres; 6 individual cottages on 30 wooded acres on Whidbey Island, near Seattle; writer furnishes own typewriter or computer. **Financial arrangement:** free room and board. **Guidelines:** woman writer of any age, published or unpublished; women of color encouraged to apply. **Application procedure:** send SASE for application; submit completed application, project description, work sample and $15 fee. **Deadline:** 1 Oct 1999 for winter–spring 2000; 1 Apr 2000 for summer–fall 2000. **Notification:** 2 months. **Dates:** year-round. (See entry in Development.)

HELENE WURLITZER FOUNDATION OF NEW MEXICO

Box 1891; Taos, NM 87571; (505) 758-2413, FAX 758-2559
Michael Knight, *Director*

Open to: playwrights, composers, screenwriters. **Description:** 11 studio/apartments available to writers, composers and poets (performing artists ineligible); length of residency flexible, usually 3 months; residencies currently booked through 2002. **Financial arrangement:** free housing and utilities; resident provides own meals; no financial aid; write or fax for application. **Application procedure:** completed application, project description, work sample and resume. **Deadline:** ongoing. **Dates:** 1 Apr–30 Sep; residencies available on limited basis 1 Oct–31 Mar.

ISLE ROYALE NATIONAL PARK ARTIST-IN-RESIDENCE

800 East Lakeshore Dr; Houghton, MI 49931; (906) 482-0984
(general information), 487-7152 (Greg Blust), FAX 482-8753;
E-mail greg-blust@nps.gov; Web http://www.nps.gov/isro/
Greg Blust, *Coordinator*

Open to: playwrights, composers, lyricists, solo performers. **Description:** 1 artist at a time housed for 2–3 weeks in cabin on remote island near Lake Superior; no electricity; resident must bring 2–3 week supply of food. **Financial arrangement:** free housing. **Guidelines:** writer with artistic integrity, ability to live in wilderness environment and to relate to park through their work; must donate 1 work to park and communicate experience of residency through programs for public. **Application procedure:** completed application form, project description, work sample and resume. **Deadline:** 16 Feb 2000. **Notification:** 15 Apr 2000. **Dates:** Jun–Sep.

THE JAMES THURBER WRITER-IN-RESIDENCE
The Thurber House; 77 Jefferson Ave; Columbus, OH 43215;
   (614) 464-1032, FAX 228-7445
Michael J. Rosen, *Literary Director*

Open to: playwrights. **Description:** 4 residencies a year, each for 1 academic quarter (2 for journalists, 1 for playwright, 1 for poet or fiction writer); writer teaches course at Ohio State University. **Financial arrangement:** $6000 stipend; furnished apartment provided. **Guidelines:** playwright who has had at least 1 play produced by a major theatre; teaching experience helpful. **Application procedure:** letter of interest and curriculum vita. **Deadline:** 15 Dec 1999. **Notification:** 2 months. **Dates:** winter or spring 2000.

THE JOHN STEINBECK WRITER'S ROOM
Long Island University–Southampton Campus Library;
   Southampton, NY 11968; (516) 287-8382, FAX 287-4049;
   E-mail sclibrary@sunburn.liunet.edu
Robert Gerbereux, *Library Director*

Open to: playwrights. **Description:** small room, space for 4 writers; carrel, storage space, access to reference material in room and to library. **Financial arrangement:** free. **Guidelines:** writer working under contract or with specific commitment. **Application procedure:** completed application. **Notification:** 1 week. **Dates:** year-round.

KALANI OCEANSIDE ECO-RESORT INSTITUTE
FOR CULTURE AND WELLNESS
RR2 Box 4500; Pahoa-Beach Road, HI 96778; (808) 965-7828,
   FAX 965-0527; E-mail kalani@kalani.com; Web http://www.kalani.com
Richard Koob, *Director*

Open to: playwrights, translators, composers, librettists, lyricists, solo perfomers, visual artists, screenwriters, television writers. **Description:** up to 20 artists share 4, 500–1000-square-foot studio spaces for 2-week to 2-month residencies at 113-acre coastal resort spa with private rooms, communal kitchen facilties and shared or private baths. **Financial arrangement:** artist eligible for 50% discount on regular daily room rates of $65–120; artist has option of preparing own food or paying an additional $27 per day for resort's meals. **Guidelines:** any artist with demonstrated ability to complete projects. **Application procedure:** completed application, project description, work sample and resume with $10 fee. **Deadline:** ongoing. **Notification:** within 1 week of receipt of application. **Dates:** ongoing, but discounted rates more available May–Nov.

LEDIG HOUSE INTERNATIONAL WRITERS' COLONY
59 Letter S Rd; Ghent, NY 12075; (518) 392-7656, 392-2848
David Knowles, *Executive Director*

Open to: playwrights, translators, screenwriters, television writers. **Description:** residencies of 1 week–2 months for up to 10 writers at 150-acre farm in upstate NY with library and computer access; private sleeping and work space; communal living and dining rooms; all meals provided. **Financial arrangement:** free room and board. **Guidelines:** published and unpublished writers proficient in English. **Application procedure:** project description, work sample, resume and letter of recommendation with SASE for notification; call or fax for guidelines. **Deadline:** 31 Nov 1999. **Notification:** 31 Dec 1999. **Dates:** spring session 1 Apr–26 Jun 2000; fall session 20 Aug–31 Oct 2000.

LEIGHTON STUDIOS FOR INDEPENDENT RESIDENCIES
The Banff Centre for the Arts; Box 1020, Station 28; 107 Tunnel Mountain Dr;
    Banff, Alberta; Canada T0L 0C0; (403) 762-6180, (800) 565-9989,
    FAX (403) 762-6345; E-mail arts_info@banffcentre.ab.ca;
    Web http://www.banffcentre.ab.ca/CFAindex.html
Office of the Registrar

Open to: playwrights, composers, performance artists, screenwriters, television writers. **Description:** residencies of 1 week–3 months for writers, composers, musicians and visual artists at studios situated in mountains of Banff National Park; 8 specially designed studios, each with washroom and kitchenette; living accommodation (single room with bath) on Centre's main campus; nearby access to all amenities of Centre, including dining room, library and recreation complex. **Financial arrangement:** resident pays for studio, room and optional meals; discount on studio cost only available for those who demonstrate need. **Guidelines:** artist who can demonstrate sustained contribution to own field and show evidence of significant achievement. **Application procedure:** write, e-mail or visit Web site for application and further information. **Deadline:** open; apply at least 6 months before desired residency. **Notification:** 2 months. **Dates:** year-round.

THE MACDOWELL COLONY
100 High St; Peterborough, NH 03458-2485; (603) 924-3886, (212) 535-9690,
    FAX (603) 924-9142; E-mail info@macdowellcolony.org;
    Web http://www.macdowellcolony.org
Cheryl Young, *Executive Director*

Open to: playwrights, composers, screenwriters, video writers. **Description:** residencies of up to 2 months for writers, composers, visual artists, video/filmmakers, architects and interdisciplinary artists at 450-acre estate; studios and common areas accessible for those with mobility impairments. **Financial arrangement:** voluntary contributions accepted; travel grants available. **Guidelines:** admission based on talent. **Application procedure:** send SASE, call for application or download from Web site; submit completed application, work samples, names of 2 professional references and $20 fee; collaborating artists must apply separately. **Deadline:** 15 Sep 1999 for Jan–Apr 2000; 15 Jan 2000 for May–Aug 2000; 15 Apr 2000 for Sep–Dec 2000. **Notification:** 2 months. **Dates:** year-round.

MARY ANDERSON CENTER FOR THE ARTS

101 St. Francis Dr; Mount St. Francis, IN 47146; (812) 923-8602, FAX 923-0294;
    E-mail maca@iglou.com
Debra Carmody, *Executive Director*

Open to: playwrights, translators, composers, librettists, lyricists. **Description:** residencies of 1 week–3 months for 7 writers and visual artists concurrently at center on beautiful 400-acre wooded site with lake, 15 minutes from Louisville, KY; private studio/bedroom, communal kitchen and dining room. **Financial arrangement:** resident pays suggested minimum fee of $150 a week for room and board; possibility of funded residencies; write for information. **Guidelines:** formal education and production credits are not requirements but will be taken into consideration when applications are reviewed. **Application procedure:** completed application, project description, work sample, resume and 2 references. **Deadline:** ongoing. **Notification:** 2–4 weeks. **Dates:** year-round. (See entry in Membership and Service Organizations.)

THE MILLAY COLONY FOR THE ARTS

444 East Hill Rd; Box 3; Austerlitz, NY 12017-0003; (518) 392-3103;
    E-mail application@millaycolony.org; Web http://www.millaycolony.org
Gail Giles, *Assistant Director*

Open to: playwrights, composers, screenwriters. **Description:** 1-month residencies for up to 6 writers, composers and visual artists concurrently at 600-acre estate in upstate NY; studio space and separate bedroom; colony accommodates artists with disabilities. **Financial arrangement:** free room, board and studio space. **Application procedure:** send SASE or e-mail for application; submit completed application and supporting materials. **Deadline:** 1 Sep for Feb–May; 1 Feb for Jun–Sep; 1 May for Oct–Jan. **Notification:** 12–15 weeks after deadline. **Dates:** year-round.

NEW YORK MILLS ARTS RETREAT

24 North Main Ave, Box 246; New York Mills, MN 56567;
    (218) 385-3339, FAX 385-3366; E-mail nymills@uslink.net
Kent Scheer, *Coordinator*

Open to: playwrights, composers, librettists, lyricists, solo performers, screenwriters. **Description:** 1 artist at a time housed for 2–4 weeks in small farming community in north central Minnesota; housing ranges from bed and breakfast to retreat house; some meals provided. **Financial arrangement:** $750 stipend for 2 weeks, $1500 stipend for 4 weeks. **Guidelines:** emerging artist of demonstrated ability; must donate 8 hours per week during residency to community outreach. **Application procedure:** completed application form, project description, work sample, resume and 2 letters of recommendation. **Deadline:** 1 Oct 1999; 1 Apr 2000. **Notification:** 8 weeks after deadline. **Dates:** Sep–May.

NORCROFT

32 East First St, #330; Duluth, MN 55802; (218) 727-5199, FAX 727-3119
Tracy Gilsvik, Managing Director

Open to: playwrights, translators, librettists, screenwriters, television writers. **Description:** 4 concurrent residencies of 1–4 weeks for women writers in all genres at remote lodge on shores of Lake Superior; private bedroom and separate individual "writing shed." **Financial arrangement:** free housing; groceries provided, resident does own cooking. **Guidelines:** women only; artist whose work demonstrates an understanding of and commitment to feminist change. **Application procedure:** completed application, five-page writing sample and description of project to be pursued at colony. **Deadline:** 1 Oct 1999. **Notification:** 1 Apr 2000. **Dates:** May–Oct.

RAGDALE FOUNDATION

1260 North Green Bay Rd; Lake Forest, IL 60045; (847) 234-1063,
    FAX 234-1075; E-mail ragdale1@aol.com
Sonja Carlborg, *Director*

Open to: playwrights, composers, librettists, lyricists. **Description:** residencies of 2 weeks–2 months for writers, composers and visual artists from all over the U.S. and abroad on property situated on edge of prairie, 1 mile from center of town. **Financial arrangement:** resident pays $105 a week for room and board; partial or full fee waivers awarded on basis of financial need. **Guidelines:** admission based on quality of work submitted. **Application procedure:** send SASE for application; submit completed application, description of work-in-progress, work sample, resume, 3 references and $20 fee. **Deadline:** 15 Jan for Jun–Dec; 1 Jun for Jan–Apr. **Notification:** 15 Apr for Jan deadline; 1 Sep for Jun deadline. **Dates:** year-round except for May and last 2 weeks in Dec.

SNUG HARBOR CULTURAL CENTER

1000 Richmond Terr; Staten Island, NY 10301-9926; (718) 448-2500,
    FAX 442-8534
Rental Coordinator

Open to: playwrights, composers. **Description:** studio workspace in performing and visual arts center with theatre, art galleries, shops, museum, meeting rooms and banquet hall, located in 80-acre historic park. **Financial arrangement:** current monthly rental approximately $12–15 per sq. ft.; renewable 1-year lease; tenant must carry own insurance. **Guidelines:** professional artist. **Application procedure:** work sample with resume. **Dates:** year-round.

STUDIO FOR CREATIVE INQUIRY
Carnegie Mellon University; College of Fine Arts; Pittsburgh, PA 15213-3890;
(412) 268-3454, FAX 268-2829; E-mail mmbm@andrew.cmu.edu
Marge Myers, *Associate Director*

Open to: playwrights, translators, composers, librettists, lyricists, solo performers, screenwriters, television writers. **Description:** residencies of 6 months–3 years concurrently for artists in all disciplines; residency provides studio facility located in Carnegie Mellon's College of Fine Arts building, including office and meeting space, work area, computers, sound and video editing equipment; fellows may also use resources of university, including library. **Financial arrangement:** stipend; assistance in finding housing in community. **Guidelines:** writer interested in technology and interdisciplinary teamwork; admission based on quality of work, clear statement of intention, experience with collaboration and project feasibility. **Application procedure:** concept proposal, work sample and resume. **Deadline:** ongoing. **Notification:** 2 months. **Dates:** year-round.

THE TYRONE GUTHRIE CENTRE
Annaghmakerrig; Newbliss; County Monaghan; Ireland; 353-47-54003,
FAX 353-47-54380; E-mail thetgc@indigo.ie
Resident Director

Open to: playwrights, composers, librettists, lyricists, screenwriters, television writers. **Description:** residencies of 1 week–1 year for artists in all disciplines at former country home of Tyrone Guthrie, set amid 450 acres of forested estate overlooking large lake; private apartments; music room, rehearsal/performance space and extensive library. **Financial arrangement:** non-Irish artists pay about Irish £2000 (about $2800) a month for housing and meals; self-catering houses also available at reasonable rents; fees may be negotiable depending on factors such as length of stay, nature of project, involvement with Irish artists or institutions, etc. **Guidelines:** artist must show evidence of sustained dedication and a significant level of achievement; prefers artist with clearly defined project; artist teams (e.g., writer/director, composer/librettist) welcome; several weeks reserved each year for development of projects. **Application procedure:** write for application and further information. **Deadline:** ongoing. **Dates:** year-round.

UCROSS FOUNDATION RESIDENCY PROGRAM
30 Big Red Lane; Clearmont, WY 82835; (307) 737-2291,
FAX 737-2322
Sharon Dynak, *Executive Director*

Open to: playwrights, translators, composers, librettists, lyricists. **Description:** residency of 2 weeks–2 months at "Big Red," restored historic site in the foothills of the Big Horn Mountains; 8 concurrent residencies for writers, composers and visual artists; opportunity to concentrate on own work without distraction and to present work to local communities, if desired. **Financial arrangement:** free room, board and studio space. **Guidelines:** criteria are quality of work and commitment. **Admission procedure:** completed application, project description and work sample; send SASE for application and further information. **Deadline:** 1 Oct for

Feb–Jun; 1 Mar for Aug–Dec. **Notification:** 8 weeks. **Dates:** year-round except Jan and Jul.

THE U.S./JAPAN CREATIVE ARTISTS' PROGRAM

Japan-U.S. Friendship Commission; 1120 Vermont Ave NW, Suite 925;
    Washington, DC 20005; (202) 275-7712, FAX 275-7413;
    E-mail jusfc@compuserve.com; Web http://www.dgsys.com/~jusfc
Eric J. Gangloff, *Executive Director*

Open to: playwrights, composers, librettists, lyricists, solo performers, visual artists, screenwriters, television writers. **Description:** residencies of 6 continuous months for 3–5 artists each year; residents find own housing in location of their choice in Japan. **Financial arrangement:** monthly stipend of ¥400,000 (about $3320) plus ¥100,000 (about $830) for housing and ¥100,000 (about $830) for professional expenses; free travel and pre-departure Japanese language instruction. **Guidelines:** U.S. citizen or permanent resident; mid-career professional artist with compelling reason to work in Japan and whose work "exemplifies the best in U.S. art." **Application procedure:** completed application, work sample and resume. **Deadline:** TBA (29 Jun in 1998).

VILLA MONTALVO ARTIST RESIDENCY PROGRAM

Box 158; Saratoga, CA 95071-0158; (408) 961-5818, FAX 961-5850;
    E-mail kfunk@villamontalvo.org; Web http://www.villamontalvo.org
Kathryn Funk, *Artist Residency Program Director*

Open to: playwrights, composers, screenwriters. **Description:** residencies of 1–3 months for 5 writers, musicians and visual artists concurrently on grounds adjacent to 175-acre Mediterranean-style villa; rural setting close to major urban center. **Financial arrangement:** free housing; resident provides own meals, transportation; 7 fellowships available. **Guidelines:** spouses welcome; no children or pets. **Appli-cation procedure:** send self-addressed label and .55¢ postage (or adequate foreign postage voucher for 1.5 oz) for application and guidelines. **Deadline:** 1 Sep for Apr–Sep; 1 Mar for Oct–Mar. **Notification:** 4 months. **Dates:** year-round.

VIRGINIA CENTER FOR THE CREATIVE ARTS

Box VCCA, Mt. San Angelo; Sweet Briar, VA 24595; (804) 946-7236,
    FAX 946-7239; E-mail vcca@vcca.com; Web http://www.vcca.com
Director

Open to: playwrights, translators, composers, librettists, lyricists, screenwriters. **Description:** residencies of 2 weeks–2 months for writers, composers, and visual and performance artists at 450-acre estate in Blue Ridge Mountains; separate studios and bedrooms; all meals provided. **Financial arrangement:** resident pays suggested minimum of $30 a day for room and board or as means allow; financial status not a factor in selection process. **Guidelines:** admission based on achievement or promise of achievement. **Application procedure:** completed application with work sample, resume and 2 recommendations. **Deadline:** 15 Sep for Feb–May; 15 Jan for Jun–Sep; 15 May for Oct–Jan. **Notification:** 3 months. **Dates:** year-round.

WALDEN RESIDENCY PROGRAM

Extended Campus Programs; Southern Oregon University; 1250 Siskiyou Blvd; Ashland, OR 97520; (541) 552-6901, FAX 552-6047; E-mail friendly@sou.edu
Brooke Friendly, *Arts Coordinator*

Open to: playwrights. **Description:** 3 6-week residencies for writers of drama, fiction, poetry and creative nonfiction at farm near Ashland, OR; 1 writer at a time housed in cabin with kitchen facilities, which opens onto meadow surrounded by forest. **Financial arrangement:** free; no meals provided. **Guidelines:** OR resident only; send SASE for full application. **Application procedure:** completed application, project description, work sample and list of publications or productions. **Deadline:** 30 Nov 1999. **Notification:** mid-Dec 1999. **Dates:** Mar–Jul 2000.

WILLIAM FLANAGAN MEMORIAL CREATIVE PERSONS CENTER

Edward F. Albee Foundation; 14 Harrison St; New York, NY 10013; (212) 226-2020

Open to: playwrights, translators, composers, librettists, screenwriters. **Description:** 1-month residencies for up to 5 writers, composers and visual artists concurrently at "The Barn" in Montauk, Long Island. **Financial arrangement:** free housing. **Guidelines:** admission based on talent and need. **Application procedure:** completed application, script (recording for composers) and supporting materials; write for information. **Deadline:** 1 Apr 2000; no submission before 1 Jan 2000. **Notification:** May 2000. **Dates:** 1 Jun–1 Oct 2000.

THE WRITERS ROOM

10 Astor Pl, 6th Floor; New York, NY 10003; FAX (212) 533-6059; Web http://www.writersroom.org
Donna Brodie, *Executive Director*

Open to: playwrights, translators, composers, librettists, lyricists. **Description:** large room with 35 desks separated by partitions, space for 300 writers each quarter; open 24 hours a day year-round; kitchen, lounge and bathrooms, storage for files and typewriters, small reference library; monthly readings. **Financial arrangement:** $50 application fee; $175 fee for 3-month period. **Guidelines:** writer, emerging or established, must show seriousness of intent. **Application procedure:** completed application and references; all inquiries by mail or through Web site (no visits without appointment).

THE WRITERS' STUDIO
The Mercantile Library Association; 17 East 47th St; New York, NY 10017;
(212) 755-6710, FAX 758-1387; E-mail mercantile_library@msn.com;
Web http://www.fictionlibrary.org
Harold Augenbraum, *Director*

Open to: playwrights, composers. **Description:** carrel space for 17 writers (3 reserved for writers of children's literature) in not-for-profit, private lending library of 175,000 volumes; storage for personal computers or typewriters, library membership, access to special reference collection and rare collection of 19th-century American and British literature. **Financial arrangement:** $200 fee for 3 months, renewal possible for up to 1 year. **Guidelines:** open to all writers; unpublished writer must submit evidence of serious intent. **Application procedure:** completed application and work sample or project outline.

YADDO
Box 395; Saratoga Springs, NY 12866-0395; (518) 584-0746, FAX 584-1312;
E-mail yaddo@yaddo.org
Admissions Committee

Open to: playwrights, composers, performance artists, screenwriters. **Description:** residencies of 2 weeks–2 months for artists in all genres, working individually or as collaborative teams of up to 3 persons, at 19th-century estate on 400 acres; approximate total of 200 residents a year (15 concurrently Sep–May, 35 concurrently May–Labor Day). **Financial arrangement:** free room, board and studio space. **Guidelines:** admission based on review by judging panels composed of artists in each genre; quality of work submitted is major criterion; send .55¢ SASE for application and further information. **Application procedure:** completed application with work sample, resume, 2 letters of support, $20 fee and SASP for acknowledgment of receipt. **Deadline:** 15 Jan 2000 for mid-May 2000–Feb 2001; 1 Aug 2000 for 1 Nov 2000–mid-May 2001. **Notification:** 1 Apr 2000 for Jan deadline; 15 Oct 2000 for Aug deadline. **Dates:** year-round except early Sep.

Membership and
Service Organizations

What's included here?

A number of organizations that exist to serve either the American playwright or a wider constituency of writers, composers and arts professionals. Some have a particular regional or special-interest orientation; some provide links to theatres in other countries. Taken together, these organizations represent an enormous range of services available to those who write for the theatre, and it is worth getting to know them.

THE ALLIANCE OF LOS ANGELES PLAYWRIGHTS
7510 Sunset Blvd, Suite 1050; Los Angeles, CA 90046-3418;
  (323) 957-4752
Dan Berkowitz and Dick Dotterer, *Co-Chairs*

Founded in 1993, ALAP is a support and service organization dedicated to addressing the professional needs of the Los Angeles playwriting community. ALAP's programs and activities include the Playwrights Expo, which brings together L.A. playwrights and dozens of representatives of local and national theatres; the series In Our Own Voices, in which members read from and share their work; the C. Bernard Jackson Award given in recognition of individuals and organizations that nurture, develop and support L.A. playwrights; symposia and panel discussions; and networking and social events. ALAP's publications include *HotLine* and the bimonthly *NewsFlash*, which keep members posted on upcoming events; the journal *InterPlay*; and an annual *Membership Directory*. Annual dues are $29.95.

THE ALLIANCE OF RESIDENT THEATRES/NEW YORK

575 Eighth Ave, Suite 17S; New York, NY 10018; (212) 244-6667,
  FAX 714-1918; E-mail artnewyork@aol.com
Virginia P. Louloudes, *Executive Director*
Mary Harpster, *Deputy Director*

A.R.T./New York is the trade and service organization for the New York City not-for-profit professional theatre, serving more than 300 New York theatre companies and professional affiliates (theatres outside NY, colleges and universities, and organizations providing services to the theatre field). Publications of interest include the *Member Directory* ($10) and *Rehearsal and Performance Space Guide* ($25), which provides information on various theatre spaces currently available for rent.

ALTERNATE ROOTS

1083 Austin Ave; Atlanta, GA 30307; (404) 577-1079, FAX 577-7991;
  E-mail altroots1@earthlink.net;
  Web http://www.home.earthlink.net/~altroots1/
Greg Carraway, *Managing Director*

Alternate ROOTS is a service organization run by and for southeastern artists. Its mission is to support the creation and presentation of original performing art that is rooted in a particular community of place, tradition or spirit. It is committed to social and economic justice and the protection of the natural world and addresses these concerns through its programs and services. Founded in 1976, ROOTS now has more than 260 individual members across the 13 states of the Southeast, including playwrights, directors, choreographers, musicians, storytellers, clowns and new vaudevillians—both solo artists and representatives of 65 performing and presenting organizations. ROOTS aims to make artistic resources available to its members through workshops; to create appropriate distribution networks for the new work being generated in the region via touring, publications and liaison activity; and to provide opportunities for enhanced visibility and financial stability via publications and periodic performance festivals. Opportunities for member playwrights include readings and peer critiques of works-in-progress at the organization's annual meeting. Artists who are residents of the Southeast and whose work is consistent with the goals of ROOTS are accepted as new members after a year's provisional status. Annual membership dues are $50. The organization's meetings and workshops are open to the public and its triannual newsletter is available free to the public.

THE AMERICAN ALLIANCE FOR THEATRE & EDUCATION (AATE)

c/o Department of Theatre; Arizona State University; Box 872002;
Tempe, AZ 85287-2002; (480) 965-6064 (Mon–Thur, 8:30–4:30),
FAX 965-5351; E-mail aateinfo@asum.inre.asu.edu;
Web http://www.aate.com
Judith Rethwisch, *President*
Christy M. Taylor, *Administrative Director*

AATE is a membership organization created in 1987 with the merger of the American Association of Theatre for Youth and the American Association for Theatre in Secondary Education. AATE provides a variety of services to support the work of theatre artists and educators who work with young people and to promote theatre and drama/theatre education in elementary and secondary schools. To encourage the development and production of plays for young audiences the AATE Unpublished Play Reading Project annually selects and publicizes promising new plays in this field. AATE also sponsors annual awards for the best play for young people and the outstanding book relating to any aspect of the field published in the past calendar year; only the play or book's publisher may nominate a candidate for these awards. AATE's publications, which are free to members, include a quarterly on-line newsletter with a Playwright's Page; the yearly *Youth Theatre Journal;* and the quarterly *STAGE of the Art.* Membership is open to all and costs $55 for students, $65 for retirees, $90 for individuals and $120 for organizations; please add $20 (U.S. funds) for foreign members (outside the U.S. and Canada).

THE AMERICAN FILM INSTITUTE (AFI)

2021 North Western Ave; Los Angeles, CA 90027; (323) 856-7600,
FAX 467-4578; E-mail info@afionline.org; Web http://www.afionline.org
Jean Picker Firstenberg, *Director & CEO*
James Hindman, *Co-Director & COO*

The American Film Institute (AFI) is the preeminent national organization dedicated to advancing and preserving the art of film, television and other forms of the moving image. Founded in 1967, AFI trains the next generation of filmmakers, coordinates nationwide film preservation efforts and explores new technologies in moviemaking. AFI exhibits and celebrates the best of the film arts through a major film festival in Los Angeles, by maintaining the AFI Theater in the John F. Kennedy Center in Washington, D.C. and by administering the annual AFI Life Achievement Award. Of special interest to writers is AFI's annual Television Writers Workshop, held in L.A., which provides 3 weeks of intensive advanced training for 10–12 competitively selected writers and the Sloan TV Writing Workshop, which provides training for writers in the one-hour drama format with a focus on creating accurate portrayals of science and technology in the media; participants pay a fee of $695 for each workshop; tuition scholarships are available; interested writers should call (323) 856-7722 or visit the Web site for guidelines and application information.

AMERICAN INDIAN COMMUNITY HOUSE
708 Broadway, 8th Floor; New York, NY 10003; (212) 598-0100, FAX 598-4909;
  Web http://www.abest.com/~aichnyc/
Rosemary Richmond, *Executive Director*
Jim Cyrus, *Director of Performing Arts*

American Indian Community House was founded in 1969 to encourage the interest of all U.S. ethnic groups in the cultural contributions of the American Indian, as well as to foster intercultural exchanges. The organization now serves the Native American population of the New York City region through a variety of social, economic and educational programs, and through cultural programs which include theatre events, an art gallery and a newsletter. Native Americans in the Arts, the performing arts component of the Community House, is committed to the development and production of works by Indian authors, and presents staged readings, workshops and full productions in The Circle, their in-house performance space. The Community House also sponsors several other performing groups, including Spiderwoman Theatre, Coatlicue Theatre Company, the actors' group Off the Beaten Path, the Thunderbird American Indian Dancers, the Silver Cloud Singers and the jazz-fusion and traditional singing group Ulali. A showcase for Native American artists is presented to agents and casting directors once a year.

AMERICAN MUSIC CENTER (AMC)
30 West 26th St, Suite 1001; New York, NY 10010-2011; (212) 366-5260,
  FAX 366-5265; E-mail center@amc.net; Web http://www.amc.net or
  www.newmusicbox.org
Richard Kessler, *Executive Director*
Leonard Lionnet, *Information Services Manager*

The American Music Center provides numerous programs and services for composers, performers and others interested in contemporary American music. The Jory Copying Assistance Program helps composers pay for copying music and extracting performance materials. The center's library contains more than 60,000 scores and recordings, including a large collection of opera and music-theatre works, available for perusal by interested performers. The AMC provides information on competitions, publishers, performing ensembles, composers and other areas of interest in new music, and its publication *Opportunities in New Music* is updated annually. Membership is open to any person or organization wishing to support the center's promotion of the creation, performance and appreciation of American music. Annual dues are $55 for individuals ($35 for students under 25 and senior citizens). Members receive discounts on AMC publications and monthly "Opportunity Updates." New members receive a free packet of information and articles of interest to the American composer. All members may vote in the annual board elections and attend the annual meeting.

AMERICAN TRANSLATORS ASSOCIATION (ATA)

1800 Diagonal Rd, Suite 220; Alexandria, VA 22314-2840;
 (703) 683-6100, FAX 683-6122; E-mail ata@atanet.org;
 Web http://www.atanet.org
Walter W. Bacak, Jr., *Executive Director*

Founded in 1959, the ATA is a national not-for-profit association which seeks to promote recognition of the translation profession; disseminate information for the benefit of translators and those who use their services; define and maintain professional standards; foster and support the training of translators and interpreters; and provide a medium of cooperation with persons in allied professions. Active membership is open to U.S. citizens and permanent residents who have professionally engaged in translating or closely related work and have passed an ATA accreditation examination or demonstrated professional attainment by other prescribed means. Those who meet these professional standards but are not U.S. citizens or residents may hold Corresponding membership; other interested persons may be Associate members. All members receive the monthly *ATA Chronicle* and a membership directory. Other publications include a *Translation Services Directory* containing professional profiles of individual members. ATA holds an annual conference and sponsors several honors and awards (see American Translators Association Awards in Prizes). Interested persons should contact ATA for a membership application, or visit the ATA Web site. Annual dues are $50 for Associate-Students; $95 for Active, Corresponding and Associate members; $120 for institutions; and $175 for corporations.

ASCAP (AMERICAN SOCIETY OF COMPOSERS, AUTHORS AND PUBLISHERS)

1 Lincoln Plaza; New York, NY 10023; (212) 621-6234, FAX 724-9064
Michael A. Kerker, *Director of Musical Theatre*

ASCAP is a not-for-profit organization whose members are writers and publishers of musical works. It operates as a clearinghouse for performing rights, offering licenses that authorize the public performance of all the music of its composer, lyricist and music publishing members, and collecting license fees for these members. ASCAP also sponsors workshops for member and nonmember theatre writers (see ASCAP Musical Theatre Workshop in Development). Membership in ASCAP is open to any composer or lyricist who has been commercially recorded or "regularly published." Annual dues are $10 for individuals.

ASIAN AMERICAN ARTS ALLIANCE

74 Varick St, Suite 302; New York, NY 10013-1914; (212) 941-9208,
 FAX 941-7978; E-mail artsalliance@earthlink.net;
 Web http://www.AAartsAlliance.org
Lillian Cho, *Executive Director*

Asian American Arts Alliance is a not-for-profit arts service organization founded in 1983 to increase the support, recognition and appreciation of Asian-American arts. The Arts Alliance strives to assist Asian-American artists and arts groups and works to raise the awareness of the diversity of Asian-American arts and cultures. The organization provides information resources, networking and advocacy services, and professional assistance through technical aid, public forums and roundtables, a resource library and publications including the *Directory of Asian American Arts Organizations and Touring Artists,* a bimonthly *Asian American Arts Calendar/Resources and Opportunities* and a semiannual art magazine, *Dialogue.* Public programs and special projects include Artist Series forums, Nuts & Bolts technical assistance workshops and the Chase SMARTS Regrant Program for New York City Asian American arts groups. There are 7 membership levels: Starving Artist, $20; Mover & Shaker, $45; Arts Organization, $60; Project Leader, $100; Arts Patron, $250; Philanthropist, $500 and Leadership Council, $1000. Members receive discounts on advertising, special publications and events; additional benefits are provided to major donors.

A.S.K. THEATER PROJECTS

11845 West Olympic Blvd, Suite 1250 W; Los Angeles, CA 90064;
        (310) 478-3200, FAX 478-5300; E-mail askplay@primenet.com;
        Web http://www.askplay.org
Mead K. Hunter, *Director of Literary Programs*

Since 1989, A.S.K. Theater Projects has been an arts service organization dedicated to playwrights and new playwriting. Each year A.S.K. develops numerous works in progress, either through public readings or in a private writer's retreat, out of which 2–3 plays are selected for workshop productions (see A.S.K. Theater Projects in Development). Allied programs supported by A.S.K. include: the A.S.K. Unpublished Plays Project, a repository of plays that premiered in southern California, housed in the L.A. Central Library; the international playwriting program at London's Royal Court Theatre; 3 playwright exchange programs, one each with the Playwrights' Center, the Royal Court and New Dramatists; the Audrey Skirball-Kenis Playwrights Program at Lincoln Center; the Mark Taper Forum's New Work Festival; the UCLA Playwriting Award and the UCLA Playwriting Fellowship; the Los Angeles Drama Critics Circle Ted Schmitt Award; the playscript publication in TCG's *American Theatre* magazine; the Playwrights-in-the-Schools program; and the *L.A. Weekly* Playwriting Award. A.S.K. sponsors symposiums, salons and labs, which serve as forums wherein issues may be explored or practical approaches to writing shared. A.S.K.'s publications include summary booklets of the symposium series entitled *Inventing the Future;* the *Directory of Los Angeles Playwright Groups;* the texts of plays given workshop productions; and *Parabasis,* a news magazine for, by and about playwrights. For information about additional programs and publications, contact A.S.K.

ASSITEJ/USA (INTERNATIONAL ASSOCIATION OF THEATRE FOR CHILDREN AND YOUNG PEOPLE)

724 Second Ave S; Nashville, TN 37210; (615) 254-5719, FAX 254-3255;
    E-mail usassitej@aol.com
Steve Bianchi, *Membership Director*

ASSITEJ/USA is a not-for-profit theatre agency which advocates the development of professional theatre for young audiences in the USA and facilitates interchange among theatre artists and scholars of the 60 member countries of ASSITEJ. ASSITEJ/USA sponsors festivals and seminars, operates an international playscript exchange and, with ASSITEJ/Japan, is founder of the Pacific-Asia Exchange Program. Members are theatres, institutions and individuals concerned for the theatre, young audiences and international goodwill. Members receive *Theatre for Young Audiences Today* and priority consideration for participation in national and international events. Membership costs $25 for students and retirees, $30 for libraries, $50 a year for individuals, $100–300 for organizations (depending on size of budget). Write or call for membership application.

THE ASSOCIATED WRITING PROGRAMS (AWP)

Tallwood House, Mail Stop 1E3; George Mason University; Fairfax, VA 22030;
    (703) 993-4301, FAX 993-4302; E-mail awp@gmu.edu
David Fenza, *Executive Director*

Founded in 1967, AWP is a not-for-profit organization serving the needs of writers, college and university writing programs, and students of writing by providing information services, job placement assistance, publishing opportunities, literary arts advocacy and forums on all aspects of writing and its instruction. Writers' Conferences & Festivals (WC&F), an association of 88 nonacademic conferences for writers, is now a division of AWP. Writers not affiliated with colleges and universities but who support collective efforts to improve opportunities are also represented by AWP. The *Writer's Chronicle*, published 6 times annually and available for $20 a year, includes listings of publishing opportunities, grants, awards and fellowships; interviews with writers; and essays on teaching creative writing. *The AWP Official Guide to Writing Programs* (9th edition, $26.95 including shipping) offers a comprehensive listing of writing programs and an expanded section on writing conferences, colonies and centers. Write or call AWP for information on membership requirements.

ASSOCIATION FOR THEATRE IN HIGHER EDUCATION (ATHE)

Box 9098; Berkeley, CA 94709-0098; (888) 284-3737,
    FAX (510) 526-8964; E-mail nericksn@aol.com;
    Web http://www2.hawaii.edu/athe/ATHEWelcome.html
Association Manager

Founded in 1986, ATHE is an organization composed of individuals and institutions that provides vision and leadership for the profession and promotes excellence in theatre education. Membership services include insurance benefits, scholarships, annual professional awards including the Jane Chambers Playwriting

Award (see Prizes) and assistance with issues such as tenure and alternate employment opportunities. Each year, members convene for the annual conference that brings together theatre scholars, educators and professionals from all over the world in workshops, performances, plenary sessions and group meetings. ATHE publishes several periodicals of interest to the theatre professional, including *ATHENEWS*, a quarterly newsletter that includes a list of teaching positions available at member organizations; *Theatre Topics*, a semiannual journal; *Theatre Journal*, a quarterly journal; a membership directory and pamphlets on various topics such as assessment guidelines for higher education theatre programs and tenure. There are 5 annual membership levels: Students, $50; Retirees, $80; Individuals, $105; 2-Person Households, $155; Organizations, $195. Members receive all publications.

THE ASSOCIATION OF HISPANIC ARTS (AHA)

250 West 26th St, 4th Floor; New York, NY 10001; (212) 727-7227,
    FAX 727-0549; E-mail aha96@aol.com
Sandra Perez, *Executive Director*

A not-for-profit organization founded in 1975, AHA promotes the Latin American arts as an integral part of this country's cultural life. It acts as a clearinghouse for information on all the arts, including theatre, and 6 times a year publishes a newsletter, *¡AHA! Hispanic Arts News*, that provides information on playwriting contests, workshops, forums and other items of interest to Latin American artists. AHA also provides technical assistance to Latin American artists seeking funding.

ASSOCIATION OF INDEPENDENT VIDEO AND FILMMAKERS (AIVF)

304 Hudson St, 6th Floor; New York, NY 10013; (212) 807-1400,
    FAX 463-8519; E-mail info@aivf.org; Web http://www.aivf.org
Elizabeth Peters, *Executive Director*

The Association of Independent Video & Filmmakers (AIVF) is the membership organization of the Foundation for Independent Video and Film (FIVF). Founded in 1975, its mission is to increase the creative and professional opportunities for independent video and filmmakers and to enhance the growth of independent media by providing services and information such as health and production insurance, networking seminars and events, a resource library and publication of books and directories, as well as *The Independent Film & Video Monthly*. As one of the largest organizations serving and representing independent flim and video makers, as well as public television and cable access producers, AIVF consists of media artists working in all genres, including documentary, animation, experimental, narrative, interactive and multimedia.

BALTIMORE THEATRE PROJECT, INC.

45 West Preston St; Baltimore, MD 21201; (410) 539-3091, FAX 539-2137
Bobby Mrozek, *Artistic Director*

Founded in 1971, Baltimore Theatre Project is a presenting theatre of new and innovative works, with special focus on Baltimore-area theatre companies.

Additional services include workshops, roundtables, seminars, open auditions and a shared database of Baltimore-area affiliated artists.

BLACK THEATRE NETWORK (BTN)

2603 Northwest 13th St, Suite 312; Gainesville, FL 32609; (352) 495-2116
FAX 495-2051; E-mail manicho@aol.com
Lorna Littleway, *President*

Black Theatre Network (BTN) is a national network of professional artists, scholars and community groups founded in 1986 to provide an opportunity for the interchange of ideas; to collect and disseminate through its publications information regarding black theatre activity; to provide an annual national forum for the viewing and discussing of black theatre; and to encourage and promote black dramatists and the production of plays about the black experience. BTN members attend national conferences and workshops and receive complimentary copies of all BTN publications, which include the quarterly *Black Theatre Network News*, listing conferences, contests, BTN business matters and other items of interest from across the country; *Black Theatre Directory*, which contains over 800 listings of black theatre artists, scholars, companies, higher education programs and service organizations; *Dissertations Concerning Black Theatre: 1900–1994*, a listing of Ph.D. theses on black theatre; and *Black Theatre Connections*, a quarterly listing of jobs in educational and professional theatre, and other career development opportunities. *Black Voices*, a catalogue of works by black playwrights, is available from BTN for $20. Annual dues are $35 for retirees and students, $75 for individuals, $110 for organizations.

BMI (BROADCAST MUSIC INCORPORATED)

320 West 57th St; New York, NY 10019-3790; (212) 586-2000, FAX 262-2824
Jean Banks, *Senior Director, Musical Theater and Jazz*

BMI, founded in 1940, is a performing rights organization which acts as steward for the public performance of the music of its writers and publishers, offering licenses to music users. BMI monitors music performances and distributes royalties to those whose music has been used. Any writer whose songs have been published and are likely to be performed can join BMI at no cost. BMI also sponsors a musical theatre workshop (see BMI-Lehman Engel Musical Theatre Workshop in Development).

The BMI Foundation (President, Theodora Zavin) was established in 1984 to provide support for individuals in furthering their musical education and to assist organizations involved in the performance of music and music training.

BROADWAY ON SUNSET

10800 Hesby St; North Hollywood, CA 91601; (818) 508-9270, FAX 508-1806;
E-mail brdwysunst@aol.com; Web http://members.aol.com/brdwyonss
Kevin Kaufman, *Executive Director*
Allison Bergman, *Artistic Director*

Broadway on Sunset, a not-for-profit organization established in 1981, is sponsored by the National Academy of Songwriters (N.A.S.) (see entry in this section). The organization provides an individually structured developmental program for musical theatre writers (composers, lyricists, librettists) of all skill levels, which emphasizes a full understanding of the principles and standards of Broadway-level musical theatre craft, and provides writers opportunities to test their material at each level. Since its inception, Broadway on Sunset has presented more than 100 original musicals as well as interviews and symposiums. There are no membership dues but writers may pay a nominal fee to participate in classes, readings and workshops. Writers and composers need to have access to the Los Angeles area to benefit fully from the workshops, although weekend intensive workshops may soon be offered for out-of-town writers.

CENTRE FOR CREATIVE COMMUNITIES

(Formerly British American Arts Association)
118 Commercial St; London E1 6NF; England; 44-171-247-5385,
FAX 44-171-247-5256; E-mail baaa@easynet.co.uk;
Web http://www.creativecommunities.org.uk
Jennifer Williams, *Executive Director*

A not-for-profit organization promoting community development through arts and education, CCC conducts research, organizes conferences, produces a quarterly newsletter and is part of an international network of arts and education organizations. As well as a specialized arts and education library, CCC has a more general library which houses information on opportunities for artists and performers both in the U.K. and abroad. CCC is not a grant-giving organization.

CHICAGO ALLIANCE FOR PLAYWRIGHTS (CAP)

Theatre Building; 1225 West Belmont; Chicago, IL 60657-3205;
(773) 929-7367, ext 60, FAX 338-3060
Allan Chambers, *Board Member*

The Chicago Alliance for Playwrights is a service organization founded in 1990 to establish a network for Chicago-area playwrights and others committed to the development of new work for the stage. Members of the coalition include Chicago Dramatists (see listing below), Columbia College New Musicals Project, New Tuners Theatre/Workshop, Studio Z and Writers Bloc. The alliance sponsors forums of interest to writers and publishes an annual directory of Chicago-area playwrights and their principal works. Write or call for membership details; annual dues are $25 for individuals and $100 for groups.

CHICAGO DRAMATISTS
1105 West Chicago Ave; Chicago, IL 60622; (312) 633-0630, FAX 633-0610
E-mail newplays@aol.com
Russ Tutterow, *Artistic Director*

Founded in 1979, Chicago Dramatists is dedicated to the development and advancement of playwrights and new plays. It employs a variety of programs to nurture the artistic and career development of both established and emerging playwrights. These programs include play readings, productions, classes, workshops, symposiums, discussions, panels, festivals, talent coordination, marketing services, collaborative projects with other theatres, national playwright exchanges and referrals to producers.

The Resident Playwright program seeks to nurture and promote the work and careers of dramatists who will make potentially significant contributions to the national theatre repertory. At no charge, Resident Playwrights benefit from Chicago Dramatists' fullest and longest-term support (a 3-year, renewable term), with complete access to all programs and services. Admittance to the program is selective, with emphasis on artistic and professional accomplishment or potential. While most Resident Playwrights are from the Chicago area, dramatists from around the country who are able to spend substantial time in Chicago may also apply; however, there are no stipends for travel or housing. Interested playwrights should contact Chicago Dramatists for full information and details of the application procedure, which includes the submission of 2 plays, a resume and letters of recommendation and intent. *Deadline:* 1 Apr each year (no submission before 1 Mar).

The Playwrights' Network provides any U.S. playwright the opportunity to form an association with Chicago Dramatists. For an annual fee of $95, Network playwrights receive written script critiques, consideration for all programs (including productions and the annual New Voices Festival), class discounts, free admittance to events and other benefits.

Classes and the quarterly 10-Minute Workshop are open to all playwrights. Quarterly flyers announce events and programs, and include application procedures.

THE CHILDREN'S THEATRE FOUNDATION OF AMERICA (CTFA)
Box 8067; New Orleans, LA 70182; (504) 283-8868, (FAX) 866-0502
Orlin Corey, *President*

Founded in 1958, The Children's Theatre Foundation of America (CTFA) is a not-for-profit organization which seeks to advance the artistic and professional interests of theatre and theatre education for children and youth by funding proposals of artists and scholars working in those fields. In the past CTFA has funded playwriting grants, scholarships, research, performances and lectures, theatre festivals, conferences, symposiums, publications and crisis-management assistance. CTFA also administers the annual Aurand Harris Children's Theatre Grants and Fellowships (see Fellowships and Grants), as well as awarding a Medallion for significant achievement in the field of children's theatre.

COLORADO DRAMATISTS
Box 101405; Denver, CO 80250; (303) 675-6500; E-mail osbornep@mscd.edu
Pamela Osborne, *President*

Founded in 1981, Colorado Dramatists, with chapters in Denver and Boulder, is a service organization for playwrights at all levels of development. In addition to bimonthly public readings, the organization sponsors small, private developmental groups; readings; workshops; seminars; an annual showcase; a program that enters playwrights in regional 10-minute play festivals; a mentoring program; and is in the process of developing a new play festival. Members receive a monthly newsletter, *The Colorado Theatre Guide,* and access to rehearsal space. Annual membership dues are $10 for actors and students, $30 for all other individuals.

CORPORATION FOR PUBLIC BROADCASTING
901 E St NW; Washington, DC 20004-2037; (202) 879-9600, FAX 783-1019;
Web http://www.cpb.org
Vice President, Programming

The Corporation for Public Broadcasting, a private not-for-profit organization funded by Congress and by private sources, promotes and helps finance public television and radio. CPB provides grants to local public television and radio stations; conducts research in audience development, new broadcasting technologies and other areas. The corporation helped establish the Public Broadcasting Service and National Public Radio (see entries in this section). It supports public radio programming through programming grants to stations and other producers, and television programming by funding proposals made by stations and independent producers.

THE DRAMATISTS GUILD OF AMERICA, INC.
1501 Broadway, Suite 701; New York, NY 10036; (212) 398-9366
FAX 944-0420; E-mail tstratton@dramaguild.com
Peter Stone, *President*
Christopher Wilson, *Acting Executive Director*

The Dramatists Guild of America, founded over 75 years ago, is the only professional association governed by and established to advance the rights of playwrights, composers and lyricists. The Guild has more than 6000 members worldwide, from beginning writers to Broadway veterans. The Guild has 4 levels of membership: 1. Active ($125 a year): writers who have been produced on Broadway, Off-Broadway or on the main stage of a LORT theatre; 2. Associate ($75 a year): theatrical writers who have been produced in other venues or who have completed a full script; 3. Student ($35 a year): full-time students enrolled in an accredited writing degree program; 4. Estate ($125 a year): representatives of the estates of deceased authors. Membership benefits include a business affairs toll-free hotline, which offers advice on all theatre-related topics, including options, commissions, copyright procedures and contract reviews; model production contracts, which provide the best protection for the writer at all levels of production; collaboration, commission and licensing agreements; seminars led by experienced professionals concerning pressing topics for today's dramatist;

access to a national health insurance program and a group term life insurance plan; free/discounted tickets to Off-Broadway/Broadway performances; and a meeting room that can accommodate more than 50 people for readings and backers auditions, available for a nominal rental fee.

The Guild publishes *The Dramatists Guild Newsletter,* issued 6 times a year with up-to-date business affairs articles and script opportunities; *The Dramatist,* a magazine that contains interviews as well as articles on all aspects of theatre; *The Dramatists Guild Resource Directory,* a biannual collection of contact information on producers, agents, contests, workshops and production companies. The periodicals are available to nonwriters on a subscription basis: Individual Subscribers ($25 a year): individuals receive *The Dramatist* only; Institutional Subscribers ($135 a year): educational institutions, libraries and educational theatres receive all 3 periodicals and have access to audio tapes of Guild seminars; Professional Subscribers ($200 a year): producers and agents receive all 3 periodicals.

THE FIELD

161 Sixth Ave; New York, NY 10013; (212) 691-6969, FAX 255-2053; E-mail thefield@aol.com
Katherine Longstreth, *Executive Director*

The Field is a not-for-profit organization dedicated to helping independent performing artists develop artistically and professionally through a variety of performance opportunities, workshops, services and publications. The Field does not engage in curatorial activity; all artists are eligible to participate in its programs. Of special interest to New York metropolitan area playwrights wishing to produce their own work are programs such as Fielday, a showcase of 12-minute work and Fieldwork, 10-week workshops for works-in-progress, guided by trained facilitators, culminating in performances. Writers should also note Artward Bound, 6 free 10-day summer residencies at various rural locations on the East Coast for multidisciplinary groups of 6–10 artists with at least 3 years professional experience; transportation, room and board, rehearsal space, workshops and career guidance seminars all provided; send resume and completed application. The Field assists artists with many aspects of producing their work, including grant writing, fund-raising, project management, securing performance and rehearsal space, and cooperative promotional efforts. Publications include *Self-Production Guide; Funding Guide for Independent Artists; Space Chase Guide to New and Lesser Known Performance Opportunities,* a listing of local performance spaces throughout New York City as well as out-of-town festivals, residencies and artist colonies; *Healing Guide,* a listing of artist-recommended healing practitioners who work on a sliding scale basis; and *Gone with the Field Guide,* a listing of performing possibilites for independent artists in 25 cites across the United States. All programs are available to members and non-members; members receive publications free, discounts on programs and may use the Field as an umbrella organization, falling under its not-for-profit status. Annual membership costs $75; individual programs range in cost from $15–75. Field programs are also offered in Atlanta, Chicago, Dallas, Houston, Miami, Philadelphia, Salt Lake City, San Francisco, Seattle, Tokyo, Toronto and Washington, DC.

FIRST STAGE

Box 38280; Los Angeles, CA 90038; (323) 850-6271, FAX 850-6295;
    E-mail firststge@aol.com
Dennis Safren, *Literary Manager*

Founded in 1983, First Stage is a service organization for playwrights that holds staged readings, which are videotaped for the author's archival purposes; conducts workshops; provides referral services for playwrights; and publishes *First Stage Newsletter*. Services are free to nonmembers, except for workshops, which are available to members only. Membership dues are $35 per quarter or $120 per year; $58 per year for nonlocal members.

THE FOUNDATION CENTER

National Libraries:
1001 Connecticut Ave NW; Washington, DC 20036; (202) 331-1400
79 Fifth Ave; New York, NY 10003; (212) 620-4230, FAX 807-3677;
    Web http://www.fdncenter.org
Judith Margolin, *Vice President, Public Services, New York Library*

Field Offices:
312 Sutter St; San Francisco, CA 94108; (415) 397-0902
Hurt Bldg, Suite 150, Grand Lobby; 50 Hurt Plaza; Atlanta, GA 30303;
    (404) 880-0094
1422 Euclid, Suite 1356; Cleveland, OH 44115; (216) 861-1934

The Foundation Center is a nationwide service organization established and supported by foundations to provide a single authoritative source of information on foundation giving. It disseminates information on foundations through a public service program and through such publications as *The Foundation Directory* and *The Foundation Grants Index*. Of special interest is *Foundation Grants to Individuals*, which lists scholarships, fellowships, residencies, internships, grants, loans, awards, prizes and other forms of assistance available to individuals from approximately 3800 grantmakers (1999 edition $65). The center maintains 5 libraries and a national network of more than 213 cooperating collections. For the name of the collection nearest you or for more information about the center's programs, call toll free (800) 424-9836 or visit the Web site.

GREENSBORO PLAYWRIGHTS' FORUM

c/o City Arts; 200 North Davie St, Box #2; Greensboro, NC 27401;
    (336) 335-6426, FAX 373-2659; E-mail gsoplaywrights@juno.com;
    Web http://www.ci.greensboro.nc.us/leisure/drama
Stephen D. Hyers, *Director*

GPF was founded in 1993 to facilitate a monthly gathering for playwrights to discuss works in progress, pool knowledge and encourage each other's artistic growth. Programs include cold and staged readings of member's plays and the annual North Carolina New Play Project open to NC playwrights; winner receives $100 and workshop production; *deadline:* 12 Jan 2000. GPF also provides members with studio space for play development and publishes *New Play Catalog*, which lists plays written by members. Membership is open to anyone. Annual dues are $25.

THE HARBOR THEATRE WORKSHOP
(Formerly The Harbor Theatre Lab)
160 West 71st St, PHA; New York, NY 10023;
   (212) 787-1945
Stuart Warmflash, *Artistic Director*

The Harbor Theatre Workshop, a not-for-profit organization founded in 1994, is a developmental lab for 10 member theatre writers and a company of 30 actors cast specifically for writers' projects. Membership is available to playwrights, composers and librettists who have a body of work; are committed to rewrites and who work well in a supportive, professional atmosphere. The Workshop meets every Thursday in New York City for 3 hours and provides cold and/or rehearsed readings, followed by a short, playwright-driven critique from Workshop members. Full productions and public readings of developed work are produced by the Harbor Theatre Company (see Production) at least once during the season. Dues for the 1998–1999 season were $350. The organization is especially, but not exclusively, seeking minority playwrights.

HATCH-BILLOPS COLLECTION
491 Broadway, 7th Floor; New York, NY 10012-4412; (212) 966-3231,
   FAX 966-3231 (call first); E-mail hatchbillops@worldnet.att.net
James V. Hatch, *Executive Secretary*

The Hatch-Billops Collection is a not-for-profit research library specializing in black American art and theatre history. It was founded in 1975 to collect and preserve primary and secondary resource materials in the black cultural arts; to provide tools and access to these materials for artists and scholars, as well as the general public; and to develop programs in the arts which use the collection's resources. The library's holdings include 1800 oral-history tapes; theatre programs; approximately 300 unpublished plays by black American writers from 1858 to the present; files of clippings, letters, announcements and brochures on theatre, art and film; slides, photographs and posters; and more than 4000 books and 400 periodicals. The collection also presents a number of salon interviews and films, which are open to the public; and publishes transcriptions of its annual "Artist and Influence" series of salon interviews, many of which are with playwrights. The collection is open to artists, scholars and the public by appointment only.

HISPANIC ORGANIZATION OF LATIN ACTORS (HOLA)
250 West 65th St; New York, NY 10023-6403; (212) 595-8286, FAX 799-6718;
   E-mail holagram@aol.com; Web http://www.hellohola.org
Manuel Alfaro, *Executive Director*

Founded in 1975, HOLA is a not-for-profit arts service organization for Hispanic performers and related artists. HOLA provides information, a 24-hour hotline, casting referral services, professional seminars and workshops. The organization publishes a biennial *Directory of Hispanic Talent* and a newsletter, *La Nueva Ola*, that lists job opportunities, grants and contests of interest to Hispanic artists. Members pay annual dues of $49.

INDEPENDENT FEATURE PROJECT (IFP)

104 West 29th St, 12th Floor; New York, NY 10001-5310;
    (212) 465-8200, FAX (212) 465-8525; E-mail ifpny@ifp.org;
    Web http://www.ifp.org
Michelle Byrd, *Executive Director*

The Independent Feature Project (IFP), a not-for-profit membership-supported organization, was founded in 1979 to encourage creativity and diversity in films produced outside the established studio system. The IFP produces the Independent Feature Film Market (IFFM), which features 300 American independent features, shorts, works-in-progress, documentaries and feature scripts. The IFP and IFP/West publish *Filmmaker*, a quarterly magazine. IFP also sponsors a series of screenings, professional seminars and industry showcases, including a conference on screenplay development. Group health insurance, production insurance, discounts, a Resource Program, publications and a series of transcripts of previous seminars and workshops are available to members. Membership dues start at $100 a year ($65 for students).

INSTITUTE FOR CONTEMPORARY EAST EUROPEAN DRAMA AND THEATRE

Graduate Center of the City University of New York; 33 West 42nd St;
    New York, NY 10036-8099; (212) 642-2231, -2235, FAX 642-1977;
    E-mail seepjour@email.gc.cuny.edu
Daniel C. Gerould, *Director*

The Institute for Contemporary East European Drama and Theatre, under the auspices of the Center for Advanced Study in Theatre Arts (CASTA), publishes a triquarterly journal, *Slavic and East European Performance: Drama, Theatre, Film*, which is available by subscription ($10 a year, $15 foreign) and includes articles about current events in the East European and Slavic theatre, as well as reviews of productions and interviews with playwrights, directors and other theatre artists. The Institute also has available 2 annotated bibliographies of English translations of Eastern European plays written since 1945: *Soviet Plays in Translation* and *Polish Plays in Translation* ($5 each, $6 foreign). The institute is interested in hearing of published or unpublished translations for possible listing in updated editions of these bibliographies; translators may submit descriptive letters or scripts.

INSTITUTE OF OUTDOOR DRAMA

CB #3240; University of North Carolina; Chapel Hill, NC 27599-3240;
(919) 962-1328, FAX 962-4212; E-mail outdoor@unc.edu;
Web http://www.unc.edu/depts/outdoor/
Scott J. Parker, *Director*

The Institute of Outdoor Drama, founded in 1963, is a research and advisory agency of the University of North Carolina. It serves as a communications link between producers of existing outdoor dramas and is a resource for groups, agencies or individuals who wish to create new outdoor dramas or who are seeking information on the field. The institute provides professional consultation and conducts feasibility studies; holds annual auditions for summer employment in outdoor drama; sponsors conferences, lectures and symposiums; and publishes a quarterly newsletter, as well as information bulletins. Writers should note that the institute maintains a roster of available artists and production personnel, including playwrights and composers. It seeks to interest established playwrights and composers in participating in the creation of new outdoor dramas, and to encourage and advise new playwrights who wish to write for this specialized form of theatre.

INTERNATIONAL THEATRE INSTITUTE OF THE UNITED STATES (ITI/US)

47 Great Jones St; New York, NY 10012; (212) 254-4141, FAX 254-6814;
E-mail info@iti-usa.org; Web http://www.iti-usa.org
Martha W. Coigney, *Director*

Now operating centers in 92 countries, ITI was founded in 1948 by UNESCO "to promote the exchange of knowledge and practice in the theatre arts." ITI assists foreign theatre visitors in the U.S. and American theatre representatives traveling abroad. The ITI International Theatre Collection is a reference library which documents theatrical activity in 146 countries and houses over 12,700 plays from 97 countries. American playwrights, as well as other theatre professionals, frequently use the collection to make international connections; to consult foreign theatre directories for names of producers, directors or companies with a view to submitting plays abroad; and to research the programs and policies of theatres or managements. ITI answers numerous requests from abroad about American plays and also provides information on rights to foreign plays to American producers, directors and literary managers. Building upon its commitment to theatre professionals, ITI's University and Theatre Partner Programs enables it to work more closely with institutions interested in international exchange.

THE INTERNATIONAL WOMEN'S WRITING GUILD

Box 810, Gracie Station; New York, NY 10028-0082; (212) 737-7536,
FAX 737-9469; E-mail iwwg@iwwg.com; Web http://www.iwwg.com7
Hannelore Hahn, *Executive Director*

The International Women's Writing Guild, founded in 1976, is a network of women writers in the U.S., Canada and abroad. Playwrights, television and film writers, songwriters, producers and other women involved in the performing arts are included in its membership. Workshops are offered throughout the U.S. and annually at a week-long writing conference/retreat at Skidmore College in Saratoga Springs, NY. Members may also submit playscripts to theatres who have offered to read, critique and possibly produce IWWG members' works. *Network*, a 32-page newsletter published 6 times a year, provides a forum for members to share views and to learn about playwriting contests and awards, and theatre- and TV-related opportunities. The guild offers contacts with literary agents, group health insurance and other services to its members. Annual dues are $35 ($45 for foreign membership).

LA TELARAÑA
2626 North Mesa, #273; El Paso, TX 79902; E-mail tatiana@utep.edu
tatiana de la tierra, *Director*

La telaraña supports Latina lesbian writers by providing information, referrals, access to resources and a connection to each other through *el telarañazo*, a newsletter that includes current news and information on contests, calls for writing submissions and retreats; and a networking/support list of members for members. Annual membership is $13.

LATIN AMERICAN THEATER ARTISTS
30 Grant Ave; San Francisco, CA 94108; (415) 439-2425, FAX 834-3360
Luis Oropeza, *Artistic Director*

Latin American Theater Artists is a performing and support organization. As a theatre, LATA "embraces Latino theatre from its indigenous roots in Spain and the Americas through its classical development and its contemporary expression." LATA annually produces one full production and a children's show; LATA accepts new plays year-round. As an organization, LATA offers a casting and referral service to local and nonlocal Latino and Latina actors and artists.

LEAGUE OF CHICAGO THEATRES/
LEAGUE OF CHICAGO THEATRES FOUNDATION
228 South Wabash, Suite 300; Chicago, IL 60604; (312) 554-9800,
    FAX 922-7202; E-mail theleague@aol.com;
    Web http://www.theaterchicago.org

Founded in 1979, the League of Chicago Theatres/League of Chicago Theatres Foundation is the trade and service organization for Chicago's theatre industry. The League provides marketing, advocacy and membership services to more than 125 Chicago area theatres; acts as an information clearinghouse; offers vendor discounts including a cooperative advertising program; conducts workshops and the annual Chicago theatre industry retreat; publishes the bimonthly Chicago Theatre Guide; oversees the unified non-Equity auditions; and implements marketing initiatives such as Sears Theatre Fever and the Chicago Transit Authority Adopt-a-Station program. The League's Hot Tix program sells full- and half-price theatre and concert tickets.

LEAGUE OF PROFESSIONAL THEATRE WOMEN/NEW YORK
c/o Shari Upbin; 300 East 56th St., 2A; New York, NY 10022; (212) 583-0177,
FAX 583-0549
Shari Upbin, *President*

Founded in 1979, the league is a not-for-profit organization of theatre professionals providing programs and services which promote women in all areas of
professional theatre; create industry-related opportunities for women; and
highlight contributions of theatre women, past and present. Through its salons,
seminars, educational programs, social events, awards and festivals, the league
links professional theatres with theatre women nationally and internationally and
provides an ongoing forum for ideas, methods and issues of concern to the
theatrical community and its audiences. Programs include the Lee Reynolds
Award, given annually to a woman or women whose work for, in, about or
through the medium of theatre has helped to illuminate the possibilities for
social, cultural or political change; the annual Short Plays festival; the Oral
History Project, which seeks to chronicle and document the contribution of
significant theatre women; a membership directory; and panels discussing topics
of interest to women theatre professionals with well-known experts in the field.
Regular monthly meetings enable members to network, initiate programs and
serve on committees. To be eligible for membership in the league, playwrights,
composers, librettists and lyricists must have had a work presented in a First Class
production in the U.S. or Canada; or in a New York City theatre under Equity's
Basic Minimum Contract, excluding showcases; or at least 2 productions
presented in a resident theatre, as defined under Equity's Minimum Basic
Contract for Resident Theatres. All other theatre professionals must meet criteria
listed in brochure. Annual dues are $100. For further details of membership
eligibility and application procedure, write or call for Membership Information
brochure.

LITERARY MANAGERS AND DRAMATURGS OF THE AMERICAS (LMDA)
121 Avenue of the Americas, Suite 505; New York, NY 10013; (212) 965-0586,
FAX 699-6940; E-mail gproehl@ups.edu; Web http://www.lmda.org
Geoff Proehl, *President*

LMDA is the professional service organization for American and Canadian literary
managers and dramaturgs, founded in 1985 to affirm, examine and develop these
professions. Among the programs and services it offers to members are a toll-free
telephone job line; discussion and announcement listservs; Early Career
Dramaturgs, which identifies and encourages new members of the profession and
works to establish them in productive professional affiliations, as well as
publishing a guide to internships; the University Caucus, which acts as a liaison
between training and liberal arts programs and the profession, in addition to
publishing a guide to training programs, source books for teachers of dramaturgy
and an annual bibliography; and the Advocacy Caucus which examines and
reports on current working conditions of dramaturgs and literary managers.
Publications include the quarterly *LMDA Review*, the *LMDA Script Exchange*, and
the *Production Notebooks Project* that documents the conception, research, planning
and realization of oustanding theatre productions. Each June, LMDA holds an

annual conference. Voting membership is open to dramaturgs and literary managers only. Associate membership is open to playwrights, artistic directors, literary agents, educators and other theatre professionals interested in dramaturgy. Dues are $20 for students, $35 for associate members, $45 for voting members and $100 for institutional memberships.

LUMINOUS VISIONS

267 West 89th St; New York, NY 10024; (212) 581-7455, FAX 581-3964
Carla Pinza, *Co-Founder and Artistic Director*

Founded in 1976, Luminous Visions is a multicultural, not-for-profit organization dedicated to developing the creative skills and culture of film and television writers, directors and actors seeking employment within the English-speaking film and television mainstream. The organization sponsors a weekly workshop for writers, an annual Writers Forum and a spring Staged Reading Festival.

MARY ANDERSON CENTER FOR THE ARTS

101 St. Francis Dr; Mount Saint Francis, IN 47146; (812) 923-8602,
    FAX 923-0294; E-mail maca@iglou.com
Debra Carmody, *Executive Director*

The Mary Anderson Center, founded in 1989, is a not-for-profit organization dedicated to providing artists with a quiet place where they can concentrate and work on their craft. Named after the 19th-century actress from Louisville who rose to become an international celebrity, the center is located on 400 acres in southern Indiana. The center's goal is to provide retreats and residencies for artists in many disciplines (see the organization's entry in Colonies and Residencies). As part of its outreach effort to the Midwest and the nation, the center sponsors symposiums, conferences and other gatherings which explore, in a multidisciplinary mode, topics of major interest to society and to artists. Contributors to the center receive a quarterly newsletter featuring center activities and news of area artists.

MEET THE COMPOSER

2112 Broadway, Suite 505; New York, NY 10023; (212) 787-3601,
    FAX 787-3745
Omus Hirshbein, *Director*

Meet The Composer, a national grant-making agency, was founded in 1974 to increase opportunities for composers by fostering the creation, performance and dissemination of their music. A not-for-profit organization, Meet The Composer raises money from foundations, corporations, individual patrons and government sources, and designs programs that support all styles and genres of music—from folk, ethnic, jazz, electronic, symphonic and chamber to choral, music theatre, opera and dance. MTC provides artist fees to not-for-profit organizations that perform, present or commission original works. Its programs include Commissioning Music/USA, New Residencies (see Meet The Composer Grant Programs in

Fellowships and Grants), the Meet the Composer Fund and Affiliate Network, and New Music for Schools.

MIDWEST RADIO THEATRE WORKSHOP

KOPN; 915 East Broadway; Columbia, MO 65201; (573) 874-5676,
    FAX 499-1662; E-mail mrtw@mrtw.org; Web http://www.mrtw.org
Sue Zizza, *Executive Director*

MRTW is a national resource center for radio theatre in the areas of writing, directing, acting and sound design. Founded in 1979, it is a project of KOPN Radio/New Wave Corporation, a not-for-profit community radio station serving central Missouri. MRTW holds an annual script contest to identify and promote emerging and established radio writers. Winning scripts may be produced during one of a series of radio theatre workshops held each year (see the organization's entry in Development). MRTW provides information and referral services and technical assistance to interested individuals and groups, distributes educational tapes and publishes a quarterly Journal, an annual Scriptbook, as well as the *MRTW Audio Dramatists Directory*, a listings guide to audio artists, producers, programmers and professional resources.

MISSOURI ASSOCIATION OF PLAYWRIGHTS

830 North Spoede Rd; St. Louis, MO 63141; (314) 567-6341; FAX 647-0945
Jo Lovins, *President*

Missouri Association of Playwrights (MAP) was founded in 1976 to assist playwrights in developing their skills. The association's activities include monthly meetings which are open to the public (Sep–Jun) at which members' scripts are presented as fully staged readings or workshops; guests from the theatrical arena speak; seminars on writing for the theatre are offered. Periodically the Association presents a fully staged production of one-act plays. Script submission for full productions and staged readings are limited to works of MAP members only. Membership is open to all playwrights, but most members live in the greater St. Louis area (including southwest IL and out-state MO). Annual dues are $20.

NATIONAL ACADEMY OF SONGWRITERS

6255 Sunset Blvd, Suite 1023; Hollywood, CA 90028; (323) 463-7178,
    (800) 826-7287, FAX (323) 463-2146; E-mail nassong@aol.com;
    Web http://www.nassong.org
Randy Sharp, *President*

Founded in 1973, NAS is a not-for-profit organization dedicated to educating, assisting and protecting songwriters. Members and the public may call a toll-free number for answers to questions about the music business, have songs evaluated by industry professionals and, as proof of authorship, deposit songs in the academy's SongBank. NAS sponsors seminars, workshops and song evaluations; produces the Lifetime achievement awards dinner; and presents the Songwriters Expo. Members receive the *Songwriters Musepaper* monthly. Annual dues are $110 for General Membership, $125 for Pro Membership (those who have had at least

1 song commercially released and distributed; must have royalties statement for verification) and $200 for Gold Membership (those who have a certified gold single or album).

NATIONAL ALLIANCE FOR MUSICAL THEATRE

330 West 45th St, Lobby B; New York, NY 10036-3854; (212) 265-5376,
   FAX 582-8730; E-mail namtheatre@aol.com;
   Web http://www.bway.net/namt
Helen Sneed, *Executive and Artistic Director*
Trudi Biggs, *Membership and Programs Coordinator*

The National Alliance for Musical Theatre, founded in 1986, is the national service organization for musical theatre. The Alliance's goal is to serve as a champion of the musical and to foster its continued growth, both by providing national networking and collaboration opportunities, and by nurturing the creation, development, production and recognition of new musicals. It has 104 member organizations in 30 states including theatres, light opera and opera companies, and performing arts centers that produce or present musicals. As part of its services, the Alliance organizes two annual conferences, maintains a Web site and publishes newsletters and a Membership Directory. The Alliance also produces an annual Festival of New Musicals in New York City, which aims to encourage further productions of the showcased works. Works to be considered for the Festival should be submitted to member theatres, not to the Alliance.

THE NATIONAL FOUNDATION FOR JEWISH CULTURE

330 Seventh Ave, 21st Floor; New York, NY 10001; (212) 629-0500,
   FAX 629-0508; E-mail nfjc@jewishculture.org;
   Web http://www.jewishculture.org
Richard A. Siegel, *Executive Director*

The National Foundation for Jewish Culture (NFJC) is the central cultural agency of the American Jewish community. Founded in 1960, the NFJC has been dedicated to the enhancement of Jewish life in America through the support and promotion of the arts and humanities. Rooted in the principle that memory, knowledge and creativity are essential to Jewish continuity, the NFJC encourages innovation and excellence in artistic, scholarly and communal expression of Jewish culture. For the past 30 years, the NFJC has been a leader in advancing Jewish scholarship and preserving the Jewish cultural heritage in America. In recent years, the NFJC's program has expanded to include supporting new creativity in the arts, as well as bringing Jewish culture to local communities throughout North America.

The NFJC provides programs and services to cultural institutions, local communities and individual artists and scholars in every region of the country. It serves as: advocate and coordinator for the fields of Jewish culture through its Council of American Jewish Museums and Council of Archives and Research Libraries in Jewish Studies; sponsor of grants and awards to artists, scholars and major cultural institutions such as YIVO, Leo Baeck Institute, American Jewish Historical Society, Histadrut Ivrit and the Jewish Publication Society of America;

cultural innovator through conferences, symposiums, publications, media productions, traveling exhibitions, residencies and performances which promote an understanding and appreciation of contemporary Jewish life and culture; and presenter of the annual Jewish Cultural Achievement Awards recognizing outstanding contributions to Jewish life in America through the arts and scholarship.

THE NATIONAL LEAGUE OF AMERICAN PEN WOMEN, INC.
1300 17th St NW; Washington, DC 20036-1973; (202) 785-1997,
FAX 452-6868; E-mail nlapw1@juno.com;
Web http://members.aol.com/penwomen/pen.htm
Judith La Fourest, *National President*

Founded in 1897, NLAPW is a national membership organization for professional women writers, composers and visual artists. Its local branches meet monthly. It holds annual State Association meetings, a National Biennial Convention and a National Art Show, and will sponsor 3 Mature Women Scholarship Awards in 2000 (see Fellowships and Grants). Members, who receive a bimonthly magazine, *The Pen Woman,* and a National Roster, pay national dues of $30 a year; dues for individual branches are separate and vary.

NATIONAL PUBLIC RADIO
635 Massachusetts Ave NW; Washington, DC 20001-3753; (202) 414-2399,
FAX 414-3032; E-mail atrudeau@npr.org
Andy Trudeau, *Director, Program Acquisition and Production*

National Public Radio is a private not-for-profit membership organization which provides a national program service to its over 500 member noncommercial radio stations. It is funded by its member stations, the Corporation for Public Broadcasting and corporate grants. Among the programs available to member stations is *NPR Playhouse,* which presents 29-minute dramatic programs, series and serials. Writers should note that NPR does not itself read or produce plays. It acquires broadcast rights to produced packages. It will consider fully produced programs or works-in-progress on tape only.

THE NATIONAL THEATRE WORKSHOP OF THE HANDICAPPED
354 Broome St, Loft 5-F; New York, NY 10013; (212) 941-9511, FAX 941-9486;
E-mail ntwh@aol.com; Web http://ntwh.org
Rick Curry S. J., *Founder and Artistic Director*

Founded in 1977, the National Theatre Workshop of the Handicapped (NTWH) is a not-for-profit organization founded to provide persons with disabilities the opportunity to learn the communication skills necessary to pursue a life in professional theatre and to enhance their opportunities in the workplace. NTWH advocates for persons with physical disabilities in the theatre and offers a forum for dramatic literature on themes of disability. In addition to offering professional instruction in acting, classes are also offered in singing, voice, movement, playwriting and fine arts. Classes are held at the NTWH studio in New York City, and workshops are offered at NTWH-Crosby, the fully accessible residential facility in Belfast, ME. Persons with disabilities who are interested in participating in these training program should contact NTWH for more information. Of particular interest to playwrights is the NTWH Playwrights Workshop, a 2-week program held each spring for 4 playwrights to develop new works in residence in ME; selected works to be fully produced later; write for more information.

NEW DRAMATISTS
424 West 44th St; New York, NY 10036; (212) 757-6960, FAX 265-4738;
    E-mail newdram@aol.com; Web html://www.newdramatists.org
Paul Alexander Slee, *Executive Director*
Todd London, *Artistic Director*

New Dramatists is the nation's oldest playwright development center, designed to provide member playwrights with the resources they need to create plays for the American theatre. Rather than producing plays, New Dramatists aids playwrights in the development of their craft through play readings and workshops; dramaturgy; a resident director program; musical theatre development and training; ScriptShare (a national script distribution program); fellowships, awards and prizes; a free ticket program for Broadway and Off-Broadway productions; writing spaces and accomodations; and photocopying. All services are provided free of charge to members.

In addition, New Dramatists hosts several playwright exchanges, including the Mary Lea Johnson Richards Exchange with Beit Lessin Theatre, Israel; the Brooks Atkinson Exchange/Max Weitzenhoffer Fellowship to the Royal National Theatre, England; the Sumner Locke Elliott Exchange to the Australian National Playwrights Centre; and exchanges with the Tyrone Guthrie Center, County Monaghan, Ireland and A.S.K. Theater Projects, Los Angeles.

Membership is open to emerging playwrights living in the greater New York area, and to those living outside the area who demonstrate a willingness to regularly travel to New York and actively participate in this community of artists. Playwrights interested in applying for membership should write for guidelines.

NEW ENGLAND THEATRE CONFERENCE
Department of Theatre, Northeastern University; 360 Huntington Ave;
    Boston, MA 02115; (617) 424-9275, FAX 424-1057;
    E-mail netc@world.com
Corey Boniface, *Manager of Operations*

Founded in 1952, New England Theatre Conference is a membership organization primarily but not exclusively for New England theatre people, including playwrights, teachers, students and theatre professionals. Services include an annual conference, publication of a member directory and annual summer theatre auditions. NETC also administers both the John Gassner Memorial Playwriting Award and Aurand Harris Memorial Playwriting Award (see Prizes). The organization publishes *New England Theatre Journal* and *NETC News*. Membership dues are $20 for students, $35 for individuals and $80 for groups.

NEW PLAYWRIGHTS FOUNDATION

c/o 608 San Vicente Blvd, #18; Santa Monica, CA 90402; (310) 393-3682;
    Web http://www.newplaywrights.org
Jeffrey Lee Bergquist, *Artistic Director*

Founded in 1968, New Playwrights Foundation is a service organization for writers working in theatre, film, television and video. The foundation runs developmental workshops, holds readings, occasionally coproduces video and film projects and assists members in furthering their careers. Membership in NPF is limited to a maximum of 15 writers who must be able to attend meetings in Santa Monica every other Monday. Applicants for membership attend meetings before submitting materials to be reviewed by the group. Annual membership dues are $25.

THE NEW YORK PUBLIC LIBRARY FOR THE PERFORMING ARTS

Library Annex; 521 West 43rd St; New York, NY 10036; (212) 870-1639,
    FAX 870-1868; E-mail rtaylor@nypl.org; Web http://www.nypl.org
Bob Taylor, *Curator, The Billy Rose Theatre Collection*

The Billy Rose Theatre Collection, a division of the Library for the Performing Arts, is open to the public (aged 18 and over) and contains material on all aspects of theatrical art and the entertainment world, including stage, film, radio, television, circus, vaudeville and burlesque. The Theatre on Film and Tape Project (TOFT) is a special collection of films and videotapes of theatrical productions recorded during performance, as well as informal dialogues with important theatrical personalities. Tapes are available for viewing by appointment (call 870-1641) to students, theatre professionals and researchers.

NON-TRADITIONAL CASTING PROJECT

1560 Broadway, Suite 1600; New York, NY 10036;
    (212) 730-4750 (voice), -4913 (TDD), FAX 730-4820;
    E-mail info@ntcp.org; Web http://www.ntcp.org
Sharon Jensen, *Executive Director*

Founded in 1986, the Non-Traditional Casting Project is a not-for-profit organization which exists to address and seek solutions to the problems of racism and exclusion in the theatre and related media, particularly those which involve creative personnel: including, but not limited to, actors, directors, writers, designers and producers. The project works to advance the creative participation of artists of color and artists with disabilities through both advocacy and specific projects. Key NTCP programs include Artist Files/Artist Files Online, a national talent bank; roundtable discussions with industry leaders; forums; and a national Information and Consulting Service. Writers of color and/or with disabilities, who are citizens or residents of the U.S. or Canada and have had at least one play given a professional production or staged reading should send a resume for inclusion in Artist Files/Artist Files Online, indicating their cultural identification and, in the case of disabled artists, any accommodation they may use; those interested in contacting listed artists will call them or their agents directly.

NORTHWEST PLAYWRIGHTS GUILD

Box 1728; Portland, OR 97207; (503) 452-4778;
E-mail bjscript@teleport.com;
Web http://www.teleport.com/~bjscript/nwpg.htm
Bill Johnson, *Office Manager*

Northwest Playwrights Guild is an information clearinghouse and support group for playwrights. The guild sponsors public readings, holds workshops and produces regional conferences on theatre that include the full production of original scripts. The guild publishes a quarterly, *Script*, that contains articles on theatre in the Northwest, as well as update newsletters that provide information on current script opportunities. Membership dues are $25 a year.

OLLANTAY CENTER FOR THE ARTS

Box 720636; Jackson Heights, NY 11372-0636; (718) 565-6499,
FAX 446-7806
Pedro R. Monge-Rafuls, *Executive and Artistic Director*

Founded as a multidisciplinary Hispanic arts center in 1977, OLLANTAY has developed a Hispanic Heritage Center for the Arts in America with a view to providing the knowledge and resources needed to pursue research and develop new programs and initiatives in the field. The center maintains a resource bank of video and audio tapes, slides, books, plays and articles, which may be consulted by writing for an appointment. Its unique Playwriting Workshop, an annual intensive course of 2–4 weeks, provides an opportunity for playwrights wishing to write in Spanish to work under the direction of major Latin American playwrights who reside outside the U.S. *OLLANTAY Theater Magazine* is a biannual journal in English and Spanish which gives local playwrights, critics and scholars the opportunity to share their knowledge and experience of Hispanic theatre within the framework of American and world drama. The magazine, which publishes at least one play in each issue, is available to subscribers. Annual subscription is $20 for individuals, $35 for organizations.

OPERA AMERICA

1156 15th St NW, Suite 810; Washington, DC 20005-3287; (202) 293-4466,
FAX 393-0735; E-mail frontdesk@operaam.org
Jamie Driver, *Managing Director, Artistic & Audience Initiatives*

Founded in 1970, OPERA America is the not-for-profit service organization for the professional opera field in North America and allied international members. OPERA America provides a variety of informational, technical and financial services to its membership, and serves as a resource to the media, funders, government agencies and the general public.

The Next Stage, a program of OPERA America is designed to increase the number of North American works in the standard repertory by providing financial, technical and informational assistance to professional opera companies for productions of existing, under-performed works by North American artists.

Application for grants awarded through the program are accepted only from Professional Company Members of OPERA America. Individual artists and other organizations may request information about the program.

PEN AMERICAN CENTER
568 Broadway; New York, NY 10012; (212) 334-1660, FAX 334-2181;
E-mail pen@pen.org; Web http://www.pen.org
Karen Kennerly, *Executive Director*

PEN is an international association of writers. The American Center is the largest of the 130 centers which comprise International PEN. The 2700 members of PEN American Center are established North American writers and translators, and literary editors. PEN activities include the Freedom-to-Write program; monthly symposiums, readings and other public events; a prison writing program; and a translator-publisher clearinghouse. PEN's publications include *Grants and Awards Available to American Writers*, a biennially updated directory of prizes, grants, fellowships and awards (1998–99 edition $15 postpaid); *The PEN Prison Writing Information Bulletin*; and *A Handbook for Literary Translators*, available for free on the Web site. Among PEN's annual prizes and awards are the Gregory Kolovakos Award, PEN–Book-of-the-Month Club Translation Prize and the PEN/Laura Pels Foundation Awards for Drama (see Prizes); and Writing Awards for Prisoners, awarded to the authors of the best fiction, nonfiction, drama and poetry received from prisoner-writers in the U.S. The PEN Writers Fund and the PEN Fund for Writers & Editors with AIDS assist writers (see Emergency Funds).

PHILADELPHIA DRAMATISTS CENTER
1516 South St; Philadelphia, PA 19146; (215) 735-1441;
E-mail pdc@libertynet.org; Web http://www.libertynet.org/pdc
Ed Shockley, *Artistic Director*
Jon Dorf, *Managing Director*

Philadelphia Dramatists Center is a service organization for professional playwrights, screenwriters and musical theatre writers. Programs include developmental readings, writers' circles, chats with area artistic directors and literary managers, free craft development workshops, actor/director files, ticket discounts to participating theatres, rehearsal space, a telephone hotline listing upcoming events and publication of the bimonthly newsletter *First Draft*. Annual membership dues are $15 for students and $25 for individuals, which includes a subscription to *First Draft*.

PLAYMARKET
Box 9767; Wellington; New Zealand; 64-4-382-8462, FAX 64-4-382-8461;
E-mail plymkt@clear.net.nz; Web http://www.playmarket.org.nz
Guy Boyce, *Director*
Susan Wilson, *Script Advisor*

Playmarket is a service organization for New Zealand playwrights, established in 1973 as a result of a growing interest in plays by New Zealand writers and a need to find new writers. The organization runs a script advisory and critiquing service, arranges workshop productions of promising scripts, and serves as the country's principal playwrights' agency, preparing and distributing copies of scripts and negotiating and collecting royalties. Playmarket's publications include *The Playmarket Directory of New Zealand Plays and Playwrights*, and a script series *New Zealand Theatrescripts*.

THE PLAYWRIGHTS' CENTER

2301 Franklin Ave East; Minneapolis, MN 55406-1099; (612) 332-7481;
E-mail pwcenter@mtn.org; Web http://www.pwcenter.org
Carlo Cuesta, *Executive Director*

The Playwrights' Center is a service organization for playwrights. Its programs include: developmental services (cold readings and workshops using an Equity acting company); fellowships; exchanges with theatres and other developmental programs; a biannual journal; the Jones commissioning program; PlayLabs (see Development); playwriting classes; year-round programs for young writers; and the Many Voices program, designed to provide awards, education and lab services to new and emerging playwrights of color. The Center annually awards 5 Jerome Playwright-in-Residence Fellowships, for which competition is open nationally; 2 McKnight Fellowships, for which competition is open by professional nomination; 3 McKnight Advancement Grants open to Minnesota playwrights; and 3 Many Voices Multicultural Collaboration Grants (see The Playwrights' Center Grant Programs in Fellowships and Grants). The annual Young Playwrights Summer Conference, open to students grades 8–12, offers 2 weeks of workshops and classes for 30 young writers, with daily workshops and readings of students' work; participants, who are selected on the basis of writing samples and recommendations, receive college credit; scholarships are available; applications are available 15 Dec 1999; *deadline:* 19 Apr 2000; *dates:* 9–22 Jul 2000.

A broad-based Center membership is available to any playwright or interested person. Benefits of general membership for playwrights include discounts on classes, applications for all Center programs, eligibility to apply for the Jones commission and script-development readings, and the Center's journal. Core (must be MN resident) and Associate Member Playwrights are selected by a review panel each spring, based on script submission. They have primary access to all Center programs and services, including developmental workshops and public readings. Write for Membership information.

THE PLAYWRIGHTS FOUNDATION

Box 460357; San Francisco, CA 94146; (415) 263-3986;
E-mail Playwrights_Fdn@hotmail.com
Belinda Taylor, *President*
Jayne Wenger, *Artistic Director*

The Playwrights Foundation provides developmental support to playwrights throughout the U.S., with emphasis on the northern California region. It produces the annual Bay Area Playwrights Festival (see Development) and is developing a new year-round playwright services program, New Play Resources.

PLAYWRIGHTS THEATRE OF NEW JERSEY

33 Green Village Rd; Madison, NJ 07940; (973) 514-1787, FAX 514-2060
Joseph Megel, *Artistic Director*

Founded in 1986, the Playwrights Theatre of New Jersey is both a service organization for playwrights of all ages and a professional developmental theatre. In addition to its New Play Development Program (see Playwrights Theatre of New Jersey New Play Development Program in Development), PTNJ co-sponsors, with the New Jersey Council on the Arts, the New Jersey Writers Project, a statewide program which teaches prose, poetry and dramatic writing in schools. Specialized programs include a playwriting-for-teachers project; adult playwriting classes; children's creative dramatics classes; acting classes; and "special needs" playwriting projects which include work in housing projects and with senior citizens, teenage substance abusers, persons with physical disabilities and court-appointed youth, as well as a playwriting-in-prisons initiative; and a program that teaches Spanish-language prose, poetry and dramatic writing. Young playwrights festivals are held in Madison and Newark, in addition to a statewide festival which is part of the New Jersey Young Playwrights Program. Gifted and talented playwriting symposiums, hosted by well-known playwrights, provide intensive 2-day experiences for up to 60 students from various school districts.

PLAZA DE LA RAZA

3540 North Mission Rd; Los Angeles, CA 90031; (323) 223-2475,
    FAX 223-1804; E-mail admin@plazaraza.org;
    Web http://www.plazaraza.org
Rose Cano, *Executive Director*

Founded in 1970, Plaza de la Raza is a cultural center for the arts and education, primarily serving the surrounding community of East Los Angeles. Of special interest to playwrights is the center's Nuevo L.A. Chicano TheatreWorks project, designed to discover, develop and present the work of Chicano playwrights. Initiated in 1989 and recurring approximately every 4 years, depending on funding, as part of the Nuevo L.A. Chicano Art Series cycle (Visual Arts, Music, Dance and Theatre), the project develops new one-acts through a 2-week workshop with director and actors, culminating in public readings; some plays are selected for subsequent full production. Latino playwrights who are California residents should contact the center for information on when and how to apply for the next round of the program. In addition to its playwrights' project, Plaza de la Raza conducts classes in drama, dance, music and the visual arts; provides resources for teachers in the community; and sponsors special events, exhibits and performances. Membership in Plaza de la Raza is open to all.

PROFESSIONAL ASSOCIATION OF CANADIAN THEATRES/ PACT COMMUNICATIONS CENTRE

30 St. Patrick St, 2nd Floor; Toronto, Ontario; Canada; M5T 3A3;
    (416) 595-6455, FAX 595-6450; E-mail pactcomm@idirect.com;
    Web http://webhome.idirect.com/~pact/
Pat Bradley, *Executive Director*

PACT is the national service and trade association representing professional English-language theatres in Canada. PACT was incorporated in 1976 to work on behalf of its member theatres in the areas of advocacy, labor relations, professional development and communications. The members' newsletter *impact!* is published quarterly. PACT Communications Centre (PCC) was established in 1985 as the charitable wing of PACT in order to improve and expand communications and information services. PCC publishes *The Theatre Listing*, an annual directory of English-language Canadian theatres, rehearsal and performance spaces, government agencies and arts service organizations; and *Artsboard*, the monthly bulletin of employment opportunities in the arts in Canada.

PUBLIC BROADCASTING SERVICE

1320 Braddock Pl; Alexandria, VA 22314-1698; (703) 739-5000,
    FAX 739-0775; E-mail www@pbs.org;
    Web http://www.pbs.org/independents
Corporate Communications

The Public Broadcasting Service is a private not-for-profit corporation that acquires and distributes programs to its 349 member stations. The PBS Program Management Department can advise independent producers about the development of specific projects. Information about the preparation, presentation and funding of projects can be obtained from the PBS Program Management Department or by visiting the Web site.

THE PURPLE CIRCUIT

921 Naomi St; Burbank, CA 90515; (818) 953-5096, -5072;
    E-mail purplecir@aol.com
Bill Kaiser, *Coordinator*

The Purple Circuit is a network of gay, lesbian, queer, bisexual and transsexual theatres, producers, performers and "Kindred Spirits" (theatres which are not exclusively gay or lesbian in orientation but are interested in producing gay or lesbian material on a regular basis). The Purple Circuit publishes news, information and articles of interest to its constituency in its quarterly newsletter, *On the Purple Circuit. The Purple Circuit Directory* lists theatres and producers around the world, including "Kindred Spirits," that are interested in presenting gay, lesbian, bisexual and transsexual works. The Purple Circuit Hotline (818) 953-5072 provides information on gay and lesbian shows currently playing in California and advises travelers on shows around the U.S. and abroad, as well as providing information for playwrights, journalists and others interested in promoting gay/lesbian/bisexual/transgender theatre and performance.

THE SCRIPTWRITERS NETWORK

11684 Ventura Blvd, #508; Studio City, CA 91604; (323) 848-9477;
    Web http://scriptwritersnetwork.com
Bill Lundy, *Chair*

Though the Scriptwriters Network, founded in 1989, is predominantly an affiliation of film, television and corporate/industrial writers, playwrights are welcome. Meetings feature guest speakers; developmental feedback on scripts is available; and staged readings may be arranged in conjunction with other groups. The network sponsors members-only contests and publishes a newsletter. Prospective members submit a professionally formatted script and a completed application; membership is not based on the quality of the script. There is a $15 initiation fee, and dues are $50 a year for nonlocal members, $60 for Southern California residents.

THE SONGWRITERS GUILD OF AMERICA

1560 Broadway, Room 1306; New York, NY 10036; (212) 768-7902,
    FAX 768-9048; E-mail songnews@aol.com;
    Web http://www.songwriters.org
George Wurzbach, *National Projects Director*

Head Office:
1500 Harbor Blvd; Weehawken, NJ 07087-6732; (201) 867-7603
Los Angeles Office:
6430 Sunset Blvd; Hollywood, CA 90028; (323) 462-1108
Nashville Office:
1222 16th Ave; Nashville, TN 37212; (615) 329-1782

The Songwriters Guild is a voluntary national association run by and for songwriters; all officers and directors are unpaid. Among its many services to composers and lyricists, the guild provides a standard songwriter's contract and reviews this and other contracts on request; collects writers' royalties from music publishers; maintains a copyright renewal service; conducts songwriting workshops and critique sessions with special rates for members; issues news bulletins with essential information for writers; and offers a group medical and life insurance plan. Full members of the guild must be published songwriters and pay dues on a graduated scale from $70–400. Unpublished songwriters may become associate members and pay dues of $55 a year. Write for membership application.

S.T.A.G.E. (SOCIETY FOR THEATRICAL ARTISTS' GUIDANCE AND ENHANCEMENT)

Box 214820; Dallas, TX 75221; (214) 630-7722, FAX 630-4468
Tracy Goodwin, *Managing Director*

Founded in 1981, S.T.A.G.E. acts as an information clearinghouse for theatre artists and theatre organizations in the north Texas region. The society maintains a library of plays, theatre texts and resource information; offers counseling on agents, unions, personal marketing and other career-related matters; posts listings of miscellaneous job opportunities; and maintains an audition callboard for regional opportunities in theatre and film; sponsors an actor's showcase, Noon Preview; sponsors annual general auditions; and produces Stages Festival of New Plays, the longest running new play festival in Dallas. Send SASE for festival guidelines. Members of S.T.A.G.E., who pay annual dues starting at $45 (for volunteers), $65 (for all others), receive a monthly publication, *CENTERSTAGE.*

THEATRE BAY AREA (TBA)

657 Mission St, Suite 402; San Francisco, CA 94105; (415) 957-1557,
FAX 957-1556; E-mail tba@best.com; Web http://www.theatrebayarea.org

TBA is a resource organization for San Francisco Bay Area theatre workers whose members include 3200 individuals and more than 260 theatre companies. Its programs include TIX Bay Area, San Francisco's half-price ticket booth; TIX By Mail, a half-price ticket catalog; professional workshops; and communications and networking services. Annual dues of $37 (add $12 for 1st-class postage) include a subscription to *Callboard*, a monthly magazine featuring articles, interviews and essays on the Northern California theatre scene, as well as information on play contests and festivals, and listings of production activity, workshops, classes, auditions, jobs and services. TBA also publishes *Theatre Directory of the Bay Area*, which includes entries of local theatre companies; the *Performance and Rehearsal Rental Directory of the Bay Area* with listings of rehearsal and performance spaces; *Sources of Publicity*; and *Management Memo*, a monthly newsletter for theatre administrators and artistic directors. The Web site includes a playbill calendar, ticket information and sample *Callboard* articles.

THEATRE COMMUNICATIONS GROUP

355 Lexington Ave; New York, NY 10017-0217; (212) 697-5230, FAX 983-4847;
E-mail tcg@tcg.org; Web http://www.tcg.org
Ben Cameron, *Executive Director*

Founded in 1961 as the national service organization for the not-for-profit professional theatre, Theatre Communications Group (TCG) offers a wide array of services in line with its mission: to strengthen, nurture and promote the not-for-profit American theatre. TCG's programs and services encompass four primary areas of activity: artistic programs, including grants to artists and theatres; management programs, including conferences and forums, industry research and management training; advocacy, serving as the primary national advocate for the field, in conjunction with the American Arts Alliance; and publications. Each of TCG's programs is designed to address at least one of the following central strategies: increasing the organizational efficiency of TCG's member theatres, cultivating and celebrating the artistic talent and achievements of the field and promoting a larger public understanding of and appreciation for the theatre field.

During 1998–99, TCG claimed 17,000 individual members, including theatre professionals, educators, students, theatre enthusiasts and a network of more than 330 member theatres in 44 states, representing a wide range of institutional sizes, structures and aesthetics. In the belief that the diversity of the theatre field is its greatest strength, TCG's membership criteria have been changed recently to embrace a wider range of theatres and practices.

TCG's artistic programs available to playwrights include the National Theatre Artists Residency Program, funded by The Pew Charitable Trusts, which supports extended relationships between theatres and individual artists by providing the resources for long-term residencies; the NEA/TCG Theatre Residency Program for Playwrights, which provides $25,000 grants to help playwrights create new works and strengthen relationships with theatres; and Extended Collaboration Grants, funded by Metropolitan Life Foundation, which help theatres hire playwrights for extended developmental work with other collaborators. (For more information, see TCG Artistic Programs in Fellowships and Grants.)

In addition to *American Theatre* magazine, which provides an up-to-date perspective on theatre throughout the country and includes the full texts of five new plays annually, other TCG publications of interest to theatre writers include *Theatre Directory*, a pocket-sized directory, which provides complete contact information for more than 360 not-for-profit professional theatres and related organizations across the U.S.; *Stage Writers Handbook: A Complete Business Guide for Playwrights, Composers, Lyricists and Librettists*, by Dana Singer; *The Production Notebooks: Theatre in Process, Volume I*, edited by Mark Bly; *Stage Directors Handbook: Opportunities for Directors and Choreographers*, edited by the SDC Foundation; and *ArtSEARCH*, a biweekly bulletin of job opportunities in the arts. TCG also publishes plays and musicals, and books on actors and acting, directors, designers, playwrights, theatre history, criticism and theory, and resource books on the not-for-profit professional theatre. (For further information, see the Publications and Useful Publications chapters, and Related TCG Publications in the back of this book. A complete publications catalogue is available from TCG and, beginning in September 1999, will be included as part of TCG's Web site.)

Individual members receive a free subscription to *American Theatre* magazine, discounted tickets to performances at more than 220 theatres nationwide and discounts on all TCG books and books from other select theatre publishers' distributed by TCG. Other benefits include a no-fee affinity credit card and discounts on car rentals, hotel accommodations and express delivery service. Individual memberships are available for $35 a year, $20 for students. (See the TCG membership application in the back of this book.)

THEATRE LA

644 South Figueroa St; Los Angeles, CA 90017; (213) 614-0556,
FAX 614-0561; E-mail theatrela1@aol.com;
Web http://www.theatrela.org

A not-for-profit association of over 150 theatres and producers, Theatre LA was founded in 1975 to unite, represent and promote theatre in greater Los Angeles. Theatre LA administers the annual Ovation Awards; provides cooperative advertising, a job bank and information and referral services for members; and runs a half-price ticket booth. Publications include *Theatre LA News*, a newsletter with information about advocacy and opportunities for playwrights; and *Opening Night Calendar*, which includes listings of member theatres' showtimes. Full membership in the organization is open only to theatres and producers on an annual sliding scale of $220–$1200. Individuals may become associate members for $35 annually. Businesses may become associate members for $50 annually.

THE THEATRE MUSEUM

1E Tavistock St; London WC2E 7PA; England; 44-171-836-7891,
    FAX 44-171-836-5148

The Theatre Museum, a branch of the Victoria & Albert Museum, is Britain's national museum of the performing arts. In addition to its regular displays, which feature 400 years of the history, technology, art and craft of theatre, and its special exhibitions, the museum houses the U.K.'s largest archive of performing arts materials, including play texts, photographic and biographical files, theatre programs and reviews, and books about the theatre. The archive and study room is available by appointment (call during office hours) Tuesday to Friday, 10:30–1:00 p.m. and 2:00–4:30 p.m. The museum's innovative education department runs workshops and study days on theatre practice and set texts for children, students and teachers. The museum also runs a program of celebrity play readings, seminars and events to give visitors insight into current theatre production.

UBU REPERTORY THEATER

95 Wall St, 21st Floor; New York, NY 10005; (212) 509-1455, FAX 509-1635;
    E-mail uburep@spacelab.net; Web http://www.nytheatre-wire.com
Françoise Kourilsky, *Artistic Director*

Ubu Repertory Theater, founded in 1982, is a not-for-profit theatre center dedicated to introducing translations of contemporary French-language plays to the English-speaking audience (see theatre's entry in Production). In addition to producing several plays a year, Ubu commissions translations and schedules reading programs, photography exhibits, panel discussions and workshops. Ubu publishes a series of contemporary plays by French-speaking playwrights in English translation, distributed nationally by TCG, and houses a French-English reference library of published plays and manuscripts.

VOLUNTEER LAWYERS FOR THE ARTS

1 East 53rd St, 6th Floor; New York, NY 10022; (212) 319-2787 (administrative
    office and Art Law Hotline), FAX 752-6575
Amy Schwartzman, *Executive Director*

Volunteer Lawyers for the Arts arranges free legal representation and legal education for the arts community. Individual artists and not-for-profit arts organizations unable to afford private counsel are eligible for VLA's services; VLA can be especially useful to playwrights with copyright or contract problems. There is an administrative fee per referral of $50–150 for individuals, $150–500 for not-for-profit organizations and $250 for not-for-profit incorporation and tax exemption. VLA's education program offers biweekly seminars on not-for-profit incorporation and evening seminars held regularly to educate attorneys and artists in specific areas of art law. Publications include *Model Contracts for Independent Contractors: Sample Provisions and Job Descriptions* ($15 plus $2.50 postage and handling); and the *VLA Guide to Copyright for Visual Artists* ($5.95 plus $2.50 postage and handling). For more information about VLA's publications and the 40 VLA affiliates across the country, contact Natalie E. Charles (ext 10) of the

New York office; referrals can be made to volunteer lawyer organizations nationwide.

WOMEN'S THEATRE ALLIANCE (WTA)

407 South Dearborn, Suite 1775; Chicago, IL 60602; (312) 408-9910;
    Web http://www.wtac.org
Ester Lebo, *Outreach*

Founded in 1992, the Women's Theatre Alliance (WTA) is dedicated to the development of dramatic works by, for and about women and to the promotion of women's leadership within the Chicago theatre community. Programs of special interest to playwrights include the Play Development Workshop and New Plays Festival which unites women writers with a director and actors for a development process culminating in a 2-week festival of staged readings; Solo Voices, which facilitates the creation of one woman shows and performance pieces; and the Salon Series, an informal presentation of new work offering social networking opportunities. WTA also publishes a monthly newsletter. Membership is open to all Chicago-area residents. Annual dues are $30.

THE WOW CAFE

59–61 East 4th St; New York, NY 10003; (212) 777-4280

The WOW (Women's One World) Cafe is a women's theatre collective whose membership is primarily but not exclusively lesbian. WOW produces the work of women playwrights and performers. It has no permanent staff and its members are encouraged to participate in all aspects of the group's operations. In lieu of dues, members volunteer their services backstage on fellow members' productions in exchange for the opportunity to present their own work. Each show is produced by the member who initiates it. Women interested in becoming members of the WOW Cafe may attend one of the collective's regular meetings, which are scheduled every Tuesday at 6:30 P.M.

WRITERS GUILD OF AMERICA, EAST (WGAE), AFL-CIO

555 West 57th St; New York, NY 10019-2967; (212) 767-7800, FAX 582-1909
Mona Mangan, *Executive Director*

WGAE is the union for freelance writers in the fields of motion pictures, television and radio who reside east of the Mississippi River (regardless of where they work). The union negotiates collective bargaining agreements for its members and represents them in grievances and arbitrations under those agreements. It also makes credit determinations for the writing of its members. The guild gives annual awards, and sponsors a foundation which currently teaches film writing to disadvantaged high school students. WGAE participates in reciprocal arrangements with the International Affiliation of Writers Guilds and with its sister union, Writers Guild of America, west. The guild publishes a monthly newsletter, which is available to nonmembers by subscription; and a quarterly journal, *On Writing*. Write for information on WGAE's service for registering literary material, or call (212) 757-4360.

WRITERS GUILD OF AMERICA, WEST (WGAW)

7000 West 3rd St; Los Angeles, CA 90048-4329; (323) 951-4000, FAX 782-4800;
   Web http://www.wga.org
John McLean, *Executive Director*

WGAw is the union for writers in the fields of motion pictures, television, radio and new media who write both entertainment and news programming. It represents its members in collective bargaining and other labor matters. It publishes a monthly magazine, *Written By*. The Guild registers material, including screen- and teleplays, books, plays, poetry and songs (call 782-4500). The library is open to the public Mon–Fri (call 782-4544).

YOUNG PLAYWRIGHTS INC.

321 West 44th St, #906; New York, NY 10036; (212) 307-1140, FAX 307-1454;
   E-mail writeaplay@aol.com; Web http://youngplaywrights.org
Sheri M. Goldhirsch, *Artistic Director*

Young Playwrights Inc. (YPI), founded in 1981 by Stephen Sondheim and other members of the Dramatists Guild, introduces young people to the theatre and encourages self-expression through the art of playwriting. YPI strives to identify, develop and encourage playwrights aged 18 years and younger; to develop new works for the theatre and to aid in the creation of the next generation of professional playwrights through the Young Playwrights Festival National Playwriting Contest (see Prizes), the Young Playwrights Spring Conference, and the Urban Playwriting Retreat; to expose young people to theatre and playwriting through WRITING ON YOUR FEET! in-school playwriting workshops; to train teachers through the TEACHING ON YOUR FEET! Teacher Training Institute; to develop and serve audiences that reflect the complex makeup of our society and to create the next generation of theatregoers through the TAKE A GROWNUP TO THE THEATER! ticket subsidy program, student matinees and a discount voucher program; to bring the vital experience of professional theatre free of charge to neglected inner-city public schools, community organizations and youth centers through the Young Playwrights School Tour; and to serve as an advocate for young writers regardless of ethnicity, physical ability, sexual orientation or economic status, and to ensure that their voices are heard and acknowledged by a diverse community of artists and theatregoers.

Epilogue

- **Useful Publications**
- **Online Resources**
- **Submission Calendar**
- **Special Interests**
- **Index**

Useful Publications

This is a selective listing of the publications that we think most usefully supplement the information given in the *Sourcebook*. Note that publications of interest to theatre writers are also described throughout this book, particularly in introductions to sections, in Membership and Service Organizations listings, and on the Related TCG Publications pages in the back. Before ordering you would be wise to find out if the prices given in all listings still pertain.

We have purposely left out any "how to" books on the art of playwriting because we do not want to promote the concept of "writing-by-recipe." However, we do recommend David Savran's *In Their Own Words: Contemporary American Playwrights* and *The Playwright's Voice: American Dramatists on Memory, Writing and the Politics of Culture*; *The Production Notebooks: Theatre in Process, Volume One*, edited by Mark Bly; *Stage Director's Handbook: Opportunities for Directors and Choreographers*, edited by David Diamond and Terry Berliner of the SDC Foundation (see Related TCG Publications pages); and Dana Singer's *Stage Writers Handbook: A Complete Business Guide for Playwrights, Composers, Lyricists and Librettists* (see this section).

AMERICAN THEATRE

Theatre Communications Group; 355 Lexington Ave; New York, NY
10017-0217; (212) 697-5230, FAX 557-5817; E-mail custserv@tcg.org;
Web http://www.tcg.org

1-year subscription/TCG membership $35; single issue $4.95. This monthly
magazine provides comprehensive coverage of all aspects of theatre. A special
Season Preview issue each October lists schedules for more than 300 theatres
nationwide, and monthly schedules for more than 200 theatres are published in
each issue. *American Theatre* regularly features articles and interviews dealing with
theatre writers and their works, and publishes the complete texts of 5 new plays
a year. (See entry in Publication; see Theatre Communications Group in Membership and Service Organizations, and Fellowships and Grants.)

BACK STAGE

1515 Broadway, 14th Floor; New York, NY 10036; (212) 764-7300,
FAX 536-5318; E-mail backstage@backstage.com;
Web http://www.backstage.com

1-year subscription $84, 2 years $136; single issue $2.75, $5.00 by mail. This
performing arts weekly includes industry news; reports from cities across the
country; reviews; and columns, including "Playwrights' Corner." The primary
focus is on casting, theatres; other producers sometimes run ads soliciting scripts;
workshops and classes for playwrights are also likely to be advertised here.

HOLLYWOOD SCRIPTWRITER

Box 10277; Burbank, CA 91510; (818) 845-5525;
E-mail editor@hollywoodscriptwriter.com;
Web http://www.hollywoodscriptwriter.com

1-year subscription (12 issues) $35, 6 months $25. This 16-page trade paper
contains a "MARKETS for Your Work" section that includes "Plays Wanted"
listings, as well as interviews and articles giving advice that is sometimes useful to
playwrights as well as screenwriters. A list of back issues with a summary of the
contents of each issue is available; call for information and a free sample.

LITERARY AGENTS: A WRITER'S GUIDE by Debby Mayer

Poets & Writers; 72 Spring St; New York, NY 10012; (212) 226-3586,
FAX 226-3963

1998. 172 pp, $12.95 (plus $3.90 postage and handling and sales tax where
applicable) paper. This book contains several chapters exploring the functions
of literary agents and the agent-writer relationship, and includes listings of 120
agencies which will consider unsolicited *queries* plus a listing of more resources.

LITERARY MARKET PLACE 1999
R. R. Bowker; 121 Chanlon Rd; New Providence, NJ 07974; (908) 464-6800,
(888) BOWKER-2, FAX (908) 771-7704; E-mail info@bowker.com;
Web http://www.bowker.com

1998. 2041 pp, $189.95 (plus 7% postage and handling and sales tax where applicable) paper. Also available on their Web site (various fee options and subscription rates are given). This directory of the American book publishing industry gives contact information for book publishers and those in related fields, and includes a "Names & Numbers" index over 500 pages long. The 2000 *LMP* is due out in October 1999.

MARKET INSIGHT...FOR PLAYWRIGHTS
Box 1758; Champaign, IL 61824-1758; (800) 895-4720,
FAX (217) 373-2468; E-mail minsight@aol.com;
Web http://members.aol.com/minsight/index.html

1-year subscription (12 issues) $40, 6 months $25. This monthly newsletter for playwrights provides submission guidelines for theatres, residencies, publishers and contests, as well as updates on personnel changes at theatres, special programs for women writers, and more; contest application forms and updates are provided via e-mail; call for a free sample.

MUSIC, DANCE & THEATER SCHOLARSHIPS
Conway Greene Publishing Company; 1414 South Green Rd, Suite 206;
South Euclid, OH 44121; (800) 977-2665;
Web http://www.conwaygreene.com

2nd edition, 1998. 490 pp, $24.95 (plus $4.00 postage and handling and sales tax where applicable) paper. This guide provides information on more than 1800 theatre, music and dance conservatory and undergraduate programs, as well as more than 5000 professional and educational scholarship opportunities. It also includes detailed information on audition requirements, decision processes at individual schools, special scholarship stipulations and student profiles.

PLAYHOUSE AMERICA!
Feedback Theatrebooks; 305 Madison Ave, Suite 1146; New York, NY 10165;
(212) 687-4185, (800) 800-8671, FAX (207) 359-5532;
E-mail feedback@hypernet.com;
Web http://www.hypernet.com/prospero.html

1991. 300 pp, $16.95 (plus $3.00 postage and handling and sales tax where applicable) paper. This directory contains the addresses and phone numbers of more than 3500 theatres across the country; it includes a cross-reference to specialty theatres (e.g., Dinner Theatres & Showboats, Military Theatres).

THE PLAYWRIGHT'S COMPANION, Mollie Ann Meserve, ed

Feedback Theatrebooks; 305 Madison Ave, Suite 1146; New York, NY 10165;
  (212) 687-4185, (800) 800-8671, FAX (207) 359-5532;
  E-mail feedback@hypernet.com;
  Web http://www.hypernet.com/prospero.html

1999. 396 pp, $20.95 (plus $3.00 postage and handling and sales tax where applicable) paper. This annual guide for playwrights publishes submission guidelines for more than 1800 theatres and production companies, contests, publishers and special programs. The *Companion* includes useful tips on query letters, synopses, resumes and submission etiquette, as well as a list of state arts councils, agents and playwriting programs in colleges and universities. The 2000 edition is due out in December 1999. Also available *Et Cetera, Et Cetera, Et Cetera,* an annual supplemental special interest cross reference to *Companion* listings, through Feedback Theatrebooks only for $2.95.

POETS & WRITERS MAGAZINE

Poets & Writers; 72 Spring St; New York, NY 10012;
  (212) 226-3586, FAX 226-3963

1-year subscription (6 issues) $19.95, 2 years $38; single issue $4.95. Though primarily aimed at writers of poetry and fiction, this magazine does include some announcements of grants and awards as well as other opportunities open to theatre writers.

PROFESSIONAL PLAYSCRIPT FORMAT GUIDELINES AND SAMPLE

Feedback Theatrebooks; 305 Madison Ave, Suite 1146; New York, NY 10165;
  (212) 687-4185, (800) 800-8671, FAX (207) 359-5532;
  E-mail feedback@hypernet.com;
  Web http://www.hypernet.com/prospero.html

1991. 28 pp, $4.95 (plus $1.75 postage and handling and sales tax where applicable) paper. This booklet provides detailed instructions for laying out a script in a professional manner, includes a "Margin and Tab Setting Guide" and sample pages of script.

SONGWRITER'S MARKET, Tara A. Horton, ed

Writer's Digest Books; 1507 Dana Ave; Cincinnati, OH 45207;
  (513) 531-2690, ext 423, FAX 531-7107; E-mail songmarket@fwpubs.com;
  Web http://www.writersdigest.com

2000. 522 pp, $22.99 (plus $3 shipping and handling and sales tax where applicable) paper. This annually updated directory, which lists contact information for more than 2000 song markets, includes a section on musical theatre. It also lists associations, contests and workshops of interest to songwriters. The 2000 edition is due out in September 1999.

STAGE DIRECTIONS MAGAZINE

SMW Communications; 250 West 57th St, Suite 420; New York, NY 10107;
(212) 265-8890, FAX 265-8908; E-mail stagedir@aol.com;
Web http://www.stage-directions.com

1-year subscription (10 issues) $26, 2 years $48; single issue $3.50. This magazine provides information on royalty issues, play publishing, new play festivals and workshops/seminars for playwrights. A special Season Planner issue each November contains a directory of royalty houses.

STAGE WRITERS HANDBOOK: A COMPLETE BUSINESS GUIDE FOR PLAYWRIGHTS, COMPOSERS, LYRICISTS AND LIBRETTISTS by Dana Singer

Theatre Communications Group; 355 Lexington Ave; New York, NY 10017-0217;
(212) 697-5230, FAX 983-4847; E-mail custserv@tcg.org;
Web http://www.tcg.org

1997. 328 pp, $16.95 (plus $3 postage and handling for 1 book, $1 for each additional book) paper. This comprehensive guide, written by the Associate Director of the Dramatists Guild, covers such topics as copyright, collaboration, underlying rights, marketing and self-promotion, production contracts, representation (agents and lawyers), publishers, authors' relationships with directors, and videotaping and electronic rights.

THEATRE DIRECTORY 1999–00

Theatre Communications Group; 355 Lexington Ave; New York, NY 10017-0217;
(212) 697-5230, FAX 983-4847; E-mail custserv@tcg.org;
Web http://www.tcg.org

1999. 190 pp, $9.95 (plus $3 postage and handling for 1 book, $1 for each additional book) paper. TCG's annually updated directory provides complete contact information for more than 330 not-for-profit professional theatres—including new TCG Constituent and Associate theatres that join after this *Sourcebook* is published—and more than 100 arts resource organizations.

THEATRE PROFILES 12

Theatre Communications Group; 355 Lexington Ave; New York, NY 10017-0217;
(212) 697-5230, FAX 983-4847; E-mail custserv@tcg.org;
Web http://www.tcg.org

1996. 240 pp, $22.95 (plus $3 postage and handling for 1 book, $1 for each additional book) paper. Useful for finding out about this country's not-for-profit professional theatres, the 12th volume of this biennial series contains artistic profiles, production photographs, financial information and repertoire information for the 1993–95 seasons of 257 theatres.

U.S. COPYRIGHT OFFICE PUBLICATIONS

Library of Congress; Copyright Office; Publications Section, LM-455;
101 Independence Ave SE; Washington, DC 20559; (202) 707-3000

There are many ways to receive free informational circulars and registration forms. You can call or write to receive them by mail; call (202) 707-9100 and key in your fax number to receive them by fax; or download them from their Web site at http://www.loc.gov/copyright. Note: if you write for information expect to wait a long time for a response.

THE WRITER

120 Boylston St; Boston, MA 02116-4615; (617) 423-3157, FAX 423-2168;
E-mail writer@user1.channel1.com;
Web http://www.channel1.com/thewriter/

1-year subscription (12 issues) $29, 2 years $55, 3 years $78. This monthly magazine announces contests in a "Prize Offers" column and publishes a special "Where to Sell Manuscripts" section, which includes lists of play publishers in the September issue.

WRITER'S MARKET, Kirsten Holm, ed

Writer's Digest Books; 1507 Dana Ave; Cincinnati, OH 45207;
(513) 531-2690, ext 287, FAX 531-7107;
E-mail writersmarket@fwpubs.com; Web http://www.writersdigest.com

2000. 1120 pp, $27.99 (plus $3 postage and handling and sales tax where applicable) paper; it is also available in a book/CD-ROM package for $49.99. This annually updated directory lists more than 4000 places where writers may sell their manuscripts. It includes many opportunities for playwrights and screenwriters. The 2000 edition is due out in September 1999.

Online Resources

Internet help for playwrights.

The Internet is an exciting place to be whether you are a gardener, a doctor or a playwright. A mobile, global library—it is elastic, ever-expanding and ever-changing. It's powerful in its ability to transport you and transform itself. But the site you landed on this morning, could pack up tomorrow at a moment's notice and move somewhere else or nowhere at all. A topic search today might bring up ten sites, only to surprise you with thirty next week.

The focus of this chapter is to give a basis for getting around what is an infinite map of locations and sublocations. We have focused only on the basic Web, and have included comprehensive sites that can lead you to just about all areas of the global theatre community. There are as many ways to go about finding information through the Internet as there are individuals, but what we hope we've done here is to give you a starting point.

But of course, most of you have been around the Internet block and can show us more than a few things. So, please E-mail any helpful information regarding the Internet, any incredible sites that eluded us to: sova@tcg.org, so that we may continue to expand this chapter with each edition.

Note: Names listed in bold are either Internet addresses or topics within sites that can be selected, and then transport you to other locations. Remember this is not an all-encompassing list, but a sampling of what we have found. There are also many Web and E-mail addresses included within the individual listings of this book which should be referred to as well.

How do I get around?

You can type a site's address directly (for example: **www.playbill.com**) into an Internet browser, such as Netscape or Internet Explorer; you can also type in a key word like "playwright" into one of the many search engines, such as Yahoo, Excite, Lycos, etc., which are accessed through a browser. (Note: all Web addresses contain the **http://** prefix, but not always the **www** prefix.) At this point the whole world opens up, and you can find yourself bumping from Web site to Web site; or into chat rooms; or news groups at some university somewhere to discuss your favorite playwright, commedia dell'arte or your one-act play about the runaway turnip.

Conduct a general search.

By typing in **playwright** in Yahoo, for example, you get listings for everything from the complete text for Aristophanes' *The Birds* to **The Playwriting Seminars** (**www.vcu.edu/artweb/playwriting/**), a "228-page site" which calls itself "a professional manual of the playwright's craft," littered with quotes by play-wrights; once you select **Regional Theatres on the Web**, it can link you to regional theatres around the country, and a few in Canada and England. It will also link you to the alternative theatre movement's **RAT** conference page. Since Web sites do like a change of scenery now and then, much like we do, and perhaps won't leave a change of address, much like us, you can always type in the organization's name, etc., in a search engine such as Yahoo, and see if they can link you to their new site.

Comprehensive Web sites.

Here are a few sites, in a reasonably alphabetical order, which together create a good foundation.

A.S.K. THEATER PROJECTS

www.askplay.org/ can pretty much hook you up to any site of relevance to playwrights. Click **Other Web Resources** and you will find many sites of interest, including: **Essays on the Craft of Dramatic Writing** (contains essays on scriptwriting and **Script Opportunities**); **New Dramatists** (includes information on their organization and their members); **Screenwriters/Playwrights Page** (lots of general information for screenwriters and playwrights, which will take you into more specific topics, such as **Internet for Writers**, **Agents**, **Release Forms** and **Tips from Pros**).

Under their **Theatre Link Directories** column you can be transported to **Theatre Central**; **Brief Guide to Internet Resources in Theatre and Performance Studies** (then by selecting **Plays and Playwrights** you will find even more playwright sites, and links to journals, indexes and other major theatre sites).

www.askplay.org/ also provides connections to **Theatres** (professional and university) and other **Service Organization** sites, such as the **Stage Directors and Choreographers Foundation.**

BACK STAGE

www.backstage.com/ From the East Coast's casting/theatre news weekly, this site contains articles, the latest Broadway cash register tallies, show listings, etc. Membership permits you to get their current and past issues online. Under **Performing Arts Service Directory** you will find **Information on Acting Schools/Coaches**, **Resume/Mailing Service** and **Theatre/Rehearsal Space**. Under **Career Corner** you can **Post Your Play** and select **Upcoming Talent Showcases** to view your listings and other posted play synopses.

CITYSEARCH

www.citysearch.com/ is a comprehensive, "what's happening" site in which you can place national searches for arts events, restaurants, etc., by city, date or subject. It also contains articles and reviews.

CULTURAL RESOURCES COMMISSION

By typing **Theatre History Resources** in a Yahoo search, you are given the opportunity to select **Cultural Resources Commission**, then **Useful Links (www.freenet.tlh.fl.us/Cultural_Resources/links.htm)**, which will bring you into the Local Arts Agency for Tallahassee and Leon County's in-depth Web site, which in addition to covering the arts for this Florida region, connects you to national and other regionally specific sites. They will link you to the **National Endowment for the Arts; Basic U.S. Patent Trademark & Copyright Information**; a **Festivals** site (**festivals.com**); **The Art Deadlines List**, which contains contest and submission opportunities; and **All-New York Theatre Guide** (**www.allny.com/the-ater.html**), a comprehensive listing of New York area theatres, among many others.

THE DRAMA DESK AWARDS

dramadesk.buybroadway.com/contents.htm provides a look at previous and upcoming Drama Desk Awards, and provides general theatre arts information.

JOE GEIGEL'S FAVORITE THEATRE RELATED SOURCES

www.on-broadway.com/links/default.htm is another in-depth site, which links you to a comprehensive group of theatres around the world, and provides links to other concentrated areas such as **Professional Resources** (which lists organizations of use to playwrights); **Indices** (which links you to sites that provide indexes to theatre-related services); **Newsgroups/Chat Rooms**; and **People** (which links you to theatre people and their Web sites).

NEW YORK THEATRE WIRE

www.nytheatre-wire.com contains articles, publication information, Broadway and Off-Broadway listings, reviews, a museum directory and classifieds.

PLAYBILL

www.playbill.com is an excellent place to begin. In addition to providing an online ticket service, the site also contains news for Broadway, Off-Broadway, regional and international theatres. It provides a link to **Theatre Central**, a site chock-full of theatre information, including **Celebrity Sites** (which when selected in **Sites**), leads you to **Playwrights and Composers**, which links you to related articles and Web sites of playwrights. In **Theatre Central** you can also select **Connections**, a resource for communicating with theatre professionals (from actors to business managers to technicians) around the world.

STAGEBILL ONLINE

www.stagebill.com/ has articles on the national theatre scene and a national **Performance Finder**.

THE TONY AWARDS

www.tonys.org/mainframe/html has general theatre news and links to Web sites of Broadway shows. It will also link you to **Call Board**, the **Los Angeles Times**, the **League of American Theatres and Producers**, **Theatre Central** and **Theatre Development Fund**.

THE U.S. COPYRIGHT OFFICE

lcweb.loc.gov/copyright/ contains information on copyright issues as well as the actual application forms (**Application Forms**) for downloading.

Internet Play Publishing and Online Playwriting.

There are many, many Online classes offered via the Internet. There are also more sites that post scripts and host Online writing cooperatives than listed here. What follows are a few sites that offer such opportunities and provide helpful links. There are also sites listed above that may help in this area.

Note: Once you post your play on the Internet, it becomes part of the world-at-large. It is still your property, but control of its use and protection of its content become hard to manage. Consider the copyright and reprint issues. You will need to be your own advocate. This is still unchartered territory.

THE DRAMATIC EXCHANGE

www.dramex.org makes entire scripts available on their Web site, and is updated every couple of months, though when we last checked it had stopped accepting submissions in Mar 1998 due to a backlog of manuscripts.

ELAC WRITERS WORKSHOP

www.perspicacity.com/elactheatre/workshop/collect.htm posts plays (it is free and they accept all). You can look up other posted scripts by selecting **ELAC Online Plays**. They ask that you send your submission via ASCII or html text to: **mckayc@aol.com** or **elac@perspicacity.com**

By choosing **Online Playwriting Collaborations, How to Collaborate**, you can participate in an Online playwriting challenge with other writers. You submit your play idea, write the first scene, and then someone writes the next, etc.

SCREENWRITERS & PLAYWRIGHTS HOME PAGE

www.teleport.com/~cdeemer/scrwriter.html can guide you to courses around the country (**Online Classes**), articles on how to write (**Dramatic Sturcture**), tips for getting around the Internet and a guide to what you'll find there (**Internet for Writers**), and Online play posting sites of new and classic work (**Stage Plays Online**).

Submission Calendar

September 1999–August 2000

Included here are all *specified* deadlines contained in Production, Prizes, Publication, Development, Fellowships and Grants, Colonies and Residencies, and Membership and Service Organizations. Please note that suggested submission dates for theatres listed in Production are not included. There are always important deadlines that are not available at press time and so cannot be included here.

September 1999

1   Attic Theatre Ensemble's One-Act Marathon   *116*
1   Dorland Mountain Arts Colony (1st deadline)   *244*
1   15 Minute Play Festival (1st Deadline)   *103*
1   Great Plains Play Contest   *125*
1   Lee Korf Awards   *132*
1   Millay Colony for the Arts (1st deadline)   *249*
1   NEH Collaborative Research grant   *221*
1   Scholastic Writing Awards (1st deadline)   *143*
1   SummerNITE, New Play Studio   *195*
1   Villa Montalvo Residency Program (1st deadline)   *252*

Contact for exact deadline during this month:

October 1999 ────────────────────────────

November 1999 _____

December 1999 _____

January 2000 ─────────────────────

February 2000 ─────────────────────────

March 2000

Contact for exact deadline during this month:

April 2000 ⸺⸺⸺⸺⸺⸺⸺⸺⸺

May 2000 _____

June 2000

1 ASF Translation Prize   *116*
1 Coe College New Works Competition   *119*
1 George R. Kernodle Contest   *125*
1 HRC's Annual Contest   *127*
1 Jackie White Children's Playwriting Contest   *127*
1 New Professional Theatre Festival   *139*
1 Ragdale Foundation residencies (2nd deadline)   *250*
1 SETC New Play Project   *145*
1 Women's Work Project   *199*
2 Headlands Center for the Arts   *245*
15 TCG National Travel Grants (4th deadline)   *226*
26 U.S./Japan Creative Artists' Fellowships   *220*
30 Main Street Arts Flying Blind Festival   *57*
30 Next Stage (2nd deadline)   *186*
30 Siena College International Playwrights Competition   *144*
30 West Coast Ensemble Musical Stairs   *151*

July 2000

1 First Stage One-Act Play Contest   *177*
1 Henrico Theatre Company One-Act Competition   *126*
1 Many Voices Multicultural Collaboration Grants   *224*
1 Many Voices Playwriting Residency Awards   *224*
1 Maxim Mazumdar Competition   *134*
1 Orange County Playwrights' Page to Stage Contest   *187*
1 Plays-in-Progress May Festival   *188*
1 Theodore Ward Prize for African-American Playwrights   *148*
15 Altos de Chavon   *241*
15 James H. Wilson Award   *120*
15 Paul T. Nolan Award   *120*
31 Play Pen   *188*

Contact for exact deadline during this month:
Frederick Douglass Workshops (4th deadline)   *178*
NYFA Sponsorship Program (3rd deadline)   *185*

August 2000 ——————————————

Special Interests

Here is a guide to entries which indicate a particular or exclusive interest in certain types of material, or which contain an element of special interest to writers in certain categories. Under Young Audiences, Media, Multimedia, Performance Art and Solo Performance, we list every entry of interest to writers in these fields. In the case of adaptations, musicals, one-acts and translations, there are numerous theatres willing to consider these types of material; we list here only those theatres and other organizations that give major focus to them. The Multicultural category is for those organizations expressing general interest in multicultural works. Under African-American, Asian-American, Hispanic/Latin-American and Native American Theatre, we have included only those organizations specifically seeking work by or about people from these ethnic groups. The Student/College Submissions category refers to college writing students or students in an affiliated writing program. Young Playwrights is a special interest category only for playwrights 18 or under.

Adaptation

African-American Theatre

Asian-American Theatre

Gay and Lesbian Theatre

Hispanic/Latin-American Theatre

Jewish Theatre

Media (Film, Radio and Television)

Multimedia

Multicultural Theatre

Musical Theatre

Native American Theatre

One-Acts and Short Plays

Performance Art
(see also Experimental Theatre)

Solo Performance

Student/College Submissions

Young Audiences

Young Playwright Programs

Index

Remember the two alphabetizing principles used throughout the book: First, entries beginning with a person's name are alphabetized by the first name rather than the surname. However, you can find these entries indexed by both names. Hence you will find the Robert J. Pickering Award for Excellence under R and P, the Alden B. Dow Creativity Center under A and D and the Helene Wurlitzer Foundation of New Mexico under H and W. Second, regardless of which way "theatre" is spelled in an organization's title, it is alphabetized as if it were spelled "re," not "er."

O

About Theatre Communications Group

Theatre Communications Group (TCG), the national organization for the American theatre, offers a wide array of services in line with our mission: to strengthen, nurture and promote the not-for-profit American theatre. Artistic programs support theatres and theatre artists by awarding $1.5 million in grants annually, and offer career development programs for artists. Management programs provide professional development opportunities for theatre leaders through workshops, conferences, forums (including teleconferences and on-line) and publications, as well as industry research on the finances and practices of the American not-for-profit theatre. Advocacy, conducted in conjunction with the dance, symphony, opera and museum fields, includes guiding lobbying efforts and providing theatres with timely alerts about legislative developments. The country's leading independent press specializing in dramatic literature, TCG's publications include *American Theatre* magazine, the *ArtSEARCH* employment bulletin, plays, translations and theatre reference books. Through these programs, TCG seeks to increase the organizational efficiency of our member theatres, cultivate and celebrate the artistic talent and achievements of the field, and promote a larger public understanding of and appreciation for the theatre field. TCG serves over 340 member theatres and almost 17,000 individual members.

Related TCG Publications

Catalogue available upon request

American Theatre
The national, 10-issue-per-year theatre magazine containing news, features and opinion; includes complete texts of 5 plays a year.

The Playwright's Voice: American Dramatists on Memory, Writing and the Politics of Culture *by David Savran*
Interviews with playwrights: Edward Albee, Holly Hughes, Tony Kushner, Suzan-Lori Parks, Anna Deavere Smith, Paula Vogel, Mac Wellman and others.

The Production Notebooks: Theatre in Process, Volume One
Editor Mark Bly; dramaturgical casebooks of Shelby Jiggets (*The Love Space Demands* at Crossroads Theatre Company), Christopher Baker (*Danton's Death* at Alley Theatre), Jim Lewis ("The Clytemnestra Project" at the The Guthrie Theater), Paul Walsh (*Children of Paradise: Shooting a Dream* at Theatre de la Jeune Lune).

Stage Directors Handbook: Opportunities for Directors and Choreographers *prepared by Stage Directors and Choreographers Foundation, David Diamond and Terry Berliner, eds*
Listings of training programs, service organizations, grants, foreign festivals and other oportunities available to directors and choreographers for the stage.

Stage Writers Handbook: A Complete Business Guide for Playwrights, Composers, Lyricists, and Librettists *by Dana Singer*
Contains information on the business end of playwriting, covering copyright issues, contracts, representation, collaboration and more.

Theatre Directory
The annual pocket-sized contact resource of theatres and related organizations.

Playwrights

A Fair Country; Mizlansky/Zilinsky or Schmucks; The Substance of Fire and Other Plays; Three Hotels: Plays and Monologues *by Jon Robin Baitz*

The Essential Bogosian: Talk Radio, Drinking in America, FunHouse and Men Inside; Notes from Underground; Pounding Nails in the Floor with My Forehead; Sex, Drugs, Rock & Roll; subUrbia *by Eric Bogosian*

Evoking Shakespeare; The Open Door; The Shifting Point *by Peter Brook*

Blue Heart; Cloud Nine; Light Shining in Buckinghamshire; Mad Forest; The Skriker; This Is a Chair *by Caryl Churchill*

Flyin' West and Other Plays *by Pearl Cleage*

Tales of the Lost Formicans and Other Plays *by Constance Congdon*

Culture Clash: Life, Death and Revolutionary Comedy *by Culture Clash*

Love & Science: Selected Music-Theatre Texts; Unbalancing Acts *by Richard Foreman*

A Lesson from Aloes; Blood Knot and Other Plays; The Captain's Tiger; Cousins; My Children! My Africa!; Playland and A Place with the Pigs; The Road to Mecca; Valley Song *by Athol Fugard*

The Necessary Theatre *by Peter Hall*

Approaching Zanzibar and Other Plays; Coastal Disturbances: Four Plays; Pride's Crossing *by Tina Howe*

Golden Child; Trying to Find Chinatown: The Selected Plays *by David Henry Hwang*

People Who Led to My Plays; Sleep Deprivation Chamber *by Adrienne Kennedy*

Self Torture and Strenuous Exercise: Selected Plays *by Harry Kondoleon*

Angels in America, Part One: Millenium Approaches; Angels in America, Part Two: Perestroika; A Bright Room Called Day; Death and Taxes: Hydriotaphia and Other Plays; A Dybbuk, *adapted from S. Ansky*; The Illusion *freely adapted from Pierre Corneille*; Thinking About the Longstanding Problems of Virtue and Happiness: Essays, a Play (Slavs!), Two Poems and a Prayer *by Tony Kushner*

Reckless and Blue Window: Two Plays; What I Meant Was: New Plays and Selected One-Acts *by Craig Lucas*

The Floating Island Plays *by Eduardo Machado*

Testimonies: Four Plays (Annulla, Still Life, Execution of Justice, Greensboro) *by Emily Mann*

The Weir and Other Plays *by Conor McPherson*

Insurrection: Holding History *by Robert O'Hara*

The America Play and Other Works; Venus *by Suzan-Lori Parks*

Marisol and Other Plays *by José Rivera*

Etiquette and Vitriol (The Food Chain and Other Plays); Raised in Captivity *by Nicky Silver*

Company and Getting Away with Murder *by Stephen Sondheim and George Furth*; Gypsy *by Stephen Sondheim and Arthur Laurents*; Into the Woods and Passion *by Stephen Sondheim and James Lapine*

Driving Miss Daisy; The Last Night of Ballyhoo *by Alfred Uhry*

The Baltimore Waltz and Other Plays; The Mammary Plays: How I Learned to Drive/The Mineola Twins *by Paula Vogel*

The Collected Short Plays of Thornton Wilder, Volumes I and II; The Collected Adaptations and Translations of Thornton Wilder, Volume I *by Thornton Wilder*

Jelly's Last Jam, *book by George C. Wolfe, lyrics by Susan Birkenhead*; Spunk: Three Tales by Zora Neale Hurston *adapted by George C. Wolfe*

TCG INDIVIDUAL MEMBERSHIP

As a *Sourcebook* user, you're invited to become an Individual Member of **Theatre Communications Group** — the national organization for the American Theatre and the publisher of **American Theatre** magazine.

As an Individual Member of TCG, you'll get inside information about theatre performances around the country, as well as substantial discounts on tickets to performances and publications about the theatre. Plus, as the primary advocate for not-for-profit professional theatre in America, TCG will ensure that your voice is heard in Washington. We invite you to join us today and receive all of TCG's benefits!

MEMBERS RECEIVE THESE SPECIAL BENEFITS

- A FREE subscription to *American Theatre*—10 issues…5 complete playscripts…artist profiles…in-depth coverage of contemporary, classical and avant-garde performances…3 special issues—including *Season Preview* (October), *Summer Festival Preview* (May) and Theatre Training (January).
- Discounts on tickets to performances at more than 220 participating theatres nationwide.
- 15% discount on resource materials including *Theatre Directory, ArtSEARCH, Stage Writers Handbook, Stage Directors Handbook* and *Dramatists Sourcebook*—all musts for the theatre professional or the serious theatregoer.
- A FREE catalogue of publications.
- 10% discount on all books from TCG and other select theatre publishers.
- Your personalized Individual Membership card.
- Opportunity to apply for a customized TCG Credit Card.
- Special discount for Hertz Rent-A-Car and Airborne Express.
- Up to 60% off regular hotel rates from Hotel Reservations Network.

TCG
INDIVIDUAL MEMBERSHIP

American Theatre magazine, available 10 times per year, provides up-to-the-minute coverage of the trends, artists and topics shaping American theatre today. In addition to all the articles, you'll also receive 5 full-length plays—the newest works by prominent playwrights like Tony Kushner, Suzan-Lori Parks, David Rabe, Paula Vogel and Wendy Wasserstein. Plus 3 special issues including "Season Preview" in October, listing the complete performance schedules for more than 300 theatres across the U.S.; "Summer Festival Preview" in May, listing theatre festivals worldwide; and "Theatre Training" in January, reporting on the opinions, evolution and theory of theatre education in America.

Members get a **FREE**

Subscription to **American Theatre**

Take Advantage NOW and SAVE!
Become a **TCG INDIVIDUAL MEMBER** and
Receive Extraordinary Benefits

☐ **YES**, I would like a one-year Individual Membership to TCG, which includes a subscription to *American Theatre.*

    ☐ Individual Membership ~~$35.00~~ $30.00.

    ☐ Student Membership (enclose copy of ID) $20.00.

☐ I prefer a two-year membership.

    ☐ Individual Membership ~~$70.00~~ $55.00.

Not only would I like to become a member, but I would like to take advantage of my discounts right now!
(Discount prices are only good if you are a member. If you are not a member, please use the full price for your order.)

☐ Please begin my one-year subscription to *ArtSEARCH.*

    Individual ☐ with E-mail ~~$64.00~~ $54.40 ☐ without E-mail ~~$54.00~~ $45.90

    Institutional ☐ with E-mail ~~$90.00~~ $76.50 ☐ without E-mail ~~$75.00~~ $63.75

☐ **TOTAL ORDER** _____

To order, you may: Send this form to: TCG Order Dept., 355 Lexington Ave., NY, NY 10017-0217 or Call (212) 697 - 5230, ext. 260; Fax (212) 983-4847; or send E-mail to: orders@tcg.org. Credit card orders: please include your billing address if it is different than your mailing address.

☐ Check is enclosed. ☐ Please charge my credit card. ☐ VISA ☐ MC ☐ AMEX

NAME _____

OCCUPATION/DATE _____

ADDRESS _____

CITY _____ STATE _____ ZIP _____

*PHONE/FAX/E-MAIL _____

CARD# _____ EXP. DATE _____

SIGNATURE _____

* All orders must have telephone number

For Individual Membership outside the U.S., please add $12 per year (U.S. currency only, drawn from a U.S. bank). Allow 6-8 weeks from receipt of order.

[Mkt. code: DDSB00]